ON YOUR KNEES

The Detectives of Hazel Hill
Book Three

ON YOUR KNEES

The Detectives of Hazel Hill
Book Three

Liz Bradford

Copyright © 2019 Liz Bradford
All rights reserved.

Stand on the Rock Publishing
Lizbradfordwrites@gmail.com
Lizbradfordwrites.com

Print ISBN: 9781687760777

Cover Design by Alyssa at Alyssa Carlin Designs
www.alyssacarlindesign.com

Editing by Teresa Crupmton at AuthorSpark, Inc. authorspark.org

Formatting by Kari Holloway at KH Formatting. Facebook.com/KHFormat

Scripture quotations are taken from the *Holy Bible,* New Living Translation, copyright © 1996, 2004, 2007 by Tyndale House Foundation. Used by permission of Tyndale House Publishers, Inc., Carol Stream, Illinois 60188. All rights reserved.

Scripture quotations are also taken from THE HOLY BIBLE, NEW INTERNATIONAL VERSION®, NIV® Copyright © 1973, 1978, 1984 International Bible Society. Used by permission of Zondervan Bible Publishers.

All songs quoted are in the Public Domain.

This novel is a work of fiction. Names, characters, businesses, places, events, locales, and incidents are either the products of the author's imagination or used in a fictitious manner. Any resemblance to actual persons, living or dead, or actual events is purely coincidental.

To everyone who is a survivor of rape.
May God bring healing beyond
your understanding.

CHAPTER 1

Adam Jamison adjusted his sweaty grip on the casket. *Don't drop it.* He needed to wipe his hands and his forehead. The July sun was relentless. Sweat dripped down his neck, soaking the collar of his dress uniform. Adam, along with Jared, Doug, Captain Baker, and two other men, carried the casket from the hearse to the graveside. The sound of the bagpipes playing Amazing Grace echoed through the air leaving an eerie presence in its wake. This shouldn't be happening. *I should be the one lying in that casket, not Rick.* Rick Miller had a family. They needed him. No one needed Adam. When he got home after a long day of work the only one who greeted him was his dog. Rick had a wife and two grade-schoolers.

I should have gone through that door first.

Adam tried to put his self-destructive thoughts out of his head throughout the graveside service. He just needed to make it through this. He and Miller had been partners for years; they had always had each other's backs. Adam thought he'd had Rick's back that day less than a week ago, but apparently not well enough, because Rick was gone.

As the pastor spoke, Adam couldn't stop his mind from replaying the day he failed his old partner.

A Monday, like any other... There was no reason to believe that anything would go awry. He and Amelia had been partners for a year and a half since the Special Victims Unit had been sanctioned. They had just wrapped up a case that morning, and Adam was wandering around the station looking for something to do other than his paperwork. Doug was out sick, so Rick asked if Adam would tag along to question a person of interest in a case he was working. Adam readily agreed. He was feeling on top of the world and maybe even invincible after a successful weekend of, as his mother would put it, worldly indulgences.

He rode along beside Miller that day, just as he had so many times before. Rick drove, and Adam read through the case file. Once they arrived at their destination, they got out of the unmarked police sedan and walked up to the rundown house. A gentle rain fell bringing the heat of the day down, but raising the humidity to uncomfortable levels, even for Adam, a native of Hazel Hill, North Carolina. They climbed the three wooden stairs to the rickety old porch. Rick raised his hand to knock, but yelling and a crash inside the house froze Rick's hand mid-air.

Both men drew their pistols and flanked the door. Adam banged on the door and announced their presence. More scuffling came from inside, and a male voice said, "I gotta get away. Do whatever you have to."

They had no choice but to breech the door.

As was customary for Rick and Adam, they both put their fists out for "rock, paper, scissors" for who would go in first. In all their years of working together, Rick had only twice thrown anything but scissors. Adam took advantage of this knowledge and threw out rock. Thus, Rick went in first. He pushed himself off the wall to the left of the door and kicked in the door with his Glock pointed straight in front of him.

Before Adam could even lift himself completely off the wall two shots cracked in his ears. Adam's heart froze. One from Rick's Glock and the other from someone inside, but Rick's shot had not been fast enough. *NO!*

Rick hit the ground; blood poured from his chest. Adam's emotions shut off. He turned into the doorway and unloaded half his magazine in the young man who had just shot his former partner. He cleared the little house. No one else was there. The screeching of tires drew his vision out the back window. A car sped down the alley.

Adam turned back to Rick and pulled out his cell. Adam called it in and collapsed to his knees beside Rick. "Officer down." He relayed the address, but the phone slipped from his hands.

"Jamison," Miller coughed out, "tell my wife and kids I love them."

Adam put his hands over the wound and applied pressure. "No, man, you have to tell them yourself. You're going to be fine."

"You know that's not true. Don't lie."

"Hey, you need to stay with me."

"Adam, turn to Jesus; it's the only way."

"Rick, come on. If Jesus cares, he'll get you through this. Come on, stay with me…"

Doug elbowed Adam bringing him back to the present. It was time to fold the flag that lay across Miller's casket. Adam and Doug folded the flag with care, and Adam presented it to Captain Baker. He was grateful that he didn't have to present it to Rick's wife like the Captain did. He wouldn't have been able to contain his grief and guilt; he was barely holding it in as it was. He clenched his jaw. His throat burned from choking back his emotion, and he endured the remainder of the service.

As the crowd dispersed, Jared turned to Adam. "Jamison, we're having people over to our house for dinner. We'd love to have you join us. I know Caleb and Amelia are coming. So are Doug and Paige, and I think the Captain said he would come, too."

Adam looked at his feet and across the way towards the people Jared had mentioned. "I don't know. I'll think about it."

Instead of walking with Jared towards where his friends were gathering, Adam turned to leave. He really had no interest in being around a bunch of Christians tonight. All he wanted to do was go to the bar and maybe get wasted. And there would be no alcohol, especially at Jared and Becca's. He might find a beer in Caleb's fridge, but he really wanted something stronger tonight.

He had only made it a few yards when he heard Amelia's voice calling. He stopped and turned to see his partner jogging toward him, her dress jacket flapping in the wind as she could no longer button it over her slight, yet growing belly. "Jamison, wait."

"Yes, Scully?" he teased her just as he had since she labeled a stack of cold missing persons cases as abductions her first month at HHPD.

Holding her belly, she caught up with him along the edge of cemetery by a large oak tree. "Adam, please come to Jared and Becca's tonight." Her southern accent was deeper than normal.

"Why should I?" He was more comfortable being honest with her than Jared.

"You shouldn't be alone right now."

He raised his eyebrows to hide the fact that he knew she was right. "Who said I was going to be alone?"

"You're going to go to the bar, drink yourself stupid, and pick up some easy tramp?"

He reached out and picked at the bark on the tree to avoid making eye contact with Amelia. "Sounds like a plan."

"A lousy plan." She gently gripped his arm.

"You are not my mother." He tried to pull his arm away.

Her grip grew tighter. "I *am* your partner."

He tried harder to pull his arm away, but she wouldn't let go. "Might not be the safest job to have right now."

"I didn't sign up for safe. I'm just trying to look out for you. It's my job, so deal with it."

He sighed. He really did appreciate her honesty with him. She never let him get away with anything, which was good and bad.

Her grip on his arm loosened, but she pulled on him slightly. "At least come for a little while. And if we really are that horrible to hang out with, I'm sure Caleb would take you to the bar."

He was having a difficult time coming up with a reason to say no to her. These were his friends, and even if they were Christians, they never tried to force their religion down his throat. They weren't like other Christians, either. They really put in an effort to live what they believed rather than being two faced in what they said versus what they did. He could share a beer with Caleb, but never once in all the years he had known Caleb had the man gotten drunk. These guys were different. Adam wasn't sure why, but they were. Maybe they wouldn't spend the evening preaching at him like others might.

"Fine, I'll come for a little bit. But I'm going to the bar."

"Good. See you over there in a bit."

"All right."

She turned and practically skipped away in her victory. He shook his head. She knew that he wouldn't go back on his word. That was something Adam had learned to never do. Because not following through on what you say can lead to broken relationships, and he'd had enough of those in his life.

———•———

Some might call him a killer or a rapist, but he preferred to think of himself as a performer. Not a circus performer, but an actor. He could play the part of a policeman or a security officer with no one else the wiser. But his greatest performance was with the women he took. And today he would continue the performance in Hazel Hill, North Carolina. The first act had played out seventeen years ago. This was the place that had initially inspired him in his craft, and tonight the second act curtain would fall for the first of the women he had performed with so many years ago.

He had moved all about the country over the years. He knew better than to stay in one place for too long, but for the last five years he had been longing to return to the place where it all began. He had to finish a job. At the time he didn't realize he hadn't completed the play; he had been satisfied with the performance, but as he expanded his practice, he realized even greater satisfaction came when they breathed their last.

He parked his car along the side of the road. His plan for tonight would be flawless. He would recreate that first night; it had been such a rush to find her walking through the park. It was the first time he had shown a complete stranger that he was a man that wouldn't take *no* for an answer. He had asked her to help him find his dog. But there was no dog. He smiled as he saw her the next day at the police station. She didn't recognize him! He had kept his ball cap low enough over his eyes, and it had been so dark. He had learned not to risk it with the next though, and a ski mask became part of his attire.

But tonight, he would let her see his face. It was likely that she wouldn't recognize him immediately, but he would be sure she would remember before the night was over. He looked over to the seat next to him. Everything he needed was right there. He unzipped the bag and removed his folding knife. He flipped open the blade. Warmth filled his being as he anticipated the pleasure he'd experience when it cut her flesh. He closed the blade and slid the knife into his pocket. Next, he shoved the roll of duct tape into the pocket his leather jacket. The August evening was a little warm for wearing a jacket, but it was necessary.

She was home alone. He had been sure of that. He pulled the hood release and the trunk release before he exited the car. He propped open the hood, that was essential for this to play out correctly. He walked up to the front door and adjusted his jacket and depressed the tiny white button that sounded the doorbell. *Sorry Kimberly, but this isn't FedEx.* He pressed his lips together to suppress his laughter.

A moment later a woman in her mid-thirties opened the door. She was dressed in a baggy, gray t-shirt and a pair of pink flannel pajama pants. Fuzzy slippers adorned her feet. "May I help you?"

"Yes, it seems that my car broke down, and my cell phone is dead. Could I bother you to use your phone to call a tow?"

"Wait, you're Officer... oh, I'm sorry I don't remember your name, but I believe you helped look for the person that attacked me years ago."

Perfect, her defenses were down. He intentionally lifted his eyebrows. "Oh my. Are you Kimberly Arden?"

"Yes, it's Vogel now, but yes. Please come in. How have you been?"

"Life has been good." He shut the front door behind himself. Excitement fluttered through his insides. They were alone.

"That's wonderful. Well, let me go grab my phone for you."

She turned, and the time had come. He pulled his knife from his pocket and flipped open the blade. He took a step forward and wrapped his arm around her neck. As the blade gingerly touched her neck, he whispered in her ear, "On your knees, Kimberly."

"It was you?!" Her voice cracked.

The desperation and shock in her voice awoke every cell in his body. "Yes, yes, it was." Time for the second act.

CHAPTER 2

Wednesday morning Ella Perkins shifted in the hard, plastic chair during the teacher's in-service at Lincoln Elementary School having a hard time believing it was already the end of August. *Where did the summer go?* She had spent her summer relaxing as much as possible, but also getting ready for her seventh year teaching third grade. She loved teaching third. After four years of teaching other grades, it only took one week of teaching third grade to know she'd found her niche.

    Ella inwardly laughed at herself. Teachers really are the worst students. For the last twenty minutes she had spent more time talking to Andrea, one of the second grade teachers than listening. They had chatted about their class lists. She tried so hard to not make judgments about her students before the year began, but the other teachers loved to talk about them. Ella had Molly Banik and Callie Palmer-Johnson, better known as the "cop cousins" in her class this year. She knew the girls from church and was looking forward to getting to know them better, even if Andrea had been sure to point out how talkative the pair was. Ella giggled. Molly was just as extroverted as her mother. Ella and Amelia had been in the same Bible study over the summer and had become close.

Ella whispered to Andrea, "No worries, their desks are on opposite sides of the room."

Ella's mind wandered to her classroom and all the work she had to do before the first day on Tuesday, but Principal Withers' voice interrupted.

"This afternoon we will be meeting over at the high school for some district-wide meetings."

Her stomach lurched.

"Ella, are you okay?" Andrea asked. "You look like you've seen the ghost of school years past."

"I'm fine." Honestly, though, she wasn't fine. She might have well eaten a rotten egg salad sandwich because she was queasy enough. She hadn't stepped back in that building since two weeks before the end of her junior year of high school. She had managed to avoid going in there for over sixteen years because she dreaded the flashbacks that would inevitably come as a result of walking in those hallways again.

When the principal dismissed them for lunch a couple of the other teachers invited Ella to go out to lunch with them on the way over to the high school, but she politely declined. She retreated to her classroom where she ate the ham sandwich she had brought and spent some time with her Heavenly Father.

Oh Abba, I don't know that I can do this. I have avoided that building for good reason. I just don't know if I can face those halls. Help me please.

An hour later, Ella stepped out of her Honda Civic and walked toward the all too familiar high school. *Please give me strength, God.* She took in a deep breath, opened the door of the main entrance, and made her way inside. The halls hadn't changed one bit. The fresh coat of paint even made it look exactly the way it did sixteen years ago. She paused and debated which way to go to the gym where they were meeting. One way, the most direct and shortest route, would take her by her old locker and the exact memory she wanted to avoid the most, but the other direction would be out of the way. With another deep breath she turned toward the quickest way.

That was a mistake. As soon as she could see her old locker the flashback came in waves of images and sensations. *The hand of Hazel Hill High School's most notorious bully rested on the locker next to her. The oversaturated sent of his cologne threatened to empty her stomach.* Even today the nausea returned as it was so ingrained in the memory. *The image of her books being knocked out of her hands flooded her eyes. The sound of the textbooks and binder hitting the floor came next. The sneering look on the bully's face. The betrayal of a friend who she hoped was coming to her rescue.* The flashback was more than she could bear.

She wobbled on her feet. She tried to keep walking. *Just one foot in front of the other, Ella.* As she passed the locker, she choked back a few tears.

"Hey, Miss Perkins." She tried to pull herself together before looking up and meeting Mr. Withers' eyes as he came up beside her.

She gave him a weak smile.

"Are you all right? You don't look like you feel well."

"I don't really." She tried to be honest, all the while hoping he wouldn't ask more questions.

"Well, if you aren't feeling well, go home. All we are doing this afternoon are 'team building' activities, which I know aren't your cup of tea anyway."

Boy, was he right about that! She hated anything that forced any physical contact with others. "Really, would that be all right?"

"Absolutely. Don't worry about it. Go home, and we'll see you in the morning. We'll have a brief meeting in the morning, and I plan to let you all have the rest of the day to work in your rooms."

"Oh, good. Thank you. I really appreciate it. I will go if that's all right. A nap might help."

"Yep, go." He turned and walked toward the gym.

Ella managed to make it all the way back out to her car without running into anyone else. She drove away, but only made it a few blocks before she had to pull the car over. Her eyes were dry, but she couldn't focus on driving. Her emotions were a mess. She couldn't pinpoint exactly what she was feeling, was it grief? Anger? Dejection? She wasn't sure, but either way she was overwhelmed by it.

She prayed aloud, "God, why? Why did I have to step back in that building? My junior year of high school was absolutely the worst year of my life. Why did I need to face that again?" Tears welled up in her eyes. "But thank you for giving me an out. I don't understand, Jesus, I thought we had dealt with all of this already…"

She sat there on the side of the road for a few minutes not even sure what words to pray. She sat until she was able to regain her composure. Her favorite thing in the world was to sing, especially old hymns. They hardly sang them anymore in church, but she had grown up singing them and continued to this day, especially when flashbacks came. Singing praises to the Lord was the only thing that could bring her out of a funk like the flashbacks sent her into.

As Ella drove home, she started singing.

I need Thee ev'ry hour, most gracious Lord,
No tender voice like thine can peace afford
I need Thee, oh, I need Thee; ev'ry hour I need Thee!
Oh, bless me now my Savior; I come to Thee!
...I need Thee ev'ry hour, In joy or pain;
Come quickly and abide, Or life is vain.
I need Thee, oh, I need Thee; ev'ry hour I need Thee!
Oh, bless me now my Savior; I come to Thee!

———••———

Adam sat at his desk in the police squad room rubbing his forehead Thursday morning. He was hungover, yet again. Ever since Rick had died over a month ago, Adam was drinking a little more than he should, but he appreciated it's numbing effects. He was trying so hard to hide it from everyone, but he wasn't doing a good enough job to keep it from his partner. And today had already been long, and it was only nine o'clock in the morning.

The call had come in at three, waking Adam from a very restless still slightly inebriated sleep. Amelia picked him up, which was good because there was no way he was in any shape to drive. She had met him outside his house with a large cup of coffee. He had been grateful, especially as she gave him the run down as they headed to the scene.

A sixteen-year-old girl had been raped. His stomach turned over at the thought. How could any man do that to anyone, let alone a young girl? It made his blood boil.

"Hey, Jamison, here's a refill." Amelia walked back over to their desks that were facing each other against the wall of the large squad room where most of the detectives of the Hazel Hill PD resided. She handed him another large cup of coffee.

"Thanks, Amelia, but you really don't have to keep bringing me coffee. I can get it myself."

"I know, but you're looking extra rough today. So, I thought I'd help out."

"You're just hoping to absorb some of the caffeine through the air."

"Ha! Right. I have my tea. This baby isn't keeping me from all caffeine, just keeping me from multiple cups of coffee."

His partner had hit the cute pregnant lady stage of pregnancy. As she leaned back against her desk, her little belly protruded from her denim jacket, since it could no longer wrap around her belly. He was so glad that his friend Caleb had found this wonderful lady to marry. Caleb deserved her. He was also glad he was friends with his partner's husband. Having a partner of the opposite gender had the potential to be awkward, but being good friend's with said partner's husband reduced any awkwardness on all sides. And Caleb counted on Adam to keep her safe.

"Have we heard any more from the hospital? How is Ava doing?" Amelia turned towards him.

"I haven't heard anything. Hopefully she is sleeping now." They had stayed with the young lady until the doctors gave her something to help her sleep in the wee hours of the morning.

"Yeah, hopefully."

"I just don't get it. No matter how long I do this job, I still get sick at what these scumbags are capable of."

"Don't ever stop getting sick because of it, Adam. That's what makes you a good detective, a good special victims detective."

"I guess."

Silence fell between them, and Amelia took a seat at her desk. There wasn't much they could do on the case until the lab work was processed since they had no leads from the scene. Adam had a bad feeling that this would be a tough case to solve.

Becca, Amelia's sister-in-law, came over to their desks. "How's it going? You were both here early today."

Adam filled her in and asked, "How's the case you and Gavin have been working going? Any leads?"

"Nope, none. It's been a week, but we're still having a difficult time piecing together what happened. Kimberley's body was found at a park on the opposite side of town. It doesn't really make any sense. She doesn't have any kids, so the playground doesn't fit. We have no clue why she would have been on that side of town, especially considering her keys, purse, and car were all at home. There was no sign of forced entry, so we're investigating anyone she knows. All we know is that her husband discovered her missing only hours before her body was found."

"Is the husband a suspect?"

"No, he's got a solid alibi. He's a doctor and was at the hospital at the time of death."

"I hope you figure it out," Adam said.

"I'm sorry, Becca." Amelia fell silent, but her eyes shifted, and he knew she had something else to say.

"What's with you?" He gave her an opening.

"Have I got a story to tell you." She shifted in her seat and leaned forward. "So clumsy pregnant lady here. Yesterday morning, I'm coming up stairs from the lab. I had the folder full of the pictures Jocelyn had taken of the domestic violence case we are wrapping up, and I totally tripped. It was comical to see, I'm sure, but the folder went flying out of my hand, gruesome pictures fly across the lobby floor just feet away from a group of girl scouts here for a tour. I couldn't catch them and myself, so of course the baby took precedence." She sat back and rubbed her belly. "I look up and who's standing there, but Patrick." She met Adam's eyes.

Adam's stomach twisted. There were few people in the world that he truly hated, and Patrick was one of them.

Becca twisted her hair. "As in Jocelyn's husband? Patrick North?"

Amelia scrunched up her nose and nodded. "That man makes me so uncomfortable." She looked back at Adam. "I do not understand how your cousin married him."

Neither did Adam. He shook his head "He's a real pretentious jack, err, jerk." Jerk was not a strong enough word for the man, but Amelia had asked him to not swear, and he respected his partner enough to honor her wishes.

"But that's not the end of the story. Patrick, as expected, was a jerk. Trash talk spewed out of his mouth, and he kicked the pictures away from me as I tried to pick them up. That's when my gallant knight appeared."

"Caleb came by yesterday?" Becca raised one eyebrow.

Amelia laughed. "Not like that. No, a guy I had never seen before appeared out of nowhere. Told Patrick to knock it off, by name."

Adam tilted his head. "This guy knew Patrick?"

"Yeah, like they go back. But he put Patrick in his place and helped me clean up the mess."

Becca leaned forward onto Amelia's desk. "Who was this knight?"

"His name's Scott, and he's going to be working in here doing office stuff."

Adam swept his arm across the room. "Where is he? I need to thank him for saving my partner from my cousin's jerky husband."

Amelia giggled. "I haven't seen him yet today. Oh wait, there he is." She pointed towards the Captain's office.

Adam looked over. Something about the man was familiar. But the thinning hair didn't fit.

Scott walked towards them. Adam continued to try to place his face.

"Well, if it isn't little Adam Jamison." Scott stopped beside his desk.

"Scott Rebus?" Adam resisted the urge to stand up and show Scott that he was over six foot, no longer the little kid Scott used to know.

"The one and only. Saved this lovely lady yesterday from North."

"So I heard. Thanks. Amelia's my partner."

"Lucky guy then. Can I just say? It's hard to believe Patrick ever became a cop, thought he would've stayed in the Army."

Adam just nodded.

Scott's eyes locked with Adam's. "How's Heather?"

A shudder course through Adam's spine. "She's fine, doesn't ever talk about you." Adam could only picture his big sister's tears from around the time she had dated Scott over twenty years ago. She would not want Scott to know anything about how she was doing, no matter how kind he seemed today.

Scott shrugged and left.

Adam shook his head and looked back at his notes.

"I suppose I should go catch a murderer." Becca turned towards her desk.

"And we've got a rapist to catch. Scully, what's our next step? My brain's too foggy."

Amelia looked down at her notes. "That's what happens when you drink so much."

His pulse increased. "I heard that."

She looked up at him with kind eyes. "Adam, I just... never mind..."

"What?" He folded his arms on his desk and leaned forward.

"You've heard it all before. Let's get back to the case. What are some of the distinguishing elements of the MO?"

Adam appreciated that she dropped it and got back to the case. "Duct tape, cut as opposed to ripped clothes, ski mask... oh and this one gets me, the phrase he used: 'On your knees.'" A shudder coursed through him. "This guy really has a superiority complex."

———•••———

Adam's eyes stung as he woke up in a hung-over fog as usual, but this time was different. He was pretty sure it was Sunday morning, but he didn't know where he was. A quick look around the bedroom revealed a vaguely familiar woman sleeping on the other side of the unfamiliar bed. He pulled his clothes on and continued to assess the situation. He couldn't remember much of anything from last night, including her name... This was a new low, even for him. He had always prided himself in the fact that he could still name every woman he had ever been with. But as his mom always said, "Pride comes before the fall." She was right.

He slipped his shoes on, grabbed his fedora, and as quietly as possible, exited the apartment. He was out of control. His insides burned, but it wasn't because of the remnants of alcohol in his system. Amelia had already threatened him with an intervention, so as he walked down the steps out of the building, he decided he needed to call on himself before his friends had to. Adam sat down on the steps and pulled out his phone. The sun was just starting to light up the horizon. He looked at his phone. It wasn't even 6:30 yet. He knew exactly who he should call, but part of him hesitated because he knew that Amelia would know who called her husband this early on a Sunday morning. Hopefully, Caleb wasn't working.

He sucked it up and dialed Caleb's cell phone; Caleb answered after the second ring. "Hey, Adam. Everything okay?"

"Hey. Was wondering if you could give me a ride? I'm not sure where I left my car."

"Sure, man. Where are you?"

Adam got up and looked at the signs. "Looks like I'm at Glen Street Apartments."

"I know where that is. I'll be there in a jiffy. Basketball or breakfast?"

Adam chuckled. His friend knew this was more than just a request for a ride. After all, he could have called a cab if all he needed was a ride. He rubbed his head. "Both?"

"Sounds like a plan."

Adam hung up, slid his phone into his back pocket, and rubbed his temples. He debated going back to sit on the steps, but he needed to be as far away from the unknown woman as he could get, so he walked around the sign and hung out on the curb.

After Adam had paced back and forth for a few minutes, Caleb pulled up to the curb. It was amazing how fast he arrived. Adam climbed into the Camaro. "Do I need to give you a speeding ticket?"

Caleb chuckled. "So, what first? Back to your place to change and then hit the court?"

"I could beat you even in jeans and dress shoes, but yeah, let's go change." Adam set his hat on his knee.

Caleb pulled away and cut to the chase, "What's going on with you?"

Adam inhaled deeply. He wasn't sure he was ready to go into it. "On more than one occasion, your wife has threatened me with an intervention. I figured I'd call it on myself before she had to."

"Sounds like Amelia. The drinking going too far?"

"Yeah. I don't remember much of last night."

"That's too far."

The conversation halted as they picked up coffee and stopped by Adam's house. They were on the basketball court at the gym before either of them said anything else of consequence. The court was empty, and Adam found a ball and practiced a few free throws, not missing one. Some say he wasted his talent by becoming a cop instead of going all the way to the NBA, but he knew that was one decision in his life that he had made correctly.

Caleb claimed a spot just inside the three-point line. "I'm going to give it to you straight."

"Wouldn't expect anything else." Adam passed the ball to Caleb.

"You know the answer, don't you?" Caleb took a shot.

"I know what you're going to say, but I'm not sure it's the answer."

"You tell me. What do you think I'm going to say?" Caleb retrieved the ball and threw it to Adam.

He caught it. "That Jesus is the only answer." Adam shifted on his feet to balance out the uncomfortable shift in his stomach. "That I need to surrender my life to him. Yadda-yadda."

"You know the Gospel better than you let on." Memories of endless mornings sitting on a cold metal folding chair listening to Sunday school teachers drone on flashed through his mind. "That junk doesn't apply to me."

"Jesus died for you just as much as he died for me." Caleb's voice was soft but punched hard.

"So, I've heard." Adam spun the ball around in his hands. "How does that even begin to get me out of the rut I've fallen into?"

Caleb rubbed his hands together and stepped toward Adam. "You have to rely on His strength. By surrendering your life to him, it changes you at the deepest level. When you have his Spirit inside of you, He will lead you, and He does all the work to help you overcome the depression you are feeling."

"Who said anything about depression?" Adam said a bit more defensively than he had intended.

"Adam, don't be a fool. Anyone who knows you can see that you've had a cloud of depression and maybe... guilt... hanging over you since Rick died."

Adam's jaw went taut, and he squeezed the basketball in his hands. The image of Rick going into that house, the sound of the guns, the blood.

"Let Jesus take that from you." Caleb's voice was tight. "He promises to ease our burdens if we give them to him."

Adam fought the urge to fall to his knees. Instead he threw the ball straight down at the floor. It bounced back up into his hands. He stared at it. The lines worn just like the defenses around his pride. "But it's my fault." Adam looked up.

Caleb pursed his lips together and shook his head. "You weren't holding that gun."

Adam chucked the ball into the bleachers. The clang echoed through the small gymnasium. "I might as well have. I should have gone through that door first."

Caleb retrieved the ball as if the ball had just bounced across the court on its own. "Weren't you were tagging along on his case? Why on earth would you have gone through that door first?"

"It's stupid." He explained the rock, paper, scissors.

"Rick always threw paper on purpose. If you'd won, he'd have insisted that he go in first." Caleb tossed the ball back to Adam.

Adam dribbled the ball and took another shot. It bounced off the rim towards Caleb. "My life. I feel out of control." His legs felt weak underneath him. But he refused to drop to his knees. He needed hold himself together.

Caleb put his hand on Adam's shoulder. "Trust it into the hands of the Creator of the Universe. Let Him be in control."

Adam sighed again. Control. He hated the idea of letting someone else be in control of his life. "Easier said than done."

"I'm not saying it's easy. I'm just saying it's the only way to have hope and joy in this world."

"I hear what you're saying, but… I don't know."

"Just think about it. Ready for breakfast?"

"Yeah."

They headed out of the gym and to their favorite local diner.

After they had ordered, Caleb started up conversation again, "So, anyone special last night?"

Adam shook his head. "No. Actually, I'm kind of embarrassed by it; I don't even know her name. I'm sure she told me, but I have zero recollection of it."

Caleb grimaced. "That's bad, Adam."

"Yeah, I know. Even for me. I can't believe it. I may not be the type to get in a serious relationship, but I'm not the type for one-night stands either."

"That's why you called me. What made you realize you had hit rock bottom."

"Yep." Adam stirred his coffee even though he hadn't added anything to it.

Their breakfast platters arrived, and Adam picked up a piece of bacon and popped it in his mouth.

Caleb picked up his fork and stabbed his sausage. "Do you think you would ever settle down? I know you've joked about not wanting to deprive any ladies by being attached to just one, but in reality, do you think you would?"

Adam had been thinking about that very thing more in the last month than he had in a long time. He finished chewing. "You know, if the right girl came along, I might consider it."

Caleb's eyebrows lifted in surprise and almost dropped his fork. "Really? Think she's out there?"

Adam looked down at his plate. "I know she is. But even if she did come back into my life, there is no way that anything would ever happen."

"Why?"

"There's so much water swirling under that old bridge, the rickety thing's been washed away." Regret seeped from his voice.

"You never know, man. God works in mysterious ways."

"Well, let me tell you that would take a frikin' miracle."

CHAPTER 3

Tuesday morning, with a tune in his head, Adam pushed through the squad room door. He whistled even though he couldn't remember the whole song. He had refrained from drinking last night and worked out instead. Definitely better than getting wasted. While he felt better this morning, something didn't feel right on the inside. It was as if his soul itself ached. There was a piece of him that knew Caleb was right, but there was no way he was going to accept that. There had to be another solution—other than God. Adam strode to his desk on the far side of the squad room, draped his blazer over the back of his chair, set his coffee down on his desk and looked up. Amelia strode straight towards him her speed accentuating her slight limp. Her eyebrows were tightly furrowed. His merry mood evaporated. "What's wrong, Scully?" He picked up his coffee and lifted it to his mouth.

"Mrs. Broderick just called. Ava didn't make it home last night."

The travel mug stopped short of his lips. "And they just now called?"

"She's been known to crash at her friend's house."

That didn't sound right. He put the cup down and coffee sloshed on the desktop. "On the first day of school?"

"But she wasn't there. She's missing, Adam." Amelia's voice cracked.

"Let's find her." Adam grabbed his jacket and moved towards the door. "Where to first?"

"Her parents." Amelia fell into step with him. "Then to the friend's house."

So, she was there at some point.

The next several hours were spent trying to discover what had happened to Ava. Her parents and friend both said that Ava was coping well. She was emotional as would be expected after being the victim of such a horrific crime, but she displayed no signs of being suicidal and gave no indication that she was thinking about running away.

Adam had a bad feeling. By eleven o'clock they had finished talking to everyone who had seen Ava the day before. So, they headed to the high school to find out who had seen her. But they had only driven a block when Adam's phone rang. "Jamison."

The dispatcher said, "We have an apparent homicide at the West Street Office Max. The description matches your missing white female."

His chest tightened. "We're on our way."

"What is it, Adam?"

"They found Ava where she was raped, and it's not good."

"Oh, no!" Amelia's face went pale.

Less than ten minutes later, they arrived at the scene. The alley beside the Office Max was already taped off and the crime scene technicians were already at work. His cousin, Jocelyn, the department's crime scene photographer was pulling equipment out of the CSU van. Adam asked if it was Ava, but Jocelyn had just arrived.

Adam followed Amelia under the tape and went to where the body lay. Immediately, Adam recognized Ava. Swearing, he punched the dumpster that was next to the one she was tied to.

Amelia put a hand on his arm and whispered, "Get control, Jamison."

He rubbed his sore knuckles and knelt beside the body. She was in the exact position she had been found in the night she was raped. Hands duct taped together above her head and taped to the handle on the side of the dumpster. Her throat had been slit. Bile rose into Adam's mouth. He slipped his hand in a glove and reached over and closed her eyes. *No way God cares about any of us if He'd let something like this happen.*

Henry, the medical examiner, came over. "As far as I can tell it is what you see. Throat slit. There are some bruises on her arms; looks like she put up quite the fight. Her pants are intact, so it doesn't look like he raped her."

Adam forced himself to breathe. Every muscle in his body was tense, and he wanted to lay into Henry for his flat description of what happened to this innocent girl. But Adam knew Henry well enough to know the man spoke flatly about it to keep his own emotions out of the situation. Adam could learn a thing or two from the ME."

Amelia tapped Adam's shoulder. "Ava said her attacker got spooked and left in a hurry the other night."

He looked up at her. "This is what he was planning the whole time?"

"It appears so." Her voice barely made it to his ears.

Adam stood up with a huff. He swore again. Amelia paced with him. He stopped and turned towards her. "We should have caught this guy before he could killer her." His voice came out more biting than he meant.

Amelia grabbed his arms with both of her hands. "I wish we had, but we had no way to, Adam. Zero leads. We've done the best we can. Now we have to find her killer and bring him to justice."

Adam pulled away from Amelia's grip and walked down the ally. Justice wouldn't be enough.

———•———

Ella waved to her last student at the end of the first half day of school. She glanced at the clock, 11:40. *That has to be some sort of record. Only ten minutes to get all 25 kids out of here on the first day!* She smiled at herself. This was going to be a good year. These kids had already proven themselves to be a riot. Her classroom-management skills would definitely be put to the test since there must be at least five class clowns, but if she could keep them under control, they would have a really fun year.

Callie and Molly had talked incessantly during their fifteen-minute recess this morning. She already loved those two.

As she packed up her things and headed out the door, she sang softly. *Joyful, Joyful, we adore Thee, God of Glory, Lord of love...*

She had one errand to run before going to her parents' for an afternoon of making cookies with her mom. She needed to get a few more clipboards from Office Max since over the summer a couple of hers had mysteriously broken.

Ella pulled into the parking lot and into the first spot she found. It would be a bit of a walk, but she didn't mind. She was feeling great after such a wonderful first day. She was surprised the parking lot was so full, but she didn't pay much attention, until the yellow police tape caught her eye, and she stopped.

Heat rushed through her chest as another flashback threatened to come. She had to break her gaze from the tape to keep the flashback from forcing her into the past. *Oh God, help me.* She knew this store had exactly what she wanted, and it was on sale. She just needed to ignore the police presence and go into the store. She resumed her path towards the store.

But *he* caught her eye. Tall and lean, as he had always been, although he had filled out since childhood. His short, dark hair styled haphazardly a top his head. He wore jeans and a dark grey blazer over his dress shirt and tie. His strong jaw line and broad shoulders made him as handsome as ever. Her breath caught in her throat, and she quickly hid herself behind an SUV.

"Good grief," she uttered out loud. "You have got to be kidding me." *God, why on earth are you doing this to me? Ok 'doing to me' isn't what I mean. I mean allowing this to happen. First, the school the other day, and the caution tape. But seriously, Adam? Why on earth is he here?* She slowly remembered that he had become a cop, she had even seen him around a bit when another teacher, Samantha, had been murdered by a serial killer a few years back. But in sixteen years, she had skillfully avoided Adam Jamison.

God, what is going on?

Deep in her soul Ella felt more than heard the words, *I'M PREPARING YOU.*

Her heart constricted. *Preparing me? For what? What on earth, God?*

No more answers came. But Ella was feeling a little woozy from fighting off the flashback and seeing Adam. She reached out her hand to steady herself and touched the SUV. The alarm rang out. "Oh, good grief!"

She scurried away from the vehicle, but a uniformed officer appeared around the front of the SUV. "Everything okay, Miss?"

"Yes, sorry, I, uh, just caught my balance on this car. I'm fine. Sorry."

"Are sure you're okay? You look a little pale."

"Yes, I'm fine. The sight of the police tape just made me a little dizzy." *Why did I say that?* "May I ask what happened?"

"I'm sorry, I'm not at liberty to discuss it."

"Oh, of course." She was grateful for his discretion; she just hoped the cops around her crime scene seventeen years ago had been so kind. "Thank you"—she looked down at his name plate—"Officer Cooper."

"No problem. Would you like me to escort you anywhere? You headed into the store? It is open."

"No, I'm fine. And yes, I'm headed into the store. Thanks."

She felt like a fool. Ella quickened her pace and tried desperately to keep her head down, hoping Adam wouldn't see her. The last thing she needed right now was an awkward reunion with him. Once inside the office supply store she felt herself breathe again. She wandered up and down the aisles aimlessly, forgetting the whole reason she came. She was able to avert the flashbacks from high school, but memories from her childhood began to come back.

A warm sense of nostalgia washed over her. Adam and Ella had been best friends as kids. That was the good part. They had lived just down the block from each other, and they had spent most of their free hours playing together before they were even in grade school. But that had changed. They weren't friends anymore. Her heart hit the floor.

God, why is it I feel like I have to forgive him all over again every time I see him? Didn't I already forgive?

The clipboards she was looking for caught her eye. She grabbed what she needed and wandered around a little longer. Maybe Adam would be gone by the time she came out of the store. She could only hope. Eventually she made her purchase but hesitated at the door. The cops were still walking around, and the coroner's van was there. *Oh no, someone died.* Suddenly, running into Adam seemed like a silly worry.

She walked out to her car. Adam wasn't there, and she breathed a little easier.

CHAPTER 4

Tuesday and Wednesday had produced very little in the way of discovering Ava's killer. In fact, the detectives really had absolutely nothing. By Thursday afternoon, the other detectives were avoiding Adam and Amelia as they'd become beyond irritable. Adam was at his desk working on paperwork on when Captain Baker came out of his office.

"Jamison, Johnson, Palmer, Riley. In my office, now." The Captain's face was straight, no emotion showing through. That was unusual. His normally jovial presence was MIA.

Amelia's eyebrows furrowed as she and Adam rose from their desks.

"What did you do?" Adam nudged her shoulder with his fist.

She cocked her head to the side and glared at him. "It's probably Gavin and Becca's fault." She puckered her mouth to suppress a giggle.

Becca threw a grimace over her shoulder. "Shut it. You two have been the cranky ones."

Adam shook his head. He wished he had a clue why the Captain was calling the four of them in. He gestured for the women to go first into the Captain's office, and he followed Gavin in.

The Captain stood in front his desk with his arms crossed. "Shut the door and sit down."

Adam was confused. Were they all in trouble? They weren't all working on one case, so he couldn't think of anything they could have done wrong. What on earth? The women each took a seat in the chairs that faced the Captain's desk. Adam and Gavin remained standing.

"What is it, sir?" Gavin asked.

Captain Baker's face had turned long. "I can't believe I didn't see it sooner. The cases y'all are working are connected. Yesterday evening when I was reviewing your case files, when your"—he looked at Gavin and Becca—"murder victim, Mrs. Vogel, was first found, I thought she looked familiar, but her married name didn't fit. When Miss Broderick was raped, the MO seemed familiar, but I couldn't put a finger on it."

Adam shifted to his other foot.

"It wasn't until I had both files side by side that it dawned on me. I've worked this case before."

"Really?" Amelia's voice squeaked.

The Captain nodded. "I did a little more research and pulled the case files." He motioned to three file boxes in the corner.

Adam recognized the top box as the one he'd had in his hand briefly a year and a half ago. If they had gotten to those cold cases, could they have prevented what happened to Ava? He hated the thought.

"A serial rape case that I worked seventeen years ago: five young women were raped, and their attacker was never caught. We just assumed he had moved or died in an accident, because he just stopped after a string of attacks that were all identical. Kimberly Vogel, Kimberly Arden, was the first victim. And now I know why she was found in that park across town. That is where she was raped."

Adam wanted to punch something but kept still and silent with the rest of them.

Gavin Riley finally spoke, "So he's come back to 'finish' the job, so to speak."

"Why didn't he just kill Ava when he raped her, why find her and take her back to the place he raped her?" Becca asked.

Adam answered, "From Ava's own testimony we know that something spooked him, and he ran off before he had a chance."

"What about those other four victims he'd attacked before?" Amelia asked the Captain.

"That's where I was headed. I've looked into them; only two are left in town. One moved away, I think she changed her name, too, because I couldn't find her. The Captain pressed his lips and eyes shut. "Another committed suicide a few years after the attack." He looked at his detectives. "That leaves two." He picked up two files off his desk and handed one to Gavin and one to Adam. "These are the ladies we need to inform and protect."

Adam stepped back to where he had been standing next to Amelia's chair. He opened the file and gasped. He grabbed the back of the chair to steady himself. *It can't be!*

"Jamison," Amelia said softly, "you okay?"

He tried to nod, but all he could do was stare at the picture of sixteen-year-old Ella Perkins. *Ella was raped?* How had he not known? Images of his childhood best friend flooded his mind. First, he saw five-year-old Ella chasing him with a frog she had captured down by the lake. He remembered eight-year-old Ella and the hours they spent playing cards, especially War and Go Fish on her trampoline. He also remembered her voice; she had always been singing. Most poignantly he remembered preteen Ella. They had been so close. Tears threatened to fill his eyes. He took in a sharp breath and choked them back.

"Adam?" Amelia said again.

"I know her." He handed the file to Amelia. He couldn't bear to look at the rest of it, feeling like he would be somehow violating Ella just by knowing what that man had done to his precious Ella. But he already knew, from Ava's testimony, what that despicable human being had done. Anger filled him now, and he could feel himself beginning to shake.

"Ella?" Amelia questioned.

"You know her, too?"

"Yes, she's Molly's and Callie's teacher this year. But she's also my friend."

Adam couldn't believe his ears. How long had his partner been friends with his long-lost Ella?

The Captain interrupted. "Well, go talk to these ladies and find them a safe place to stay until we get this guy. They both live alone, so I don't think they are safe in their own homes. He was able to find Kimberly despite her married name, so I'm sure he'll be able to find them as well. Go."

The detectives left the Captain's office. Adam looked at his watch. School wasn't out yet, so Adam and Amelia decided to hold off and let her finish the day in peace. But they waited parked in the school parking lot. Adam wanted to keep an eye out, just in case this guy was lurking around watching her. When they finally went in at 3:30 the secretary informed them she was in a meeting, so they waited longer. Adam's insides were fumbling all over themselves in anticipation of seeing Ella. He didn't know how she would react. It had been too long, and he had no idea if she still hated him.

———•———

Ella smiled. The meeting with Aidan's parents had gone beautifully. They were all on the same page as to how to help the boy succeed this school year. She sang "Blessed Assurance," one of her all-time favorite hymns, and erased the white board. But she was interrupted by a knock at her door. She turned and found Amelia Johnson, Molly's mom, standing in the door way.

"Amelia, come on in. Molly is doing fantastic." Ella turned towards her desk. As she turned, she noticed a man come in behind Amelia and assumed it was Caleb. She grabbed a paper off her desk. "Molly did great on her math paper today! Didn't miss a one..." Her voice trailed off as she locked eyes with Adam Jamison's. Her entire body went rigid. She quickly broke his gaze and looked at Amelia. "But I'm guessing that you aren't here to talk about Molly if *he's* with you." The disdain in her voice surprised her.

"We need to talk to you about something." Amelia motioned to the table at the back of the classroom. "Can we sit down?"

"Just tell me Amelia." She was starting to tremble. *Why were they here?* She couldn't even imagine, but she had a bad feeling about it.

"Ella, really, we should sit."

"No, just tell me!" She pressed her heel into the floor fighting the urge to stomp her foot on the floor.

"Well," Amelia took a step closer, but Adam hung back.

Ella couldn't even bring herself to look at him again.

Amelia rubbed the palm of her hand. "Ella, we were handed a file this afternoon, and it was yours."

Ella closed her eyes, and Molly's paper dropped from her hand.

"We believe your attacker is back in town."

Sheer terror coursed through her body. Ella shook, her breathing erratic. Her worst nightmare was coming true.

"Let's sit." Adam's strong voice surprised her; the boyish tenor she remembered had become a rich baritone.

She nodded and headed to the table at the back of the classroom. She sank into one of the chairs, and Amelia and Adam each sat in a chair on either side of her. She gripped the table in front of her. Her world was crashing down. Not only did Amelia now know about her past, now Adam did, too. The very thing she had kept a secret for so long… she knew Adam would put the pieces together.

"Elly, breathe." She looked up at Adam. She hadn't heard that nickname in ages; he was the only one who ever called her that. She closed her eyes and obeyed, taking several deep breaths and slowly letting them out.

"Office Max. He killed someone?" She looked at Amelia.

"Yes, he killed a young girl that he had raped a few days earlier. But he's also killed one of his victims from seventeen years ago," Amelia said.

Adam put his hand on the table near hers, so she pulled her hands into her lap. It was impossible to miss the hurt and regret that flashed across his face.

"Ella, we want to keep you safe," Amelia said.

"Security at my apartment is pretty tight." Her voice came out more confident that she expected. Because even though it was secure, she wasn't sure she'd feel safe anywhere right now.

"Ella, that's not enough." Amelia folded her hands on the table.

Where could she stay? *It's not like I would stay with Adam. Where did that thought come from?* "I guess I could stay with my parents."

Adam replied, "No, Ella, they still live in the house you grew up in. He'd be able to find you there."

"I already talked to Caleb, if you are okay with it, we'd like you to stay with us."

"Are you sure? I don't want to be a—"

"Keeping a friend safe could never be a burden."

"Okay." Ella tried to process all that was happening. She feared the flashbacks that were likely to come back at the news of her attacker being back. He was supposed to be dead in a ditch somewhere, not still alive and still taking victims.

"Are you ready to go? We can go back to your place and pack a bag and then go to my house."

"No. There's no way I'm going to be able to teach tomorrow. I need to prep for a sub and let the office know."

"That makes sense," Amelia asked. "Would you like me to go talk to the office, while you do what you need to?"

"Yes, that would help. Maybe they won't ask you questions."

"Okay, I'll do that." Amelia got up and left the room, but Ella just sat there next to Adam, unable to move.

"Ella, I had no idea," Adam finally spoke.

She waved a hand at him. "Don't, Adam." That gave her the motivation she needed to get up and go to her desk. She started pulling things together for a sub and making notes. Initially, Adam stayed at the table but eventually wandered to the front of the room and leaned against one of the student desks in the front row and watched her.

She nervously tucked her hair behind her ear. Her hair was normally very unruly, but she had managed to get up early enough to straighten it this morning, but now she just wanted it up in a ponytail. She searched her desk, her purse, her school bag. Finally, she found a hair tie and pulled her hair up.

As she finished her last note to the sub, Amelia came back into the room. "Wow, I'm glad you let me tell them. They asked me a ton of questions, of which

I answered very little. I can only imagine how hard they would have been on you."

"Especially since I would have had a hard time just saying, 'I don't feel well.'"

Amelia and Ella exchanged a brief smile. At least it was Amelia that was here and not another detective.

They headed to her apartment, leaving Ella's car at the school. She rode in the backseat of the unmarked police sedan while Adam drove. Adam pulled into a parking spot near her building and turned to Ella, "I'm going to go up and check it out first, just in case, all right?"

"Okay." She handed him her keys. It was a little weird to think about Adam going into her apartment without her. She quickly thought through how she had left it that morning. Not too bad, as far as she could recall. Adam exited the car and went into the building.

Amelia turned to her, "How are you holding up?"

"Okay for now, I guess. I know it will catch up to me eventually though."

"Know that I'm here for you. I may be the detective on the case, but I'm your friend first."

"I know, thank you, Amelia." Tears nearly pooled in her eyes, but she was able to blink them away.

Amelia's phone rang. "All clear for us to come up?" She asked without even saying hello.

Ella could hear Adam's answer, and the fear in his voice, even though the phone was up to Amelia's ear. "No! Don't get out of the car. I already called it in. CSU is on their way. Can you find someone to get

Ella, maybe see if Caleb or Jared can come get her? I'm going to need you up here."

"Okay. What happened?"

"You'll have to see it, but not Ella. You can get her stuff for her. She is NOT to come up here."

"Yes, sir." Amelia hung up and turned to Ella.

Ella stared out the front of the car. All air drained from her lungs. *What on earth happened up there?* She was officially scared out of her mind. She blinked her eyes and tried to keep her mind in the present despite the tunnel threatening to close in on her.

"Ella, Caleb's at work, so I'm going to call Jared, and see if he can come get you, okay?"

Ella nodded. She kind of knew Jared and Becca from church. Becca had always seemed intimidating but nice enough. Jared and Becca were cops, so at the very least Ella knew she could trust them with her safety.

She remained in a fog of fear as squad cars and a CSU, or crime scene unit, van pulled into her parking lot. Jared pulled up next to them. Ella followed Amelia's lead as she exited the car and went to Jared. She left with Jared and went back to his and Becca's house, while Adam and Amelia investigated whatever had happened in her apartment.

CHAPTER 5

Adam stood in the middle of Ella's apartment holding a broken picture frame. The picture of him and Ella down at the lake when she was twelve and he was thirteen made him smile. He couldn't believe she had kept it in a frame in her living room even after all that happened. He stared at the mess an intruder, most likely the unsub or unidentified subject, had left.

Amelia entered the apartment and apparently saw the message on the wall, which appeared to be written in blood. She let out a little shriek. "Oh my!"

Sorry I missed you. See you soon, Ella. The message made Adam's skin crawl. That man had been in Ella's apartment intent on killing her tonight.

"Hey." Amelia stepped across the room to stand beside him and put a hand on his arm. "Are you okay?"

"I think so. We have to get this—"

"We will, Jamison, we will. But I have to ask you a question. What on God's good earth happened between you and Ella? I need to hear it from my partner before I hear her side."

He looked back down at the picture in his hand. "Let's just put it this way. We were best friends, but I was a jerk to her in high school. That's the super short version. Basically, she has every right to hate me."

"I'm not sure she hates you, but clearly she was uncomfortable around you. Are you going to be okay working this case?"

"Yes, I will. I'm sure it made her even more uncomfortable considering why we were there. I had no idea she had been raped." He couldn't decide if wanted to collapse in a hole or beat somebody up. He knew he could do his job, but this was pushing what he could handle.

They worked the scene for a while before leaving the rest to the CSU crew. Right before they left, one of the techs called out to them. "Hey, Jamison, Johnson. I think we can definitively say that the message was written in cat blood."

The two detectives went to the balcony where the tech had called from. Adam followed him out with Amelia right behind him; there they saw where he had moved a chair revealing the filleted corpse of an orange tabby.

"Oh, gross!" Adam had a tough stomach, but the sight of the cat threatened to bring up any contents of his stomach. He immediately blocked Amelia's way knowing the pregnant lady wouldn't be able to hold her cookies.

Amelia turned away. "All right, I don't need to see that. Ella wasn't here, so he decided to kill her cat. That's just..."

"Repulsive?"

"Among other things. Let's get out of here and check on Ella."

"Please."

They went to the station to get their personal cars before heading to Jared and Becca's. It was already past seven, anything else that needed to be done would have to wait until morning.

At Jared's, Amelia went straight to the family room where Ella was sitting on the couch with Becca. Adam stayed in the kitchen with Jared, who offered him the leftover Chinese that was scattered across the island.

"How's she holding up?" Adam nodded towards Ella.

"I think they've stayed off the topic of what is happening, but I have a feeling once she starts talking about it, she'll break down. That's how Becca always is anyway."

"Tough on the outside, not so much on the inside? That sounds like the Ella I used to know, but that was a long time ago."

Adam turned to the women and asked if they needed anything.

Amelia said, "I need to eat, but I can get it myself, Adam. You eat."

Once Adam had fixed himself a plate, he pulled a dining chair into the family room and sat across from where Ella sat on the couch.

"Adam, tell me what happened in my apartment, please."

He looked deep into her dark brown eyes. The fear there was intense, but so was the sorrow. He knew the sorrow was partially his fault, and he would have to rectify that, but this wasn't the time or place. "It's not pleasant, Ella."

"I don't doubt that. But I need to know."

"Well, clearly there was an intruder. They emptied your bookshelves, several of the picture frames that hit the floor broke, and the cushions were pulled off the couch and slit open clearly in a fit of rage. We believe that he was expecting you to be home, and when you weren't, he got angry."

"I *am* normally home. Anyone who knows anything about me knows I'm always home by four on Thursdays, so I can make it to my kickboxing class by five. But I was still at school with you guys at five. You guys saved my life... How did he get in?"

"Not sure. There was no sign of forced entry. But there's more, Ella."

"What?"

"You have a cat, right?"

"Yeah, I really dislike that thing, but he came to me a few years ago and wouldn't leave, so I let him stay. Wait, what happened to the cat?"

"Well, he killed it. And Ella..." he hesitated.

"Spit it out, Adam!"

"He wrote a message on your wall: 'Sorry I missed you. See you soon, Ella.'"

He watched a shudder work its way through her entire body. All he wanted to do was draw her into his arms but based on her reaction to the closeness of his hand earlier that wasn't going to be a good idea.

"Seriously, the cat? That's just ridiculous. Good thing I wasn't very attached to it... but still." Her expression grew a little darker; her eyebrows were deeply furrowed, and her shoulders slumped a little further forward.

"Hey, we are going to keep you safe. You understand?" She was looking at her hands in her lap. He searched her face, hoping she would look up. She finally did and met his eyes.

She nodded.

"Call me if you need anything. You'll be safe with Caleb and Amelia, but don't hesitate to call me. You are not to be alone, got it?"

A slight smile lifted one side of her lips as if she was amused by his overbearing reassurance. "Okay, Adam. Thank you."

He pulled a business card out of his pocket. It seemed such a silly way to give Ella his number, but it was the easiest since his cell phone number was on the card. She took it.

"Are you ready to go back to my place and get some rest?" Amelia asked.

"I am. Not sure how well I'll sleep, but I need to try and relax at the least. Thanks, Becca. Adam." She got up.

Adam jumped to his feet. He deposited his plate in the kitchen and walked them to the door. Amelia and Ella left, and Adam turned to back to their hosts.

"Jared, Becca, thanks. And thanks for dinner."

"No problem." Becca pulled him into a hug.

"Are you going to be okay, Jamison?" Jared asked.

"Yeah, I'm fine." He lied. He wasn't fine. He knew that as soon as he got home, he would open his liquor cabinet. Today had been too much.

"Thanks for opening your home to me, Amelia." Ella set her bag down in Amelia's entry way.

"You're welcome. Caleb will be home around midnight, and the kids are staying at my folks tonight."

"I feel bad to have displaced them."

"Not a problem. They sleep over there on a fairly regular basis; it's not displacement at all. I thought it would be better for you tonight to not have to worry about disturbing them."

"Yeah, that does help a bit. Thanks. I haven't had flashbacks in a long time, but they have a tendency to not be pretty."

"Let me know what you need. Don't hesitate to wake me. I'll probably be up going to the bathroom anyway." Amelia rubbed her belly.

Ella nodded. She was tired but knew that she wasn't going to be able to sleep. In fact, she feared going to sleep because she knew the flashbacks would come as soon as she turned off the light.

"I'm going to get my pajamas on and have a cup of tea. Want to join me?"

"I'd like that. Where should I settle in?"

Amelia motioned for her to follow her up the stairs. "I was thinking you could sleep in Carter's room. He can bunk with his sister since she has a double bed. Hope you don't mind sleeping in a race car bed. At least it's a twin and not a toddler bed."

"Sounds good." She let out a slight chuckle.

Amelia pulled some sheets out of the linen closet

in the hall and helped Ella make the bed. Once Ella had changed, she met Amelia downstairs where she'd already started the water for tea. Ella sat down at the breakfast bar. But had no words to say.

Amelia spoke instead. "I don't want you to think about the case at all this evening, so I'm going to ask you something else that I hope isn't off limits."

Ella's curiosity was spiked. *What is she going to ask?*

"You and Adam clearly have a past. When I walked into your apartment this evening, he was holding a picture of a much younger version of the two of you. He told me a little, but I'd love to hear your side of the story."

Of course, that's what she would ask. Why didn't I think of that? Ella didn't try to stop the goofy smile that she felt slip up the corners of her mouth. "Oh goodness. That's a can of worms that doesn't end pretty."

"You're blushing. Now you have to tell me."

She laughed at her friend. "You need sleep. Heaven forbid I keep the pregnant lady from her rest."

"Oh, I'm fine. Already talked to the Captain, too. I don't have to come in until you are up to talking about the case. So, we can sleep in tomorrow."

Ella shook her head. She wasn't getting out of this. "Fine, to the couch. It's a long story." Both ladies grabbed their mugs of tea and went to the family room. Ella took a seat on the couch and debated where to start. She could tell stories about her and Adam for the next year. "All right, well, where to start? I know." She knew exactly the part of their story that Amelia would want to know most. "Adam was my first kiss, and I was his."

Amelia's eyebrows rose. "Oh really?"

"Yep."

CHAPTER 6

Twenty Years Ago

The oscillating fan blew across thirteen-year-old Ella on a hot day at the end of June. She was stretched out on her bed reading another one of her mom's Nancy Drew books.

"Elly?" Adam's voice come from downstairs. The screen door slammed behind him. They had been best friends for years, having always lived just three doors down from the other. They had an open-door policy at each other's homes; if the door was unlocked, come on in.

"In my room!" she hollered down to him.

She heard him run up the stairs two at a time, his long legs making it easy. "Hey!" He swung around the doorway and entered her room. He had easily grown another six inches in the last six months, so he now towered over her. It had only been two years ago that she had been taller than him. It was short lived, but she had rubbed it in his face.

"Hey. What's up?"

"Want to go swim down at the lake?"

She jumped up off her bed and tossed her book onto the pillow. That was the best idea she had heard all day. "Let's go!"

Adam left her room long enough for her to change. She pulled on her one-piece swimsuit over her newly curvy body. Just over the last year her body had dramatically changed. She was no longer a lanky little girl, but her body was quickly becoming that of a woman. She threw on a pair of cutoff jean shorts and grabbed a towel and her sunglasses. She met Adam at the bottom of the stairs.

"Mom, is it okay if Adam and I go swimming down at the lake?" She stuck her head around the corner so she could see her mom.

"Sure, have fun and be careful. Just be back in time for dinner."

"Ok; thanks, mom!"

They headed out the door, grabbed their bikes, and rode the two miles to the lake with the semi-public beach. They were surprised that hardly anyone was there, just a group of older teenagers they didn't really know. They leaned their bikes up against a tree, and while Ella took off her shorts, Adam took off his shirt. She surprised herself by blushing a little at the sight of him without his shirt. It wasn't, by any means, the first time she saw his bare chest, but recently she was developing a bit of a crush on her best friend. And apparently, she wasn't alone. She looked at Adam and was even more surprised by the shimmering in his eyes as he watched her. The heat in her cheeks increased.

She shoved him aside and ran towards the water; Adam was in quick pursuit.

He caught her once she hit the water and wrapped his arms around her waist but tossed her into the water. She laughed uncontrollably, and a splashing war commenced. They both gave up eventually, and Adam said, "Want to swim out to the raft today? There's nobody out there."

"Sure, but no racing! I'm still out of breath from all the laughing." They leisurely swam out to the wooden raft that was anchored down in the middle of the small lake. There was no ladder on the raft, so as always Adam helped Ella climb up by letting her use his knee as a step. Once on the raft they both laid back and basked in the bright mid-afternoon sun.

They were growing up fast and were beginning to feel like they were. Ella was finally an official teenager, and Adam was going to start high school in the fall and turn fifteen in October.

Silence lingered for a few minutes, until Adam sat up and finally spoke. "Ella?"

"Yeah?" she said without even opening her eyes.

"Ella..."

She sat up at his hesitation. "What is it?"

"Well, I was talking to a few of the guys from basketball and well, apparently I'm the only one that hasn't kissed a girl yet. Supposedly, if you haven't kissed by the time you get into high school you get made fun of pretty badly."

"Oh. Guess you have to find yourself a girlfriend this summer, huh?" Her heart hurt at the thought. She didn't want to share Adam. He was her Adam.

"Or... or well, I was thinking... who better to kiss than your best friend?"

Her eyes shot up and met his. "Really? You want to kiss me?"

"I don't want to kiss anyone else."

She smiled. He smiled back. Was he going to kiss her now?

"Well, may I?"

"Now?"

"When else? Unless you want to do it somewhere else."

"No, here is fine."

They both looked at each other nervously, both completely unsure as to what to do. They scooted closer to one another until they were facing, and their knees touched with how they were both sitting, legs crisscrossed. Ella sat up straighter and bit her lip nervously. Adam fiddled with his hands in his lap, clearly not sure what do to with them. They giggled.

"Okay," Adam said, "we can figure this out. Should we just go for it?"

Ella nodded. Adam's face came toward hers, and she leaned towards him. As soon as their lips touched, her eyes slammed shut. The kiss didn't last but just a few seconds, but in that time Ella's heart took flight. She had no idea what she was feeling, but she liked it. Adam pulled back and smiled at her.

"Well, you can't say you've never kissed a girl, now."

Adam just smiled the stupidest grin she had ever seen on his face.

She giggled. "You can kiss me again if you'd like." A slight tease danced in her voice.

"I would like." And he leaned forward and kissed her again. This time his hands didn't stay in his lap, instead they caressed her upper arms. His lips moved more this time, and she matched every move he made. As they kissed, they scooted closer to each other so that Ella's knees rested on Adam's thighs. His hand stroked her back, and she put her arms around his neck. Her spirit soared. She couldn't believe she was kissing Adam, her Adam. Finally, they breathlessly pulled away from one another. Ella turned and dipped her feet into the lake. Her heart was beating so hard she thought it might launch into space, and her smile was so wide that her cheeks felt like they were going to split open. Adam came over and sat super close and put his arms around her shoulders. She leaned into him and looked into his face. His smile matched hers. She giggled, and he laughed in return.

This is going to be the best summer ever!

And it proved to be. Adam and Ella spent every possible minute together. Hours were spent down at the lake both swimming and making out. On raining days, they spent the days at one or the other's house. However, their parents caught on to their developing romance and stopped allowing them to spend any time in each other's bedrooms. They balked at the new rule but obeyed. So, they spent the rainy days in each other's family rooms. Adam had just learned to play the guitar, so they would sit and sing together for hours. Adam's favorite song to play and sing to Ella was "Brown Eyed Girl" by Van Morrison. She loved it and would always add some harmonies to his boyish soprano that by the end of the summer had become a tenor.

One Friday evening in the beginning of August, Ella and Adam had been out on the trampoline in her backyard. They had been jumping and trying to best each other in flips, but now had lain down with their heads near each other and looked up at the stars. When Ella's mom came out the squeaky back door, they both groaned since they were sure she was coming out to send Adam home. But to their surprise she said, "Hey, you two want some popcorn and Cokes?"

"Yes, please, Mom. Thank you!" Ella rolled onto her stomach and looked at her mom.

"Yes, thank you Mrs. Perkins," Adam added.

"No problem, you two. It's a gorgeous night. Enjoy a bit of it before Adam has to go home." There it was. "I'll be back in a few minutes."

Ella rolled back to her back, and Adam grabbed her hand. She intertwined her fingers in his and looked over and smiled at him. Neither of them said anything until after Ella's mom had brought out the popcorn and Cokes. They sat up and enjoyed their snack.

Adam swigged his Coke. "Ella?"

"Yes, Adam?"

"You'll marry me when we grow up, right?"

She smiled. "Of course. Just don't forget about me when you're in high school without me this next year."

"I could never forget you. I love you, Ella."

"I love you, too, Adam."

He scooted closer to her and wrapped his arm around her. She leaned her head onto his chest. She wanted that moment to last forever.

But it didn't.

The first day of school came way faster than either of them had wanted. It was the first time since Adam was in kindergarten that they hadn't gone to the same school. He had always been a year ahead since he was over a year and a half older, but their school had gone through eighth grade, so they had always been together. Not as much as when she was in second and he was in third. That year they had even been in the same second/third split class. That was the year they had become completely inseparable. But this year, they didn't even ride the same bus. Adam's bus left an entire half hour before hers. But on the first day of school she met him at the bus stop.

"You didn't have to come out here and wait with me, Ella."

"I know, but I wanted to. I wanted to send you off to a good first day of high school."

He smiled and kissed her deeply. They stood there hugging until his bus pulled up.

"Well, I guess I have to go. Love you, my brown-eyed girl."

"Love you, too. Have a good day. I can't wait to hear about it."

He gave her a quick kiss and climbed on the bus and waved to her as it pulled away.

That was the beginning of the end.

It was a gradual drifting. As school got underway, they both became very busy. Adam joined the track team and that kept him busy after school most days. They still made time to see each other, but it was much less often than they would like. One evening, Ella was sitting on Adam's front steps waiting for him to get home. He had promised they would have some quality time that evening, but when he arrived home he was with a group of guys from school.

She jumped to her feet. "Hey, Adam!"

"Hey, Ella!" he said with a smile.

"Jamison, what the heck is she doing here? You're in high school now, you can't hang out with middle schoolers," Conner Malton said.

Ella's heart plummeted. Surely Adam would stand up for her.

Connor continued, "Get out of here, Fatso." He walked past her toward the house, and the other guys followed, except Adam.

She looked at Adam, her heart ripped a little.

"I'm sorry, Ella. But I guess you should go. I'll find you tomorrow."

He hadn't stood up for her. He chose the guys over her. He broke his promise to spend the evening with her. Her heart ripped in half.

But she didn't give up hope on him. Not yet. They still hung out some, but not nearly enough for Ella's liking. One spring afternoon Ella was once again sitting on Adam's steps. She didn't jump up at the sight of him, instead she just sat there and waited for him to come sit down next to her. She was tired of the uncertainty she felt with him. Hopefully, he would have time for her now that the basketball season was over.

"Hey," He sat down next to her.

"Hi. Can we actually hang out tonight?"

"I wish. I have so much homework, though. I have a paper due tomorrow that I haven't even started."

Her heart dropped to the ground.

"I'm sorry." He put his arm around her shoulders, and she leaned into him. "You could come in and hang out with me while I work."

"You know your mom won't let that happen. Plus, you know you won't get anything done."

He gave her a mischievous smile. "True. How about ten minutes? My mom isn't home yet. Come inside, and we can hang out for a bit?"

She liked that idea. It was her turn to give a mischievous smile. She hopped up and followed him inside. They sat on the couch and started kissing.

"Ella," Adam said as the pulled away briefly, "you know I still love you right?"

"Yes, but I miss spending time with you. And not just making out for ten minutes. I miss going places together, playing cards, singing."

"I know. I do, too. This summer, we'll do all that. I'm all yours once school is out."

She smiled. But June seemed so far away.

They kissed again, and he leaned her back onto the couch. His kisses were deep and passionate, and she matched them. But when Adam's hand started wandering, she stopped him. "Adam, no." It wasn't the first time she'd had to stop him. Last summer they had gone too far for her comfort on many occasions.

"I know, I know. I'm sorry." He lowered himself down to the couch beside her and wrapped his arms around her. She buried her head in his chest.

"I love you, too, Adam."

He kissed her head.

That was the last time they made out.

When the last day of school finally arrived. Ella found Adam sitting on her steps when she got home. She smiled, but her heart dropped.

"Ella! It's summer! I'm all yours."

"Oh, Adam." She fell into his arms.

"Ella," her mom called from in the house, "No time to hang out with Adam, you need to pack."

"Pack?" Adam asked with dismay.

"Yeah, I haven't had a chance to tell you yet. My grandmother is really sick, so my mom and I are going there to help her."

"You can't stay here with your dad?"

"No. Mom won't let me. Apparently, Dad has some business trips planned."

The look on Adam's face broke her heart. His lips were pressed together, and his eyes closed. Disappointment seeped from every pore.

"I'll be home at some point. I'll be all yours."

"Okay."

"Eleanor!" her mom called again.

"I have to go, Adam."

"Okay. Bye, Elly."

"Bye, Adam." He gave her the last kiss they would share.

That summer was awful. She never saw Adam. The few weeks she was home, he was gone, either to basketball camp, or to his dad's, since his dad had left his mom and him during the winter and had moved away with his new girlfriend.

When the new school year finally rolled around, Ella was so excited to finally be in high school. Finally, she and Adam could be something again. But he wasn't at the bus stop when the bus arrived. She climbed onto the bus and found a seat and saved one for Adam. He jumped onto the bus just before it was about to pull away. He smiled when he saw her, but before he could make it back to where she was sitting, Sandra, a tall, skinny, popular girl, grabbed his arm and pulled him into the seat where she was sitting. His rueful smile and the longing and heartache in his eyes as he surrendered to Sandra shattered Ella's heart.

And that was the end. A month later when Adam got his driver's license, he no longer even rode the bus. They hardly even saw each other anymore. They both were busy with their own activities. She was in choir and wrote for the school newspaper. He was the quintessential jock. She became an outspoken proponent for abstinence before marriage. He had a new girlfriend every couple of months. Adam Jamison and Ella Perkins were history.

CHAPTER 7

Present Day

Thursday morning Adam massaged his temples and attempted to keep his eyes open at his desk. After leaving Jared and Becca's last night he had gone home and gotten completely wasted. He had skipped the beer and went straight for the hard stuff. The news that Ella had been raped, and to find her apartment ransacked by a killer, had been too much. He was paying the price this morning, though. He hadn't made it into the station until nine, but no one said anything. Despite lots of coffee and ibuprofen, his head felt like a jackhammer was doing a polka on his skull. He tried to work through the details that the tech team had been able to come up with since last night, but it wasn't much. No sign of entry. Her apartment had been locked when he went up. He remembered that significantly as he had struggled with the lock for a second since the bolt was stiff. No fingerprints were left. They were still working on the knife used.

There wasn't much more he could do other than paperwork, so he sat at his desk most of the morning working on his reports, just waiting for Amelia to bring Ella in to give her testimony. They were going to need to have her go back through what was probably the worst day of her life. But it was necessary.

Around noon he looked up and saw them walk into the squad room. Ella looked as beautiful as always. Her strawberry-blonde hair was pulled back in a low ponytail, and her makeup was subtle, but that's what made her so much more beautiful than most of the women he dated who gobbed on the makeup. Ella's beauty was natural. It radiated right out of her soul. Her curvy figure was graced in a pair of simple blue jeans and a striped blue blouse.

They came over to his desk. "Good morning, ladies," he greeted them and grimaced. He had moved his head too quickly.

"Good morning, Jamison. That's what I figured. That's why I brought you this." Amelia set a brown paper bag in front of him. "According to Becca and Jared, these are the best things to cure that hangover."

He was a bit embarrassed that his partner expected him to have a hangover today, but there was a good chance that Ella had told her about their history last night, so she would know how much this was affecting him. But in front of Ella? *Oh well. It is what is.* He looked in the bag, banana, a Gatorade, some crackers with honey, and an egg salad sandwich.

"Thanks, Amelia. I think you know me too well."

Amelia sat at her desk and smiled.

He looked at Ella. "I hope you don't still hate eggs."

She scrunched up her nose. "I was trying not to gag while she made it."

He chuckled and pulled a chair over to his desk for her to sit in. "How are you doing this morning?"

"Okay, I guess." She sat and looked down at her hands.

"Sleep at all?"

"Not really. Amelia and I stayed up too late talking."

"About me?" he guessed.

She smiled an adorable little smile that caused her cheeks to redden a bit. He was right. "Maybe," she replied. "Among other things. But even when I did go to bed, I didn't sleep very well."

"Flashbacks?"

"Yep."

"That's not uncommon."

"It still stinks."

"No doubt. Do you think you can handle walking us through what happened seventeen years ago? I know we have the old report, but it would help Amelia and me to hear it directly from you. But I understand if you don't want me in there. You can just tell Amelia. I think the Captain wants to sit in too since he was the detective on your case back then."

Her expression softened at his suggestion. "No, Adam, it's all right. You can be there. I think I'm as ready as I'm going to be."

Adam stood and pulled the Gatorade out of the bag and said, "Shall we?"

"Eat first, Adam," Ella said. "You look like you need it."

He smiled and lowered himself back into his seat. He ate half of his sandwich and the banana. "Okay. Happy now?" He teased Ella.

She responded with a curt nod and a satisfied smile.

Is she actually warming up to me? He hoped so.

The three of them went to the Captain's office and shut the door behind themselves. "Hi, Miss Perkins," the Captain greeted her.

"Hello, Detect-, I mean Captain Baker." They shook hands, and the Captain motioned for her to take a seat on the couch along the side of his office. She took a seat at one end, and Amelia sat next to her. Adam and the Captain moved the chairs to face the couch and each sat in one. Adam sat across from Ella. He wanted so badly to take her fidgeting hands in his own and reassure her it would all be okay.

The Captain spoke. "Miss Perkins, I know this is going to be hard, and I know we've been through it all before, but it will help these detectives to hear it from you."

"I know."

"Just take your time. Okay?"

Ella nodded and looked from Baker to Amelia but didn't say anything.

Amelia said, "Ella, why don't you start by telling us what you were doing that afternoon. It was a Friday, right? What did you do when you got home from school? Talk us through even the most mundane details of that day; that may help you get to the rest."

Ella's shoulders dropped and her eyes closed. She pressed her lips together and looked as if she might cry already. She looked up at Adam with so much sorrow as if this was the piece of all pieces she wanted to leave out of the puzzle.

"Go ahead, Ella, it's okay," he tried to reassure her not knowing at all what she was going to say.

She swallowed hard and began, "After school, I went right out to the trampoline to try and do my homework, but I couldn't focus because I kept crying. I remember my mom coming outside and asking me what was wrong. I had just discovered that afternoon that my childhood best friend was having his eighteenth birthday party that evening, and I hadn't been invited. I shouldn't have been so broken up about it, because we hadn't talked in years, but... I was a teenage girl."

Her eyes met his. He tried to apologize with his eyes. *Why didn't I invite you?*

She sighed and licked her lips before she continued. "I just didn't understand what had happened between us that had torn us so far apart. I had to work that evening, but I would have gotten out of it for him... if he had just asked."

This was all his all his fault. If he had invited to her to his birthday party, she wouldn't have been anywhere near that alley that night, and she wouldn't have been raped. He could feel the heat rising in his ears as his anger, now at himself, grew.

"But it wasn't his fault I was raped." She looked right at him; she was talking to him. "Based on the fact that this man knew my name, I'm guessing he would have done it one way or another."

She was right, but that didn't ease the guilt gripping his gut.

She continued, "But anyway. I begged my mom to drive me to work that night, or to let me have the car. But it wasn't possible, my mom had a meeting, and she had to leave before I needed to be at work and my dad wasn't going to be home until after I needed to be there, so I had to ride my bike. That wasn't unusual though, I rode my bike to work often. Especially since the whole reason I had gotten a job was to save up for a car. I went to work at the little used bookstore as usual, nothing was out of the ordinary, well other than my sour mood. Two, maybe three, customers came in the shop that night. I left at my normal time and took my normal path home. I cut close to the side of another strip-mall because it was the most direct path home. That's when I heard someone calling for help from the alley." Ella closed her eyes and took a deep breath in.

Adam wished he could take this away from her, but he couldn't; it had already happened. "Take your time."

She gave him a weak smile and slowly continued. "I knew it was stupid, but I got off my bike to check it out. I pulled my keys out and put one between my fingers, just like my dad taught me, in case it was a trap. Ha. That didn't matter. He snuck up behind me. Before I even realized what was happening, he had a knife to my throat. My keys dropped to the ground, useless." Her eyes closed and her voice stopped. A flashback was coming on.

Amelia said, "Ella, you're safe. Come back to the present; here, today, in Captain Baker's office."

Ella opened her eyes, looked at Amelia, and nodded. "Sorry."

"No need to apologize. Flashbacks are part of it. Good job cutting it off. Do you need anything?"

"No, I'll be okay."

"Continue when you're ready."

"Well, next he said, 'On your knees, Ella.' All I could do was obey out of fear... he got in front of me and told me to put my hands out. He taped them together and pulled them up so high it hurt. He pulled me over to the dumpster and taped my hands to it, all while... pressing himself into my face." A shudder shook Ella's body.

Amelia placed a hand on Ella's shoulder, but she jumped, and Amelia removed it immediately. Apparently, it wasn't only his touch she avoided. But knowing what she was going to say next, he couldn't blame her.

"It happened so fast. The next thing I knew he had ripped my pants off and... and... was in me." She looked as if she was about to crumble into a thousand pieces.

Adam hated this and hated the man responsible for hurting sweet Ella. That word wasn't strong enough; Adam felt something much deeper than hate.

She took several deep breaths. "He washed me. I remember him saying something like, 'don't want to leave any evidence.' Then he was gone. He just left me exposed and taped to the dumpster. The police found me a couple hours later after my mom called and insisted that they go look for me since I hadn't shown up at home."

"Ella, can you tell us what he looked like or what he was wearing?" Amelia asked softly.

"He was wearing all black, black shoes, black jeans, black shirt, black leather jacket, black gloves, and a black ski mask. I have no idea what he looked like other than I know he was Caucasian. His eyes, I'll never forget his eyes, but they were a very ordinary blue. He was probably just under six foot and an average build."

"Good job, Ella. Is that everything you remember?" Amelia said.

Ella nodded and even accepted a squeeze of Amelia's hand as she sighed deeply. "Captain Baker, one thing I wanted to ask, what ever happened to the DNA evidence?"

The Captain shook his head. "There wasn't any recovered."

Ella's eyebrows furrowed. "But I specifically remember the nurse who did my rape kit said there was."

The Captain stood and picked up a file off his desk. He flipped it open and sat back in his chair. "Hmm... I don't see anything in the file. Jamison, follow up with that when we're done here."

"Yes, sir."

Baker closed the file. "Ella, is there anything else?"

She shook her head.

But Adam knew she had left something out. The pieces had come together instantly in his mind. "Ella, you're not telling us something."

Her eyes shot up at him, wide in horror. She shook her head.

"Ella, you know it matters."

"No, it doesn't." Her breathing became rapid. She clearly didn't want to acknowledge the truth.

He leaned forward and rested his elbows on his knees. "You are a smart woman, Ella. You know it's important and why." Even though he was staring at Ella, out the corner of his eye he couldn't miss the Captain's and Amelia's confused expressions.

Surrender washed over her, and her rigid body relaxed. "Well, what I'm about to say can*not* leave this room." They all nodded. "A month later I realized that I was pregnant. I didn't tell anyone for the longest time, not even my mom or my counselor, but they both caught on within a few months."

The Captain leaned forward. "Miss Perkins, you never told us."

"I didn't figure it would make any difference. By the time I admitted it, the case had gone cold."

"Were you offered the morning after pill at the hospital?" the Captain asked.

Adam knew that wouldn't have mattered.

"I was, but I turned it down on ethical principle."

Adam smiled. "You probably said it just like that, too. Didn't you?"

She weakly returned his smile. "You're right; I probably did." Her soft laugh pulled on his heart strings.

"So, what did you do?" Amelia asked gently.

"I gave the little boy up for adoption."

"Was it a closed or open adoption?" the Captain asked.

Ella's brows furrowed. "It was open, why?"

"Miss Perkins, since it seems like we don't have any DNA from any of the crime scenes, if we could get a sample of the child's DNA–"

"No. You can't. His parents don't even know that I was raped. They, just like everyone else, thought I was simply a promiscuous teenage girl. I didn't want the boy growing up with the stigma that his biological father was a rapist."

They all sat in silence. Adam knew they would have to get the child's DNA; it would be the biggest break in the case in seventeen years. But they had to be tactful about it, and he did not want to go about it without Ella's consent. But he was also afraid to push her. Their connection was so fragile at this point.

"Ella," Amelia said, "Do you understand the significance of the child's DNA?"

"I do. And I want to catch this guy, of course. But I want to protect Kyle more than anything. Is there any way you could get what you need without having to explain the situation? Kyle is a great kid, doing well in school, an active member of his church youth group. He's a sixteen-year-old boy, trying to figure out who God made him to be. He doesn't need this. And most importantly, I'm afraid for his life. If this guy is trying to kill off his former victims, that couldn't even identify him seventeen years ago, what is he going to do if he discovers one of those girls he raped gave birth to his son? Kyle won't be safe."

Amelia clenched her hands. "Those are all very valid and important factors. I promise we will use the greatest discretion we can. Captain, is it safe to say we can keep this information between the four of us?

I don't see why the lab techs would even need to know where the sample is from or how we obtained it."

"That is completely reasonable," the Captain agreed. "Miss Perkins, you have my word. No one else will know about this. The boy's safety is of utmost importance, as is yours. I will have Jamison and Johnson handle everything, even the collection of the sample. For now, we get permission from the parents for data and search purposes only. If we need the proof for court as well, we'll cross that bridge when we land on it."

Ella slipped her fingertips under her legs. "Thank you, Captain Baker." Ella's face was pale and her eyes sunken in; she was exhausted.

"Ella, you need to get some rest," Adam said.

She gave him a rueful smile and nodded.

Amelia said, "I agree with Adam. Let's take you back to my place."

They all stood. And Adam watched Ella leave with Amelia. He wanted to go with them. He didn't want to leave Ella's side, but she probably needed time away from him right now. He could throttle himself for not inviting her to his birthday party.

"Are you all right, Jamison?" The Captain went and sat at his desk.

"Yes, sir."

"Close the door. Let's talk for a minute."

Adam closed the door slowly and turned back towards the Captain.

"A few things, Adam. First off, we have a problem, and you need to rectify it. You are no longer to come to work hungover. If this continues, I'm going to put you back on desk duty and send you back to the counselor. Understand? Get it under control yourself, or I'll help, and you won't like it." The Captain sure was good at saying it like it is.

"Yes, sir." Adam lowered his head and sighed. *How could I have let it get this bad?*

"Secondly, I can tell that Ella means a lot to you. Is that going to interfere with your ability to work objectively on this case? Are you too close to this?"

"No, sir." He looked back up at the Captain. He would give up drinking completely for Ella. He would do anything to keep her safe and find her rapist.

"Good, because I think the personal connection will help you if you don't let it get the best of you. Also, were you the friend she was talking about?"

"Yes, sir."

"Okay, that's what I thought based on the expressions you exchanged. Chin up, okay. You heard her. She doesn't blame you, but she was clearly hurt. You need to clear things up between the two of you."

"I intend to, sir. I'm just not sure how."

"Well, one thing women want more than anything is an apology. If you've done something wrong, or even if you just inadvertently hurt their feelings, the best thing you can do is acknowledge their feelings and say you're sorry. I know, I was married for nearly twenty years, and that doesn't happen if you're prideful." Sorrow flashed through Baker's eyes.

Adam swallowed. "But I'm not sure she should forgive me, Captain."

"Adam, I think she already has. If she was spiteful and unforgiving, she would have been more malicious in how she talked about the party. She didn't even say your name. The way she talked about it showed her grief from the loss of your friendship, not anger toward you. Apologize and give her space. But be available. I think you'll be surprised; relationships can be mended."

"Thank you, sir. I appreciate the advice." Adam's dad had been so distant, especially after running off, so it was nice to receive some fatherly advice even if the Captain was only ten years his elder.

"Any time, Adam. On a personal note, aside from being your boss, I wanted to let you know I'm praying for you. Miller's passing has been hard on you, I know. It's been tough on all of us, but you've taken the brunt. Keep processing it though, don't hole up in a bottle of liquor, because that isn't going to cut it. Trust me, I know. Let me know if you need anything, all right?"

"Thanks, Captain, I will." The prayers surprised Adam. This man had been through a lot too. Not only had he lost a detective under his watch, but this year had been tough on Baker personally. Why would a man whose wife was ripped away from him by cancer be so ready to pray? Adam knew the Captain had gone to the same church he had when Adam was a kid. Apparently, his faith had withstood time. Adam wanted to believe that prayers could make a difference. He wanted to believe that God was up there looking down on all of them actually caring what was happening. But if that was the case, why would He have taken Baker's wife, and why would he have ever allowed such awful things to happen to Ella?

Ella followed Amelia out of the police station. She was exhausted. The nightmares hadn't been too bad last night, but they had come. She didn't really remember the dreams, for which she was thankful, but they had left her with a knot in her chest and heaviness in her head.

They approached Amelia's minivan and Amelia asked, "You okay?"

"I guess, as well as I can be." Ella climbed into the passenger's side and pulled her phone out of her purse. She had put it on silent last night and figured she should check it. "Oh my."

"What's up?"

"Looks like my mom is trying to reach me... She's left five voicemails, three in the last half hour alone, and a zillion texts."

"Oh no. You never did call her last night, did you?"

"No. I just couldn't even talk about it. All she's going to do is worry."

"But you need to tell her." Amelia pulled out of the parking space.

"I know, but what am I going to say?"

"The truth."

"Well, of course, but you've met my mom. She's going to totally overreact."

"True. Should we go over there together?"

"That would probably be good."

"Then that's what we'll do. She should be at home, right?"

"Yep." Ella dialed her voicemail as Amelia drove. The first message from her mom was from yesterday evening. She sounded calm and just wanted to chat and see how Ella's first week of school was shaping up. The next message was from this morning, asking if everything was okay. The next three messages were the ones she had just left; her mother's frantic voice urging her to call immediately.

Amelia turned into Ella's old neighborhood, and Amelia's phone rang. "Is this your mom's number?" Amelia held the phone where Ella could see it.

Ella sighed. "Yes, just ignore it, we'll be there in just a minute." Ella's heart raced. She was more nervous to tell her mom what was happening than she was to talk about that night seventeen years ago, even with Adam there.

No sooner than Amelia had turned into the driveway than did Ella's mom come bursting out the door and out onto the veranda. Ella got out of the van and her mom came running down the stairs.

"Oh, thank heavens! I thought you were dead! Why didn't you return my calls, young lady!? I've been worried sick. You didn't answer. The school said you were out, and they wouldn't tell me why! Explain yourself." Her mom ended her reprimand with a heavy hand on Ella's shoulder, but she quickly removed it. Her mom was not one for physical affection, especially since Ella had been raped. It was like she was afraid to touch her.

"I'm sorry, Mom, I just got your messages. I've been..."

Amelia stepped forward. "I'm sorry, Mrs. Perkins, she's been with me."

"Mom, let's go inside and talk."

Ella's mom put her hands on her hips. "What's wrong?"

"Please, let's go sit down." Ella crossed her arms.

"Okay, do you ladies want some coffee or tea?" Ella smiled; her mom's southern hospitality could never let up.

"Coffee would be nice. Thanks, mom. Amelia?"

"I'm good, maybe just a glass of water."

Ella and Amelia followed her mom up the steps, through the front door, and into the large country kitchen. They sat at the kitchen table while her mom fixed a pot of coffee. Once the coffee was brewing, she brought Amelia a glass of water and sat.

"Now, tell me, what is going on. Ella, you look awful. Oh no, you're having flashbacks again, I can see it in your eyes."

"Yes, I am."

"But why ever so, hasn't it been a while? Has something triggered it?"

"Yes, Mom." Ella swallowed. The knot in her stomach tightened. "He's back."

"Huh? What are you talking about?"

Ella looked down at her hands. They were shaking in her lap. She could really use that cup of coffee to help calm her nerves. "He's back. My rapist. He's back."

"What?!"

Ella looked over to Amelia. She couldn't say anymore. Amelia gave her a little nod.

"Mrs. Perkins, someone is committing crimes, just like what happened to Ella seventeen years ago, but now he's also killing his victims. He's also killing the women he hurt seventeen years ago."

"Oh, sweet Jesus!" Ella's mom was starting to panic. "You mean he's going to try to kill you now, as if he hasn't hurt you enough!"

"Mom, breathe."

"How do you expect me to breathe at a time like this? Why are you so calm? You'll just have to go live with your grandmother for a while. You can't stay in Hazel Hill if someone is trying to kill you here." Her mom stood sending her chair flying over backwards.

"Mom, I can't go to Grandma's, I have to teach."

"How can you teach at a time like this?" Her mom started pacing and wrung her hands together.

"Because I'm in good hands. God is with me no matter what happens, even at a time like this. You taught me that. Plus, Amelia and Adam are on the case, and I have faith that they will catch him."

"No one was able to catch him seventeen years ago. How is anyone—wait, you said Adam? As in Adam Jamison?"

"Yes, Mom, he's Amelia's partner." Ella clenched her hands together and braced herself for the rest of her mom's fury.

"What? No. You tell them that he's not allowed to work on your case. That good for nothing boy should not have anything to do with this."

"Mom!"

"Don't defend him, Ella. You've done that for far too long. He was awful to you."

"Don't you think I know that, Mom. I lived it, remember?" Ella's heart raced as she grew angry herself. Her mother, who would preach the gospel until she was blue in her self-righteous face, couldn't forgive the boy who had broken her daughter's heart.

"You need to forgive him, Mom."

"*I* need to forgive him? No, I won't."

"Well, he's not getting off this case. You'll just have to deal with it."

"Don't take that tone of voice with me, young lady—"

"Mom, I'm not a little girl anymore. I don't mean to be disrespectful, but you need to give him a chance."

Ella shot a look to Amelia hoping for a rescue.

"Mrs. Perkins, I can vouch for Adam. He's a great partner and an even better detective, probably one of the best ones we have in Hazel Hill. Trust me. I trust Adam with my life."

"I don't know. I don't like him being involved."

Ella spoke again and kept her voice as calm as she could, "I know, Mom, but please give him a chance. I'm going to."

Her mom sighed and picked up her chair and sat back down. She looked at her hands as she folded them on the table. She took another deep breath and let it out slowly.

Ella waited.

"Fine. I'll give him a chance, but if there are any problems you tell whoever's in charge that he has to go."

"Okay, I will."

"But you need to be careful, Ella. That boy broke your heart too many times. You keep your distance."

"I'll be careful, but I also want to reconcile with him eventually. That doesn't mean anything will happen between us, but I hate having a rift in our friendship."

"Oh Ella, be careful."

"Mom, I just said I will be. And I'm staying with Amelia, okay. She and Caleb have graciously opened their home to me. I know they will both keep me safe."

"Oh good. I still think you should go away until this is all settled."

"I understand, but I need to work. And not just for the kids, but for myself, I need the distraction. It will be better for me to keep as much of my normal routine as possible."

Amelia said, "We are going to keep Ella safe; I promise. Someone will be with her as soon as school is over, and Caleb or I will take her every morning."

"Okay." Ella's mom stood again. "Let's have that coffee now."

"That would be good."

CHAPTER 8

Saturday afternoon Ella sat in Amelia's living room watching TV and folding laundry.

"Ella, what are you doing?"

Ella looked up from the laundry to see Amelia standing beside the loveseat with her hand on her hip. She just wanted to laugh at her friend but restrained herself. "Folding laundry, what does it look like? I was bored, and it was just sitting here. Hope I'm not folding it wrong. And that Caleb won't think it's weird."

Amelia laughed. "You do not need to fold our laundry."

"I know. But like I said, I was bored. I have plenty of things I could be doing at my apartment, but since I'm still not allowed in there, I'm going to make myself useful here."

"Heaven forbid you just enjoy a little down time."

"I'm watching a movie, too." She gestured toward the TV.

Amelia shook her head. "And don't worry about your apartment today. We should be able to go over and clean it up tomorrow. Jared and Becca said they would help."

"Yep, we'll make it good as new." Caleb walked into the room and put his arms around Amelia's round waist. They were just too cute together.

"Thanks; although I'm not sure I could ever live there again..."

Amelia tilted her head. "That makes sense."

"Guess we can help you pack up, too." Looking back at his wife, Caleb asked, "Will you ladies be all right on your own tonight?"

"Yes, but why? Where do you think you are going, Mr. Johnson?" Amelia teased.

Caleb's smile faded as his expression became more somber. "I'm worried about Adam. I think he would be better off with some company tonight. I'm hoping to keep him from the bar and on the basketball court."

"You are such a good friend, Caleb," Amelia said.

Ella sat frozen with one of Molly's dresses only half-folded resting in her lap. "Adam Jamison? You're friends with Adam?"

Caleb answered, "Yeah, have been for a number of years now, ever since I moved to town. Amelia said something briefly about you and him going way back."

"That's one way to put it. Can I ask what's been going on for him? I don't want to gossip, so if it is don't tell me. I'm just curious."

"I'm not sure where exactly that line is, but you should ask him at some point. But I will tell you his former partner was killed this summer, and it shook him up pretty badly. But he's asking the right questions. I really feel like God is doing something in him. So ladies, be praying for him."

"Have been. Every day for over twenty years. I won't stop now. Thanks, Caleb."

"Is it all right if we potentially come back here after basketball?" Caleb asked Amelia.

Ella felt her whole body tighten up. Was she okay with that? But it wasn't her place to have a problem with it.

Amelia answered, "I'm fine with that, but are you, Ella?"

"Honestly, I don't know."

"Caleb, why don't you just give us a call if you guys want to, and then we'll give you an answer?"

"That works. Ella, if you don't want us to, we won't. Answer honestly."

She smiled at Caleb's sensitivity even though he had no idea what her issue was. "I will. Thank you."

"All right, Ladies, I'll call if we are thinking of coming this way. But for now, I'll take my leave. Have a good evening." Caleb kissed his wife, told the kids goodbye, and left to hang out with Adam.

Amelia came and sat down near Ella. "Seriously, Ella, don't hesitate to tell us if you aren't comfortable with Adam coming over."

She smiled at her friend. "Thanks. But there is part of me that wants to see him. I have such mixed emotions about it, because the other part of me wants to be as far from him as possible. I almost wonder if we just need to face our past, but I'm not sure what there is to say…"

"You'll figure out what, if anything, needs to be said."

"I guess."

The ladies didn't talk about Adam the rest of the afternoon or evening. Ella even managed to forget about him for a few hours, until Amelia's phone rang while she was upstairs putting Molly and Carter in bed. Ella picked up her phone and looked at the screen to see who was calling. It was Caleb. Instantly, she remembered why he would be calling, and her indecisiveness resurfaced. She went ahead and answered it.

"Hi, Caleb. It's Ella, Amelia's upstairs."

"Hey, was wondering if you felt up to having Adam come over. We'll bring some pie with us."

"Oh, you drive a hard bargain with the pie. I guess it's okay. Can I request apple?"

"Ah, good choice. We'll get ice cream, too."

"Awesome."

"We'll see you ladies in a bit."

"Okay, bye." As Ella hung up, her stomach sank. Was she really okay with seeing Adam in a nonprofessional atmosphere? She was adjusting to the idea of him being one of the detectives on the case, but this would be an informal, just friends hanging out, kind of interaction. *Ugh. Why am I so nervous?* It was as if her very soul trembled at the thought of being around Adam.

Amelia came down the stairs. "Was that Caleb?"

"Yes, I went ahead and answered it; hope that's okay."

"Totally. So, what did you say?"

Her shoulders dropped. "I said okay... but he said they'd bring pie, so how was I supposed to say no?" She chuckled at herself.

Amelia snickered too. "Ella, I get the feeling that there is more to the story between you and Adam than you've told me."

Ella bit her lip and looked at the floor. "Yeah, a little bit. But I don't want to get into it right now. Not right before they show up. Another time I'll tell you."

"You don't have to, if you don't want to."

"No, I want to. Just not now."

"Understandable."

Ella changed the subject. "The kids go down okay?"

"They did. They think it's great camping out together."

The ladies went to the kitchen and fixed some coffee to go with the pie. Ella tried to ignore the nerves that were eating her stomach and tried to steel herself against any emotions. But the ten minutes she had before the guys walked in the door were not enough. There he was standing in the place she was temporarily calling home, looking more handsome than ever. He was quite good looking in his dress coat and tie, but something about seeing him in basketball shorts and a t-shirt reminded her entirely too much of the young teenager she had been madly in love with all those years ago.

"Hi, Ella." Adam gripped his hands in front of himself as Caleb greeted Amelia with a kiss.

"Hi."

"How are you doing?"

"Well as can be, I guess. You?"

"I'm okay," he sighed. But one corner of his lips turned up in a slight smile setting her a little bit more at ease. Knowing he was having a rough go of life lately and knowing that her situation was affecting him helped soften her heart toward him.

God please help us to be at least civil with each other through all of this. Help me know what to say to him...

Once everyone had their pie a la mode and coffee, the four made their way to the dining room and sat around the table, the ladies on one side and the guys on the other.

Amelia started the conversation, "So did you guys have a good time playing ball?"

Adam responded, "Of course."

"Yeah, thankfully, Jamison here went easy on me tonight."

"I have to every once in a while, old man. Otherwise you won't want to play anymore."

"Eh, if I want to win, I just have to play Jared in a little one on one."

Both men laughed. Ella was amused, but also a little confused. "Is Jared no good?" she asked.

Caleb replied, "Oh, he's good, but I know exactly how to distract him, so I can get a few extra shots in. All you have to do is ask him about Callie or Dani. He is so smitten with his little girls that he completely loses focus."

They all laughed.

The conversation stayed lighthearted and on safe topics for everyone. The longer they sat there though, the more questions Ella wanted to ask Adam, but she really wanted to ask them one on one. However, she was deathly afraid of being alone with Adam. She wasn't sure her emotions could handle it yet, but maybe one day they would be able to sit down and talk, just the two of them. But not yet.

When Amelia started yawning and excused herself to go to bed, Ella followed suit. "I'm going to turn in, too."

Adam's eyes locked with hers, and he smiled. There was something in his eyes that she couldn't quite decipher. Was it longing? If so, longing for what? Was it sorrow? She couldn't be sure, and she wasn't about to ask him.

"Good night, Adam." She pushed herself up from the table and genuinely added, "It was good to see you."

"You too, Ella. Sleep well. I'll see you again soon." He gave her a reassuring nod, as if to say that she could believe him this time.

Amelia kissed her husband and told Adam goodnight, and the two ladies went upstairs together.

"Ella." Amelia stopped at the top of the stairs. "You did well tonight. It was interesting to see the two of you interact away from Adam being a cop on your case. You two clearly need to deal with some things before you can be friends again."

"You could say that."

Amelia turned fully toward Ella and rubbed the palm of her hand with her thumb. "Do you want to be friends with him again? Do you want to mend that broken relationship? Because I don't want to push you."

Ella smiled at her friend's concern. "I think I do, Amelia. I really think I do. But it's all so sudden. I've tried so hard to forget about him, but here he is, back in my life. I'm not sure I'm ready to deal with all of that mess yet, but one day. But part of me isn't even sure if we can be 'friends' after all that happened between us. I loved him so much that it's hard to think of him as anything but the boy I loved. And I'm not exactly the type of girl Adam Jamison dates, so... I don't know." *I'm no size four.*

"One day at a time, Ella. I'm praying for you and Adam. God's got His hand on this situation."

"How do you know that? I mean, I've always believed in God's sovereignty and that He works things together for the good of those He's called, but I just don't even see how this is all working together."

"Well, for one, we can't see the big picture. But we can have faith and hope in God. Plus, Caleb had one of those feelings I've told you about when I told him about that you and Adam knew each other when you were younger."

"A good feeling or a bad one? One like he had about you when he met you or one like he had when you went to Richmond for that hearing?"

"One like when he met me, a very good one." Amelia's entire face formed a smile.

Ella smiled in return. She couldn't, wouldn't, hope for love again with Adam, but maybe friendship could be a reality.

———•———

"All right, Adam, you've got some talking to do."

With eyebrows raised, Adam looked over at his friend. They walked out of the dining room towards the kitchen with their plates and coffee cups. "What on earth are you talking about?"

"I'm talking about Ella. You've managed to avoid the topic, and well, it's time to fess up."

Adam set his dishes in the sink and moved out of the way for Caleb. "I don't know what you are expecting me to say."

"How about you start with whether or not she is the woman you were talking about in the diner on Sunday morning?"

Adam let out a long, exaggerated sigh.

"Oh, so she is?"

Adam leaned against the counter. "Yes. She is. But I seriously messed that up years ago. I'm not even expecting her to ever be my friend again, let alone anything more."

"Don't underestimate her. You may have screwed things up, but that doesn't mean the friendship can't be mended."

"Dude, you have no idea. I was a total jerk to her. I completely betrayed her. I let her go because some stupid bully said she wasn't worth my time. And because, apparently, I valued what other people thought of me more than her. Which is so completely stupid, because she meant more to me than anything. I cared more about what she thought of me than anyone, but I took for granted the fact that she always saw the best in me. I told you, Caleb, it would take a miracle. And I'm not sure I believe in those, so I wouldn't hold your breath."

"Adam, God is a God of miracles; that's what He does. If He can mend his relationship with mankind, I think He can handle your and Ella's friendship. I was so messed up, yet God redeemed me. He can do the same for you."

"Okay, now you aren't talking about Ella and me..."

"No, I guess not. But it comes down to humility, Adam. Humble yourself before God, humble yourself before Ella, and those relationships can be mended and redeemed."

Adam didn't respond. He did know how. What could he say? He had no argument for Caleb, even if he didn't like what he said. Humility was not a quality that Adam knew much about. But it seemed like God was forcing him to his knees with one bad experience after another. But could he willingly go to his knees? Could he ever admit that he wasn't enough on his own? And could God actually forgive him for all the ways he had screwed up? Could Ella?

CHAPTER 9

Adam was sitting at his desk Monday morning digging further into Ella's case file from seventeen years ago. He had spent all of Friday afternoon in the evidence locker scouring for the missing DNA. But he had found nothing. This morning's search was turning up nothing as well. Either no DNA was logged, or someone deleted every trace of it.

Amelia looked up at him and said, "It's nice to have you back to normal, Jamison."

"Normal?" He met her eyes.

"Not hung over and whistling."

"I was whistling?"

"Yep."

"Oh, sorry." He shot her a non-apologetic smile. He considered Amelia for a moment, not sure if he should ask the question that was on his mind.

"Just ask, Adam."

"Am I really that transparent?"

She laughed. "Yes, but only when you aren't trying to hide things."

He shook his head. "Fine. I was wondering if you think Ella would be willing to spend some time alone with me. I'd like to talk to her about some things."

A knowing smile came across Amelia's face, clearly she knew the whole story. He sighed. He wasn't quite sure how he felt about her knowing all about his relationship with Ella, but at the same time he was somehow comforted by the fact that Ella had someone she could talk to about what had happened. What surprised him though, was the fact that Amelia didn't seem to judge him for how he had treated Ella.

"Adam, I believe she is willing, but she doesn't think she's ready. I'm not sure she ever will. But she's more ready than she'd let on. Actually, tomorrow evening we have Bible study at our house, and I think Ella would rather not be there for it. Would you like to pick her up from school and hang out with her?"

His heart jumped. "Really? You think she'll be okay with it?"

"I'll ask her to be sure. But I think it would be good for both of you."

"Thanks, Amelia."

Silence fell between the detectives, and they continued to work. More information had come back from the crime lab, but it wasn't much to go on. So far Adam's research had come up empty. The crime lab had determined that the same kind of knife had been used to kill Kimberly, Ava, and the cat, but they still hadn't determined what make and model of the knife. All they knew is the blade was probably around four inches long and was a straight edge, not serrated. Not much to go on.

Adam was looking back at the case file when his cell phone vibrated on his hip. He grabbed it and looked at the caller ID. He didn't recognize the number, but he knew it was a local cell phone based on the prefix. He answered, "Detective Adam Jamison."

"Hi, Adam." It was Ella. Why was she calling him in the middle of the school day? And why him and not Amelia.

"Ella, hey. What's going on?" Amelia looked up from her paperwork and tilted her head to the side with one eyebrow up.

"We are out at recess and a couple of my students came up to me and said they saw a strange man looking at us from the bushes." Her voice shook.

Adam jumped to his feet and grabbed his jacket and keys. "We're on our way."

"No, Adam, just you. Amelia will freak. It was Molly and Callie who saw him."

He stopped; Amelia stood. "Oh. It's too late though; she's already curious. I'm not going to be able to leave her here."

Amelia's eyes narrowed.

"Oh well. Okay. Just come. I'm taking the kids back inside."

"We'll be there as fast as we can." He wanted to say more but wasn't sure what. He wanted to reassure her that it would be okay, and he would take care of her. But he couldn't say that right now.

"Thank you, Adam." They hung up, and Adam went straight for the door. His pregnant partner on his six.

They walked by Jared's desk, and he asked, "What's up?"

"Wanting to know myself," Amelia said from behind him.

Adam stopped and turned toward them. He rubbed the back of his neck. "Ella called; a couple of her girls saw a guy in the bushes."

Amelia glared at him. "That's why Ella said not to bring me. Which girls?"

He closed his eyes. "Molly and Callie."

"What?" Becca exclaimed from her desk a few feet away.

"Well, we are coming too." Jared said.

"Fine, but the three of you are staying outside and looking around. I'll go in and talk to Ella and the girls. The last thing your daughters need is their parents coming to school all freaked out." All three parents looked at Adam, surprised by his forthrightness. "You know I'm right."

They all nodded and the four headed out and to the school. When they arrived, Adam stuck to what he said and made the three parents stay outside while he went in. The secretary met him at the door. "Hi, Detective. Miss Perkins said you were coming. We've gone on soft lock-down and are keeping all the kids inside the building until further notice. She and the girls who saw the man are in their classroom. Do you know where that is?"

"I do. Thank you. I have three other detectives outside; they are going to start looking around."

"Okay. Thank you."

Adam made his way down the hallway to Ella's classroom. The door was open, so he stepped into the doorway. Molly was the first one to see him and waved enthusiastically. He smiled at her. Ella turned from where she was standing in front of the class and smiled at him too. His heart did a little flip. To have her smile at him was the best thing he could ever imagine. For a brief second, he completely forgot why he was there.

But Ella's words brought him back to reality. "Ad— I mean, Detective Jamison, thank you for coming." She walked over to him but turned to her students and said, "Keep working, please."

"You all right, Ella?" Adam whispered.

"I am, I think; thanks, Adam. What do you need from us? I didn't see anything. I looked over where the girls pointed, but I saw no one. If it had been anyone else, I might write it off, but Molly and Callie are always truthful. And with all that's been happening... Plus the looks on their faces... they were scared, Adam. That scared me more than anything."

"Scares me too, but we'll find him. I need to talk to Callie and Molly individually and see what they can tell me about what they saw and hopefully what he looks like."

"Okay. There's a little table in the hall. That would probably be a good place to talk to them."

"Perfect. I have to say I'm glad they both know me, hopefully they will feel comfortable enough."

"They will. They both looked happy when I told them I was calling you." Color rose in her cheeks.

He couldn't help but wink at her. He took Molly into the hall first and then Callie, but they couldn't give him much detail. The only thing they really agreed on about how he looked was that he had blue eyes. That fact set a chill down his spine. One thought he was wearing green, the other blue. One thought he had dark hair, the other said it was gray. Not super helpful, but it was something. He took both girls outside afterward so that they could show him exactly where they had seen the man.

All four detectives came inside after they had thoroughly searched the area the girls indicated. They found Ella alone in her classroom.

"Hey, all," she greeted them. "Did you find anything?"

Adam answered, "Unfortunately, no."

Jared said, "Could have just been their overactive imaginations."

"I don't know," Ella said. "They looked really scared. And I know I don't know them as well as you do, obviously, but it doesn't seem to be their norm to overreact to something. Maybe I'm just scared and made it more than it is. I'm sorry."

Adam didn't like where she was going. "No, Elly, don't apologize. I'm not willing to risk that it wasn't something. If that creep is hanging around, I don't want you to be here without someone right here with you."

Amelia said, "I agree with Adam."

"I feel like I'm safe if the kids are here. There is no way he could get in here and take me while they are around."

Adam said, "Yeah, but after school, I don't think you should hang around without one of us here with you."

"And we will be," Amelia added. "If for some reason Jamison or I can't come we'll send someone to be here as soon as school lets out."

Ella smiled. "Thank you." Her shoulders relaxed a little.

He hoped beyond all hope that she would be fine, and that they would catch the unsub before he was able to hurt Ella, or anyone else.

Tuesday afternoon, Adam pulled into the school parking lot, his mouth dry. He was so glad that Ella had agreed to let him be her chauffeur tonight, but his nerves were wreaking havoc on him. Yet, he had a slight spring to his steps as he entered the building. He couldn't wait to see Ella. He hoped they would be able to talk tonight, but he had no idea how he would even start the conversation.

He walked down the hallway and could hear Ella's sweet voice filling her classroom.

O soul, are you weary and troubled?
No light in the darkness you see?
There's light for a look at the Savior,
And life more abundant and free!

He felt a little guilty but couldn't resist leaning up against the doorpost just out of sight. He took in the sound of her voice, but the words, not just her voice, pulled at something deep in his soul.

Turn your eyes upon Jesus, Look full on his wonderful face,
And the things of earth will grow strangely dim
In the light of his glory and grace.

He lifted himself off the door frame and knocked gently as Ella started on the second verse. Part of him just wanted to stay out there and listen to her sing, but that would be rude. Plus, he didn't want to deal with what the words of her song were pleading for him to do. He wasn't ready to turn his eyes upon Jesus. What had Jesus ever done for him?

"Hey, Adam, come on in."

He smiled at her.

"So, you get to be my babysitter tonight, huh?" Her eyes were wide, and she bit her lip.

His tense muscles relaxed; he wasn't the only one that was nervous. "It seems so. I hope that's okay." He locked eyes with her, desperate to read anything in her eyes. She just stared back at him as if she was trying to do the same thing.

Finally, she said, "I think it's okay." She turned towards the whiteboard and continued erasing the work from the day. He couldn't take his eyes off of her. Her long, green shirt clung to her hips and flowed over a pair snug brown pants. He diverted his eyes.

In effort to keep his eyes off Ella, he glanced around the classroom. It was bright and colorful. He couldn't imagine all the time she must have spent stapling pictures up on not one but four bulletin boards. "Is there anything I can help you with, Ella?"

She turned back towards him and tilted her head. "Really?"

He nodded.

"Sure. Actually, can you hang these up?" She reached for a stack of funny looking owls that had clearly been created by her third graders. "There are paper clips hanging from the ceiling around the room. Just put them up randomly around the room."

"Sure." He took the projects from Ella; his hand brushed hers slightly sending a tingling sensation up his entire arm. He hung the owls and wondered if it would be the same to hold her hand as it had been when they were teenagers. Would her lips taste the same as they did back then? What would it be like— *Stop it, Adam!* He needed to not continue down that line of thought.

"Adam?" Thankfully, Ella broke into his thoughts with a question of her own.

He looked up at where she now sat at her desk working on a stack of papers.

"Now tell me. How did you end up becoming a cop? I thought you were headed to the NBA? I thought basketball was your life."

He paused what he was doing and smiled ruefully at her. Basketball had been his life, and that's part of how he'd managed to lose her. "I was in college when I realized that there was more to life than basketball. Wish I had realized sooner, but... Anyway, I was at a party my sophomore year, when I saw a guy slip something into his date's drink. I didn't think anything of it; I had already had a few drinks and wasn't fully there. Plus, there was a piece of me that thought I should just mind my own business. Well, after I left the party and was walking across campus, I heard someone crying. Thankfully, I hadn't gotten wasted knowing I had practice the next morning. I found the same girl hiding behind some bushes all battered and bruised. Her skirt and legs were all bloody and instantly I knew what had happened."

"Oh no, that poor girl," Ella said with the most genuine, understanding sympathy Adam had ever heard. It crushed him to think that Ella knew exactly how that girl felt.

"I gave her my jacket and called 911. She told me that he had tried to roofie her, but she hadn't had anymore of her drink once she realized she had left it alone for a moment. So, he got angry and beat her and forced himself on her. I stayed with her until the paramedics and cops got there. I was able to give my statement to the cops and ended up testifying at the trial."

"Did he go to prison?"

"Yes, he did. Cops said that was thanks to my testimony."

"Wow, Adam."

He smiled. "That's when I realized I could do a lot more good as a detective than as a professional basketball player. I continued to play—I was there on scholarship after all—but I changed my major and headed down the road that brought me to where I am today."

The smile she gave him made him forget how to breathe. He hung the last of the owls and walked toward her desk. "What do you want to do this evening? Have errands you need to run? Want to eat out? Or I could make us something back at my place, although I'm not sure what I have, or we could get takeout? We could watch a movie or something?" He stuffed his hands in his pockets.

"Hmmm… Definitely in the mood to keep it low key. I guess get takeout."

"I have all three 'Back to the Future' movies; we could watch one or all of them."

He got the smile he was hoping for. "Those are still some of my favorites."

The air couldn't come in and out fast enough. *Breathe, Adam.* "I thought so."

"All right. It's a plan. I'm not quite done here yet." He took a step forward but pushed his feet into the floor. He wanted to eliminate the space between them, but he didn't dare. "Anything else I can help with?"

"I don't think so unless you think you can grade penmanship papers?"

He laughed. "Do your kids write solely in caps?"

"Do you really still do that?"

He pulled his hands from his pockets and lifted his palms to the ceiling. "More than ever."

She shook her head and laughed at him. "Just a couple more stacks to grade, and then we can get out of here."

"Okay." He wandered around the room while she worked. He read every last thing displayed on the walls. It was the only way to keep his mind from dwelling on what could have been.

Ella finished her work about twenty minutes later, and just before 4:30 they headed out of the school building. Neither spoke until they arrived at his car.

"Wow!" Ella voice sang. "You still have your dad's old '67 Chevy Impala! I thought you totaled it in high school."

"I did, and my dad was furious. He was like 'I didn't keep that car in mint condition and give it to you so you could wreck it.' But I kept the wreckage and started fixing it up after college. Completely rebuilt her; just finished a few years ago."

"She's a beauty." Ella ran her fingers along the car's hood.

"Yes, she is." But he wasn't looking at the car.

———•———

Ella couldn't believe she'd agreed to hang out with Adam. Once they'd decided what to get for dinner, the ride back to his place was quiet. They needed to talk. So much needed to be said, but she had no idea where to even start. *Lord, will Adam and I ever be able to clear this tense air? Help us, please. Help us to at least have a good evening even if we don't talk about anything.*

Adam drove, and Ella practiced in her head what she might say to him, but nothing made sense enough to say. All that she managed to do was create a knot in her stomach.

Adam turned down a familiar street. "Ella, sorry I've been quiet."

"No, it's okay. Me too. You live down here?"

A sheepish grin appeared on his face.

"What?"

He licked his lips. "Yes, I do. Bought a little house a few years back, I think you'll like it." Adam pulled into the driveway of a cute little bungalow.

She let her mouth drop open, and her heart froze in place. "You didn't!?"

"I did." His little grin had become a full smile, but the worry lines remained. His concern for her thoughts about it was endearing.

She smiled back at him. "I was wondering who was on the other end of the bidding war."

"That was you?!" His eyes grew wide. It was his turn to looked shocked.

"Yep. I would have kept going, but I was too unsure about living on my own, so I decided to let it go."

They got out of the car. Ella adjusted her bag on her shoulder, and they walked to the door. She couldn't believe Adam had actually bought the house they had talked about getting together when they were kids. The little bungalow was on their bike route to the lake. They had ridden past this house and dreamed of how they would fix it up and live happily ever after in it. Apparently not every dream had died for either of them. Adam handed her the bag of takeout and unlocked the door.

A loud bark resounded from behind the door. "Hope you still like dogs." Adam pushed the door open, and a great big golden retriever greeted them with a boatload of enthusiasm.

"Down, Rusty." Adam pushed past the dog while giving him a generous rub on the head. Adam turned the lights on and pushed a few buttons on an alarm panel by the door.

Ella knelt and greeted the dog. "Rusty, huh?" She nuzzled the affectionate dog.

"His fur was so red... Reminded me of the color your backend would be after I'd gave you a ride in that rusty old wagon." Adam's cheeks were nearly as red as the dog.

"His fur's gorgeous." She looked back at Rusty. "You're a good boy, aren't you?"

"He is. Best protector from those horrible Hazel Hill squirrels." Rusty barked and ran towards the side door. "See. All you have to do is say squirrel."

Warmth filled Ella's chest. Not only had Adam bought the house they'd dreamed of, he got a dog just like they'd talked about. She stood and looked around the house.

Adam put his messenger bag on the coat rack to the left of the door and let Rusty out the side door.

Ella followed him to her left. The side door was in a small dining room with a simple dark table and chairs. She set the bags of takeout on a counter that divided the dining area from the kitchen, whose modern decor with white cabinets and stainless-steel appliances was stunning. She wandered back towards the interior of the house. A hallway with four doors cut down the middle of the house. She walked past the hallway and into a little living room graced with a plush, black leather sofa with an array of colorful pillows, an Ikea chair, and a large-screen TV. She wandered in and set her bag by the couch. Along the far wall, an old upright piano held the focus of the room even over the large TV. Several guitars sat near the piano. She smiled. The light gray walls were adorned with black-and-white photographs, and the dark hardwood floors created a seamless look among the rooms. She stepped closer to one of the photographs.

Adam came to her side. "Like it?"

"Did Jocelyn take this one? It has her flair."

"She did. Thankfully she doesn't only use her skills behind the lens to solve crimes. Did you see that one?" He pointed across the room to the wall between the TV and the piano.

She shook her head and took a step in that direction. "The lake." She could almost feel the warmth of the late summer breeze coming off the lake.

"Do you remember taking that one?"

She looked up and met his grey eyes. "Of course. That was our summer." She let her voice fade. When Adam didn't say anything, she added, "I guess it's no different than me having a picture of us from that summer in my living room."

Slight lines appeared at the corners of his eyes, and he drew his lips in.

She stepped towards the kitchen and away from the strange fuzzy feeling that was invading her insides. She complemented him on the house, and they both went into the kitchen.

Adam retrieved plates from the cabinet, and they fixed their plates. While they ate, Adam told her all about the gutting the house and the fun he'd had doing the renovation. He also told her how his friendship with Caleb had grown during the process of them hanging drywall.

Adam took another bite of his Szechuan. After he'd finished telling Ella about the time Caleb had dropped the drywall on Adam's foot and Ella's laughter had faded, they fell into an uncomfortable silence. The unspoken words were going to eat him with more vigor than he'd eaten his Chinese. How did he even begin to apologize for all he had done to her?

"Ella?" Her name barely slipped from between his lips.

"Yeah?" She looked up at him; the forkful of rice loomed near her lips that almost seemed to quiver.

"I... uh..." He couldn't find the words as his mind took him back to the day that he had betrayed their friendship.

Adam shifted from one foot to another and listened to Mr. Withers berate him for the paper he had turned in the day before.

"Adam, you could risk losing your scholarship to UNC if you don't pass my class. You only have two weeks left before graduation. Don't blow it now. This paper is lousy, and I know you are capable of better. Fix it! And have someone proofread it for you, for crying out loud. I want it back on my desk tomorrow morning. If it is up to the standard that I know you can achieve you'll pass the class, but if it's not, I'm going to have to fail you."

He sighed and took the paper back from his English teacher. "Yes, sir."

Mr. Withers dismissed him with a nod.

Adam turned and all but stormed out of the classroom. He rolled up the paper and stuffed it in the back pocket of his jeans. Why did Mr. Withers hold him to such a high standard? English was not his subject. Before high school Ella had always helped him with his grammar homework, and she was a grade behind him! Oh, how he missed her, and not just for her way with words. He missed everything about her. Why had he let that relationship fade away? Why had he been so distant from her? Here he was about to graduate, and he had nothing but regrets. Maybe he should seek her out. He had thought about it probably a million times over the last three years. His heart tightened.

He had just been dumped by another bimbo, but that wasn't why he felt this way. Every time a relationship ended, he just wanted Ella. She was the one he was supposed to be with.

He walked down the hallway, taking the long way to his locker so he would pass by Ella's and hopefully at least catch a glimpse of her before he went home.

His heart tripped up when he saw her, despite the gloom of the paper that still hung over him. But then he caught sight of her round belly. How could she? He clenched his teeth, and his ears grew warm with anger. She had claimed that she wanted to wait until she was married, but clearly, she had just meant that she didn't want to have sex with him.

He slowed his pace. Connor, his supposed friend, knocked Ella's books on the floor. Adam's stomach lurched. He was conflicted as always, stand up for Ella or let Connor just be Connor? A glimpse of Ella's "True Love Waits" poster in her locker fueled his anger though, and he walked up to them. She was such a hypocrite.

"Leave me alone, Connor!" Ella pleaded.

"Oh, come on, it'll be fun. Just come back to my place. Clearly, you're a little floozy. Let me show you a good time."

"Go away, Connor!"

"Hey, Adam! Don't you agree?" Conner's sleezy voice made Adam want to punch him.

But Adam stayed silent.

"You guys are no fun." Connor walked away but not before kicking Ella's books further across the hall.

He hated the way Connor treated Ella, but he was so mad that he couldn't say anything. He just stood there and watched Ella struggle to lean over and pick up her things.

"Why, Ella? Why would you go and get yourself knocked up? You're such a hypocrite!" He reached into her locker and ripped her "True Love Waits" poster out and tore it into pieces as Ella stared at him, tears streaming down her cheeks. He threw the shredded poster at her and turned and walked away.

A huge knot formed in his throat. He instantly regretted his behavior, but it was too late. Words and actions couldn't be taken back. He tried to blink back the tears that pooled in his eyes, but they were too big. Ella's sobs echoed off the walls from behind him. What had just happened? Why had it come this far?

Adam looked up to where Ella sat next to him at the little square table and wiped his face with the heel of his hand. How could he even dare to ask for her forgiveness? But her beautiful brown eyes were full of compassion.

He stood and took their plates to the sink. When he turned, she stood there, just waiting for him.

In a soft voice, she said, "Let's go sit on the couch."

He just nodded, afraid his voice would crack if he spoke. His throat was so tight.

She led the way to the couch. She went to the far side and picked up a brightly striped pillow off the couch and hugged it as she sat. "I have to say Adam, the pillows are an unexpected, almost feminine touch."

He smiled. "Totally Becca. She got them for me as a house-warming gift when I finished renovations."

"That doesn't surprise me one bit. They do look like they are straight from her living room."

He watched her, but she was still waiting for him. He needed to say what was on his heart. He sat down at the opposite end of the couch and learned forward putting his elbows on his knees. "I'm so sorry, Ella. I... I can't even express how much I regret how I treated you, especially that day in the hallway with Connor... I don't expect you to forgive me. I just want you to know how sorry I am. And now that I know what happened... I feel even worse. You were the only thing that ever mattered to me, and I let you go and treated you like garbage..." He leaned further forward and buried his head in his hands. His stomach burned from his shame.

Her hand came to rest on his shoulder shooting electricity through his body. Ella was touching him! He lifted his head and met her eyes. He hadn't even heard her scoot over next to him. She slowly removed her hand. Her eyes moved back and forth as she kept them locked to his and in conjunction with a quick, sharp breath gave away her conflicting emotions at having made physical contact. He wanted so badly to pull her into his arms and just hold her and tell her he would never mistreat her again. But he didn't deserve her. He didn't deserve her forgiveness.

"Adam," her tender voice broke into his thoughts, "I forgive you."

"What?" He couldn't believe she would.

"I forgive you."

"Really? Why?"

"Because, I do. Why isn't the easiest question to answer, but frankly because I want to. I have missed you so much. But it's more than that. Christ has forgiven me and calls me to forgive in the same way. Like it says in Ephesians, forgive 'just as in Christ God forgave you.'"

"What have you ever done that needs forgiveness?"

"Plenty. Trust me."

"I don't believe you." He gave her a sideways glance.

She laughed. The sweet music of her laugh lifted his heart further. "Oh, Adam, if you must know an example…" her laughter floated out the window, and a very serious expression overtook her face and darkened her eyes. "I am having a very hard time not dwelling on what I would do to that b- monster given the opportunity. Let's just say, it's *not* what Jesus would do."

It was his turn to laugh. He shook his head.

She shrugged.

"I still can't believe you would forgive me."

She smiled. "Believe it, because I do."

"Thank you." He ran his hand through his hair. "Can I ask you a question?"

"Of course." She folded her hands in her lap.

He turned toward her. "Did you come back to school after that day in the hall? I didn't see you."

"That's because I didn't go back. I couldn't. Mom coordinated with my teachers, and I finished the last two weeks of my junior year at home and homeschooled my senior year. I couldn't step back in that building after that. Well, until I had to two weeks ago."

"What was two weeks ago?"

"We had an in-service thing over at the high school. Actually, I had a flashback that day because of that."

The ache in his stomach returned. "I'm sorry."

"Don't. I really think God was preparing me to face all of this."

He couldn't understand her faith, especially with all she'd been through. "I don't get it, Ella, how can you trust a God who would let all this happen to you?"

"Because no matter what I go through He is still good."

"I don't know." Rusty came over and nudged Adam's hand with his snout. He petted the dog. Part of him wished he could have the blind trust in God that Ella and his other friends had, but it seemed impossible.

As if reading his mind Ella said, "It's not just some blind faith. He's proved himself over and over again. I went through all this awful stuff, but He was always there for me. I found comfort in His Word and in His presence."

He smiled at her. She was as passionate for Christ as ever. No wonder she and Amelia were such good friends.

Ella's phone rang. She got up, retrieved it from her bag, and answered it. He watched her. She was the most gorgeous creature on earth. He tried to not stare at her while she talked, but she made that very difficult as she paced back and forth. She turned back around and hung up.

"Amelia says everyone is gone."

"Where did the evening go? So much for watching the movie. I guess you want to get to bed soon." He looked at the clock; it was already eight thirty.

"I don't have to leave yet, unless you want to take me now." She smiled shyly.

His heart spun. "No. You can stay a bit longer. How about some dessert? I have some ice cream in the freezer."

"That would be perfect."

Adam could barely lift himself off the couch. He was dumbfounded at how this evening was going with Ella.

———•———

"Okay, spill it."

Ella had barely walked in the door of Amelia's house when the tiny pregnant woman demanded details from Ella's time with Adam. She laughed, and her cheeks flushed. "We had a good time, if you must know."

"Of course, I must! How good a friend would I be if I didn't pull it out of you?" She winked at Ella.

Ella shook her head. "Only if I get a cup of that amazing tea."

"But of course. You can thank Becca for that. She's the one that got this southern girl drinking herbal tea."

Ella dropped her bag by the steps and followed Amelia to the kitchen. "The kids in bed already?"

"Yeah, Caleb is up there reading to them."

"What a great dad!"

"I agree." Amelia put the pot onto boil, and Ella sat in one of the stools at the breakfast bar. "So, tell me. Obviously, it went well, better than you expected, huh?"

"Yeah, he apologized."

"Really? Now, I know you haven't told me everything, because while I totally agree that you deserve an apology for the way he abandoned your friendship, I had a sense that there was more of a betrayal..."

"You'd be right about that." Ella went on to tell her about that day with Connor in the hallway at school.

Amelia fixed their tea and slid it across the counter. "Oh, Ella..."

She pursed her lips in a frown. "Yeah, it hurt. I wanted so badly to just yell at his back as he walked away that I had been raped and had only ever wanted him. But I really thought it wouldn't matter, but maybe it would have. Maybe he would have turned around and pulled me into his arms. That's what I needed. Amelia, I can't believe the sorrow I saw in his eyes as we talked tonight. I just wish he would repent to God the way he repented to me. My heart breaks for him. He needs Jesus." She brought her mug to her mouth and blew on the hot liquid.

"But you represented Jesus to him tonight. You showed him forgiveness he didn't deserve. Just like Jesus."

"I'm so far from a perfect representation of Jesus."

"I didn't say perfect, just a picture of Him."

Ella let that sink in. Maybe her forgiveness would help Adam see that God can forgive him, too. *Oh God, please help Adam see you. Reveal yourself to him. Heal his heart. And help me protect mine...*

CHAPTER 10

The next day, Adam sat at his desk twirling his pen and waited for Amelia to get off the phone. Hopefully she had good news regarding the case. It had been two days, and they still had no idea if the little girls had actually seen someone watching at the school or if their imaginations had gotten the best of them.

"Thanks, Mr. Withers. We'll be there shortly." Amelia hung up her phone.

"Well?"

"Another class of kids saw the guy again, thankfully this time they got to the teacher before he disappeared. Looks like we have a more credible witness than my daughter and her cousin."

"Give Molly credit. This proves she was right!" He stood up and pulled his blazer off the back of his chair and slid his arms in.

Amelia slowly stood and followed him out to the car. As they drove to the school, Amelia kept looking over at him. "What is it? Is Carter's drawing of me with a unicorn horn coming true?"

"Sorry, no." Her cheeks flushed.

"What did Ella tell you?"

"She just told me about last night. I'm really glad you guys are able to reconcile. I'm proud of you for apologizing."

"Has she told you the whole story?"

"Yes."

"Then You know why I had to. I still can't believe she forgives me."

Amelia smiled. "She's not the only one who will forgive you."

He shook his head. Caleb had always been good at not preaching at him about God's forgiveness, but Amelia, not so much.

"Yeah, I know what you're going to say, and you can save it."

"Adam, I'm just saying."

"I know… How 'bout this? I'll think about it. And you know if I say something, I'll do it." He smiled at her.

"Yes, I do. And now I understand your motivation to always be true to your word."

"Indeed. I messed up the best thing that ever happened to me by not keeping my word; so, never again. If I say something you can count on me. I'll think about it, Scully." And he already had been. Ever since last night, the idea that maybe God could really forgive him had been eating at his mind.

He pulled into the school parking lot.

Once inside Adam and Amelia split up. Adam spoke with the teacher. Her description of where they saw the man was exactly what Molly and Callie had seen two days ago.

"I was also able to get a picture of him. It's not very good, as I was so far away, but the kids came to me without causing a ruckus, so I was able to pull my phone out and snap a photo before he knew anyone had seen him."

"Mrs. Brown, this is perfect. May I?" He held out his hand for the phone.

"Of course."

He took the phone. "I'm going to send it to myself, so I can send it to the techs. That should be sufficient. They'll be able to enhance the photo some to give us a better idea of what he looks like. Thank you." From what little he could see in the small picture, the man had dark hair with a spattering of gray. Molly and Callie had both been right their descriptions.

Once he had sent the photo, he gave the teacher back her phone. He took another student's statement before heading back to the front office to wait for Amelia to finish her interviews with the students. As he walked past Ella's classroom, he saw her waving to her students as they left for what he assumed was PE based on the number of gym shoes worn by the kids.

A grin overtook her face when they made eye contact, making his heart act like it was on a trampoline.

"Hey, Detective Jamison. What brings you to Lincoln Elementary today?"

"Hello, Miss Perkins," he said matching her professional tone. "Looks like we've got another sighting of your peeping tom. Even have picture evidence the cousins weren't making it up."

"Oh, good... well, not good... but you know what I mean."

He chuckled. "I do. How's your day going?"

"Good. Thanks again for yesterday. It was really nice spending time with you."

"Likewise."

"Jamison!" Amelia called out from behind him.

He turned to see his partner. She stood near a pair of doors that led outside with alarm written all over her face. "What is it?" He jogged towards her, Ella right behind him.

"There!" She pointed out the window. "Do you see it? It looks like a shirt hiding behind that bush."

"I do!" He pulled his phone out of his pocket. Putting in the passcode he looked at the picture that was still open and showed it to Amelia. "Looks exactly like the flannel shirt our creeper was wearing just a bit ago. Call it in, Johnson. I'll go out the doors by Ella's classroom and sneak around and try to nab him. Everyone is to stay inside."

"I'll go tell the office," Ella said.

He reached over, squeezed her arm, and headed towards her classroom.

"Be careful," she yelled after him.

He ran down the hallway and out the door.

Amelia had spotted the man around the east side of the modular building that sat just to the north side of the school, so he went around the west.

Adam pulled his Sig Sauer from his holster and quietly snuck around the side of the building. With slow, steady breaths he rounded the northwest corner, but a twig snapped under his foot. The simple little noise resounded like a gong.

He picked up his pace along the north side of the modular building, but when he was halfway to the other end flannel-shirt-man started running across the clearing toward the wooded area. Adam took off after him.

One foot after the other, Adam sprinted after the man. "Stop. Police," he yelled and tried to catch up to the middle-aged man. Adam tried to take a breath to calm himself even as his heart sped up. The running accelerated his heart, but so did his anger. That man not only was sneaking around a school where his pseudo-nieces went to school, but he could also be Ella's rapist. His heart pounded as hard as his feet did against the soft earth.

The man darted into the trees. Adam was gaining on him but taking him down in the trees would be more difficult. He side stepped a tree. "STOP. POLICE." The man didn't stop. The man was more athletic than Adam would have expected. Adam was in excellent shape and should have caught the guy in the clearing, but this guy was fast. The guy jumped over a log. The underbrush was slowing him down, but it was also slowing Adam down.

Adam hurdled the log with ease. "I said STOP." He yelled again. The guy didn't look armed so Adam popped his gun back in its holster as they left the woods and entered someone's backyard. Tackling a suspect was easier, and safer, without a firearm in hand. Just a few more steps.

Adam's heart thudded against his ribs. He had to time the takedown just right. If he didn't, the man could get away. A few more pounding steps. Adam threw his body forward and grabbed the guys shoulders. They both went flying forward. The ground came rushing at their faces. As the man's body hit the ground, the impact reverberated through his body and into Adam's. He struggled to catch his breath. The other guy was in worse shape.

Keeping his weight on the man, Adam reached for his arms. The man tried to wriggle away, but Adam's hours at the gym paid off, and he was able to overpower the suspect. Once he had the man's arms behind his back Adam lifted himself up and restrained the man with one hand and a knee on his back. Adam reached under his blazer and pulled his handcuffs out from where they were tucked into his waistband. He took a deep breath and slapped the cuffs on the man's wrists. "You're under arrest."

"For what?"

Adam yanked the man off the ground. "Seriously, you were lurking around an elementary school and ran away from a police officer. That's just for starters."

"You mean there's more?"

Was this guy a complete bonehead? "Right now, you're our top suspect in… other crimes as well."

"What?!?!"

"Get moving." He pushed the guy back towards the woods.

———•———

Ella headed back down the hallway towards where she'd left Amelia after going to tell the office what was going on. The school was now on soft lock down, no one in or out of the building, but activities would continue as usual. Amelia was right where Ella had left her but was now on the phone and pacing back and forth. Amelia's normal pleasant expression had been replaced with worry lines and wide eyes.

"Where's Adam?" Ella asked. Her stomach twisted in on itself.

Amelia moved the phone away from her mouth. "The suspect took off running, and Adam chased after him. Last I saw them they were entering the wooded area over there."

Ella's chest tightened. What if something happened to Adam? What if the guy got away?

"Hey, don't worry. Adam will get him." Amelia moved her phone back to her mouth and turned back towards the window. "Yes, Sarge? Correct. Wait, I see him. Looks like Jamison got him. We'll bring him in now. Thanks."

Ella looked out the window and smiled. Something quickened in her heart at the sight of Adam escorting a bad guy in cuffs. She shook it off.

"You okay?" Amelia asked.

She shook her head to clear it. "Yeah, I'm good."

"Okay. Maybe this is the guy, and it'll all be over."

"I hope so."

Amelia's smile returned. "Well, if things go well, and we get a full confession, I'll be here to pick you up by four o'clock."

"Let's pray it's that simple."

"If not, I think Caleb will be able to come get you."

"Okay. Go get that confession."

Amelia left. Ella went back to her classroom and prayed for Adam and Amelia to get to the bottom of this, for God's favor and protection, and for this all to be at an end.

She sat at her desk and tried to focus on the papers that needed her attention, but she couldn't. She picked up her phone. The clock face on the screen said 11:37, only twenty minutes since Adam left. Maybe Adam would text her once they knew something. She set the phone down and tried to push away the thoughts, but the events of the morning plagued her mind.

At lunch, she barely listened to the other teachers' chitchat. She couldn't stop her mind from wandering to the image of Adam hauling that guy out of the woods. She picked up her phone. 12:37. Would Adam or Amelia text her an update? She set her phone down and poked at her salad.

She gave the students extended independent work time throughout the afternoon, and after they walked out the door at the end of the day, Ella tried to gather her things while Molly cleaned the white board. She wanted to get out of school. She picked up her phone from her desk. 3:37. She was tempted to text Amelia or even Adam. She was itching to know what was going on down at the police station. Was the guy she saw Adam with the guy who had raped her seventeen years ago? Was it the guy that was threating her life now? The guy who'd killed her cat? She tossed her phone in her bag.

Knock, Knock. Ella jumped. She turned and found Caleb and Carter standing in the doorway.

"Sorry, didn't mean to startle you," Caleb said.

"Dad!" Molly ran over and gave him a hug.

Ella smiled. "It's okay. My mind is elsewhere."

"I bet. Sounds like it was an exciting morning around here."

"Indeed! Do you know how things are going down at the station?" She leaned forward in anticipation.

"No, I just got a simple text from Amelia asking to pick you and the kids up."

Her shoulders dropped. "Oh."

"Sorry. We can leave whenever you're ready, no rush. We don't mind sticking around."

"Actually, I'd really like to get out of here today. I just need to write tomorrow's assignments on the board, and I'm ready. Just give me five minutes."

"No problem." Caleb and the kids went to the back of the room and sat on the bean bags and read a book while Ella finished up.

Once she was finished, she slid her lesson plan book, grade book, and a stack of papers into her bag and lifted it onto her shoulder. She looked back at Caleb and the kids. She always loved seeing dads with their kids. Caleb truly was their dad, not just a stepfather. Both Molly and Carter called him dad, and sometimes she completely forgot that he wasn't their biological father. Something she couldn't identify stirred deep in her soul. Was it longing? Hmmm... *Lord, I've always thought being a mom would be nice, but I just don't see that happening. I've never felt it so strongly as now. Why?* She shook her head trying to dismiss the thought. Having kids would mean letting someone get close. She wasn't sure she could ever handle that. She couldn't predict when the flashbacks would come. One time in church some overly zealous man tried to give her a hug after a small group of them had prayed together, and it sent her spiraling and running out of the room before it paralyzed her. The only people she was able to receive physical affection from were her students.

"Ready?" Caleb said looking up at her.

She snapped out of her thought. "Yep."

The kids jumped up and ran towards the door, Carter grabbed her hand. She smiled and let the four-year-old drag her out the door.

Once they were back at the house, Ella had a snack with the kids before diving into some grading. She sat at the breakfast bar doodling when Caleb came into the kitchen.

"Doesn't look like you're getting much grading done."

She laughed. "Nope. Waiting to hear from Amelia or Adam is driving me crazy. I want to know what's going on. I can't concentrate at all."

He opened the fridge and pulled out a package of ground beef. "Well, I heard from Amelia, but no news."

Her hope jumped but was smashed in one sentence. "Oh."

"Yeah, she just said she wasn't going to be home in time for dinner."

"That's no good." She crossed her arms and slumped onto the counter.

"My thoughts exactly. Well, good thing it was my night to cook anyway." He pulled a jar of spaghetti sauce from the cabinet and held it up.

"You two have such a great system down."

"It just makes sense with both of us working that I make dinner when I'm home. I can't cook as well as she can, but, oh well."

She raised her pointer finger. "But you knock dessert out of the delicious ballpark."

He bowed slightly. "Thanks. But I can't make pie for the life of me."

"But you can buy a mean one."

They both laughed.

"Anything I can help with?" she asked.

"No, just get your grading done."

"Yes, sir." She looked back down at her papers and actually got to work. The quick conversation with Caleb was just the distraction she'd needed. She finished her grading just in time for dinner.

After dinner, she settled on the couch and watched a short movie with the kids. She braided Molly's hair and colored a picture with Carter during the movie to keep herself occupied. Once Caleb took the kids up to bed, she sat back into the couch and scrolled through Netflix. She desperately needed to keep herself distracted. The worry was eating at her stomach, and she couldn't sit still for the life of her. When would Amelia come home? It was driving her crazy.

She flipped past a few crime dramas, definitely not what she was in the mood for. Romantic comedy? No, thank you. This wasn't working. Nothing looked appealing. She got up and went into the kitchen. Maybe a snack and another glass of water would help. She rummaged through the cabinets without any aim. Why hadn't they heard anything from Amelia? And why on earth was she so anxious to see Adam?

CHAPTER 11

"It's late, Scully, I'll just go home." Adam walked with Amelia back to their desks after meeting with the Captain. Amelia had invited him for dinner hours ago when they thought they might be able to leave at a reasonable hour. But that hadn't happened.

"No, you won't. Caleb said there is plenty of food left over from dinner, plus I know you want to see Ella."

He felt his cheeks grow warm. Of course, he wanted to see Ella, but he had hoped he wasn't so obvious. "I am hungry, and I'm not sure I have much at home to make other than a bowl of cereal."

"So, it's settled."

Adam retrieved his blazer while Amelia got her purse. He really could use a cold beer, but he'd rather see Ella, so going to Amelia's was definitely the best bet. He just hoped Ella would still be up. It had been a long day, and he needed to know she was safe.

Ten minutes later Adam followed Amelia into the house through the side door that led into the kitchen. Amelia opened the door and a squeal followed by a thud came from the kitchen.

"Oh, Ella, I'm sorry," Amelia said, "I didn't mean to startle you."

"Ah, don't worry about me. I've been jumpy all—Adam, hey." She bent over to pick up the jar of peanut butter and knife she had dropped.

"Hey." The look on her face was priceless. Her big brown eyes smiled right back at him. *She's glad to see me, too.* His heart soared. He went into the kitchen and grabbed a paper towel and cleaned up the peanut butter that had splattered on the floor.

"Thanks. Ok, guys, I've been going nuts all day. Amelia, it's your turn to spill it. Tell me. What happened? Is it him? Am I safe now?"

Adam's lungs deflated. He had known hours ago that the guy they were holding wasn't her rapist. Why hadn't he thought to tell her?

"It's not, is it? I can see it on both of your faces." Her hands shook.

Adam reached over and took the knife and peanut butter out of her hands and set them on the counter next to her plate and crackers. "No, it's not him. A creep, but a different creep."

"I'm sorry, Ella," Amelia said. "I know you were hoping. Should have thought to tell you earlier in the day. It just got crazy as we figured out who he was."

Adam watched Ella carefully. Her eyes had glazed over slightly, and her hands trembled where she held them out in front of herself.

"Ella, what did you guys do today?" He needed to bring her back to the here and now. He had seen people experience traumatic flashbacks, and she was displaying the first signs.

She blinked and looked at him.

Good.

"Nothing much." She took a stabilizing breath. "Graded papers, ate dinner, and watched a movie with the kids. You guys have to be hungry. Let's get you some food."

He sighed. Crisis had been averted. "That'd be great."

"I'm famished," Amelia added. She nodded at Adam as to tell him "good job."

"You two sit. I'll get it for you."

"Thanks, Ella, I'm going to run upstairs to kiss the kids first."

"Okay, but you need to put your feet up," Ella pointed at Amelia.

"What are you my mother now?" The teasing sparkle in Amelia's eyes made Adam laugh.

Ella was clearly amused, too. "Ha. When are you going to be on desk duty anyway? I swear you look more pregnant in just the last week."

Amelia put her hands on her hips and feigned offense. "What you're saying is I look fat?"

In the most sarcastic tone she could manage, Ella kept the teasing alive, "Yeah, that's it."

"Why, thank you." The women laughed.

Adam slid onto a stool at the breakfast bar and laughed at the exchange. Amelia went upstairs, and Ella started pulling out dinner. It was strange to have his partner and the 'girl that got away' be such good friends. He was so grateful that Ella has someone as great as Amelia in her life. "How'd you and Amelia get so close?"

Ella turned towards him and told him about how they'd been in a small group at church together. "I always dreamed about what it would be like to have a sister, and this is exactly what I imagined it would be like. Speaking of sisters, how's Heather? I haven't seen her in years, either. Are you two close these days?"

He took a weighty breath. "Not as close as I'd like to be. She lives up in the D.C. area with her husband and two boys. Don't see her as much as I'd like. Guess that's mostly my fault. I could go up there more often than I do. We talk on the phone about once a month though. She jokes that I replaced her with Becca."

"Really? I didn't realize you and Becca were that close."

"Yeah, Becca makes a great big sister. But I keep telling Heather that no one could replace her." He smiled at the thought of his sister's jealousy about Becca. It was mostly teasing, but he did tend to dote on Callie and Dani more than his nephews, but that was because he saw them more regularly, plus they were girls. Maybe he should go see Heather and the boys soon.

The conversation lulled. Ella heated up the leftover spaghetti in the microwave, scooped it into bowls, and dumped some salad from the bag into another pair of bowls. She turned and handed Adam his bowls. "Would you like a glass of water or milk? I'm not sure they have anything else."

Adam knew Caleb kept beer in the fridge in the basement, but even though he really wanted one he was determined to fight the desire tonight. Because he knew he wanted way more than one. "Water's great."

He watched her as she reached in the cabinet for a glass. Her curvy figure accentuated by the way her loose sweater clung to her body. It didn't matter how modestly she dressed, he found her attractive.

She turned and handed him his glass of water. Her expression had darkened. "So, can you tell me anything about the guy that you found today?"

Not really what he wanted to talk about after dealing with the creep all day.

Amelia showed back up with Caleb before Adam could answer Ella's question.

Amelia said, "Thanks, Ella, I'm going to eat in the family room, so I can put my feet up like I was told to."

They all followed her. Ella carried Adam's glass for him and sat down near him on the couch while Amelia and Caleb took the love seat.

Adam took his first bite and just soaked up being near Ella.

She reached over and poked his knee. "You really took him down, didn't you?"

He looked at the grass stains on his gray slacks. "I did. Chased him all the way through the woods and into someone's backyard before I was able to tackle him."

Her smile gripped his heart. "Wow. I'm impressed."

He shrugged as if it wasn't a big deal, but he loved her praise. "I haven't forgotten your question."

"Yes, what can you tell me?"

"Well, turns out the guy was a pedophile. A search of his house revealed some very... unpleasant things. He's been officially arrested, and let's just say, probably won't see the light of day anytime in the next fifty years. But he's definitely not the guy we were hoping for."

"Yikes. I don't understand people like that..."

"Me neither."

"Okay," Amelia said, "on to happier subjects. How much trouble did Molly get in at school today? I have to say I love having an in with her teacher this year."

Ella leaned her head back and let out a giggle.

Adam clutched his fork to keep his hand from reaching out to her. How he long to feel her touch.

———•———

Adam pulled a piece of paper off the notepad sitting on his desk the next morning.

"Is everything set?" Amelia asked as she came back to their desks after yet another trip to the bathroom.

"Yes." Adam had just gotten off the phone with Kyle Young's father. "Spoke to the boy's father. He didn't ask any questions and is expecting us in an hour."

"Really? No questions?"

"None. Kyle's at school. So, we'll just speak to the parents."

"That's good. He might ask more questions than they will."

Adam stood and flipped his fedora on his head. Despite not getting enough sleep he was feeling great. Ella had seemed so open to him last night at Amelia's house and had even agreed to hang out with him this evening. But first he and Amelia had to drive to Charlotte to talk with the parents of the boy Ella gave birth to.

"Where you guys headed so early? It's not even nine yet," Becca asked as they passed her desk.

"Uh." They really should have decided on the cover story.

Amelia's quick thinking saved them, "We have to follow up on a lead. Even though Jamison was the arresting officer yesterday, Ramirez is taking care of most of it. You guys have any leads you're following up on today?"

"I wish. Gavin and I are planning on staring at pictures from all the crime scenes today."

Gavin added, "Should be a blast! It would have been really helpful if this guy would have left some fingerprints or DNA."

"No kidding," Adam said. But hopefully they would have some DNA by the end of the day.

Adam and Amelia left and began the hour drive to Charlotte in silence.

Adam checked his side mirror as he merged with traffic on the interstate, and Amelia finally broke the silence. "I'm dying to know how you are feeling about this whole thing. We're going to talk to the parents who adopted the kid who Ella gave birth to in high school. Is it totally weird for you, or am I just reading too much into things again?"

Adam chuckled and rolled his eyes. His partner really had a way of prying, but he knew it was useless to avoid her questions, especially since they were stuck in a car together. If he didn't answer, she'd just keep rewording the question. He had never met someone so persistent at getting things out of him. He told her it was weird and that he kept trying to reimage his memories of pregnant Ella with the facts he now had. But that didn't satisfy Amelia, she continued to ask a barrage of questions.

He finally asked, "Is this 'twenty questions'?"

She giggled. "Yes. But I understand if you don't want to talk about it; I'm just curious."

"As always." He laughed but let the serious nature of her line of questions take over. Did he really want to delve into this with her? Maybe it would help to talk about it with someone other than Ella. Should it come up with her, he'd like to have sorted through the emotions beforehand. He checked his mirrors again as he switched lanes and proceeded unloaded his thoughts about Ella and the situation.

However, it was clear that Amelia already knew all that he was telling her.

"She really told you everything, didn't she?"

"She did. I hope that's okay."

"Of course. Guess that makes you our little shrink, hearing both sides and sorting it all out for us."

"Something like that."

The conversation lulled, and after another twenty minutes of driving, they pulled up in front of a modest two-story suburban home. Adam turned off the engine and rubbed the back of his neck. Why was he so nervous about this?

"You ready?" Amelia asked.

"As I'm going to be. This could totally be the break we need in the case, but if we screw up somehow this kid's life could be in danger."

"So, we don't screw it up. That's the whole reason we're taking the sample to a private agency here in Charlotte, and they pride themselves in discretion. My friend with the Charlotte PD has worked with them before and says they're the best. No one back home will even know we were here today. Well, other than Ella and the Captain."

"Jared doesn't even know?"

"Nope. He knows what we are doing today has to do with Ella's case, but he knows no details."

"Okay. Let's do this; but remember, they don't know how Ella conceived."

"I know, Adam."

Adam's stomach twisted in on itself as they got out of the car and walked up to the door. He knocked on the door with three firm raps and waited. A moment later a middle-aged man opened the door. "Mr. Young?"

"Yes. You must be the detective from Hazel Hill I spoke with earlier."

"Yes, sir. I'm Detective Adam Jamison, and this is my partner Detective Amelia Johnson."

Mr. Young shook both of their hands. "Please, come in." He turned and called up the stairs, "Linda, those detectives are here."

A nicely dressed woman in her late forties came down the stairs. "Welcome, detectives, would y'all like some coffee or sweet tea?" She looked at Amelia. "The tea is decaf."

"Some tea would be wonderful," Amelia said.

"Sounds good to me, too," Adam added.

"It'll be right up; please have a seat."

They followed Mr. Young into the semi-formal living room. The mantel held several family pictures, Mr. and Mrs. Young and two children. A teenage boy, obviously Kyle, his big brown eyes looked just like Ella's, beside him was a younger girl, whose different features made it clear she was also adopted. The bookshelves opposite of the fireplace held a number of trophies and awards. Adam smiled and sat on the sofa.

Mrs. Young came back into the room with a tray of glasses and a pitcher of sweet tea. She poured them each a glass and sat on the opposite sofa next to her husband. "Now, why are a couple of detectives from Hazel Hill coming to talk to us?" She wrung her hands that she had set in her lap. "Is Ella okay?" She turned to Mr. Young, "That's where Ella is from right? Doesn't she still live there?"

Mr. Young glanced at his wife before looking back at Adam. "Yes, she does. Please tell us what this is about."

Adam pressed his lips together. He would let Amelia do the talking. She was the talker.

"Thank you for meeting with us today, Mr. and Mrs. Young. Ella is part of why we're here. It's a very delicate situation, so I'm going to seem guarded with my words, but feel free to ask questions."

The couple nodded.

"First off, Ella is safe, so you can let that worry rest. We are here because we need a sample of Kyle's DNA."

Adam expected them to be surprised by the request, but they weren't.

"Okay," Mrs. Young said. "May we ask the circumstances behind the sudden request? Why after sixteen years would that matter now?"

"That's my question, as well? Did Ella not know her attacker? We've never asked her those details. But why look for evidence now?"

Adam replied, "So you knew that Ella was raped?"

"Yes," Mrs. Young said, "she never told us as much, but as we got to know Ella it was clear that she was not the type to have... you know. It was also evident that she had been through a great deal of trauma."

"She still doesn't think you know that. But we're here now after so long because the man who assaulted her was never captured and has begun attacking women in Hazel Hill again."

"Oh, my goodness, that's terrible."

"Whatever we can do to help. Is Kyle safe?" Mr. Young asked.

"We will see to it. No one knows about him. That is part of why we are here just now. Ella never told anyone in the police department that she was pregnant. The only ones who know about Kyle are the two of us, Ella, and our Captain. We are going to have a private lab analyze the DNA as well, just to keep the need to know out of the department and out of Hazel Hill."

"So, do you need to swab his cheek like they do in the TV shows?"

"That is one option, but we can even keep him out of the loop by taking a toothbrush."

"He could probably use a new one of those anyway. I'll go get it."

───●───

The kids had left for the day, and Ella wandered around her classroom cleaning up. She still wasn't safe, and the insecurity of that was fraying her nerves. For the entire day, she had struggled to stay in the here and now. The kids had been acting up all day. She had never been so glad to see her students walk out the door as she had been ten minutes ago when they did. Guilt washed over her. She didn't want to feel that way about them. They were just a bunch of eight-year-olds, but she was spent. Thank goodness tomorrow was Friday.

At least Adam was coming to get her today. She stopped midway through picking up some scraps on the floor. Was she actually happy about hanging out with Adam? *Oh, Jesus, what's my heart doing?*

She didn't have time to process those thoughts any further. A knock sounded on the open classroom door. She stood and turned and smiled at the tall, handsome figure leaning against the door frame. "Hey, Adam."

He tipped his hat to her. "Good afternoon. How was your day?"

Her soul lifted a bit in reaction to his smile. "Awful."

His smile faded and worry lines replaced his raised brows.

"My class was a piece of work today. Wild and crazy, and I'm still recovering from yesterday's anxiety."

"I'm sorry to hear that." He came further into the room.

She threw the bits of trash away and erased the board. "It's okay. I'm just glad the day is over, and tomorrow is Friday."

"Well, tonight we shall relax. Thanks for being understanding about not going to your kick-boxing class."

"Not a problem. I could see how it's not the best place to keep me safe. What were you thinking for babysitting me tonight?"

"I wouldn't call it babysitting; it's a privilege to hang out with you. Thanks for putting up with me."

"It's nice to get out of Amelia and Caleb's hair some, but I'm also glad to be able to spend time getting to know you again." His boyish grin gave away that she had just made his day. "How was your day? Were you guys able to talk to Kyle's parents?"

"We were. It went well. Really nice family. We got what we needed, and it's being processed."

"Great. How long will it take?"

"This isn't the movies, so it could be about six weeks or so."

"Really? That long?"

"Unfortunately, yes."

Ella finished her end of day routine, and the two of them headed back to Adam's house to make dinner.

After walking in the door, she played with Rusty, and the butterflies in Ella's stomach that had fluttered the entire drive dissipated. The dog's enthusiastic affection was just what Ella needed to push any discomfort aside. Adam had gone into the kitchen to make dinner so once she finished petting the dog, she went in to join him.

"Can I help?"

"Sure, can you hand me the rice out of the cabinet next to the fridge."

"Can do." She turned and opened the cabinet and pulled out the rice, but before she could close the door, she noticed a box of brownies. Chocolate. She could use some of that. "Ooo, could we make these brownies, or are you saving them for something special?"

"No. I'm up for having them tonight."

"Awesome." She handed Adam the rice and pulled out a bowl to mix the brownies in. They quietly prepared the food.

Ella slid the brownies in the oven, and Rusty started scratching at the side door that was just off the dining room. "Apparently someone needs to go out."

Adam walked over to the door and opened it for the dog. "Oh, looks like I left the gate open, I'll be back in a second."

"Okay." Ella watched him walk out the door. She was enjoying the time with him, but her anxiety was growing again. And it wasn't about him either. She needed to distract herself, so she went to the sink and started washing the dishes she used for the brownies. But it didn't work. The tunnel was coming.

No. She needed to keep focused on the dishes. *Feel the water, Ella. God, help.* She took a deep breath. She had to fight it from coming. She didn't want to deal with a flashback in front of Adam. It was bad enough one almost came yesterday in front of him. But she had been able to shake that one. She gripped the counter. She could barely maintain her balance as her vision started to narrow.

"Hey." Adam came back into the house.

She managed to get a "Hey" out in return.

Adam tossed his keys on the counter, but they slid off and clanged on the floor. The tunnel she had been fighting to enter raced toward her. The flashback was coming hard and fast and she couldn't fight it any longer. T*he sound of the keys clanging against the asphalt, the cold steel pressing against her throat. The sound of her name, "Elly?"* Wait, he hadn't called her that nickname.

"Are you having a flashback? Elly, look at me. It's Adam. I'm here. You are safe. Can you smell the brownies you put in the oven?"

She forced her eyes to look at Adam. He was sitting on the floor next to where she had slumped against the cabinets.

"Look in my eyes. Steady your breathing. Slow deep breaths. You are at my house. You are safe."

She looked into his deep gray eyes and tried to listen, tried to calm her breathing. The terror dissipated as the compassion in Adam's eyes reached her soul.

"That's good, Ella. Deep breath. Let it out slowly."

She obeyed. "I'm sorry."

"You have nothing to apologize for. What triggered it?"

She looked across the kitchen where his keys still lay on the floor.

"Oh, I'm so sorry!"

"No, it's fine, Adam. I was fighting it before that, but the keys hitting the floor sounded the same as when I dropped my keys in the alley when I felt the knife against my neck." Her eyes glazed over as her mind when back there...

"Stay here, Elle. Focus on here and now."

She blinked and shook her head a bit before refocusing on Adam. She gave him a weak smile.

He smiled back at her. "Is there anything that helps you get past these flashbacks? A cup of tea? A—"

"Yes!" She pushed herself up off the floor using Adam's knee. Leaving him on the floor of the kitchen, she went straight to Adam's upright piano in the living room. She sat down on the bench and fingered the ivory keys.

Adam appeared at her side. "Of course."

Her fingers glided across the keys, and she played the old hymn "Tis So Sweet to Trust in Jesus" from memory. As she played and began to sing Adam picked up his acoustic guitar and gradually started playing and singing with her.

Jesus, Jesus, how I trust him, How I've proved him o'er and o'er

Jesus, Jesus, precious Jesus! Oh, for grace to trust him more.

Yes, 'tis sweet to trust in Jesus, Just from sin and self to cease,

Just from Jesus simply taking life and rest and joy and peace

Jesus, Jesus, how I trust him, How I've proved him o'er and o'er

Jesus, Jesus, precious Jesus! Oh, for grace to trust him more.

She was a little surprised that Adam remembered the old hymn but was even happier to have him play with her.

When she finished playing the entire song, she turned to where Adam sat on a little stool. "It's been fifteen years since I've had so many flashbacks."

"It makes sense. You're having to face what happened all over again. You're displaced from your home. Heck, you're having to deal with me in the process too. It's a lot."

She nodded and choked back a few tears. "It is a lot."

"I'm so sorry you're having to deal with all of this. I'm so sorry this all happened."

"Me too. But as much as I wish it hadn't happened, it's part of what made me who I am today. If I hadn't had to deal with so much heartache, I may not be as close to Jesus as I am today. And if it hadn't happened, and if he hadn't come back, I wouldn't be here with you today." She licked her lips, hesitant to say what came to her mind. "And I'm glad I'm here." She gave him a tentative smile.

He smiled, but it quickly faded. "But Ella, if I hadn't been a jerk. If I hadn't let my own desire for popularity take me away from you…"

"No, Adam, don't go there. God works it all out for good. I love Him, and He's promised that because

I'm His, He will work it all together for good. I believe that with all my life." She bit her lower lip. She hoped she wasn't getting too preachy. She didn't want to preach at him, but her love for Jesus and her desire to see Adam love Him too spilled out of her heart and spewed out of her mouth.

"I know you believe that. I can see that. I appreciate that you say it like you see it. I just don't understand how a god who says he loves you would do this to you."

"He didn't do it to me. This happened because we live in a fallen, sinful world. A place of death and destruction. But He did allow it. Why? I don't know. But I will praise Him through it. Because no matter what vileness we experience, He is still good."

"I still don't understand how you can say that. I don't want to belittle your faith, but I just don't get it. How can a good God let us experience so much pain?"

"Because He is a good God. Philosophers and theologians have wrestled with this question for eons. But I see it like this. He is good because He has allowed us free will. He didn't make us robots; He gave us freedom to choose to love him. He is good because when we sinned against Him and chose not to love him, He sent His son to die in our place. He is good because He gives us redemption. He is good because He carries and sustains us even when junk happens. He is good because He loves us."

Ella kept her eyes on Adam. He was processing what she said, but the timer interrupted before he could respond. This talk would have to continue another time.

CHAPTER 12

Friday night Adam had come over to the Johnson's house for dinner and stayed. He leaned his head back and laughed. He hadn't laughed this hard in a long time. Ella, Amelia, and Caleb were all in stitches, too. Apparently, it was getting late. A glance at his watch revealed he was right—it was pushing midnight. Once the kids were in bed, the adults had all settled in the living room. After a short board game, he and Ella had started telling stories of their childhood antics. Ella had always had a way with words, and she still did. Her flare on the stories was downright hilarious.

"But that's nothing like the brief period of time where Adam thought he wanted to be a stunt man," she said.

"Oh, Ella, no." He shook his head, but his 'no' was probably hard to believe with how hard he was laughing. "Don't tell that story." He knew exactly where she was headed with that train of thought. He looked to the other end of the couch where she sat with her feet pulled up between them.

"Come on," she nudged his leg with her toes, "Don't be a spoil sport! It's funny, and you know it."

His leg tingled at her touch. "It wasn't funny then."

"Well, not so much, but it's hilarious now, especially in my head because when I replay the memory it's completely in slow motion."

"Slow motion for me, too." His indignation showed through in his voice. "But there's nothing funny about it."

She turned off her giggles and gave him a serious look. Her brow furrowed, and her eyes narrowed. "Adam, it was funny, whether you want to believe it or not. And I think Caleb and Amelia would agree."

"You'll just have to tell us, so we can weigh in," Amelia said.

"There's nothing funny about a nine-year-old kid, a bike, a very large mound of sand, and a trip to the ER."

Ella laughed.

He stretched out his words as he said, "I said, 'nothing funny'!"

"But the look on your face as you hit the hill, oh my word. It went from 'This is awesome. I'm gonna fly!' to 'Oh, no, I'm stuck!' to 'Save me, Jesus!' in a matter of seconds." Ella was now hunched over from laughing so hard. She kicked him a little as her whole body was taken over with the giggles. He couldn't help but laugh with her.

Caleb said between his laughs, "So what happened?"

Adam replied since Ella wasn't going to regain her composure any time soon. "Well, I took off on the grass and pedaled to the sand ramp as fast as I could. We had packed the sand super tight, but it didn't matter. The sand gave way to the back tire. I'm still not even sure how the front one made it up. But halfway over the makeshift ramp I knew I wasn't going to make it. The bike was completely stuck in the sand, but I had been going so fast that my body didn't want to stop—"

"He went *flying* over the handlebars. I couldn't believe the air he got."

"Not the kind of air I had been hoping for though."

"For real. The look on your face, oh my word!"

Everyone's laughter came to an abrupt stop when Adam's phone rang. Only one phone number would likely be calling him at this hour of the night. He leaned forward and grabbed it off the coffee table where he had set it earlier in the evening. It was that number.

He squeezed Ella's ankle and rubbed the top of her foot with his thumb briefly and stood. He looked at her as he pressed the green answer button. Her face had gone ashen. "Detective Jamison." He walked out of the room and into the dining room.

He paced beside the table as the dispatcher told him that they had an apparent homicide of a woman in her early twenties. MO appeared to be the same as the case he was working. He informed them that he would let his partner know and hung up. He put his hands on the table and dropped his head as he leaned forward. How was he going to tell Ella? He definitely didn't want to leave her now. *But she is safe with Caleb,* he tried to reassure himself.

"What's going on?" He looked up and saw Amelia.

"We have another victim."

"Oh no!"

"How do I tell her?"

"Just do. Don't dance around it. And we don't know for sure yet, anyway."

"True."

He rubbed the back of his neck and walked back into the family room. Ella had grabbed a throw pillow and was hugging it, curled up in the corner of the couch. He sat down on the coffee table directly in front of her and held out his hands. He didn't know if she would take them, but he wanted her to. She sat up a little, leaned forward, and placed her hands in his. His pulse quickened.

"I'm not going to mince words or pretend nothing's happening, but there has been another murder, and initial description leads us to believe it's him again." Her hands started to shake in his; he gripped them a little tighter. "Amelia and I are going to investigate, but Caleb is here. Stay in the house, go to bed. Don't even stay down here by yourself. I don't want to scare you, but I want you to be extra cautious. We've let our guard down a little, but we have to be extra diligent."

Caleb said, "I'll keep her safe, Adam."

"Thank you." He didn't look at his friend; his eyes couldn't break with Ella's, but he knew his friend was standing behind him hugging his wife before she left for a late night of work.

"Be careful, Adam." Ella squeezed his hands.

"I will. I'll see you tomorrow."

"Okay." The tentativeness in her voice made Adam just want to pull her into his arms, but they weren't there, yet. He squeezed her hands again before letting go and stood. He turned and took in her beauty again before walking out the door with Amelia.

They climbed in his car, and Amelia said, "She'll be okay."

"I appreciate your confidence," he started the car, "but I'm sure she's going to have another flashback, and I want to be with her to help her through it. Did she tell you she had a bad one yesterday evening?"

"No, she didn't. It was in front of you?"

"Yeah, I accidentally triggered it by dropping my keys, but she had already been having a rough day."

"I know she's been having them, but she's really good at hiding it. I'm impressed she let you see it."

"She didn't have a choice. I'm worried about her. The PTSD seems to be pretty intense."

"I agree. I've encouraged her to reach out to a counselor, but she doesn't seem too keen on it."

"I wonder why." Adam was grateful she was finding ways to cope with it, but she should talk to a professional.

"I get the impression her counselor from years ago wasn't as helpful as he should have been."

"That's frustrating."

Amelia nodded.

Adam pulled into an apartment complex that was lit up with the flashing lights of squad cars. He parked his car as close to the crime scene tape as he could. The partners got out and made their way into the scene. They entered the small, first-story apartment and were greeted with a gruesome scene. The victim was tied to the refrigerator; her clothes had been removed, and her throat slit.

A hand gripped Adam's elbow. He turned to Amelia. Her face had gone stark white with a slight hint of green. "I'm thinking it's almost time for desk duty."

"You work the scene outside. Gavin and I have this." He nodded at Gavin as he came out from the backroom of the apartment.

"Thank you." She turned and went back outside.

"Hey, Riley. What ha' we got?"

Gavin looked down at his notes. "We have one Clarissa Zerillo. Twenty-one years old. Lives here alone, but when her boyfriend didn't hear from her tonight like he expected, he called. She didn't answer, so he called her work. She never showed up, so he came over to check on her."

Henry, the medical examiner said, "He just missed the killer, too. She's been dead an hour, tops."

"Sexual assault?"

"Yes. This is the most violent attack yet."

Adam took a deep breath. Amelia wasn't the only one feeling a little queasy. He did not like working homicide scenes. He preferred working with victims that could still speak with him.

"No."

Adam turned to see the Captain standing in the doorway. The man's eyes were wide and his shoulders dropped. He looked as if he had seen a ghost.

"What is it, Captain?"

"This is crazy. This is the same apartment that Brooke, the fourth victim seventeen-years ago lived in." Captain Baker avoided looking at the victim and went over to a bookshelf and picked up a picture of the victim and her boyfriend. "She even looks a bit like Brooke."

"Brooke is the victim that committed suicide, isn't she?" Adam asked.

He nodded.

"So, Captain, are you saying that you think his new victims are to replace the ones he couldn't get to?"

The Captain met his gaze after a moment of contemplation. "Maybe."

———•———

Adam leaned his elbows on his desk and rubbed his eyes. It had been a long night. He had sat with the boyfriend a long time—a mix of counseling and investigating. Adam had learned a great deal about Clarissa and her habits of coming and going. Her killer had definitely taken a risk when he attacked her when he did. Her boyfriend easily could have come over earlier and called the cops, since it wasn't Clarissa's normal night to work.

Adam had also learned a lot about the crime itself. The killer had been there for hours. Had assaulted her repeatedly before killing her. It made Adam sick. The guy had also clearly been an opportunist in the situation. He had targeted her for location as well as looks, but he had seen an opportunity to attack, and he took it. Adam was going to have to sit down and write up a profile for this guy that might help them narrow down where to look for him. It was going to be a busy weekend. So much for enjoying the holiday.

"Jamison, are you ready to leave? I really need to sleep in my bed." He looked over at Amelia. She looked completely exhausted.

"Yeah. Let's get you home. There's nothing to do that can't wait for a bit. I hope it's safe to say that we've got a little bit of time before he makes another move."

"Let's hope so."

Adam and Amelia stood and moved towards the door. "We're calling it a day," he said to Becca and Gavin.

"A day, it's not even ten a.m. yet!" Gavin teased.

"What, you gonna put in a whole day on a Saturday after being at a crime scene all night?"

"Not hardly, I'm out too. Becca?"

"Best idea I've heard in the last twenty-four hours."

The four detectives walked out together. Adam asked Becca, "So, Jared got out of this overnighter, huh?"

"Yeah, he got to stay with the girls. But I'll brief him when I get home."

"Just how he wants to start his Saturday, I'm sure."

They all let out a tired laugh and said goodbye. Adam drove back to Amelia's house. He was anxious to see Ella. He hoped that she had been able to get some sleep.

He pulled in the driveway. "Is it okay if I come in for a bit?"

"Absolutely. Why don't you stay for some breakfast? I'm starving and was thinking about having some pancakes or French toast before I went to sleep."

"That would be nice."

"It's settled. I'm sure Ella would like to know you're okay, too."

His cheeks warmed.

Amelia reached for the door handle but cocked her head to the side. "Doesn't your dog like to go outside occasionally, though?"

He laughed. "Rusty's fine. He's got a doggy door, plus Mrs. Williams next door comes over and takes care of him when I'm not home much. I already sent her a message this morning."

"Ah, nice."

They got out of the car, and Caleb and the kids came around from the back of the house. Amelia gave them all hugs and kisses.

Caleb shook Adam's hand. "You two had a long night."

"You have no idea. Your wife needs some sleep, stat."

"I see that."

"What's that supposed to mean?" Amelia feigned offense. "I got a few cat naps on the Captain's couch."

"Only after I told her to go lay down because she was falling asleep at her desk."

Amelia shrugged. "Whatever, I'm hungry. Let's get some breakfast."

"Agreed. How's Ella doing?" Adam asked Caleb.

"Don't know. Haven't seen her this morning. Part of why we came outside was to let her sleep in as long as she could. We watched a musical after you two left, so she didn't go to bed until almost two."

Amelia's jaw dropped, and she smacked her husband's arm. "You watched a musical with her? But you won't with me?"

Caleb laughed at his wife. "Well, she watched it; I read, but stayed downstairs with her like you asked, Adam."

"Thanks, man."

Caleb nodded. The kids had gone back to the backyard and the three adults went into the house. A loud scream from upstairs met them upon opening the door. Panic shot through Adam's entire body. The adrenaline propelled him up the stairs. He pulled his gun from its holster before opening Carter's door.

CHAPTER 13

She tried to fight, but he was too strong. He pulled the tape tighter around her wrists. She screamed for help, but he slapped her. Her cheek stung. He ripped her clothes. She tried to kick him. He laughed, the haughtiest, most maniacal laugh she had ever heard. It echoed through the alley. No one was around to hear her scream. And he knew that. He was on top of her.

Ella sat straight up in bed. She was safe, or was she? She tried to orient herself to her surroundings, but her head was spinning.

The door flung open, crashing against Carter's dresser. Right, she was in Carter's room at Amelia's house. She looked at the figure standing in the doorway and blinked before she realized it was Adam rushing toward her. He put his gun in the holster on his hip. She was still having a hard time sweeping the darkness from her mind. Had she screamed?

"Ella, are you okay?" Adam sat down on the edge of the bed.

She grabbed her pillow and hugged it tight. Was she okay?

"Ella, you're safe. You need to take a few deeper breaths."

She nodded and took a trembling breath in.

"Did you have a flashback in a dream?"

She nodded again. She stared at nothing.

"Ella look at me. And keep breathing."

She brought her eyes up and met his. He was smiling at her. A sweet, caring smile. A concerned smile.

"I'll be okay." She reached out and squeezed Adam's arm. His smile broadened, and he rubbed her hand with his.

"Do you want to talk about it?"

She removed her hand and shrugged. She probably should, but she didn't really want to. "It was just the same as the dreams almost always are, a replay of exactly what happened. I tried to fight him off, Adam, but he was too strong. If only I could have..."

"Don't go there. You tried, that's important." He held his hand out to her.

She debated, could she handle the contact? She risked it and put her hand in Adam's. Nothing happened, nothing other than a quickening of her heart that she couldn't tell whether it was because of her fear of the flashback or because her heart was attaching itself to Adam.

Ella smiled at Adam across the breakfast bar in Amelia's kitchen from where she stood at the sink cleaning the breakfast dishes. He had refused to go home despite how tired he was. The man hadn't slept, and he was fading fast. "Adam, you should go home and get some sleep."

"No, I'm fine. I need to do some research, and I can do that as well here as at home." His smile faded. "Unless you want me to leave."

"I didn't say that. Why don't we go hang out in the living room?" She dried her hands.

"That would be good. I'll grab my computer and meet you in there." Adam walked out the side door towards his car.

She grabbed her school bag and went to the living room. She pulled her lesson plan book and pencil out and set them on the coffee table. She settled on the floor, and Adam came back into the house, smiled at her, and settled on the couch behind her with his laptop.

"What are you working on?" Adam asked.

She leaned against the couch and looked up at him. "Lesson plans. I'm trying to make them super clear should I have a bad night and need a sub without notice. I'm telling ya, not going to school is more work than just going. What about you?"

"Research."

"What research?" She tilted her head and turned to see him a little better.

He pulled his lips in like he didn't want to answer the question. "I'm starting a clean profile of the attacker. I need a fresh look at it. We've been working with a seventeen-year-old profile. More research has been done since then, and we know more about him now."

"That doesn't sound like fun."

"It's not. I have to dive into what makes him tick and what the triggers in his life might be, to give us a clearer picture of what we're looking for. I do find it interesting, but only in the sense that it helps me catch the bad guy."

They both dove into their work and kept at it in silence for quite a while. Ella finished her plans for science and realized she hadn't heard the clacking of Adam's keyboard in a while, so she turned. He had fallen asleep. She smiled. He was an adorable man. A chunk of his dark hair had fallen down across his forehead. She took the laptop from his hand and put it to hibernate while avoiding looking at what he had up on the screen. She closed the computer and set it on the table and grabbed a blanket from the basket by the TV. She draped the blanket over him and impulsively reached up and brushed the hair out of his face. He had been so sweet to her that morning when she had woken up in such a fright. She touched his shoulder as she turned and left the room.

She needed more coffee. Her night had been nearly as long as his. Staying up watching a musical had been wise on one level, but it just prolonged the inevitable. She might have stayed up longer if she hadn't noticed that Caleb had fallen asleep on the love seat. She couldn't make him stay up all night with her. So, she had gone up to bed. But knowing that her attacker had been out there killing another woman while they had all been sitting around laughing made sleep impossible. She had taken her time getting ready for bed and sat in Carter's car bed reading her Bible until she couldn't keep her eyes open any longer. But it wasn't long until the dreams started. The rest of the night had been spent fighting her demons and willing herself to get some sleep.

Caleb came in the side door from where he had been out playing with the kids again. "Hey, Adam fall asleep?"

"Finally."

"That's good."

"Yeah, I tried to get him to go home, but he refused."

Caleb nodded. "He's worried about you."

"So, I see. Caleb, you said at one point that Adam was asking all the right questions." Caleb nodded. "Do you think he really will turn to Jesus?"

"I can't know that, Ella."

"I know, but as worried as he is for me, I'm worried about him, too."

"Me, too. He's been doing better this week than I've seen him in a long time. He hit rock bottom a couple of weeks ago, just before you came into his life again, and he is really searching in that. Have you guys had any spiritual conversations?"

"We have, a little bit. I just hope he doesn't take too much of this case on himself... if something were to happen to me... I just don't know if he could handle it."

"Let's not talk that way. If we have anything to do with it, nothing is going to happen to you. The best thing we can do in all of this is keep praying. We pray for Adam, that he'll turn to Jesus. And we pray that God will keep you safe."

Ella nodded.

Late Monday afternoon, Adam lifted the lid on the grill to check the burgers. Caleb came over to join him.

"Thanks, again, for having us over today."

Adam flipped a burger. "My pleasure. Just seemed like it would be a more comfortable situation for Ella over going to the Captain's house for his annual Labor Day barbecue."

"Definitely. She wanted to get out of the house but was not interested in hanging out with the whole squad."

"Can't blame her." Adam flipped the last burger and closed the lid. He turned and looked over to where Ella and Amelia were across the yard with the kids. "What was going on with Carter?" The boy had thrown a huge temper tantrum a few minutes ago.

"He wanted to open the gate all by himself."

"Can he even reach the latch?"

"No, but he insisted that he could do it on his own."

"Goofy kid."

"I guess they call it childish for a reason. How are you doing, Adam?"

"I'm all right." Adam grabbed his bottle of beer and took a swig.

"The drinking?"

He let out an amused snort. "Fine. I've got it back under control."

"You sure?"

"Yes." Adam tilted his head. "The Captain gave me an ultimatum. Apparently, he didn't like me coming to work hung over."

"As your partner's husband, I'm not too impressed with that either."

"It's better. I need to be at my sharpest anyway to keep Ella safe."

"Do you think it would be wiser to follow Jared and Becca's example and cut it out completely?"

"Nah, I got this."

The guys sat in the lawn chairs. Rusty came running over and shoved his tennis ball into Adam's lap. He petted the dog and launched the ball across the yard.

"Ella seems to have warmed up to you in the last week."

Adam's lips turned up and his heart palpitated. "She has!"

"I told you miracles are possible."

He raised an eyebrow at his friend. "Maybe. We'll see if it goes any farther than friendship." Rusty brought the ball back, and Adam threw it again.

"You want it to?"

"Uh, yeah. But I have no idea if she'll ever be open to that."

The dog returned the ball again. "Will you grow tired of this boy?" The dog panted in anticipation of another chance to chase the fuzzy, green ball. "Okay, fine." He chucked it as far as he could and still have it land in the yard. He looked back at Caleb. "I just wish she'd be open to staying here."

"Totally not appropriate." He was a little louder than he needed to be.

"Just so I could protect her." Adam focused on Rusty who was back yet again with the ball.

"And you're the only one who can protect her?"

"Well, no, I guess." Adam clasped his hands together. "But I know I can."

"We'll protect her, too. You know that."

"Well, yes. It's just that…"

"Arrogant much? You know what the Bible says about pride?"

"Yeah, yeah. Comes right before I fall on my arrogant face, right?"

Caleb nodded. "And 'God opposes the proud but gives grace to the humble.'"

Adam rubbed his hands on his thighs and stood. His entire body felt restless because of Caleb's admonition. "I should get those burgers off the grill." He turned and shoved the irritation with his friend aside. He didn't care if Caleb was right, Adam knew he could keep Ella safe. Not that his friends couldn't; he trusted them through and through, but he wanted to do it himself.

———•·———

Adam ran his hands through his hair Tuesday afternoon. He'd been staring at the rolling whiteboard in the squad room and at his notes for an hour straight without making any further progress on the new profile he'd spent all weekend writing. After Ella and the Johnsons had left last night he'd stayed up and worked on the profile. It should help him figure out who to look for, or at least who to rule out. The first seventy-two hours after a murder were crucial, but despite working all Friday night, a little Saturday, all day Sunday, and a little yesterday morning, he and the other detectives didn't even have a suspect list. This morning had been spent following up with witnesses, not that any one of them had seen anything substantial. The team had taken a late lunch and were now back at their desks. Amelia was working on paperwork, while he mulled over the profile.

Amelia's voice broke into his thoughts. "You do know that staring at that board won't tell you who he is, right?"

He shook his head at her, ignoring her question.

She pushed back from her desk and crossed her arms. "Let's talk through it. I want to hear what you've got over there. Have you managed to get in his head, yet?"

"I wish I hadn't. It makes me sick, Amelia. To understand his motivation just makes it even more infuriating."

"So, what's his motivation?"

"It's not so simple, because as I look at it, I see two different profiles. One from the guy from seventeen years ago, and one is the guy from today. They are clearly the same person, but a changed person. In researching the different types of rapists, we see two different types merging and then morphing into what we have today." He rubbed the stubble on his face that he hadn't bothered to shave the last two days and sat up straighter in his chair. "I would say the guy from seventeen years ago falls into the power-assertive type." Adam stood and turned the rolling white board around to the side that was blank. He picked up a marker and at the top of one half of the board he wrote "SEVENTEEN YEARS AGO" and at the other end wrote "TODAY."

"The differences we see are mostly in his method. Previously, he was much less controlled in his actions. Still methodical and angry, but back then he ripped their clothes off, whereas today he is taking the time to cut them off." He wrote those things under their headings. "In the past all his victims said he was very profane, but Ava said his language was angry and hostile but not profane."

"That seems like a strange change," Becca said. She and Gavin and Jared all moved towards him to listen to what he was saying.

"I think so too, but I believe it has to do with maturity. While I still can swear with the best of 'em, I don't swear like a sailor like I did when I was in college."

"That makes sense," Amelia said.

"Then there's the most obvious difference between then and now. He's taken up killing, which throws him now into the anger-excitation type, also known as the sadistic rapist." He wrote the types under the headings, as well. "I think back in the day we were dealing with a power-assertive with sadistic tendencies, but it's reversed now. I'd classify him today as a sadistic rapist with power-assertive tendencies. And I wonder if those tendencies are showing more because he's reliving the past attacks."

"Do you suppose he's been out there raping and killing other women over the last seventeen years?" Jared asked.

"Yes. That's why I already contacted the FBI and am running his MO through the national database. I'd be surprised if it doesn't come up in multiple places. I'd bet he goes on sprees like he did here initially and is satisfied for a while and then goes on another spree."

Gavin leaned forward in his chair. "That means there could very well be hundreds of victims out there."

"Easily. However, the other possibility is that he married and found some satisfaction in beating his wife."

An eerie silence fell across the room. Even the shuffling of papers by the other detectives in the squad room who were working other cases seemed to shuffle silently.

Adam turned his attention back to the board and wrote, "KNIFE - PROP" on the first side and "KNIFE - WEAPON" on the other. "Back then the knife he carried was only used to instill fear in his victims, but now, obviously, he's using it to kill. Those are the biggest differences between the time frames. But there is quite a bit of overlap, which is, of course, part of why we know it's the same guy." Adam continued to add to the board while he talked. "He's an angry man who gets off on hurting women. The violence of the crime is part of what he enjoys, especially now. He has become increasingly violent; we've seen that in the last two victims alone. Clarissa was tortured for hours before he finally killed her.

"He's opportunistic, but also very intentional. He's always carried what would be called a rape kit. It would include the ski mask, duct tape, his knife if he doesn't keep that on himself at all times, along with the squirt bottle and other supplies he uses to clean his victims."

"So, what does that tell you about who he is?"

Adam turned to see who had asked the question. A shiver ran down his spine as he met Scott's eyes.

"Quite a bit." Adam turned his back on Scott. "By analyzing what type of rapist, he is I can tell that he is an arrogant, guy's-guy kind of man, yet is charming and manipulative. Probably was flashy in the things he did or wore or the car he drove back then. But today probably tries to blend in a little more. He most likely works in a field dominated by men as he is likely a fairly macho kind of guy and likes to show his 'superiority' over women."

Adam absent-mindedly looked down at his watch. "Crap. It's already three o'clock."

From across the room Patrick North said, "Need someone to go pick up Ella for you?"

A shiver ran down his spine. He didn't like that man being around Ella. It was bad enough he was married to Jocelyn, but Adam didn't want him around Ella, too. What was he even doing in the squad room? "Nah, that's okay." He looked around trying to find an out. He really needed to stay as did Amelia, they were on a roll and needed to be sure everyone working this case knew what they were dealing with. Out of the corner of his eye he caught Doug Ramirez raise his hand slightly. He didn't trust many people with Ella's safety, but Doug fell onto that short list. "Doug said he would earlier." He lied. Doug had said no such thing.

"Sure did." Doug covered him. "I'm headed out now to get her." Doug stood and left.

Adam pulled his phone off his belt and texted Ella. "In the middle of something, so Doug Ramirez is coming to get you and bring you to the station. C ya soon."

Just a moment after hitting send his phone vibrated. The text back from Ella said, "K. See you shortly." Followed by a smiley face emoji. His heart skipped a beat. He looked forward to seeing her.

But right now, he needed to focus so he could leave with her as soon as possible.

"And what was his age?" Someone from the growing crowd of detectives asked.

He jumped back in. "Based on the survivors' testimony, which is congruent with the profile, he was in his early to mid-20s initially, which puts him pushing 40 today. That's the other thing that changed in his MO. He was choosing victims that were near his age or slightly younger, but now age varies, but that's because he's trying to kill the women he attacked before and if he can't like with Angela and Brooke, he's taking substitutes. Ava and Clarissa both resemble the original victims, and they were both killed in the original locations. We didn't realize that's what happened with Ava until it happened with Clarissa, but when we looked back at it, I'm quite confident that is what's going on."

"Now, wait," Becca said, "It took us a bit to connect Kimberly's murder with Ava's attack because he didn't rape Kimberly. Why?"

"Amelia and I have a few theories on that."

Amelia took over from where she sat at her desk as this was the part they had talked about yesterday morning. "One possibility is that the younger vics are his type and Kimberly was out of his age range preference. Another possibility is that he didn't because he had already done that part of the ritual with her. And the last possibility we talked about was that he didn't need to because he got off on the memory of what he did in the past since he took her to the same location where he had raped her."

"What a lovely thought..." Becca's turned up nose proved she thought the opposite of what she said.

Adam continued, "Another thing that needs to be noted is that he is becoming increasingly violent. He beat up Kimberly extensively, but it was all with his fists before he slit her throat. With Ava there were bite marks along with the beating and also several wounds from the knife. With Clarissa... well, it was incredibly violent. He raped her repeatedly, beat her, and stabbed her in multiple locations before finally slitting her throat." Adam's stomach churned. He hated what this man had done to these women. He had to force himself to unclench his fists.

"And what about Ella?" Gavin asked. "He was ready to take her that one night. Do we believe he'll try again?"

Amelia answered, "Unfortunately, I have no doubt that he will try again, especially when you consider the note he left in blood on her wall."

Jared asked, "What did that note say again?"

Amelia said, "'Sorry, I missed you. See you soon, Ella.'"

It still made Adam's skin crawl.

"That's a clear threat," Jared said. "How are things going in keeping her safe?"

Adam replied, "So far so good. I think we've kept her location outside of school a need to know basis."

"Good." Jared looked at Gavin and Becca. "How about with Hillary? We are assuming he will go for her at some point too?"

"Yes, Sarge," Adam said before Gavin or Becca could reply to the first question.

Gavin added, "Hillary hasn't been quite as cooperative as Ella. She hasn't wanted as much protection but has been willing to let one of us escort her to and from work. She's also agreed to stay in and call us if she needs to go out for anything, but I'm not sure how much she's really adhering to that."

"I'm sure Ella's personal relationships with us helps her," Amelia said.

"For sure," Gavin said.

Amelia spoke again, "So, back to my original question, what's his motivation today? Is it to 'take care of' anyone that could identify him?"

"I don't believe so. Now this is speculation, but I think he's come back to kill them out of a desire to 'finish the job' so to speak. They weren't able to identify him at all in the past, so he has no need to cover his tracks. I believe that somewhere along the way he found that he received greater satisfaction in killing them. It probably started by finding sexual satisfaction by causing his victims to suffer. He's stimulated by the pain he infli—" He stopped mid-word when he looked across the squad room and saw Ella walk in with Doug. She really didn't need to hear any of this.

"How did you come up with this?" Becca asked.

He brought his attention back and looked at Becca. "Research. A lot of research. I read case study after case study this weekend."

"Fun."

"Not really, but necessary. Anyone else have any other questions?" He looked over at Ella. She was standing by the door talking to Scott Rebus. Every muscle in Adam's body constricted, he did not like the idea of Scott being near her, either, not after the way he had treated Heather.

Jared's voice interrupted his thoughts. "I think you guys covered all the bases pretty well. Anything else we need to do today?"

Adam shook his head. With Ella here, he lost all ability to concentrate on the case.

"I don't think so," Amelia said.

"All right, who's up for calling it a day?" Jared asked.

"I am." Adam said. He grabbed his hat and blazer and headed to Ella. His palms started sweating. He was looking forward to a quiet evening with the girl of his dreams.

He slammed his car door and walked toward the pub. The entire day had been a bust. Ella was always with Adam. He had tried to follow Adam after he picked her up from school to find out where Ella was staying, just like he had more than half a dozen times over the last two weeks. But even in Adam's stupid muscle car he always managed to lose him. He was taking her somewhere he just had to find out where.

He had visualized how he would take her in a variety of situations. Maybe Adam would bring Ella to the station again. When he saw her arrive at the station yesterday afternoon his mind had started spinning. There had to be a way to get her out of there. But a building full of cops would make it tricky. He had spent all night fantasizing about what he would do if given that opportunity.

If he found out where she was staying, maybe he could break in during the night and take care of business there. He would rape her again no matter what since the alley he had first taken her in had been destroyed when they built the new Wal-Mart. He looked forward to having her again. And this time she would suffer. His heart beat a little faster about finally having his way with her. And then she would die.

He took a deep breath in and let it out slowly to regain his composure before stepping into the pub. He was looking forward to a few drinks with some of the other guys from the station. Taking a moment to relax was just what he needed. Throw back a few beers, maybe shoot some darts. And he could regroup about how to take Ella. He had already figured out where Hillary was staying, and if he had to, he would take care of her first. He had already adjusted his plan by taking the golden opportunity to take Clarissa. And she had been the perfect substitute for Brooke. Just as Ava had been for Angela. He smiled. Two more in Hazel Hill before he moved on to the other places he had lived before he discovered how satisfying it was to kill his victims.

"Hey," the bartender greeted him, "what can a get for ya?"

"I'll take a beer."

"What kind?"

"I'll take one of your best local IPAs." He leaned on the bar while he waited for the barkeep to get his beer. He looked around the pub. It was a family friendly sort of place with a large dining room with the bar along one side. At the back of the restaurant was a little stage that he presumed was for the regular karaoke nights. A couple of pool tables and dart boards were tucked into the corner.

"Here ya go."

He took his beer and took a long swig as he continued to take in the scene. The pub wasn't busy, enough patrons to keep business running on a Wednesday evening, but it wasn't crowded by any means. He went around the side of the bar and sat on a stool where he could see the door while he waited for the other guys to arrive. The bell on the door jingled, and he looked up. He smiled. She was here. He watched Ella walk across the dining area. Tonight could be the night. She was special. He preferred not to know his victims, and he had barely known the names of some of his victims, initially anyway. But he made an exception for Ella. He had wanted her; he wanted to hurt her. He had never liked the way that beautiful little redhead looked at him. He would show her who was superior once again. Now he just had to wait until she was away from the other five in her party.

CHAPTER 14

Ella slid into the large corner booth after Becca, and Adam slid in next to her. Her heart did a funny little flutter at his nearness. Maybe she shouldn't be spending so much time with him. Oh, but she was enjoying it. He had come to her classroom once school was over and helped her do little things this afternoon. They had just chatted while they moved the students' desks around, and he followed her down to the copier and held stacks of books for her while she copied worksheets for the next two weeks. It had been wonderful. And now they had gone out to dinner. Caleb and Amelia had gotten a babysitter, as had Jared and Becca, so they all went to a little pub for dinner.

"What's good here?" she asked Adam.

"The fries are always top notch. Can't really go wrong with anything."

She opened her menu and started looking at her options when a pretty young waitress came up to their table.

"Hey, Adam," she said.

"Hey, Susie."

Ella watched closely as Susie leaned close to Adam and tried to flirt with him.

"You guys going to need a few minutes? Can I get some drinks for you? Adam, you want your usual beer?" she asked as she touched Adam's shoulder.

Ella's stomach churned. It was happening. She knew what Adam was like. She was silly to think that something could happen with them. Adam leaned towards Ella and slid his arm along the back of the seat where she sat. Her heart skyrocketed. *Did he really move closer to me and away from her?*

"No beer tonight, but I'll take a coke, Ella?"

"I'll take a coke too." She smiled up at Adam.

Susie took the rest of the groups drink orders while Adam looked over her shoulder at the menu instead of picking up his own. Her body was doing crazy things in response. Her heart raced, her stomach fluttered, and her hands became incredibly sticky. A feeling she was so unfamiliar with. She hadn't felt this way since she was in junior high.

Once Susie brought their drinks, they all ordered. Ella leaned her elbows on the table as she played with her straw. She listened to the conversation her friends had but didn't participate much. She was simply enjoying spending the time with them. Before long, their dinner came, and everyone grew quiet as they ate.

During the meal a DJ got up on the little stage that was at the back of the restaurant by the bar. "It's karaoke time, folks. Y'all need to start picking your tunes and warmin' up your pipes. It's time to sing!"

"Oh, yeah, I forgot Wednesdays was one of their karaoke nights." Adam bumped her arm with his elbow. "So, what do you say, Ella?"

"Wait, what?" She looked at him as a smidgen of terror coursed through her veins.

"You and me. Let's sing a song like old times."

"Oh, Adam, I'm not going to know any of the songs they have. I hardly listen to the radio."

"Come on, I know one for sure that we can do."

"Now, how would you know I know it?"

"Because I used to sing it to you all the time when we were kids."

Her cheeks increased in temperature by a thousand degrees. She knew exactly what song he was talking about.

"Oh, do it, Ella," Amelia said.

Becca added, "We all know you have an incredible voice, so I know you can't be nervous about that!"

Adam pinched her shirt sleeve and tugged slightly while giving her the best puppy dog eyes.

She wavered. "Okay, fine."

The smile on Adam's face stretched to his ears. "Excellent. I'll go sign us up." He was gone in a flash and back just as fast.

She picked at the last few fries on her plate until it was their turn to sing. She took a swig of her coke and slid out of the booth with Adam. The butterflies in her stomach turned into a tornado. Singing never made her nervous.

They went up to the stage and picked up the microphones. She smiled at Adam, whose face was beaming. She started tapping her foot to the beat, and once Adam started singing the melody of "Brown Eyed Girl" she threw in a few harmonies here and there, until the chorus where they harmonized beautifully, just as they always had. She hadn't felt this happy in a long time. When they reached the third verse, Adam surprised her by changing the words to "swimming with you down at the lake and making out on the raft with you..." The temperature of her cheeks shot up again. And she laughed so hard she could barely finish the last chorus with him. They put their mics down and headed back to the table. As they walked, or were they floating, back Adam squeezed her arm and pulled her into a side hug. She wrapped her arm around his waist and hugged him back.

"You guys!" Amelia said. "That was awesome!"

Jared clapped. "I'm impressed."

Ella blushed a little more and managed to squeak out a "thanks."

She settled back into the booth and took a few slow breaths. *That was so much fun! Lord, thank you for laughter. And for Adam.* Her heart did a little flip. *Oh God, I'm not sure I'm ready for these feelings.* Her emotions were taking a fast turn. She needed a little air. "I'm going to have to excuse myself to the restroom. I'll be right back."

"I'll come with you," Amelia said.

She smiled at her friend. Adam slid out of the booth to let her out and squeezed her shoulder, sending her heart all over the place again. She patted his arm as she walked away with Amelia.

"You guys really sounded great. Your voices! Oh my word! They're perfect together."

She managed to say "thanks," and they walked into the bathroom.

Amelia went straight into a stall, but Ella just stood there, and as soon as the door shut behind her, the overwhelmed feeling took hold. Her chest tightened, and her lips quivered. She clenched her eyes shut and pressed her lips together. She didn't want to cry, but it was coming whether she liked it or not. The tears came. A slow trickle ran down her cheeks. She took a few steps forward towards the sink. She grabbed it to steady herself and tried not to sniffle. The stream of tears continued. She was completely overwhelmed by her emotions.

The door opened behind her, and Becca walked in. "Decided I should go, too." Ella made eye contact with Becca in the mirror and quickly diverted her eyes. "Ella?" Becca walked over and put a hand on Ella's shoulder.

Ella started at the contact, and Becca removed her hand and leaned against the sink next to the one Ella was leaning over.

"You all right?"

She shook her head. "I don't know. I'm such a hot mess. I don't get it. I was just laughing a few moments ago. And it was real, just as real as this."

Amelia came out of the stall, and Becca moved so she could wash her hands. Amelia said, "You've been through a lot lately especially with Adam."

Ella wiped her eyes and turned and leaned her back against the side of the stalls. "True. It's so confusing. I have pushed people away and avoided physical contact for so long. But I find myself just wanting to fall into his arms. It feels so weird. This feeling is so foreign. I haven't felt this way since well, since I was fourteen. Why does he have this effect on me?"

"I wonder," Amelia said, "if the physical past you have with Adam is actually helping you get beyond what happened to you that's caused you to physically push people away."

"But sometimes when he touches my arm or something, the flashbacks flare in my face. I want to let him hug me. I want to hug him. But I'm so afraid. What if I go into a full flashback? How can I ever get close to him?"

Becca answered, "One step at a time. I don't know you super well, but I do know Adam. While he's... been around the block, for lack of a better way of putting it, he's the most patient man I've ever met. He's compassionate. And if you do have a flashback with him, he'll help you cope with it. Heck, he's trained for that."

"He did help a lot when I had one at his house last week. Oh, but I'm so overwhelmed with the emotions of all of it. I loved him so much, so I can't tell if it's just my old feelings for him resurfacing or if it's new genuine feelings. I've forgiven him for all that happened, but I feel like I should still be hurt or... put off by it."

"Why should you?" Becca asked.

"I don't know. I guess it's what people expect."

Amelia said, "We don't expect you to feel that way. But we know Adam, today's Adam."

Becca added, "Yeah, the guy that learned the hard way to never go back on his word. May I ask? Are you the one he learned that lesson with?"

Ella bit her lip and nodded. "Yeah."

"Thought so. If you've moved past it, you've moved past it. It's that simple. Don't feel guilty for opening your heart to him again. You can trust him with it. I'm not sure I would tell just anyone that about him, as he's never been serious about any girl in his life since I've known him, but I've *never* seen him look at someone like he looks at you."

"So true," Amelia said. "He looks at you like he would stop heaven and hell to just be near you."

Ella blushed again and let her lips turn up at the thought of Adam wanting to be near her.

"But how do we know these emotions are real and not just sentimental?"

"Well," Becca said, "first, I know exactly what you mean. I had to weigh that when Jared came back into my life. So, when you are with him do you only think about back when you were kids or are you in the here and now?"

She looked up at the ceiling as she contemplated Becca's question. "Hmmm… here and now."

"The emotions are real not just sentimental. And some sentimental isn't bad. It's a solid building block into a renewed relationship."

Ella took in a deep refreshing breath. A smile turned her lips up, but if faded quickly. "But what about his relationship with Christ, or lack thereof. I want to see what could be there for us, but I don't want to be disobedient to God about being in a relationship with someone who's not actively walking with the Lord."

Amelia said, "That's a tough one. Because as much as I think you two are so adorable together, you're right. You're a believer, and he isn't."

"I just wish I knew why he walked away from the faith."

"Away?" Becca and Amelia said in unison.

"Yeah, you guys didn't know that he grew up in the church?"

"Not a clue!" Becca said. "Man, I really thought I knew the boy."

Amelia said, "I'm surprised by that. As much as he's not closed up, he clearly hasn't told me everything. But, Ella, I think we just keep praying. Praying that Adam turns to Christ. Praying for you as you continue to heal from the past. And praying for yours and Adam's relationship, whatever that may look like."

"Thanks! Both of you. If I was a hugger, I'd totally hug you now." All three women chuckled. Ella turned and looked in the mirror to assess the damage from crying. "Ugh, I look like a complete mess."

"Here," Amelia reached in her purse and pulled out a small makeup bag. "I learned to carry makeup in my purse after Evan died because I never knew when I would break down and need to reapply. Comes in handy still since I never know when the pregnancy hormones will send me into a fit of tears."

"Right?!" Ella touched up her face and handed the bag back to Amelia. "Thanks. And Becca, I have to say, I totally see it now."

"See what?"

"What Adam says about you being like Heather. I can't pinpoint exactly what it is, but whatever it is, you've got it just like her."

Adam looked down at his watch, the ladies had been in the bathroom for quite a while.

"Don't worry, Jamison; they're talking about you," Jared said.

"That's what I'm worried about. My partner and pseudo-big sister talking to the girl I like... that doesn't bode well for me."

"Ha. Those two adore you," Caleb said. "You've got nothing to worry about."

"You really like her, don't you?" Jared asked.

"Is it that obvious? Ah, man. I've never felt this way about anyone else. It's driving me crazy."

His friends just shook their heads. They knew exactly what he meant. He had seen the exact same look that he was sure was on his face on theirs when they fell in love with the other two women in the bathroom.

"Hey, guys," Patrick appeared out of nowhere beside their table. "How's it going?"

Adam wasn't typically a vibe kind of guy, but whenever Patrick came near him, he got a bad one.

Jared replied, "We're good, just out to dinner with the ladies. What are you up to this evening?"

"Just grabbing a drink with some of the guys." He turned and looked towards the bar where a few other police officers were gathering.

Caleb asked, "You guys going to get in on the karaoke? You just missed a rousing rendition of 'Brown Eyed Girl,' by Adam over here."

"I heard it, but nah, not my kind of thing," Patrick said.

Past Patrick, Adam saw the women walk out of the restroom smiling and talking. He smiled. Being away from Ella even for a few minutes was longer than he liked. He never wanted to leave her side. And not just because he wanted to be sure she was safe. It was a silly little feeling like when he was fourteen. He slid out of the booth, so he could let Ella and Becca in.

Patrick greeted the women as they sat down, "Good evening, Detectives. Hello, Ella."

Adam watched Ella give Patrick a slight nod and the weakest smile possible. A smile that barely even made it to her lips, let alone beyond. Adam slid into the booth after Ella and sat close to her.

Patrick was saying something to the others; Adam looked at him to try and get back into the conversation, but Ella's tender fingers drew his attention. She slid her hand into his. His heart took flight. He looked at her and his heart drooped a little. She looked very unsettled. That had not been the look on her face when she left the bathroom. What had changed? Patrick?

Adam stroked the back of Ella's hand with his thumb. She smiled at him, but her grip on his hand tightened the longer Patrick hung around. As soon as he walked away, Ella let go of Adam's hand. He leaned close to her and stretched his arm across the back of the booth. "You okay?"

"Eh. I guess. I've really never liked Patrick. He gives me the creeps."

"Know the feeling." He desperately wanted to tell her that he really liked holding her hand, but there would be time for that later.

The group sat around at the restaurant a little while longer after paying their bill. Ella couldn't figure out why she was feeling off now, maybe it was the cry in the bathroom, maybe it was seeing Patrick, or maybe she regretted holding Adam's hand? No, that last one wasn't it. She smiled to herself.

Adam still had his arm across the back of the seat behind her. An unseen force seemed to pull at her to lean against him, but she resisted. She wasn't ready for that much contact yet.

She was getting antsy.

"Can we get out of here?" She leaned a little closer to ask him quietly.

"Sure. Want to go for a walk? I could use some fresh air."

"Me, too. A walk would be nice."

She couldn't breathe. His eyes sparkled, and she felt like she was just a pile of goo in the seat. She was falling hard. She took in a shaky breath. She needed to get control over her emotions. He touched her shoulder as he removed his arm from the back of the booth. She struggled to get the air into her lungs.

While she tried to gain her composure, Adam spoke to the others, "Ok, y'all. We're gonna head out and get some fresh air. I'll bring her home in a little while."

Caleb smiled, "Don't keep her out too late; it's a school night, ya know."

"Ha. Yes, 'Dad.'" They all laughed.

"But seriously," Amelia added, "Be careful."

"Of course."

Adam and Ella slid out of the booth, and Adam grabbed his hat from the hook on the side of the booth where he had hung it when they came in. He twirled it and plopped it on her head. She giggled, and they exited the restaurant.

They turned towards the downtown avenue that was only a block away from the pub. Adam walked on her right. His hand swung next to him as they walked. She wanted to hold his hand again. His hand was strong yet gentle and fully encompassed hers. But she didn't want to presume anything. Just because he had squeezed her hand earlier and had rubbed it with his thumb, didn't mean he thought anything more of this than friendship.

She diverted her eyes back to the sidewalk in front of them. This whole thing was going to drive her crazy.

Her hand collided with Adam's. She jumped. Instead of pulling his hand away he took hers and wove his fingers between hers. She was beyond happy, all reservations swept aside. She wanted to say something to break the silence, no matter how comfortable it was, but she didn't know what to say. Everything she thought of just sounded stupid and childish.

Adam broke the silence instead. "I didn't tell you earlier, but you look beautiful this evening. Well, all the time."

Her cheeks warmed. "Well, maybe not when you burst into Carter's room the other morning when I had that nightmare."

"Even then."

"Not even—gnarly hair, plastered to my face with sweat—hardly beautiful."

He shook his head. "Yes, even. Don't argue with me about this. You're beautiful."

He was the only one who had ever told her that, well other than her mother. She had believed him when they were kids, and he said it so genuinely now that she almost believed him again.

He stopped and turned towards her without letting go of her hand. His eyebrows furrowed. "You don't believe me, do you? You don't think you're beautiful?"

She shrugged.

His eyes looked sad. His free hand came to her face and swept a loose strand of hair out of her face.

"I'm just average. I'm not a twig like that waitress. My hair is crazy most of the time. I'm not at all like the girls you've dated over the years." She instantly regretted saying that. What difference did it make if she was like the girls he had dated? Was she expecting that he would date her? That was awfully presumptuous. She wasn't his type.

"Ella, I've never dated anyone as beautiful as you. I love your hair, always have. It's gorgeous when you straighten it, but it's awesome when you don't. The wildness reminds me of how wild you were when we were little. You were always chasing me with frogs or what not. And the red in it matches the fire in your spirit. And as for your body," he looked her up and down and raised his eyebrows and a sly smile formed on his lips.

The heat rose in her neck and cheeks. She was unfamiliar with the look he gave her, but she knew what it meant, and her embarrassment caught her breath in her chest.

"Let's just say it's perfect."

She couldn't handle the attention. She started walking again and tugged on his hand.

He squeezed hers. "I don't mean to embarrass you, but I wish you'd believe me."

"I'll try." She gave him a little smirk.

His smile broadened showing his perfectly straight teeth.

They walked on, hand in hand. Until they came in front of a little convenience store on the corner, and Adam stopped. "I want to get you something."

She raised her eyebrows at him. "What?"

"You'll see. It'll just take a second."

"I'll wait out here."

Adam's face turned serious. "I don't know about that." He looked up and down the street. "Just stay under the streetlight."

"Of course. I know how to be aware of my surroundings."

"I know. I'll be back in a flash." He winked at her and spun and disappeared into the shop.

Maybe it wasn't the wisest thing to be by herself out on the street after dark, but she actually needed a minute away from Adam. This was all moving too fast for her. Or was it? She looked up and down the street, staying aware of what was going on around her. It was a quiet evening in Hazel Hill. It was pushing nine o'clock and even though most of the stores were still open, most the patrons had gone home. There was a couple walking out of a shop down the road on the other side of the street. Other than that, no one else was around. Half a dozen cars or so were parallel parked along the sidewalk on either side. Nothing nefarious seemed to lurk about. She always loved downtown Hazel Hill. It was so quaint with its old-time shops and rot iron lampposts. The cobbled crosswalks were the finishing touch that made it perfect.

Ella continued to scan up and down the street until her phone chirped in her purse that was hung across her body. She pulled it out and found a new email from her mom. Another stupid 'cute' animal video. They were her mom's new obsession that she just *had* to share with Ella. If Ella was honest, she thought they were adorable too, but the volume that her mom sent was getting obnoxious. She pressed play since Adam hadn't come out of the store yet.

She laughed at the silly antics of the baby animals. The hair on the back of her neck stood up. Someone was behind her. She dropped her phone. She tried to turn but a man's arm was around her neck before she could spin around. The cold steel of a blade against the side of her neck. He had a knife. It was him. He was going to try to rape her again and kill her.

Without a thought her training kicked in. She hadn't taken fifteen years of martial arts to let this guy get at her again. She stomped on his foot and grabbed the arm around her neck. She pulled it away from her neck and further across her body; she raised the shoulder that his arm was over. He was big. Easily six foot, it was definitely the same guy. She continued to pull on his arm and spun out and under his arm. Keeping one hand on his wrist, she rotated the other one to his upper arm and pushed down with all her might. She swung her knee up and jabbed it into his head. She took her knee to his head again pushed him to the ground with all her might.

The knife fell out of his hand, and he hit the concrete.

She dove for the knife.

He tripped her.

She fell. Her palms scraped across the ground, setting them on fire. But she was able to grab the knife. She turned over, raising the knife off the ground. He lunged toward her. His fist hit the side of her face; she swung the knife. Her vision blurred as her head reeled from the punch. She kept her arm steady and swung the knife. It made contact with his arm. She scrambled backwards away from him as she took a deep enough breath to scream. "HELP!" He lunged toward her again; his pale blue eyes glared at her from under his ski mask. She kept the knife up as she scooted farther backwards.

"ELLA!" She heard Adam scream behind her. "POLICE! STOP!"

Her assailant jumped to his feet and ran.

It sounded like Adam was a mile away. "Call 911," he yelled to someone, "tell them a plain clothes officer is in pursuit."

She watched Adam take off running after him. And watched Adam disappear down the alley that the attacker had gone down.

Ella's vision tunneled. She couldn't fight it. Everything around her seemed to disappear. She looked at the knife in her hand, but she couldn't see it. Her hands shook. Her whole body shook. Shock was setting in. Her mind replayed what just happened over and over. She couldn't get it out of her head. She was only slightly cognizant of the flashing lights and people gathering around her where she sat on the sidewalk. Someone touched her arm. She jumped.

"Ella, it's Jared; you're safe."

Her mind reeled as she processed what was said. How long had she blacked out? She slowly closed her eyes and reopened them. *ADAM!* She became fully aware. "ADAM! Where's Adam? He ran after the guy!"

"ELLA! I'm here." She lifted her head. Adam ran towards her.

"Ella," Jared spoke, "I need you to let go of the knife."

She looked at it. Jared had put an evidence bag over the knife and was holding it and her arm. She let go, and Jared took it. Her hands were still shaking. Adam collapsed onto the ground next to her and put his arm across her back. She fell into his chest.

"Shh." Adam's voice was soft, and he rubbed her back. He stroked her hair with his other hand, and she turned her face a little further into him. She clutched the front of his shirt and didn't want to let go.

"Hey, Ella," Caleb said, but she didn't want to lift her face to look at anyone. "Ella, the paramedics want to check you out. Are you hurt?"

She turned her head and looked at Caleb.

"Looks like you might have a shiner. Anywhere else hurt?"

She stared at Caleb like she didn't know what he said. Hurt? Did anything hurt? She couldn't feel anything. She let go of Adam's shirt and looked at her hands. They hurt. And for good reason, the skin was broken where they had slid against the sidewalk.

"Let's clean those up. How are you feeling?"

She sat there with Adam's arm still around her, and a paramedic in uniform started cleaning her hands. Another paramedic brought a blanket over and Adam helped him drape it across her shoulders.

"I'm okay," she finally said. "My head hurts a little too."

"Can you get up and come to the ambulance?" one of the EMTs asked. "I want to check your vitals and make sure you don't have a concussion."

"Yeah, I think so."

Adam helped her up, and she spotted his hat and her phone on the ground. She pointed to them, and Adam picked them up. They walked to the ambulance, and Gavin joined them. She knew Gavin was Becca's partner and knew him a bit from church.

"Ella," he said, "when you're ready, I'd like for you to tell me what happened."

Ella nodded and squeezed Adam's hand.

CHAPTER 15

Adam came back to the Captain's office with two cups of tea in his hands. Ella was right where he had left her, curled up on the couch. She was still shaking; it was a subtle quiver, but it consumed her whole body. They had come to the station an hour ago, so Ella would have a safe, warmer place to give Gavin her statement. They had gone into the Captain's office, and she had managed to walk them threw exactly what happened and how her training had kicked in and saved her life.

But he was kicking himself. This was all his fault. He should never have left her for even a second. He could have lost her tonight. His whole body shuddered at the thought, and a lump formed in his throat. His voice was too tight to speak, so he sat down on the couch next to Ella. She jumped. "Sorry."

"It's okay. I just can't get out of my head." She took her cup of tea from him and sighed.

"I bet. I'm so sorry."

"It's not your fault."

"Yes, it is. If I hadn't gone in that store…"

"Yeah, but if I hadn't dropped my guard and watched that stupid video…"

Silence hung between them. He yearned to pull her into his arms, but even though she had leaned into his chest earlier, he wasn't sure she would want to now.

She blew into the tiny opening on the lid of her disposable cup, before she took a sip. He was mesmerized by her. What if he had lost her? His chest felt like it was collapsing in on itself.

"Adam." She took his hand. His skin tingled at her touch. "It isn't your fault or mine. It's that evil man's fault. All blame lies with him."

He knew she was right, but that didn't wash the guilt away. He had put her at risk for a silly romantic gesture. She probably wasn't even ready for that yet. What had he been thinking?

She was still shaking. The blanket had fallen off her shoulder, but he didn't want to let go of her hand to help her with it. So, he set down his cup and reached across and lifted the blanket back onto her shoulder. He lifted her hair out from under the blanket and noticed the bruise forming on her cheekbone. That vile man had hit her. If he could get his hands on him…

"*O God, our help in ages past,*" Ella's tender voice filled the space between them, "*Our hope for years to come,*

"*Our shelter from the stormy blast, and our eternal home!*

"*Under the shadow of thy throne Thy saints have dwelt secure;*

"*Sufficient is thine arm alone, and our defense is sure.*"

He closed his eyes and let her voice and the words from the old hymn wash away his violent thoughts. He couldn't remember all the words to the song, but he did know the last verse, so when she began singing it, he opened his eyes and added a harmony. Their eyes connected as they sang.

"*O God, our help in ages past, our hope for years to come,*

"*Be thou our guard while life shall last, and our eternal home.*"

Ella had finally stopped trembling and smiled at him. "Thanks for singing with me."

"My pleasure, if I had remembered the words I would have sung more."

"I know." She sunk down a little deeper into the couch and leaned her head on his shoulder. His heart felt like it was going to beat out of his chest. She intertwined her fingers into his. He was a goner. He didn't want to leave this place ever, but she needed to get some sleep. It was getting really late now.

While the other detectives were working the case, he had been given strict orders from Amelia to stay with Ella, he should at least take her back to Amelia's house, so she could get some sleep. "I can take you home when you're ready to go get some sleep."

Her hand tightened around his. "Adam, I can't. I don't want to sleep." The fear in her voice tugged at his heart. Of course, she didn't want to sleep. It was going to be a rough night.

"I have an idea."

She lifted her head to see his face.

"Why don't we go back to Amelia's? You don't have to go to bed. We can sit up and watch a movie or something. And if you fall asleep, I'll be right there if you need me."

"That could work."

"You will need to sleep eventually."

"I know, but I'd like to avoid it as long as possible."

"So, we binge watch Netflix and eat an extraordinary amount of popcorn."

"Is it safe to leave the station? Do you think he knows where I'm staying?"

"I don't think he does. We've been careful not to talk about it at all. And you've got both Caleb and me there to keep you safe. Not that I did a real great job of that earlier..." he dropped his head, the guilt surging inside again.

"Don't. You chased him. You did good."

"No, you're the one that did good. You kicked his butt!"

She giggled. "I guess."

"I just wish I would have shot him."

"But he was running, you couldn't justify it. You wouldn't do me any good locked up in prison."

"The only reason I didn't." He winked at her.

She giggled again. And his heart did somersaults.

———•———

Adam stretched before he climbed out of his car and walked toward the police station the next morning. He was tired. The night had been long and hadn't included much sleep, and what sleep he had gotten had either been on Amelia's love seat or the floor. He felt worse for Ella though, because what little sleep she had gotten on the couch had been riddled with nightmares. He was so glad he had been there for her though. He had held her hand, stroked her hair, and sang songs with and to her. At one point she had woken him while having a nightmare and he had started singing. She settled almost instantly without waking up.

He took another swig of his coffee. He pulled the station door open and walked through.

"Hey, Adam!" He turned his head and saw his cousin, Jocelyn North, who was the department's forensic photographer coming up the stairs from the lab.

"Hey, Jocelyn."

She fell in step with him as he walked toward the squad room. "How's Ella? She looked really shaken last night."

"She's doing all right. Had a rough night but was doing better this morning."

"Glad to hear she's having a better morning. Where is she? Wait, don't tell me the fewer people who know the better, I'm sure. Tell her I'm praying for her."

"Will do. I'm sure she'll appreciate it." He held the door open for her, and they entered the squad room. "What do you have for us?"

"I have the pictures of the crime scene from last night printed out." She held up a manila folder. "Nothing too exciting. I'm going to take the individual evidence pictures when I go back down. The lab has the knife right now looking for fingerprints and taking samples of the blood from where she nicked the guy."

"Excellent." Proof that the guy that grabbed her last night was the same as the guy from seventeen years ago.

"Hey, Gavin; Becca," Jocelyn greeted the other detectives.

"Hey, guys," Adam said.

Gavin and Becca both said hello.

Jocelyn handed over the folder and the detectives looked through the stack of pictures and pulled out a few and to add to the white board. Adam walked over to his desk but stopped dead in his tracks when he saw a bouquet of daisies sitting on his desk. The hair on the back of his neck stood on end. Why were there flowers on his desk just like the ones he had gone in the store to buy for Ella last night? "Hey guys, who put those flowers on my desk?"

"No idea." Becca turned from putting the pictures on the board. "They were there when I got here this morning."

"Some of those were on the ground at the crime scene last night, right?" Jocelyn asked.

"Yeah, that's why I was away from Ella for that moment. I ran in the convenience store. I knew they had a little section of flowers and wanted to get some for her. But I dropped them when I saw the attack. Totally forgot about them."

Gavin said, "Maybe someone saw you dropped them and picked them up for you."

"Maybe…" He took the few last steps to his desk and was about to pick them up when he saw an envelope under them. He had not left that on his desk yesterday. "Maybe not..." He pulled a pair of gloves out of his desk, slipped them on, and carefully pulled the envelope out from under the flowers. Becca, Gavin, and Jocelyn all came over and gathered around his desk. Jared soon followed when Becca called him over. He opened the envelope. A single folded sheet of copy paper was inside. He set the envelope down and unfolded the paper. The note was typed in large letters. He read it.

She got away this time, but you can count on that NOT happening again. You tell your little girlfriend her days are almost over. And if you get in the way, so are yours. I may not know where she is staying, but I will find her.

His stomach dropped. He was going to be sick. That man had been at his desk. And had once again threatened Ella's life. The heat from his anger started in his toes and worked its way all the way up to his head. He dropped the letter back on the desk and ran his hands into his hair. "Who saw him? Who put these flowers on my desk? Somebody had to have seen him!" He looked at his friends. They all looked confused. He hadn't read the letter out loud. Becca stepped over and put a hand on his shoulder and leaned over his desk and read the letter. Her fingers tightened on his shoulder. He locked eyes with her. The fear in her eyes reflected how he felt.

Gavin moved toward them and used a glove to slide the letter and envelope into an evidence bag. He did the same for the flowers. "Is there anything else out of place on your desk?"

Adam looked. Everything else was just as he had left it the day before. "No. Just the envelope and flowers." He felt paralyzed. He stood there as his friends flew into action in response to the threat that had just been delivered. Gavin had put the bagged letter face up on the desk. The words stared up at Adam and seemed to mock him. He swallowed past the lump that had formed in his throat.

Becca's voice broke into his head, "You need to call Amelia."

He looked at her. She was right.

Jared asked, "Do you know if Ella was going to work today?"

"No, she didn't sleep last night. Pretty sure she's planning on taking tomorrow off too."

"Ok, call Amelia so she knows what's going on, but she needs to stay with Ella," Jared said.

He pulled his phone off his belt. How was he going to tell them? Amelia answered on the third ring. "What?" He must have woken her. After the late night she had, she had still been in bed when he left for the station at nine.

"Hey. Mornin' to you too. We have a problem."

"What is it?" Concern replaced the annoyance in her voice.

"I just received another threat on Ella's life."

"And yours too," Becca added just loudly enough for Amelia to hear too.

"Yours?"

He read her the note and explained the flowers.

"Do you want me to come in?"

"No, Sarge said to stay with Ella. Please keep her safe."

"You know I will."

"I know."

"Okay. Keep me posted."

He hung up the phone and felt the anger rising. "Someone had to have seen something. Someone doesn't just waltz into the detectives squad room with flowers and not have somebody notice!" His cheeks and ears burned.

Jared walked over to him and squared himself in front of Adam. "You're right!" He spoke in a hushed, but serious tone. "And we're going to move this to the conference room before we discuss it further. You *know* I understand exactly how you feel right now, but you have to maintain control or you're off the case."

"Yes, sir." Adam silently counted to four and turned towards the conference room. He tried not to storm into the room but paced back and forth as he waited for the other detectives to join him. They had to get this guy sooner rather than later.

Gavin, Becca, Jared, and Captain Baker came into the room. As soon as the Captain closed the door behind himself Adam said, "Wait. Where's the evidence?"

Becca sat at the table. "Jocelyn took custody of it. She's taking it down now to get pictures and have it dusted for fingerprints. You trust her, right?"

"Yeah, definitely. The question is who do we not trust? How did this guy get in here and leave it on my desk?"

"That's what we have to figure out," Jared said from where he stood by the door.

"What time did y'all get here today and were they there when you did?" Adam asked.

"Becca and I got here around eight. Becca did you say you saw them there?"

"Yep. Gavin, you were here before me? What did you see?"

Gavin answered, "I got here around 7:30. They were already there. I was also one of the last ones to leave. Didn't finish typing up Ella's statement until two."

Becca gave him a cockeyed look. "Did you sleep?"

"A little bit."

Adam was getting impatient, "But were they there when you left?"

"No. And no one else was here."

"Captain?"

"I turned the lights on when I came in at seven this morning. Unfortunately, I didn't notice if the flowers were on your desk."

Jared said, "So we have a five-hour window in which someone could have come in and put it there."

"We have security cameras. Let's pull the tapes," the Captain said.

Becca chuckled. "Captain, no disrespect, but you do know it's all digital these days."

"Yeah, yeah. Whatever."

Even Adam smiled. "Sounds like that's what we need to do first. See who came in with the flowers and arrest them."

Gavin replied, "Let's hope it's that simple."

It had better be.

CHAPTER 16

Adam leaned his head down on his arms that were folded on Jocelyn's desk. "Well, that was pointless." After six hours of staring at a computer monitor, Gavin's warning was ringing true. They had nothing. Gavin, Jocelyn, and Adam had sat in Jocelyn's office in the basement all day watching hours of video.

"I don't get it!" Jocelyn said.

They had watched the door to the squad room. Nothing. Not one person had gone through that door between when Gavin left at two and when the Captain entered at seven. After that everyone that entered belonged and no one was carrying flowers. They had looked through the video from the front door and every other entrance to the entire building.

"Okay. So," Gavin said, "no one came in outright carrying the flowers, but who could have been carrying them hidden?" They spent another hour going back through taking screen shots of every single person that entered the station carrying a bag big enough or a jacket loose enough to conceal the bouquet. They crossed that with people who entered the squad room. They had four possibilities. Two of which they couldn't tell who they were at all because one hid their head and the other had on a baseball cap. One was a woman, clearly not the attacker, but maybe she was working in cahoots with him. But the other left a weird taste in their mouths.

"That's Patrick," Gavin said.

Adam looked at his cousin. Her lips were pursed together, and her head was tipped to the side.

The air in the room was tight. What was his cousin's husband, a patrol officer, doing?

Gavin broke the silence that was hanging between the three. "Anyone know why Patrick would go up to the squad room? Makes sense that he would bring a bag to work, but why would he go in there. He was a little early for duty, but who would he have gone to see in there?"

Adam rubbed the back of his stiff neck. "He and Scott seem to be buddies. Was Scott in the squad room?" They ran back through the footage. No, Scott, unless he was one of the unidentifiable men. He came in later.

"Sorry, Joc, looks like your husband just made the suspect list." Gavin bit his lip.

"He's not the only one though, Jocelyn. We've got nothing more to go on yet." The look on his cousin's face made him know he had to ask more questions, not questions he wanted to ask. "Is there any reason to believe that he could be involved?"

"Jocelyn," Gavin interrupted, "You don't have to answer that."

Adam looked at Gavin with a furrowed brow. He was right that legally she didn't have to answer.

Adam's phone rang. He pulled it off his belt. It was Ella. His heart lifted. He stood and paced to the other side of the room and answered it. "Hey."

"Hi, Adam." Her voice was salve to his tired mind. "How's your day going?"

"Eh, not as productive as I would have hoped. How 'bout you? You doin' okay?"

"I guess, I'm so tired, but every time I close my eyes..."

"I'm sure." If only he could pull her into his arms.

"Well, I called to see if you wanted to come over to Amelia's for dinner."

"I would love that!"

"Oh good." He could hear the relief in her voice.

"I'll be there as soon as I can. I think I'm almost at a point I can leave, and I'll come straight over." His heart raced at the idea of seeing her. They said goodbye, and he turned back towards Gavin and Jocelyn who were leaning a little too close talking to one another. He raised an eyebrow but didn't say anything about it. Instead he went back to the question he had asked her before Ella called. "Jocelyn," the two jumped back from one another, "we have to talk about this at some point, because I can tell there is something more going on with Patrick. And if we need to talk just as family, let's."

"Not right now. But you can trust that I won't say anything to him about being a person of interest. But don't let your personal disdain for him cloud your judgment as a detective. Please, Adam."

"I'll try not to. I don't think he's the rapist, but I have to consider what his involvement is with the flowers."

"I know."

"Gavin, do you think we need to do much more today?"

"Well, we should run this all by Becca and Jared at least. But I can do that. I take it Ella wants to see you?"

His heart did a somersault again. He nodded. "She does. Jocelyn, can you print off the pics of the people and the note for me to show Amelia as I think she'll stay with Ella again tomorrow. And keep all of it backed up somewhere other than the station's server, just in case this guy really does have connections inside the department."

"Can do and will do. I want Ella's attacker caught and punished. Don't forget that Ella is my friend."

"I know. I still can't believe you've been friends with her and didn't tell me."

"Hey, I watched what happened between you two in high school, and I wasn't about to stir any of that up in either of you."

"Fair enough."

Jocelyn printed off the pictures Adam asked for. They would need to interview each of those they could identify and try to figure out who the other two were, but it could wait for tomorrow since today was almost gone.

———•———

Ella kept stirring the sauce. It was the only way to keep her hands from shaking. It had been a long day of nothing. She had helped Amelia sort through baby things, mostly hand-me-downs from Becca and Becca's sister, Amy. It had been a perfect distraction, but it hadn't lasted more than a few hours. Then she was back to avoiding sleep. Her nerves were fried, leaving her stomach with a perpetual state of queasiness. *O Lord, help. Bring peace to my soul. I'm so weary. I know I need to sleep, but the dreams...* She needed to refocus. She had spent the hour after Adam left and before Amelia got up reading her Bible. It had been wonderful, and the Lord had really touched her heart and given her peace, but that peace was once again dwindling.

She was also anxious for Adam to get there. They had talked almost thirty minutes ago, and given the threat he received today, she was more worried about him than ever. Hopefully, he'd show up soon.

Thunder rumbled outside. It sounded like they were in for a doozy of a storm. But the sound of thunder always reminded her of one of her favorite hymns, so she started singing softly.

O Lord my God, when I in awesome wonder, consider all the worlds thy hands have made,

I see the stars, I hear the rolling thunder, Thy pow'r thro'out the universe displayed.

Then sings my soul, my savior God to Thee, How great Thou art, how great Thou art!

Then sings my soul, my savior God to Thee, How great Thou art, how great Thou art!

She sang the last verse and chorus, and a familiar baritone joined in. Without stopping, she turned to see Adam standing at the edge of the kitchen, looking just as exhausted as she felt.

Then sings my soul, my savior God to Thee, How great Thou art, how great Thou art!

Then sings my soul, my savior God to Thee, How great Thou art, how great Thou art!

She wished he believed the words he so easily sang with her. *Jesus, please draw him to your heart.* "Hey."

"Hey." He moved closer to her.

She was sure he wanted to hug her, but she turned and attended to the food on the stove. The flashbacks were sitting on the sidelines just waiting to play, but she would do everything in her might to keep them benched. "Rough day, huh?" she asked him.

"You could say that. What did Amelia tell you?"

"Everything you told her."

Amelia walked into the kitchen. "Any developments? Any idea where the flowers came from?"

"There are a few possibilities. Where are the kids?"

"They're upstairs," Amelia said. "Go ahead and fill us in."

Ella put down the spoon she was using to stir the alfredo and stepped across the kitchen to where Adam was pulling out a stack of photographs.

"These are the only four people who entered the squad room and could have possibly been carrying the flowers." Adam laid the pictures out across the counter and held up another. "This is the note."

The words jumped off the page and hit Ella in the gut. She was already nauseated, now she felt like she might actually throw up. The fear started creeping back in.

She jumped when Adam touched her arm. Despite the fear that resided deep in his eyes, the strength of his presence eased her anxiety. She looked back at the pictures. "Is that Jocelyn's husband, Patrick?"

"It is."

"You don't think he's..."

"I'm not making any conclusions now, not until I talk to him, but I don't think so."

She looked at the other pictures. She picked up the first unidentifiable person and then the other. "It could be either of these guys. They both seem tall enough and built the same way."

"Yeah, my thoughts exactly. Gavin and Becca are going to try and identify them, and we'll interview these people specifically tomorrow. Becca and Jared spent today talking to everyone in the station."

Amelia asked, "Did they learn anything? Did anyone see anything?"

"Nothing. How can a bunch of detectives not notice anything? Aren't we trained to notice things that are out of place? I wasn't there, you think someone would be suspicious of someone at my desk."

"Unless it was someone who wasn't out of place?" Amelia took the pictures from Ella.

Ella asked him, "So it has to be one of these four people to have put the flowers on your desk?"

"The only other possibility is someone tampered with the footage. When I left Jocelyn was going back through it to see if there are any glitches or something that would indicate that it had been altered."

"Either we're looking at an inside job, or at least someone who has inside connections?" Amelia asked.

Adam nodded. "Well, that would explain what happened to the DNA and other evidence seventeen years ago."

Ella half listened as Amelia and Adam continued to discuss the case, but she went back to attending to dinner. She turned the stove off and stirred the sauce one last time. The spoon was still in her hand when Adam touched her back causing her to jump. The sauce went flying off the spoon and landed square on Adam's chest. "Oh, my goodness, I'm so sorry."

He laughed, "It's okay. I'm sorry I startled you!"

"It doesn't take much right now."

"I should have known better." He unbuttoned his shirt.

"Let me throw that in the wash for you," Amelia said.

"At least it wasn't a red sauce." Ella let out a dry chuckle.

"Thanks, here." He pulled the shirt off and handed it to Amelia.

Ella smiled at his t-shirt. "Really? Captain America under your work shirt? Someone thinks highly of himself."

He joined her laughter. "I need to do laundry."

She reached out and squeezed his arm. Heat rushed up her arm and filled her cheeks from the contact. His arm was strong, significantly more built than it had been when they were just preteens. He had been a rail, nothin' but skin and bones, now he was quite muscular while still thin and lean. Her entire face felt like it was on fire. She looked away; afraid her face was actually going to burst into flames. She busied herself pulling out plates for dinner.

They set the dining room table, and Amelia and the kids joined them. They all sat down and enjoyed a nice meal sans Caleb, who was working. Ella got the full run down about today's sub from Molly. She hadn't asked any questions about why Ella hadn't been at school, for which Ella was very grateful.

"Will you be back tomorrow?"

"No, Molly, but I should be there Monday."

"Oh good. The boys just won't listen to Mrs. Fredrick. She's nice and all, but maybe she's too nice to them."

"You're a good student, Molly. Why don't you tell those boys that I told them to behave for Mrs. Fredrick tomorrow?"

The girl's face beamed as if a rock star had told her something very important. Ella smiled at her.

"Okay, kids," Amelia said, "Time to head to Grandma and Grandpa's."

The kids took off up the stairs to grab their things for the night, and the adults cleared the table.

Ella looked at Amelia. "I feel bad that they've been so displaced from their own home."

"Don't, Ella; they're fine. They spend at least one night a week over there anymore, and it'll probably increase a little bit once the baby comes, at least on the nights Caleb has to work overnight."

"You sure?"

"Yes, stop worrying about it. Now, I'm going to take them over there and then go to the grocery store. Anything else you need?"

"Nope."

"Adam, I'm assuming you're okay with hanging out with our dear friend here for the rest of the evening."

"You bet."

Ella blushed. He hadn't hesitated at all to say yes!

Adam helped her clean up the dinner mess, and shortly after Amelia and the kids left, a loud crack of thunder shook the whole house. Ella jumped. Another bright flash of lightning flash with a huge crack sounded in quick succession.

"That one was close." She tried to make light of the situation and ignore her jumpy nerves.

Another clap sounded before Adam could reply. The lights flickered but stayed on.

Adam reached out for Ella and touched her shoulder. She saw it coming, so she didn't jump at his touch, but she pulled away and moved to the other side of the kitchen as fast as she could.

"I'm okay." She put the last of the leftovers in the fridge.

"But I'm not. *I* need to hold you."

She looked up at him. The fear she had seen in his eyes was stronger now. She knew it wasn't the storm that he was afraid of.

"I know, Adam. But I'm afraid. I'm scared of the flashbacks. I've been fighting them off all day. Every time you touch me, they threaten to take over."

"I know. But I need you to trust me. I'll help you. Let me help you create new memories of touch."

She took a step closer to him and kept her eyes locked with his. He smiled. She took in a wobbly breath. Her heart palpitated. Why was she so afraid?

His hand came to rest on her upper arm. He pulled her into his chest and started to sing softly. The words to Jack Johnson's "I Got You" washed over her. She didn't know the words very well but listened as Adam sang them. Focusing on the words and the tender sound of Adam's voice kept her in the here and now. The warmth of his body and the gentleness of his touch helped her relax into his arms. She cautiously wrapped her arms around his waist and laid her head against his chest. He rested his chin on her head and continued to sing. He led them in swaying to the rhythm of the song.

She squeezed him a bit tighter. And he stroked her back and her hair. So far, she was okay. Instead of remembering that awful night that had driven her away from touch, she was present, right here, right now in Adam's arms. *Adam's arms!*

When he had finished the song, she pulled him back to arm's length without letting go to see his face. He smiled down at her. "You did it! Any shadows creep in?"

She smiled at him. "No. Thank you."

"Looks like we've figured out exactly how to help you with the flashbacks."

Another loud crash of thunder sounded outside, and the lights went out. Ella jumped back into Adam's arms. His arms encircled her again. "Guess we can't continue our Netflix marathon tonight… and I don't even know where Amelia and Caleb keep flashlights or candles."

"No worries. We'll just sit on the couch and talk. We don't need light for that." While keeping one arm around her, he pulled his phone off his belt and turned the flashlight on. The little light chased the darkness away. He slid his hand down her arm and hand in hand they made their way to the couch.

Ella leaned her head against Adam's shoulder. They had been sitting on the couch talking for quite a while. The lights still hadn't come back on, but that was okay with Ella, she was enjoying Adam's nearness and the ability to talk without other distractions. They were snuggled together with Adam's arm wrapped around her. She wanted to take their conversation a little deeper, but she was uncertain how he would react to the question she wanted to ask. She ran her finger along the emblem on his shirt and mulled over how to word it.

"You've gotten awfully quiet." Adam broke into her thoughts.

"Sorry, I was just thinking," she said without moving her head from his shoulder.

"About what?"

She took in a slow breath and lifted her head and looked deep into his eyes. "Well, I wanted to ask you how you were doing regarding your partner's death? Caleb mentioned it a couple of weeks ago and in all our conversations we haven't talked about it."

Adam dropped his feet from where they were resting on the table and sat up straighter, pulling away from her. A dark shadow filled his eyes.

"I'm sorry; I didn't mean to pry..."

He pulled his arm out from around her and leaned forward resting his elbows on his knees. She had been worried about his reaction, but she hadn't expected it to be this bad. Her heart constricted. She didn't want to push him away; she wanted to draw him closer.

"It's okay." He rubbed his face.

She slid her feet off the couch and onto the floor and leaned close to him putting her hand on his back. "Are you sure?"

"Yeah, I've managed to keep myself focused on you the last couple of weeks and have avoided thinking about it."

"Can I ask what happened?"

He folded his arms across his knees and turned his head to look at her. He told her the whole story about tagging along, about rock-paper-scissors, about how Rick died in his arms, and about how he felt responsible. A flash of lightning filled the room, and Ella saw the tears running down Adam's cheeks.

"Adam...." She reached up and turned his face back towards hers. She wiped the tears from his face with her thumbs. "From what you just told me, it wasn't your fault at all."

"That's what everyone says, but no matter how much I hear it, the words don't take away the guilt I feel. It should have been me in that casket, not him."

"It may be super selfish of me to say, but I'm so glad it wasn't you." A few tears broke loose from her eyes.

The corners of his lips turned up.

She slid the hand on his back up and stroked his hair. *Oh, Jesus, help Adam. Free him from the guilt he's feeling. Help him to turn to you in this and let you take it from him. And thank you so much that it wasn't him. Thank you for sparing him.*

"I can't believe I left you alone last night. I just can't handle the idea of anything happening to you. I was supposed to be there to protect you, but I got stupid. If you hadn't been able to get the upper hand... I'm so sorry."

"Adam, we've gone over this already."

"I know, but again, the guilt is too heavy."

"Let it go."

"It's not that simple."

"If you give it to Jesus, it is."

He sighed and sat up straighter.

Shoot! Jesus, I don't want to make him uncomfortable. Deep in her being, as if God himself was impressing the thought into her, she knew that uncomfortable was exactly what he needed to be. *But how much do I push him?*

"Jesus can heal your heart and take on the guilt for you. Like He said, He will take your burden and give you rest."

He stood up and walked across the room. Maybe she had said too much.

"I don't know, Ella. Do you want something to drink?"

"A glass of water would be nice."

"Okay, I'll be right back." He disappeared into the dark.

She prayed for Adam the entire time he was in the kitchen. His shoulders had relaxed by the time he came back with their drinks. She eyed the beer in his hand. After seeing him hung over that day at the police station she added a new item to her worry list for the evening.

"I'm sorry I pulled away, but can we talk about something else now?" He sat down close to her.

"Of course. But please know you can talk to me any time about anything."

He put his arm back around her. "I know. Thank you."

She settled back against his chest and sighed in relief that no flashbacks were even on the sidelines as she snuggled close to Adam.

"What do you mean it's missing?!" Fire coursed through Adam's veins, but he tried to keep his voice calm Monday morning.

"Well, Detective, I mean, it's not here. It was here when I left Saturday. I logged it away, see." Mike, the lab tech, lifted the clipboard and all but shoved it in Adam's face. "I promise we followed all procedures. It should be in here. The lab was locked when I came in this morning so there's no way anyone came in."

"But obviously someone did!" He pulled his phone off his belt and dialed Amelia's phone.

He had simply come down to the lab to check on their progress. He had not expected to find the technician running around frantic, looking for the evidence.

When Amelia answered the phone he said, "We have a problem. Get the Sergeant and come down to the lab."

In a matter of minutes Jared and Amelia showed up. Jared crossed his arms. "What's up?"

"You want to tell them how you screwed up?" Adam jabbed his finger into Mike's shoulder.

"It's not my fault, I swear! Sergeant, when I left on Saturday, I properly put all the evidence, the knife, the samples I had collected, the flowers, the note, everything from Wednesday and Thursday, I put it in the box. I put it back into the evidence locker. It was all right where it was supposed to be. I locked it up. And then I locked the lab. There's no way some random person just came in and took it."

Amelia gasped. "Oh, no."

"Hadn't you started running tests already? Aren't the results in the computer? We still have something, right?" Jared asked.

The three followed the technician over to the computer. "I hope so. I had already put the DNA into the system, but that takes time to process and there's a backlog..." Mike typed away at the computer. "Oh no..."

"WHAT!?" Adam clenched his hands.

"It's gone. Everything I worked on for three days is gone." Mike's face had gone from flushed to ashen. He looked as if he might be sick. "Someone had to have tampered with it. There's no other way for all my findings and notes to be completely gone."

Adam rubbed the back of his neck. Maybe it wasn't this guy's fault that everything was gone. Maybe there was something more nefarious at hand.

Amelia's voice cracked, "So we really are dealing with someone on the inside..."

"Either that or a hacker and master thief," Adam said.

Mike snorted, "He'd have to be a brilliant hacker. The police station's firewall is tight. And the alarm on the door. You'd have to go in the system and take out the evidence that you were in here. Because look"—he pointed to the screen—"there's no record of anyone coming in or out of the lab from the time I left Saturday until I arrived this morning."

"So, what do we do now, boss?" Adam turned to Jared.

"We get to the bottom of it. If he's inside the department, that narrows our suspect list significantly. First, we find out who was around this weekend, but we don't limit our list by that, that just narrows down who we talk to about what they saw. Next, we look back at your profile, Jamison, and see who could fit it that would have had access to this area at all. If he wasn't from inside, surely someone would have noticed him lurking about."

CHAPTER 17

Adam walked to his front door, his spirit was light, the craziness of the missing evidence forgotten for a moment. For at this very second life was as it should be, and he could get used to it. In fact, he was starting to. Once again, he had left the station early, leaving everyone else to search for the person who had stolen the missing evidence, and picked up Ella after school. They had come back to his place for a nice evening together. His smile widened as he unlocked the door to the sound of Rusty's barking. The dog barely let him open the door before he was jumping up at them, begging for attention.

"Let us in, Rusty!"

Ella giggled; the sweet sound sent an electrical current though his whole body. It was definitely his favorite sound in the world. Despite Rusty's jumping, they finally made it into the house.

Ella put her school bag on the couch and dropped to the floor to play with Rusty. Adam hung his hat and messenger bag on the coat rack and went to the kitchen to start dinner. Ella joined him a few moments later as he was pulling the frying pan out of the cabinet.

"Hey, Adam, you have a new voice mail on your machine."

He glanced across the kitchen to where the answering machine sat on the counter. "Huh. Wonder who it's from. Not many people would call me on that line, sometimes I wonder why I even have it."

"To keep telemarketers from interfering with important police business." Her teasing smile lit up her whole face.

"Something like that." He smiled back. He turned and opened the fridge and said, "Go ahead and play it. Doubt it's anything important."

"K."

Adam wanted to keep watching Ella as she reached across the counter and pressed the play button but managed to turn and open the fridge.

"Hi, Adam," a disdainful female voice came out of the speaker. "I found your number in the phone book. It's Jenifer by the way. You know, the girl you abandoned three weeks ago. I can't believe you just took off like that. And didn't even bother calling me. My friends all tried to vouch for you. 'Oh, Adam Jamison, he's an upstanding guy.' 'He probably had to run off to work early.' 'He's a great guy.' They all said. So, I gave you a bit. Surely if you were such a great guy you wouldn't just leave me as a one-night stand. But have I heard from you? NO! They said you were a quality guy; well I know that's a bunch of bull. Complete hogwash." Expletives filled the message before a click ended the call and the machine stated the time and date. A beep sounded as Ella pushed a button.

His heart dropped like a bad transmission. He stood there frozen, the fridge door in his hand. He was going to be sick to his stomach. Ella had just heard about his darkest hour from a message on his machine. He was mortified. He stared into the fridge; his heart rate skyrocketed. How was he going to explain this? "Umm... Uh..." he couldn't. Nothing intelligent was coming to his mind.

"You don't have to explain, Adam."

"But I do. Ella, that's not who I am. Really, it's not. I don't just sleep with anyone. And I don't normally get so drunk that I don't remember the night before. Really."

"I believe you."

"I'm so sorry." He dropped his head; he could barely look at her.

"I'm not the one you should apologize to."

The air vanished from his lungs. He looked up at her. "You think I should call her after she told me off on my machine?"

"That's not what I meant. Although..." her voice trailed off.

"Oh. You mean God?"

"He's the one you've sinned against."

As if he didn't feel uncomfortable enough. "Yeah, I know..."

Silence filled the room, and he pulled the food for dinner out of the refrigerator.

"Should I call her? I don't want to be a jerk. Or is it too late for that?" He gave Ella a weak smile.

She set the plates she had pulled from the cupboard on the counter and smiled back at him. "It may be a little late..." She placed her hand on his elbow. "Anyway, I deleted her message." Her eyes twinkled mischievously despite her attempt at sheepish.

An ounce of joy crept in, especially as her hand lingered on his arm. But it quickly faded. "I know you say I don't have to apologize to you, but it feels as if I do. I really am sorry."

The tenderness in her gaze melted his heart. "I know."

"Why are you so stinkin' understanding?"

"Well," she looked away from him as she formed her thoughts, "because I care about you. And while I by no means approve of your behavior, which you know—"

He nodded.

"I care about *you*. Just like Christ cares about me, no matter what I do, He still loves me. He can't stand my sin, but that's why He died for us. He loves us despite our sin."

He pressed his lips together. He didn't know what to do with what she said. He knew the truth behind her words, but could he accept it?

"I'm sorry, I didn't mean to get preachy."

"You're fine. It's not preachy. I know your heart, and it's just who you are."

She squeezed his arm before releasing it. The two of them set about making dinner in silence. But once they sat down next to one another at the little square table he knew from the pensive look on Ella's face that they weren't done with the hard conversations. He popped the cap off his bottle of beer and took a long swig.

"Adam, why did you walk away from Christ? I saw you walk up the aisle at camp that summer between our fifth-grade years. Or was that not genuine?"

He covered his mouth to keep from spitting out the beer. The girl didn't beat around the bush. "I don't know, on both accounts. I guess it was real. I thought so, but it never sunk in I guess." He took another long swig of his beer and thought about her first question.

She picked up her fork and stabbed a piece of chicken but kept her gaze glued on him. He wanted to squirm, but something about her settled his spirit.

"I guess I started walking away when my dad... when my dad made a fool of himself. I just didn't understand how a so-called believer could do that."

"It seems like that happens more often than it should. I guess all those hours in the church just the two of them..."

He shook his head. "It's a stupid cliché! I just couldn't stand the hypocrisy of it all. He preached against infidelity but ran off to Atlanta with the stupid secretary!" He chugged the last of his beer.

Ella reached across the table and took his other hand and squeezed it.

"I guess if I boiled it down, I didn't want to be a hypocrite like my dad, so I decided it was easier to just not be a Christian and live however I wanted."

The conversation was getting too intense for his liking. He didn't want to let go of Ella's hand, but he had to get up. He gave her hand a gentle squeeze before pulling his away. He stood up with a weak smile and went into the kitchen. He needed another beer.

Ella watched Adam pull another bottle of beer from the fridge. *I guess two isn't anything to worry about...* Had she pushed too much? No, he needed to talk about these things whether he wanted to or not. But it grieved her to hear him imply walking away from Christ was easy. She couldn't imagine. Christ was her anchor; she would never have been able to make it through the last seventeen years without Him.

Adam sat back down, and they didn't say much as they ate the rest of their dinner. They cleared the table, and the quietness continued to linger. Ella carried the casserole dish to the sink, and intentionally bumped into Adam.

"Oh, sorry." He finally looked her in the eyes.

She smiled and shook her head. His eyes softened, and his smile returned. He slid his arm across her shoulders and gave her a little squeeze. Her hands were full, so she simply leaned in but didn't linger.

"Thanks for dinner, Adam."

"My pleasure. Thanks for putting up with me."

"My pleasure."

They settled in the living room. Adam noodled on his acoustic guitar, and Ella worked on grading papers. Rusty curled up at Ella's feet. The scene was surreal. This was exactly the picture she had imagined as a child of what adult life would be like. Only difference was the path that brought them here.

In her childhood image, they would have been married with a few children running around by the time they were the age they were. None of the heartache, trauma, and turmoil the two of them had experienced would have happened. But it had happened. God had brought them down a very different path than either of them had ever imagined.

"You aren't getting much grading done." Adam's voice snapped her out of her daydream. "You okay?"

"Yeah, just thinking about how this," she motioned around them, "is exactly the scene I imagined as a kid. You with your guitar, me sitting on the couch, Rusty at my feet…"

"Me too. Not exactly how I thought it would happen. I thought you'd be my wife…"

Rusty jumped on the couch knocking Ella's papers everywhere interrupting their moment. "Rusty!" she yelled but the dog just stuck his head between the curtains and barked uncontrollably.

Adam dropped his guitar onto the stand. He jumped up and reached for Ella. She took his hand, and he pulled her across the room and into the hallway at the center of the house. He dropped her hand, put his left arm in front of her, and tucked her behind himself. His right hand rested on his pistol.

She gripped his hand again, but more tightly and with both of hers. "Adam?" Her voice shook.

"Shh," he said softly. "Rusty likes to bark, but not like that."

After a few minutes Rusty stopped barking and trotted over to them. "Everything clear, boy?" Adam knelt and petted the dog.

"Do you think he knows where I am?" Her vision tunneled. "He's out there."

"I don't know. It's... Ella?"

"Adam—" She dug her fingers into his shoulder.

"We got this." He stood and turned to fully face her. He flipped the hall light on and placed his hand on her shoulders. She jumped. But he started singing. "Oh, Danny boy, the pipes, the pipes are calling." His rich baritone beckoned her back and soothed her nerves. "From glen to glen, and down the mountain side."

The tunnel opened, and she locked eyes with Adam. The memories vanished.

"The summer's gone, and all the roses falling." They smiled at one another.

Ella took a stabilizing breath, and Adam kept singing.

"It's you, it's you must go and I must bide." He reached the end of the song. "You okay?"

"Thanks to you."

He rubbed her arms. "Anytime!" He walked to the window where Rusty had barked and looked out between the curtains into the dusk of the evening.

Ella took a few steps forward but waited for Adam's assessment before she moved further.

Rusty jumped up on the couch next to him and growled out the window.

A shudder worked its way across Adam's shoulders. He rubbed the dog's back. "I know, boy." He stood and walked back towards Ella. "I hate that man! If he shows his face around here..."

"Don't go there."

"Fine." He said it, but she didn't believe him. With heavy steps he stormed off to the kitchen. She didn't like how his mood had changed so quickly. She understood he was angry, she was too. What bothered her more was how his breath still reeked of alcohol.

She walked over to the couch and picked up and sorted her papers that Rusty had scattered everywhere. Clearly, she needed to use paper clips around this dog. He poked his head into her face. She smiled at him and ruffled his fur. "You silly dog!"

She was vaguely aware that Adam had come back into the room and plopped into the chair behind her. She sat back on the couch and turned her head towards Adam. He set an empty beer bottle on the end table and opened yet another.

"Adam!"

"What?" Apathy speckled his voice.

"I think you've had enough."

"Not nearly."

"No, I'm serious. You've had enough to drink." She stood up and took the two steps necessary to put her right in front of Adam. Without hesitating she grabbed the beer from his hand and took it to the kitchen.

"What are you doing?" He followed her.

Good. She wanted him to see. Without words she looked at Adam to be sure he was watching and emptied the full bottle of beer into the sink. She set the empty bottle on the counter and looked back at Adam, who just stood there, mouth agape. She walked over to him and took his hand. "You will not drink yourself stupid around me. This is not the solution, Adam."

———•———

Adam walked into the empty conference room Tuesday morning, spent. This case was taking an emotional toll on him. After Caleb picked Ella up last night, he had spent time wrestling with all they had talked about. He had wanted to drown it all in a bottle of liquor, but he didn't. Instead he had sat down at the piano and tinkered around. He had tried to sleep, but it hadn't happened. It was as if an unseen force was calling his name. But he ignored it. It wasn't that he didn't believe in God. He knew the truth; he just wasn't ready to live it out. He could do this on his own... couldn't he? He was beginning to doubt that.

"Jamison." Adam looked up at Becca who followed him into the conference room.

"Hey." He tossed his messenger bag in a chair and took off his hat.

"You all right?" She cocked her head to the side slightly.

"Sure. We're meeting in here, right?"

"Yeah, in fifteen minutes."

"Okay. You have the files you pulled together yesterday? I can start looking through 'em."

She held up the folder in her hand before she set it on the table. "Yeah, but not yet. Not 'til you tell me what's going on?"

"I'm fine, Becca."

She took a step closer. "No, you're not. You know you can't lie to me. We've been friends for far too long for that."

"I just didn't sleep well."

She crossed her arms. "Nope. Not buying it. There's more to it."

"Fine." He fiddled with his hat and tried to formulate his thoughts. "We've talked about this before, albeit a long time ago, but how do you reconcile being a Christian with still messing up? Why bother trying to follow Him if you know you're just going to screw up again?"

She looked back at him with wide eyes and mouth agape.

"Ha. A little weightier than you expected, huh?" He gave her a wry smile.

"You could say that... Well..." She uncrossed her arms and looked up before looking him in the eye. "Because the more closely I follow Jesus the easier it is to say no to temptation. Not saying it is easy, just easier than it would be without Him. Because there is more joy and peace in being in a relationship with Him." She paused. Her eyes narrowed and searched Adam's face. "Let me ask you this. Do you view me as a hypocrite?"

"No."

"But I still mess up. Just last night I completely lost my temper with Callie." She shook her head and dropped her shoulders. "I totally yelled, no, I screamed at her. Is that the Christian thing to do?"

"No."

"Exactly. We can never be completely Christ-like this side of Heaven. Look at it this way." She steepled her fingers in front of her mouth before speaking again. "Think about you and Ella. You two are getting really close; you can't hide that, if you're trying, you're doing a miserable job… but anyway, let's say you two continue to get closer. Well, you want to be continually building into that relationship, right?"

"Of course."

"Okay, but what if she goes out and let's say, lies to you about something. Do you still want the relationship? Do you want her to still walk through life with you?"

"Yes. Nothing she could do would change the way I feel about her."

"Does Ella sinning against you make her a hypocrite if she tells you she loves you?"

"No, she just messed up. I'm sure there could be times when I don't like what she does, but I would still love her."

"Exactly. That's how God feels about us, about you, Adam. Even when we screw up, He loves us and wants to walk through life with us. And you know what?" Tears glistened in her eyes. "His mercies are new every morning. Every single day He gives the grace we need. Just like He said, His grace is sufficient for me and for you."

Becca's words hung in the air and seemed to beckon his heart. But before he could process further Jared, Amelia, and Gavin all came in the conference room chatting loudly. Becca reached out and squeezed Adam's arm and gave him a warm smile.

"This case is officially closed doors." Jared pulled out a chair and sat; everyone else did the same. "We don't talk about it outside of a closed room. Always be sure of your audience and keep it need-to-know only."

They all nodded.

"All right," Jared folded his hands on the table. "What do we have from yesterday? Any leads on who could have stolen the evidence or tamper with the files?"

"Well," Amelia started, "Becca and Gavin and I went through personnel files yesterday afternoon of every single person that works in this building and each came up with a list of red flags. Even just minor flags."

Becca said, "We need to compile our lists and dig a little deeper."

"All right, let's do it," Adam said.

The five traded lists around and discussed what they knew about the different individuals.

Adam sighed as his eyes fell on a familiar name.

"What is it, Jamison?" Amelia asked.

"A repeat from Thursday's short list."

"You mean," Jared said, "that someone who was on the camera on Thursday is on this list?"

"Who?" Gavin said. His brow was furrowed.

"Patrick North."

"Isn't that Jocelyn's husband?" Jared asked.

Becca nodded. "I put him on there because he has a history of losing his temper, and he's been divorced. Our criteria for putting anyone on the list was that they had two of the traits Adam outlined in his profile."

"That's pretty broad criteria," Adam said.

"Yeah, but he's also the right age. He was 23 seventeen years ago, right in the middle of the age range you suggested."

Jared asked, "What was the research that gave you the age range again, Jamison?"

He answered, "As a power-assertive rapist, like he was back then, he would have targeted women in his own age range. Ella being the anomaly since she was only 16. The rest were later teens or early twenties."

"And Patrick lived here?" Amelia asked.

"Yeah," Gavin answered. "His dad was a police lieutenant back in the day."

"What?" Jared said, "You're telling me that our current person of interest is the son of a former police lieutenant? Wife to our forensic photographer? Which makes him related to one of the detectives on this case? Oh, and he's a cop himself?"

"Yep." Adam pressed his lips together and huffed.

"Well, before we press this any further is there anyone else that stands out as a stronger candidate?" Jared asked.

They spent another twenty or so minutes throwing around a few other names off of their lists, but no one else stood out as strong as Patrick. So, they had to investigate his cousin's husband.

"So, since we've got nothing else to go on, let's talk about Officer North," Becca said.

Adam kept his mouth shut. Ever since Jocelyn started dating him eight years ago, he hadn't liked him. The man was arrogant and chauvinistic. Jocelyn deserved better. He didn't have any proof, but he was pretty sure Patrick was abusive. Jocelyn had never sported any physical evidence, but he could sense that something wasn't right in their marriage.

Amelia's voice interrupted his thoughts, "Riley, you know Patrick well, don't you?"

Gavin nodded. "Yeah, we rode together quite a bit when I was a uniform, but we go further back than that. Served in the Army together, including a few tours in the Middle East."

"What can you tell us about him? Anything that stands out about him that makes our suspicion founded?"

"He's always had a short fuse. Let's see, I met him pretty soon after I enlisted, so fifteen years ago; he had already been in for a couple of years."

Jared looked at his laptop. "According to his file, he enlisted seventeen years ago as of this coming January."

Becca looked up. "Really?"

Jared nodded.

That timing did nothing for a case for Patrick's innocence.

"Well, while serving with him, I got to know him decently, we became friends, I guess. His anger has gotten him in trouble more than once. He was also a bit of a lady's man. Back in our army days he was known to take a prostitute."

Adam's stomach churned. Not something he wanted to hear... Jocelyn deserved so much better. Why had she married such a creep?

Gavin continued, "He's pretty stuck on himself. And definitely likes to think he's better than everyone else."

Jared asked, "What can you, and you too, Adam, what can you tell us about his marriages?"

"This is so weird," Becca said, "I feel like we're invading Jocelyn's privacy on this."

Amelia replied, "I know, but what other choice do we have?"

Adam sighed. "We don't. Everyone knows that I've never thought very highly of my cousin's husband. I don't know much about his first marriage. I don't even think Jocelyn knows much about it. But I do know that I've never liked the way he treats her, always talking down to her and trying to control so much of what she does. He never puts her needs before his own. I'm surprised he actually let's her go to church and stuff like that."

"That's pretty new, really," Becca said. "While she's always been able to come to our Bible study group all the time, she used to only make it to church if Patrick was on duty, but lately she's been coming almost every Sunday."

Jared said, "I suppose that could indicate that he's busy with something else…"

Adam watched Gavin. The detective had slouched down in his chair slightly, as if pulling back from the conversation. "Riley," Adam said. Gavin looked up at his eyes wide as if caught in the headlights. What did he know about Patrick and Jocelyn that he wasn't sharing? Adam would ask him about it later. "Do you know anything about the first wife?"

"Oh, um…" he sat back up. "Not much. They got married shortly after we returned from a deployment. He seemed to ride the monogamy thing well for a few years. But towards the end that didn't last, I know he was with other women. He separated from his wife for a year, per state law, before divorcing her after four years of marriage while we were on another tour."

"Did you ever observe any abuse?" Adam asked that question more out of concern for Jocelyn than anything.

"We weren't close enough. Barely ever saw the wife."

Jared said, "Okay, so we've established that he fits the profile, but what do we have as evidence that will help a judge grant us a warrant for his arrest and a search of his home."

Adam replied, "We have the video tape from Thursday. It's totally circumstantial, but he was going somewhere he didn't belong with a bag that could easily have hidden the flowers."

Amelia added, "But after you left yesterday, we established that he was around here over the weekend. Even at times when he wasn't on duty."

"More circumstantial evidence."

Gavin asked, "But if whoever stole the evidence from the lab deleted footage of the lab entrance, and manipulated the entrance log, and broke into a secured lab, why wouldn't he delete himself from the other videos as well. If it was Patrick, wouldn't he have done that as well."

Adam ran his fingers through his hair. "Except he didn't do it before we found it, and if it was Patrick, he probably knows that Jocelyn backs up her evidence in a separate server."

"Why not just hack that too?" Gavin asked.

"Printed pics," Amelia said. "As soon as you guys found that footage you printed the pics and brought them to me. Maybe he knew that. But either way, I'm getting hungry. Can we break for lunch?"

"Of course, the pregnant woman is hungry." Adam gave her an exaggerated eye roll.

"I can't help it. Making a baby human is a lot of work."

He smiled at her, and they all agreed lunch was a good idea.

After lunch they gathered once again in the conference room and spent another hour discussing Patrick and laying out their request for a warrant. It was questionable whether or not the judge would grant a search warrant, let alone the arrest warrant, but they were hopeful. The crimes were serious enough that they needed to leave no rock unturned.

"I'll take this to the judge," Amelia offered.

They all scattered when Amelia left to talk to the DA and judge, but before Jared left the room Adam pulled him aside. "Is it all right if I go talk to Jocelyn? I'd rather her have the heads up. I know she won't alert Patrick to the situation."

"That's fine, but be sure that she doesn't call him."

"Of course."

———•◦•———

Adam bit his lip and knocked on Jocelyn's office door. He wasn't quite sure how he was going to tell her this. Was it really possible that her husband was the one who attacked Ella seventeen years earlier? Was he really the one that had tried to grab her the other night? For Jocelyn's sake Adam hoped the team was wrong, but for Ella's sake... for her sake he hoped they were right, because if they were right that would mean once they had him in custody, she would be safe again.

The door opened. "Hey, Adam, come in."

"Hey. Got a minute?" He walked into the room that was half office and half photography studio.

"Sure, what's up?"

He closed the door behind himself. "Well, I have a few questions for you." He tried to keep his voice soft and compassionate as he did not want to put her on the defensive.

"About Patrick? He really is a suspect?"

"Person of interest, but yes."

Jocelyn sighed but barely blinked.

"You aren't surprised?"

"I don't know. I've been mulling it over since we saw him on that tape... Is he really capable of the things that were done to these women? I... I just don't know, Adam."

A knock sounded on the aluminum door. Adam turned and opened it. Gavin Riley stood on the other side. "Oh, hey, Jamison." His eyes widened.

"Hey. What's up?"

"Um. Was just coming to um..."

"Come in, Gavin," Jocelyn said.

Adam stepped back far enough for Gavin to come in the room as well. "Jocelyn, I still have some questions I'd like to ask you."

"I don't doubt it, but Gavin can be here."

"You sure? I'm going to ask as your cousin, not a detective."

"I know. Gavin probably knows the answers to any of the questions you want to ask anyway."

Adam raised an eyebrow. "Really?" He looked Gavin in the eye. "You didn't seem too eager to indulge us upstairs."

"Wasn't my place."

He liked Gavin, but he seemed awful chummy with Jocelyn considering Patrick was the jealous type. "Fair enough." Adam grabbed a folding chair and turned it around and sat backwards in it. He motioned for Jocelyn to come sit by him. She pulled out her desk chair and sat face to face with Adam. Gavin grabbed the other folding chair and sat down with them. "How are things going with you and Patrick? The only way I see it being Patrick is if things are not settled at home. That could be a trigger to go back and recreate his past crimes and kill his victims as well. If you say things are going well, I'm inclined to call the whole search into him off."

Jocelyn fiddled with her hands and avoided eye contact.

"Jocelyn?"

She and Gavin exchanged a look that he couldn't quite distinguish, and Gavin nodded to her. *What's going on between those two?*

"Well, it's not that good. We've tried to work it out, but he moved out back in May."

"May? He moved out? Why didn't you tell me?"

"Because I was embarrassed. Please don't tell anyone. No one else needs to know. But yes," her eyes dropped to her shoes, "he did move out. Said it was for my protection."

"Do you believe that?"

"In some respects, yes. After all we had started fighting so much more, and he was losing his temper all the time over even the stupidest things."

"Has he ever hit you, Jocelyn?"

"Not really."

"What does 'not really' mean? He's either hit you or not."

"Well, he's never beat me. Never punched my face or anything."

"So, you're saying he has hit you though?"

"I guess a couple of times. Nothing like abuse."

"If he's hit you at all, Jocelyn, that's abuse."

"It's gotten better. He's been more agreeable since we've had time apart. I think he might move back soon."

"Why would you take him back?"

"Because he's my husband, Adam. I married him; I made a vow: 'til death do us part. I have to honor that. I thought you would appreciate that."

"I do, but not if he's abusive. There is a line that I think even God would agree; you should *not* stay with a man who would hurt you."

"I don't know. It's not like he beats me. Anyway. If he's the killer, he'll go to prison. Then you won't have to worry about me."

"Do you think he's capable of this?"

"I don't know. I really don't. I want to say no, but I feel like he has this dark side that he never lets anyone see. I saw that profile you drafted up on the board. He does fit it."

"The profile isn't everything. We need evidence and at this point we don't have much. Amelia's talking to the judge right now about a search warrant."

"Make sure it includes the cabin. That's where he's been staying. But don't—"

"I won't. Thank you, Jocelyn." Adam pulled his phone off his belt and texted Amelia, "Include Jocelyn and Patrick's cabin out at the river in the search warrant."

A moment later his phone chimed. "Got it."

"Jocelyn, it's almost time to pick Ella up, want to go with me?"

"Sure. I could use the distraction. Wait, you're also supposed to babysit me to be sure I don't alert Patrick, aren't you?"

He smiled at his cousin. "Not really, well, sorta, but I was actually thinking it would be a good distraction for you."

Gavin had been quiet during the whole conversation and stayed that way as they all left Jocelyn's office. Once they reached the top of the stairs, Adam turned to Jocelyn. "I have to go grab my keys and let Jared know I'm leaving. Be right back."

He had half expected Gavin to follow, but he hung back and stayed with Jocelyn. Adam wanted to think better of the two of them, but he was worried that they were treading on thin ice. But that was a worry for another day.

Right now, his pulse pounded at the idea of seeing Ella. He found that he was missing her whenever she wasn't around. Her smile was exactly what he needed right now. He wished they could just go back to his place tonight, but that wasn't going to happen. It was going to be a long night. Assuming Amelia had no trouble getting the warrants signed, they could have Patrick in for questioning before night fall, and if that happened, he didn't see sleep in his near future.

Ella stood up from the couch in Captain Baker's office and paced back and forth. She felt a little like a caged animal. She was having a great time visiting with Jocelyn. Her friend was sweet as always but was also clearly hiding something. Ella didn't want to be rude, but she was about to ask Jocelyn what was going on.

The activity around the station was chaotic. She had never been here when so many people were moving around looking so serious. Adam hadn't told her anything, other than that they had to come to the station today since he and the others were in the middle of something. He had said he would tell her more later, but it was already after five, and he hadn't said anything. About fifteen minutes ago, Becca, Jared, Amelia, Captain Baker, and a bunch of others headed out the door wearing bulletproof vests. Adam and Gavin hadn't gone with them. That fact alone settled her nerves about what might be going on.

She looked out between the blinds on the window into the squad room. She found her target, and her heart fluttered. Adam stood up from his desk and ran his hands through his short dark hair. The dark blue tie around his neck hung looser than it had been an hour ago. He had also shed his blazer and rolled up the sleeves of his long sleeve, blue and white striped shirt. The shirt was fitted and accentuated his muscular shoulders quite well.

"Like what you see, do you? But are you keeping your thoughts pure?" Jocelyn's teasing tone did nothing to help diminish the blush forming in Ella's cheeks.

"Shut it."

Jocelyn laughed.

Ella glanced briefly at her friend and shook her head before turning her attention back to Adam. Her heart jumped; he was coming toward her!

"You are so smitten."

In the most facetious tone she could muster, Ella said, "I have no idea what you're talking about."

"Hey, ladies!" Adam spun around the door frame and entered the room.

"Hey." The heat in Ella's cheeks increased.

"Anyone else want some dinner? I ordered pizza. Should be here in about half an hour."

"I'm hungry," Ella said, "but can I ask what's going on around here?"

The smiles on both Adam's and Jocelyn's faces faded, and Jocelyn started picking at her fingernail.

"Well, yeah, we should tell you," Adam said. "Let's sit."

"Okay..." Ella sat back on the couch next to Jocelyn and Adam took a chair across from her.

"We're going after a suspect in your case, Ella."

"Isn't that a good thing?" Her spirit rose a bit but stopped before it even reached the ceiling. Adam didn't even seem happy with it. "What's wrong?"

Jocelyn didn't look up from her hands. "The suspect is Patrick."

"What? Really? That doesn't seem right. Could he really be the guy who attacked me?"

"It's possible," Adam said.

"So that's where everyone went, and why"—she looked at Jocelyn— "you're hanging out with me this evening. You have to stick around here too don't you."

"I probably don't have to, but I want to. I'm enjoying hanging out with you, but I'm also anxious to see what happens with Patrick. I hope this doesn't make things awkward between us. If he is the guy, I had no idea."

"I know." She reached over and put her hand on Jocelyn's shoulder. "I can't even imagine what you must be feeling right now. You'll always be my friend. I know you didn't have anything to do with what he did, if it even was Patrick. Well, one easy way to clear it up is if Patrick had a cut on his right arm after last Wednesday. Did you notice a cut on his arm? I think it was near his elbow." Ella lifted her arm and pointed to where she thought she nicked the guy.

Jocelyn was still. "I didn't notice anything one way or another."

So much for that.

Every emotion possible washed through Ella. The three of them sat there and the conversation moved on to lighter topics even if her mind didn't. Her heart rose at the idea that the guy threatening to kill her could potentially be behind bars tonight, but what if it wasn't Patrick? Her stomach twisted. That would mean that evil man was still out there. And if it was

Patrick... poor Jocelyn. Patrick wasn't a great husband, and she had always thought Jocelyn deserved better, but he was still her husband. Was he really capable of doing those things?

When the pizza arrived, Jocelyn offered to go get plates from the break room and left Adam and Ella alone. Ella walked over to where Adam stood next to the Captain's desk opening a pizza box. She slid her hand in his when it fell back at his side. He turned and smiled at her. He intertwined his fingers with hers as he leaned back against the desk.

"How are you doing today, Ella?"

"All right, I guess. What about you?"

He reached up with his free hand and brushed her hair away from her face. "I'm okay. It's a mixed bag of emotions with this whole Patrick thing. I just want it to be over, I want you to be safe, but I'm worried about Jocelyn."

"Me too."

A glint of desire flashed through Adam's eyes. She hadn't seen that in nearly twenty years. Fire burned in her cheeks, so she looked down. She was not ready to kiss him yet. Instead she let go of his hand and slowly wrapped her arms around his waist.

That was a mistake. His arm wrapped around her shoulders, and her vision tunneled. Every muscle in her body constricted. Her arms shook. She couldn't stop it. She couldn't speak.

"Ella?" She heard his voice, but it was like he was in another room, not right beside her. "Ella, you're safe."

I'm safe. Jesus, help me.

Adam's voice took on the gentle melodies of a Jason Mraz song she had once heard Adam sing before. The tunnel faded.

Thank you, Jesus. She steadied her breath and urged her whole body to relax. She laid her head on Adam's chest and closed her eyes, and he kept singing.

She opened her eyes just as Jocelyn walked back in the room. She suppressed a giggle at the sight of her friend's amused smile, yet she didn't pull away from Adam.

"Are we going to eat that pizza or are you two love birds going to just stand there and cuddle while it gets cold?"

Adam and Ella reluctantly pulled away from each other and exchanged a smile. They put slices of pizza on their paper plates, but before they could turn around a loud commotion came from the lobby. Adam put his plate down and left the Captain's office. Ella followed suit and stood slightly behind Adam. Becca and Doug escorted Patrick through the lobby towards booking. A deep scowl was etched into his face. He writhed against Becca and Doug's grip and profanity spewed from his mouth.

The man fit the physical parameters of the man who attacked her. He was just about the right height and build. Patrick glared over at Adam. Ella didn't make eye contact with him, but his beady blue eyes caused a shudder to course through her body. It could be him. Doug shoved him through the doorway and out of sight, and a surprising sense of satisfaction filled Ella's gut. If it was him, she was safe.

CHAPTER 18

Adam turned back towards the Captain's office and ran into Ella. "Sorry."

"It's okay." She slid her arm around his waist.

He smiled at her and put his arm across her shoulders, and they went back to their pizza. He wanted to go find out what they had discovered, but the greater pull had her arm around his waist. Warmth filled his body.

When they got to the desk where they had both left their dinner, he let her go, picked up his plate, and took a bite of a slice pizza. They ate in an uncomfortable silence, and when he popped the last bite of his second piece in his mouth, Jared appeared in the doorway with a large evidence bag in his hand.

"Jamison, you need to see this." He was gone as quickly as he appeared.

Adam looked at Jocelyn first. Something to show didn't bode well for Patrick, and he worried about how she would handle it. Next, his eyes fell on Ella. She would help Jocelyn cope with this even though she had her own set of worries. Adam reached out and squeezed Ella's elbow. "I'll see you in a bit."

She nodded and gave him a weak smile.

He wanted to wrap her up in his arms and never let go, but he couldn't do that today. Instead he winked at her which brought a little color to her cheeks, and he left the room. He followed Jared into the conference room where they were soon joined by the rest of the team.

Thud. Jared dropped the evidence bag on the table. "Check this out." Jared pulled on a pair of gloves and took a duffel bag out of the evidence bag. Adam took a step closer, and Jared unzipped the bag. Jared proceeded to pull out and show them one item at a time and then returned each to the bag. A roll of duct tape. A folding knife. A black ski-mask.

"A rape kit?" Adam said. He felt as if someone had punched him in the gut.

"Looks like it. We found it in his car."

Adam couldn't believe it. "I really thought it couldn't be him, but I guess..."

"Is that the knife stolen from evidence?" Amelia asked.

Jared pulled it back out of the bag. "No. I got a good look at it when I took it from Ella. It's very similar, but not the exact knife."

Gavin crossed his arms. "This really doesn't look good for Patrick."

"No, it doesn't." Becca shook her head.

"Now what?" Adam asked.

Jared looked up at Adam. "We ask him about it. Maybe we'll get a confession."

Becca twisted her hair. "You want me to take the lead on the interrogation?"

"I'm not sure that would be the best," Gavin said. "He has a complex that women shouldn't be cops, so it may just close him up."

"I think I want Adam to start with him," Jared made eye contact with Adam. "I think if you appeal to him as family. As much as you don't like him, you have not wanted to believe he was responsible."

"More for Jocelyn's sake than anything."

"But still. Go in and get an explanation for this stuff," Jared swept his hand above the duffel bag.

Adam took a deep breath and blew it out throw his mouth. "Okay."

Jared put the duffel back into the evidence bag, and he and Adam walked out of the room. Adam grabbed his blazer from the back of his chair, and as he walked by the Captain's office Adam glanced in at Ella and Jocelyn. They were deep in conversation on the couch, but Ella caught his eye and gave him a sweet smile. It did wonders for his heart. He had to get to the bottom of this for Ella. She needed answers. If it really was Patrick, he would have to answer for hurting the woman he loved. *Love?* Yes, he did love her. Always had and did again. He would question Patrick as if he was the man that hurt her. He had to focus on that and not that he was Jocelyn's husband, even while appealing to him as family.

Adam pulled on his jacket and turned down the hallway towards the interrogation room. *God, it's been a really long time. Don't know if you'd listen to me, but for Ella's sake would you help me get the guy. Even if it means putting Patrick behind bars.* He couldn't do this on his own. And he finally admitted it. It felt like a punch in the gut and a wash of relief all at the same time.

Adam took the bag from Jared and opened the door to the interrogation room. There at the table sat a smug Patrick. He was sitting back in his chair with an arm up on the back of the chair next to him. His ankle propped up on the opposite knee.

"Hey. Someone read you your rights? Not that you don't already know them, but you know legal stuff..."

"Yeah, your partner seemed to enjoy reading every last word to me. But guess that's the only thing a knocked-up cop is good for. So, they sent family in to talk to me. Really? What, they think I'll talk to you, huh? Humph. They do know you can't stand me, right?"

"Yeah, but they know I care about Jocelyn, so I'm your best bet right now. Why don't you just tell me the truth, and we can all leave and be on our merry way."

"I don't know what you want me to say, Jamison."

Adam pulled the chair out from the table and turned it around and straddled it. "Well, for starters, why don't you explain why there was a rape kit in your car?"

"A what?" Patrick's face remained neutral save a slight furrowing of his brows.

"Do I really have to spell it out for you?"

Patrick dropped his arm from the chair and his foot to the floor. "Apparently since I don't have a clue what you're talking about."

Adam lifted the bag and set it on the table. "Recognize this bag?"

"Yeah, it's my gym bag. I keep it in my car, so I can work out when I have a chance."

"You keep duct tape, a knife, and a ski mask in your gym bag?"

"No, why would I do that?"

"Then explain why that's what's in this bag."

"That's ridiculous. I keep shorts, a t-shirt, shoes, and such in there."

Adam pulled a pair of gloves from his jacket pocket, stood up, and slid them on his hands. He opened the evidence bag. He pulled the red duffel out and set it on the table. "Is this your duffel bag?"

"Looks like mine."

"And you acknowledge that it should have been found in your car?"

"Yes. I keep it in the trunk."

"Ok. Then you need to explain this." Adam unzipped the bag and pulled out the ski mask.

Patrick's face contorted. "That's not mine."

"But it's in your bag."

"But it's not mine."

"What about this?" Adam showed him the roll of duct tape.

"Not mine. I'm classier than putting duct tape on my tennis shoes."

The man didn't seem to care that Adam was accusing him of three murders along with five additional rapes. "Patrick, it's in your bag. A bag you admitted is yours. Do you see we have a problem?"

"No, because those items aren't mine, and I didn't do it."

"But it sure is looking like you did."

They were getting nowhere fast. They continued to go back and forth, but it was pointless. Patrick acted as if he was above the law somehow. And making it seem like no big deal when he said someone else had to have put the stuff in the bag.

"All right, you say someone else put this in your bag, but explain why you went to the detectives' squad room last Thursday morning?"

"What does that have to do with anything?"

"Just answer the question, Patrick?"

"I had a note in my locker saying to go up there. But it amounted to nothing."

"Really, a note in your locker?"

"Yep."

"You don't happen to still have that note do you?"

"Why would I have kept it. I didn't know I was being set up."

"So, you're gonna to stick with that set up story?"

"Yes, Jamison. That's what's happening."

Adam was unnerved by how calm Patrick was remaining, especially after his angry display in the lobby. Was he guilty or not? Adam's intuition didn't seem to be working. The evidence pointed to Patrick, but he could explain everything. But, of course he could. If he was guilty, he would have thought of a way to explain everything he did. Still footage had been erased from over the weekend at the lab, but not the piece that had pointed them to Patrick in the first place.

Jared came into the room. Good, backup. Adam took a step back and leaned back against the wall near the two-way mirror where he knew Becca and Amelia were watching from the other side.

Jared took another approach with Patrick and started going hard at him. Accusing him of lying and getting in his face. Patrick remained calm. A little shiver crept its way through Adam's whole body. Something wasn't right. His stomach writhed. He searched his mind trying to figure out where the sick feeling was coming from. Was it in reaction to Patrick's calmness? No. *That's weird.* Was it the idea that maybe Patrick did force himself on Ella? Maybe, but something else was wrong. Ella? Somewhere deep in his gut he felt a pull to her. Almost a sense of needing to save her. Was he having one of those senses that Caleb got? If so, he didn't dare ignore it.

He pushed himself off the wall as the panic in his heart grew. "I'll be back," he muttered and rushed out the door.

He nearly ran into Becca and Jocelyn in the hall. *What is she doing down here?* "Where's Ella?"

"Up in the Captain's office," Jocelyn said.

"You left her there alone!"

"Yeah, she's in the police station, Adam. And you have the number one suspect in custody."

"But I don't think he did it!" Adam took off running towards the Captain's office. Hopefully, he was wrong, but... He couldn't handle the idea of losing Ella. *God, help.*

RUN, ADAM!

He didn't know where the sense was coming from, but he knew he had to find Ella.

He crashed through the squad room door and spun into the Captain's office.

She wasn't there!

"Ella!"

Back into the squad room, his eyes scanned back and forth. His heart was pounding. Where was she?

He went back through the lobby. His eyes darted back and forth. She had to be here somewhere. A group of people standing across the open lobby broke apart. There! His eyes fell on Ella, and his heart soared. But his stomach flew up into his throat. She was talking to Scott!

"Ella!" He ran to her.

"Hey, Adam."

"Jamison." Scott's voice was flat.

Adam locked eyes with Scott but said nothing. He wrapped his arm around Ella's shoulders and pulled her away from Scott.

"Don't be rude, Adam." Ella squeezed his waist with her arm.

"Later, Scott." Adam threw the words over his shoulder. He led Ella back to the Captain's office.

Ella didn't say anything else until they were in the office. Ella pulled away and turned to face him. Her body was still close to his, and it was messing with him. The terror he had felt was not leaving despite the relief he felt from having her safe in front of him.

She put her hands on his sides. "What is going on, Adam? I have never seen you look so scared."

He cupped her head in his hands. He didn't know how to explain what he had just felt, and he didn't want to scare her either. "I didn't know where you were."

"But why were you looking for me in the first place? Did you get a confession?"

His shoulders dropped. "No. I'm still not sure it was him. Ella, what were you doing out in the lobby talking to Scott?"

"I just needed to move around. I'm getting tired of being cooped up all the time. But I wasn't going anywhere. I was just trying to move around where I knew I was allowed to be. Scott came up and started talking to me. He offered me a ride since he knew you guys were busy, and it's getting late."

"Were you going to go with him?" The terror rose in his gut again.

"No! You know he makes me uncomfortable. But it was kind of him to offer."

"Did you tell him where you're staying?"

"No, Adam. You need to calm down; I'm safe. I'm right here." She pulled him into a hug and rested her head on his chest.

He slid his arms around her back and held her tight. *Thank you, God, that she's all right.*

Adam rubbed his eyes with the heels of his hands. Tired didn't even begin to cut the surface of how he felt. He looked at his watch. Two o'clock in the morning. Why was he still up? And why was he still at the station? This was ridiculous.

Ella and Amelia had left around ten, and Patrick decided he wanted a lawyer around eleven. Why he had waited that long to lawyer up, Adam couldn't even begin to guess. And of course, he picked a lawyer that was out of Raleigh, so they had to wait three hours before the guy finally arrived. And for the last hour Patrick had been in there talking to his lawyer and his field representative.

Adam resisted the urge to lay his head on his desk, because surely Jared would tell him to go home soon. What else would they be able to accomplish this late at night? Adam looked up and saw Jared coming his way. Maybe relief was in sight.

"Jamison, you're up."

"Huh?"

"Patrick won't talk to anyone but you."

He furrowed his brow. "Really?"

Jared shrugged.

Adam went to the interrogation room and found Patrick in the same place he had been hours earlier, but now he was flanked but two older men in suits. They all three had bags under their eyes, but their irises held determination. Apparently, no one was leaving before this was cleared up.

"You wanted to talk?"

Patrick sat up and leaned his forearms on the table. "Yes. Since you all haven't believed anything I've told you yet, I figured I should give you proof that I couldn't have committed at least one of the crimes you're accusing me of."

"You have an alibi?"

"Yep."

"For which crime."

"The murder of Clarissa Zerillo."

"All right. Give it up, and I'll check it out." Adam pulled his notepad and pen out of his pocket.

"Nope. I want a guarantee from you, as family, to be discreet about it. You tell Jocelyn, or anyone else for that matter, and I'll make sure the real killer knows where Ella is staying."

Adam froze mid-click of the pen. "What do you mean? Do you know who the real killer is?"

"No, but I'm sure I can get the information to him anyway."

Adam's hope faded. "You do know I have to file your alibi in my report."

"I do, but I also know that information doesn't have to be filed until the case is closed. So, it can wait, once the case is closed or at least long gone and cold, no one else will look in the file."

The man had a point. He didn't like it; he hated making accommodations for potential criminals. "Fine. I'll do what I can keep the information need to know."

"Good. And I know you're a man of your word."

"So, you going to tell me or not?"

"Give me your pad and pen."

Adam look at the items in his hands and reluctantly handed them over.

"Call this number and talk to Monty. Ask about me and the night in question. You'll have your answer. You'll see that I could never have been with Clarissa at the time of her unfortunate demise."

Adam's skin crawled and took the pad and pen back from Patrick. He looked down at the phone number. It meant nothing to Adam. "I'll go check into this. Can I call it now or in the morning?"

"You can call now. Someone will be available to talk."

He narrowed his eyes at Patrick whose lips curled upward.

He exited the room and shook his head. *That man. Ugh.*

Once Adam was back at his desk, he opened his computer and entered the number into the reverse directory. He wasn't about to call some random number blindly. "Great," Adam muttered sarcastically.

"He's giving you an alibi?" Jared came over. They were the only two left in the squad room. Everyone else, even Becca and Gavin had gone home for the night.

"Yep, for Clarissa Zerillo's murder."

"What is it? You didn't sound too thrilled."

"Well, he's threated to advertise Ella's location if I tell anyone."

"Does he actually know where she's staying?"

"Probably not, but I'm not sure I want to risk it."

"Good call. Let me know if it pans out."

"Yep."

Adam looked back at his computer screen. The listing in the directory made him blush. He didn't want to even read the name, let alone call it. He wasn't shy, but that was the kind of place he would prefer to put out of business. And it was not the kind of place he wanted to think about his cousin's husband patronizing.

He picked up the station phone and reluctantly typed in the number. A sultry voice answered, "Thanks for calling. Looking for something hot tonight?"

Bile burned Adam's throat. He swallowed. "No. Is Monty available to talk?"

"Oh, but of course. Please hold."

Thirty minutes and three phone calls later Adam had thoroughly substantiated Patrick's alibi. Adam slammed his fist against his desk. They were back at zero. Patrick couldn't have killed Clarissa. In all the killer's careful planning to point the evidence in Patrick's direction, he hadn't counted on the man's lack of inhibition.

Adam stood up from his desk and walked to the other end of the room to where Jared sat at his desk.

Jared looked up at him with tired eyes. "Please tell me it's a gaping hole, and he really is our guy, because I'm so ready to be done."

"Well, we're done for tonight anyway. It's not him. There's no way he killed Clarissa and since we're convince all these attacks were committed by the same man, Patrick isn't responsible."

Jared's shoulders dropped a little further. "Blasted!"

"Yeah, I've got four witnesses willing to testify. Three of which were with him the entire evening and night. And there's a timestamped security video." He sighed. "Now what?"

"We sleep and regroup tomorrow afternoon."

———•———

Ella set her school bag on the floor next to Adam's couch and sat down. Adam collapsed down next to her. He looked exhausted. On the way back to the house he had told her about his late night and how they had accomplished nothing this afternoon. No one else on their list seemed like a viable suspect.

That news weighed heavy on her heart now too. She still wasn't safe.

She patted Adam's shoulder. "Hey, sit up and turn. You look like you could use a little relaxing. That was why we came back here before going to Becca's for dinner."

He smiled and acquiesced.

She slid her shoes off and knelt on the couch to get a better angle to rub his shoulders. His shoulders were tight. Not that she knew what to expect them to feel like. She really didn't know what she was doing, but she had watched Caleb rub Amelia's shoulders last night while they all unwound while watching a sitcom. She couldn't believe how far she had come. Just three weeks had been enough to change her life completely. It was only by the grace of God.

She prayed and continued to rub Adam's shoulders feeling him melt like butter under her touch. *Oh, Jesus, thank you for Adam and for using him to help me get past these incredible hurdles in my life. But please, help him to turn to You. It's not even about him and me. Sure, I want something to come of this, and I don't want that to happen without him believing in You. But I really just want him to know and love You. He's gone through so much lately, and I know this case is weighing on him. Please help him. Give him, and the other detectives, wisdom and direction. Please let this be over soon and keep us all safe in the process.*

Adam's hand rested on hers. She slid her arms around his neck and leaned against him. He hugged her arms and leaned his head against hers. Her heart soared. What was this feeling? All she knew is that she didn't want to let go. She held him silently for a few minutes, but then reluctantly pulled away.

"Want something to drink?" she asked.

"Sure. A glass of water would be nice." A glint of desire flitted through Adam's eyes and she felt her cheeks warm.

"Coming right up." She turned and exited the living room as fast as she could.

She walked into the kitchen but stopped and stared at the cluster of empty liquor bottles sitting by the sink. She walked over to them, poked at them, and picked a few up. They were all empty. The whiskey, the rum, a couple bottles of wine, and half a dozen beer bottles. Every last one empty. "Adam?"

"Yeah?" he called from the other room.

She didn't know what to say. Did he drink all of it? Nah. There's no way.

"What's up?" Adam came around the corner.

She just pointed at the empty bottles and tilted her head.

"I dumped them after you left the other night."

"You didn't have to do that for me."

"I know, but I would do anything for you, Ella. Anything at all."

She smiled, but it quickly faded. "Adam... you know I'm not the solution either. I can't make you happy. I'm not what's missing in your life." She walked closer to him and set her hands on his chest. "I can't fill the hole in your heart. Only Christ can do that."

He kept her gaze. For once he didn't run away or even look away when she brought up spiritual things.

He didn't say anything, but the intensity in his eyes gave away that he was processing what she said.

———•———

Ella bit her lip and looked across the room to where Adam sat on Becca's couch. His ears were turning red.

"Absolutely NOT!" He sat up straight from the relaxed position he had finally taken. They had come over for dinner along with Caleb and Amelia. Adam had managed to relax a little until Caleb brought up that Ella was scheduled for worship team this weekend.

She gripped her hands in front of herself and walked closer to him. "But Adam, I'm so sick of being stuck in the house or school all the time. I want to go to church. I just want to sing on the worship team."

"I understand, but…"

Ella thrust her hands into her hair and pulled her hair together. She had completely forgotten that she was scheduled. "But what?" She threw her palms up. "I'll be fine. I'll be with Caleb. You could come too." She secretly loved the idea of getting Adam to come to church with her.

"But don't you know the story?"

"What story?" She looked around at her five friends who were scattered throughout the living room and kitchen; she was clearly missing something.

"I don't remember seeing you there that day," Adam said, "and I would. But I would have thought you would have heard the story."

"Again, what story?"

Ella followed Adam's gaze to Becca. Her eyes were wide, and her lips pressed together.

"Ella," Becca's voice shook. "I was taken from church."

"Wait, that happened at church?"

Becca nodded.

"Oh." She had heard Becca's story, at least parts of it.

Caleb spoke up, "But we learned from that situation. We can be a lot more strategic in our protection of Ella. If she stays with two people at all times, no matter how skilled he is he won't be able to take her, especially if it's two of us. That was our biggest mistake with what happened to Becca."

"He's right," Jared said.

Adam crossed his arms and sat back into the couch. "I still don't like it."

She closed the distance between them and sat next to him. "But I need this." She reached out and set her hand on Adam's arms.

"But I can't lose you."

"I know. And I want to promise nothing will happen. But we'll all be careful. I won't even leave the sanctuary."

He unfolded his arms and drew her to his chest. "I guess. But we set up a plan, and we don't deviate from it one iota. No mysterious texts leading us down a seemingly empty hallway."

Jared snorted a laugh. "Right!"

That one was lost on her.

On Your Knees

Adam held the basketball in his hands and tried to catch his breath. The guys had gone outside to play ball while the women sat inside having tea. Caleb and Jared were playing him hard tonight, but it probably had something to do with his lack of sleep and a little more to do with his inability to take his mind off Ella.

"Come on, Adam," Caleb said. "Take a shot."

Adam squared up the shot, dribbled the ball twice, and took the shot. Swish. He smiled.

"Finally, what's been going on with you tonight? Normally you school us?" Jared chuckled. "Oh, I know. Ella. You've got it bad, huh?"

Adam laughed. "You could say that."

"I think there's something more going on," Caleb said.

Adam and Jared both turned their heads to where Caleb was under the hoop after picking up the ball after Adam's shot.

Caleb lifted an eyebrow. "Adam, what else is going on?"

Why did Caleb have to be so astute?

Adam blinked and caught the ball Caleb threw back to him.

"It's just been a tough week, and it's only Wednesday."

Caleb nodded. "Does sound like this case is a doozy. How's the whole idea of trusting God sitting with you?"

Adam took another shot. "Well, honestly, I think I'm starting to."

"Yeah?" Caleb grabbed the ball and passed it to Jared.

Jared dribbled. "I know, for me, I wouldn't have been able to handle what happened to Becca without trusting God. It was out of my hands anyway, so leaning on Christ, knowing that His ways are higher than mine, kept my head above water." Jared shot the ball, making a basket.

"You guys just make it sound so easy. But I've been doing life on my own, on my own terms for so long. I... I just don't know..."

Caleb dribbled the ball out towards him and turned and took a shot himself. The ball hit the backboard and spun around the hoop before finally dropping through the net. "Let me ask you this: what do you have to lose in trusting God? What's it going to cost you?"

Jared ran after the ball.

"Hmm..." Adam just stood and thought about Caleb's question. What would it cost to follow Christ? "I guess it would cost... it would cost everything. Christ calls for complete surrender, right? Practically hate everything, even your own life, right? Isn't that what He said."

"In comparison, yes. The point of that verse is that when we give up everything, Christ becomes Lord and Master of all. And our devotion to Him should be to him alone, to the extent that it would seem that we hate everything else."

"I'd have to give up my approach to my relationships with women."

Jared came back up the driveway. "Which I think you've done already anyway."

He thought of Ella and smiled. He could never even think of another woman with her in his life. "I already gave up drinking."

Caleb's eyes grew wide.

"Dumped all the liquor I had at home down the drain. I'm done running to the bottle."

"So, where you going to run now?" Caleb asked.

Adam knew what his friend was suggesting, but he wasn't sure he was ready to run to Christ. He opened his hands towards Jared. Jared passed the ball, and Adam dribbled it out to the far side of the driveway from the hoop. He took a shot. "I don't know, Caleb. I'm not sure I'm ready to say I'd be okay with God if something *did* happen to Ella. I just couldn't handle it. That would be too much."

Jared retrieved the ball.

Caleb took a step toward Adam. "But you still have to trust that *He* will take care of her. That He will keep her safe, especially when you can't."

Adam lifted his hands with his palms up. "But what if He doesn't? He didn't take care of Ava or Clarissa. How do you explain that?"

"I can't, other than to say that we live in a fallen, sinful world. But despite the evil things that happen, God is good."

"Now you sound just like Ella."

"We serve the same God, a good God. Crap happens. It's possible you could lose Ella, that this guy you're hunting could win. But does that make God any less God?"

"I guess not."

"We don't have all the answers. I wish we did, but we don't. But I know with confidence that God is faithful. Even when life is awful; if we let Him, He'll sustain us through it."

"I just don't think I could handle it if something were to happen to her."

"Trust her into the Almighty's hands. Trust your own heart into His hands. Trust that He will protect her. And trust that He will hold you if something happens."

"The weirdest thing happened last night." He told Caleb and Jared about the sudden, urgent need to find Ella.

Caleb said, "Sounds like God was speaking to you and protecting Ella."

"You think?"

Both guys nodded.

Jared asked, "Who was she talking to or who was around?"

"She was talking to Scott; I didn't notice who else was around. Is Scott on our list?"

"I don't think so, but it kinda seems like he should be."

"Yeah, I'd agree."

CHAPTER 19

Ella wiped her sweaty hands on her pant legs. She stood next to Adam waiting at the check-in counter at the gun range Saturday afternoon. She wasn't sure about this. "I don't know, Adam. I've never held a gun before."

"That's exactly why I want to teach you how."

She had been so excited when Adam came over to the Johnson's this afternoon, until he told her his plan for their Saturday. She was thrilled to spend time with him, but guns made her nervous.

"Detective Jamison! Welcome."

"Hey Jack, I'm going to teach my friend Ella here to shoot, could we borrow one of the training rooms before we hit the range?"

"Absolutely. Room 2 is empty, help yourself."

"Thanks."

Ella followed Adam down a hallway and into a classroom. He set his bag on the table and pulled out a hard case. He opened the case but left his gun lying there. He turned and faced her. His tender smile eased the queasiness in her stomach.

"A healthy fear of guns is good. But they are inanimate objects that require a person controlling them. Come here." He held his arms open to her.

She stepped closer, and he placed his hands on her shoulders.

"I appreciate you letting me show you how to use it. Should you ever need to know, I keep a pistol in my nightstand drawer at all times. That's why when people's kids are over, I keep the door closed. This is my service pistol; I keep it on my hip or on the top shelf in my closet. I know Amelia and Caleb keep one in a safe on the shelf above the washing machine in the laundry room. I think they have a safe in their room too for the guns they carry regularly. Becca and Jared have a safe in their room, I believe. Not sure if they have another spot too."

"Why would I possibly need to know all of that?"

"Just in case. I want you to know Amelia's codes so that, heaven forbid, if you need one you can get to it."

"Okay." She took a deep breath.

"All right. Let's go over the basics. Before I even show you how to use it there are four rules of firearms that everyone should know. First, never point the gun at anything you are not willing to destroy."

"So, I should never point it towards you." She winked at him.

"Please don't."

"I would never."

His cheeks flushed. "I think you got the point of that one. If you follow any rule that's it. It's the most important, always point it in a safe direction. Second, always treat every gun as if it is loaded. Even if you just cleared it and checked that it was empty. The third rule is never put your finger on the trigger until you are ready to fire. Side note, can I just tell you how much it drives me nuts in TV shows and movies when the cops have their fingers on the trigger. They would know better, but anyway. The fourth rule is to always be sure of your target and what's behind it. A bullet doesn't magically stop when it hits what you've shot at. Its velocity is intense, and it will keep going, so know what's behind what you're shooting at."

She nodded. "Seems like common sense."

"Yes, but common sense isn't so common these days."

She giggled. "True."

Next, he showed her all the parts of the gun and how they functioned. He showed her how to clear the firearm, how to load it, and how to hold it properly.

"Ready to try and shoot it?" He put the gun back in the case.

She held her breath. "As ready as I'm going to be, I suppose." They went back to the check-in counter.

They put on their eye and ear protection before going through the first door. Adam reached over and squeezed her hand as they waited for the first door to shut completely before opening the inner door that would put them on the actual range. As soon as they walked through the second door Ella was overwhelmed by the volume of the fans that were running. Even through her earmuffs the sound was deafening. *Pkew!* She jumped. The sound of a gun firing nearly knocked her off her feet. Adam's hand rested on the small of her back and helped steady her. They walked through another door to another set of lanes. There was no one else in there. She let out a sigh of relief.

Adam led her to a lane and showed her the controls for moving the target forward and back. He hung a target that was a black silhouette of a man and sent it back a few yards. "Most self-defense shootings happen at a distance of around seven feet, so I put it at nine." He pulled out the pistol and loaded a magazine. He inserted the magazine into the gun and laid it down on the shelf. "Let's see what you can do."

She wiped her hands on her pants and picked up the firearm. It was heavier now that it was fully loaded. She took the stance Adam showed her and raised the gun. Her heart thudded against her ribs. She couldn't do it. She felt Adam come up close behind her. He adjusted her hold, but she couldn't focus on it. Her heart rate rose at his closeness.

"Now remember," Adam spoke loudly so she could hear through her earmuffs, "you want to shoot for center mass. You shoot to kill. Your goal in firing is to stop the threat."

She set the firearm down and turned to him. "I don't know that I could take someone's life, not even if..."

"It's not easy. It shouldn't be. But sometimes you don't have a choice."

She looked up at him and met his eyes. "Have you ever had to?"

"Yeah... twice..." he dropped his eyes.

"Really?"

"Yeah, we can talk about it later."

"Okay."

"Go ahead and take a shot."

He helped her get the right stance and stepped back.

She raised the gun and aimed. She pulled the trigger. *Pkew.* She laid the gun back down and searched the target. She had missed.

"I can't do this, Adam."

"Yes, you can. This is serious, Ella. If that"—he pointed to the silhouette—"is your attacker, and he's hell bent on killing us what are you going to do?"

"Let you shoot him."

He shook his head. "But what if I can't. Elle, he's charging at us with a knife, what do you do?"

"Tell him he shouldn't have brought a knife to a gun fight!"

"That's my girl!"

They smiled at each other.

"He's coming, Ella!" He stepped back.

She raised the gun toward the target and lined up the sights and continued shooting shot after shot until the magazine was empty. When the slide stayed back, she set the gun down and took several quick breaths. Adam stepped back to her side and brought the target home with the little touch pad screen.

"Wow! Ella, that was great!"

All fourteen rounds had hit the silhouette. Maybe this wasn't so bad.

———•———

Adam smiled to himself and pulled the bag of popcorn from the microwave. Ella had really gotten the knack of shooting before they left the range. It gave him a sense of peace to have her able to work a firearm with confidence. He had also enjoyed the closeness, and not just the physical closeness. She was letting him into her heart, which was only fair since she had stolen his.

He opened the bag and poured the popcorn into a large bowl. He grabbed two cans of coke from the fridge and went to the living room where Ella was tinkering on the piano. He set their snack on top of the piano out of Rusty's reach and sat down next to her on the bench. He slid his arm around her waist. She leaned into him and continued to play.

"Do you remember this one?" she asked.

"Maybe. Sing it. If I do, I'll join you."

Her voice filled the air.

Marvelous grace of our loving Lord, Grace that exceeds our sin and our guilt,

Yonder on Calvary's mount out-poured, there where the blood of the Lamb was spilt.

Grace, grace, God's grace, Grace that will pardon and cleanse within;

Grace, grace God's grace, Grace that is greater than all our sin.

Dark is the stain that we cannot hide, what can avail to wash it away?

Look! There is flowing a crimson tide; Whiter than snow you may be today.

Grace, grace, God's grace, Grace that will pardon and cleanse within;

Grace, grace God's grace, Grace that is greater than all our sin.

Marvelous, infinite, matchless grace, Freely bestowed on all who believe;

All who are longing to see his face, will you this moment his grace receive?

Grace, grace, God's grace, Grace that will pardon and cleanse within;

Grace, grace God's grace, Grace that is greater than all our sin.

The words and her tender voice reached deep into his soul. He let her sing the whole song and listened without joining in this time even though the words came back to him as she sang. The words nudged him to respond, but he ignored it.

When she finished the song, she turned to him and smiled. She put her arm around his waist and leaned her head against his shoulder. He kissed the top of her head. Against his chest he could feel her cheeks scrunch from her lips turning up in a smile.

They sat there for a few moments before Ella said, "How about that popcorn? It smells good."

"I agree." He stood up and Ella followed. She rubbed her arms. "You cold?"

"A little, it's that time of year I need to start taking a sweater wherever I go."

"Want a sweatshirt?"

She shrugged only one shoulder. "Sure."

He went back to his room and grabbed one of his favorite hoodies. He handed to her where she had settled on the couch.

"You want to watch a movie?"

She pulled the over-sized sweatshirt on. "No, I'd rather talk."

Oh, no... He could tell by the way her eyes had narrowed ever so slightly that she had something serious on her mind. And that seemed to always mean him talking about something that he wasn't sure about diving into. Not that he didn't trust her with his heart, but it was hard stuff that he didn't really want to deal with. He'd rather just ignore it.

"What's on your mind?" He sat down facing her on the couch.

She scooted a little closer to him and took his hand in hers. "You said at the range that you've had to shoot two people. I can't even imagine how that would be. It must be so hard. Would you mind telling me what happened?"

He took a deep breath and let it out slowly. "Well, the first time I had to kill someone was when Becca was taken. The guy that had taken her had knocked Jared to the ground from behind and was about to kill him."

"You had no choice but to protect your friend."

He rubbed the back of her hand with his thumb. "Yeah. Doesn't make it easy to take a life. But I didn't think twice about it. It was him or Jared. The other time was the guy that killed Rick..." He swallowed past the lump in his throat. He looked down at her hands where they held his and then looked back up into her eyes. "I wish... well, I didn't have a choice, he was shooting at us. I just wish I had gotten him before he got Rick."

"I know. You feel guilty for killing them? I see it in your face."

He looked down again and shook his head. "I ended someone's life, Ella. It haunts me. No matter how evil they were or how much I wanted to kill them for what they had done to people I cared about, I still hate the idea that their lives ended as a result of my pulling the trigger."

"But you were doing your job, you were doing what was necessary."

"I know. And that's why I was cleared for duty. No wrongdoing found. Justified shootings they call them. And given the opportunity to go back and redo it, in both situations, I'd do the exact same thing, but... I still don't like that I had to. Does that make sense?"

"Absolutely."

"Do you think God sees it like the courts did? Was I justified in His eyes to take the lives of those men?" He looked up at her face.

She tilted her head to the side. "I do think He would see it that way. I think you should talk to Him about it, let Him take the weight you feel."

"Yeah, maybe I will." He reached forward and grabbed the cokes off the coffee table and handed one to Ella. She leaned forward and grabbed the popcorn. When she leaned back, she turned to lean up against him, and he wrapped his arm around her shoulders. They sat and snuggled while they munched on the snack.

He continued to mull over the idea of taking his burdens to God. What would it look like to lay them down at the foot of the cross? Could he really find peace from these things that plagued his heart? He wanted to believe that it was possible. He wanted peace. But would Christ really want his mess? Not only did he have the weight of taking two lives, no matter how 'justified' it was, it didn't sit well in his stomach, but he also had really messed up a lot in life. Ella seemed so forgiving of his short comings, but could God forgive him? Every day he felt less able to handle the burdens of life on his own, but part of him thought he just needed to pull himself together and get over it. But according to Ella, and Caleb, and Becca, that would never cut it. They all said he needed Christ.

The words to the hymn Ella had just sung echoed in his mind.

Marvelous grace of our loving Lord, Grace that exceeds our sin and our guilt,

Yonder on Calvary's mount outpoured, there where the blood of the Lamb was spilt.

Grace, grace, God's grace, Grace that will pardon and cleanse within;

Grace, grace God's grace, Grace that is greater than all our sin.

Was God's grace really great enough to cover his sin? He believed that Jesus had died and that He rose again, but believing it wasn't enough, he knew that. Even the demons believed it. But could he own it? Could He let Christ into his life? Could he let someone else be the Lord of his heart?

Adam took a seat next to Becca as the first service began. They had a plan in place, and Ella should be safe. Jared was hanging out in the back while Ella was on stage. Even though the band normally went backstage after playing before coming in to find their seats, Ella would not. She would come right off the stage and sit with him. Between services was going to be the time they would need to be most vigilant, but they would all stay close to Ella and be on the lookout for anyone that seemed nefarious or out of place. It did seem a little silly to be so overly cautious at a church, but after what happened to Becca, not one of them was going to take a chance. He wasn't the only one that cared about Ella and that made him happy.

The songs started, and they stood again. Ella joined the worship leader in singing, her beautiful harmony adding richness to the song. Music had always been a component in his life and as the words to the songs he didn't know were on the screen and sung by the people around him, he took it all in. Through the songs that Voice that had been beckoning him for weeks seemed to call a little louder than before. He didn't know how to respond to it though. He looked around, Becca raised her hands as did a few others. Some just sang, others bowed their heads, a few stood stoic. He looked up at Ella where she stood on stage. The epitome of beauty, the girl who was normally so reserved with her emotions worshiped with all her being. With one hand raised all the way to heaven, her whole body seemed to feel the music and express the intensity of her emotions. His eyes fell on Caleb playing the drums, the same expression of joy and gratitude that was on Ella's face was on his as well.

The next song began, and those around him followed Ella in clapping. He joined in, not sure of what else to do. For the first time he realized how genuine his friends' faith really was. They all loved God, and it wasn't just here on a Sunday morning at church that they lived it out. It was every day during the week. The way they interacted with people. The way they coped with life's troubles. It was all firmly rooted in their relationship with Christ.

A burning sensation ignited in his stomach. A feeling he wasn't used to. Was he actually jealous of what his friends had? A little bit. He shifted his weight from foot to foot. He was not comfortable with this feeling. But he didn't know what to do about it.

The music quieted, and the worship leader prayed. Adam bowed his head and closed his eyes just like he was taught to do as a boy. This church was so different from the one he grew up in though. That stiff, emotionless church was a far cry from this place where you could actually feel the presence of God moving. That was what he felt, wasn't it? Somehow, he knew that was it.

Everything grew silent. A few strums of an acoustic guitar filled the void followed by Ella's voice.

Marvelous grace of our loving Lord, Grace that exceeds our sin and our guilt...

The very song she had sung yesterday. It once again beckoned him to acknowledge God's grace. But could that grace really be for him as well. Surely, his walking away from Christ as a teen and proceeding to live in a way that he knew displeased the Lord was too much.

Grace, grace God's grace, Grace that is greater than all our sin.

He bit his lower lip. Part of him just wanted to run from the room, run away from everything. The emotions that were churning inside him. The past. His own selfishness. The fear in his heart that he could possibly lose Ella. The weight of life. But he couldn't move. His feet were cemented to the floor. Something or Someone wouldn't let him leave.

He sat with the rest of the congregation as the pastor came on the stage. Ella came down and sat with him. She smiled at him and slid her hand into his. The resounding echo of the hymn Ella had sung was so loud in his head that he didn't feel the usual flutter in his heart from Ella's touch. He just gripped her hand tightly, and the pastor started his sermon about God's grace.

CHAPTER 20

"Amelia!" Ella said under her breath as soon as the guys walked outside to shoot a few hoops.

Amelia took the plates from Ella's hands and set them in the sink. "What?"

"Did you see the look on Adam's face during worship?"

"You know I couldn't from up at the sound board." Amelia leaned forward to hear more.

"I'm not even sure how to describe it. But God was working on him. I could just tell." Ella couldn't contain her excitement any longer. She had managed to since she noticed Adam wrestling with the words they were singing during first service. Her heart felt like it was going to burst right out from her chest.

"Oh, Ella. That's awesome. Caleb said they had a really good talk on Wednesday when they all went out to play basketball at Becca's the other night. He's so close. I really believe it."

"Me too."

The ladies fell quiet, and they finished clearing the table after Sunday lunch. Ella put the leftovers in the fridge and turned back to where Amelia was putting the dishes in the dishwasher.

"You know what I did notice at church?" Amelia raised her eyebrows.

"What?"

"You automatically holding Adam's hand as if you two were an item."

Ella's cheeks grew warm. "So?"

Amelia laughed. "I just find it amusing, two weeks ago you'd barely touch him. Three weeks ago, you weren't even sure you wanted to hang out with him alone. Yet here you are, barely able to be separated at all. I see the way you look at each other. Is this moving too fast?"

Ella's stomach dropped, and her smile vanished. "I don't know, is it? I don't want to move too fast, but it's felt so natural."

"Oh, hun. I'm not trying to accuse you of moving it too fast; I'm just checking in with you to make sure you're okay."

The air released from her lungs. "Okay. I'm so clueless when it comes to relationships. I don't want to do anything wrong."

"Ella, there's no right way or wrong way to maneuver through a relationship. There's no set speed to go at. Just be careful."

"I know."

"You two are so good for each other. You definitely bring out the best in each other, and I think that's awesome."

Ella smiled and bit her lip. "Thanks. Amelia, would you sit with me and pray for a bit?"

"Of course."

"I want to pray for Adam and our relationship too. But mostly for Adam to come to know Christ. I feel this relationship moving forward but I don't want to be 'unequally yoked.' I want us to be on the same page spiritually, and I really don't want to get in his way of knowing Christ."

"I know. Let's go sit at the dining room table."

"Good spot."

"You're just saying that because you'll be able to see Adam out the window."

She raised her palms up and looked up in an attempt to feign innocence, but her cheeks warmed again. "I have no idea what you're talking about."

"Ha. Right." Her friend shook her head and lifted her glass of sweet tea. "This can help cool those red cheeks."

Ella gigged and took a seat at the table where she had a clear view of Adam and Caleb playing one on one basketball in the driveway in their jeans and t-shirts, the button-ups they wore to church discarded. She pulled her feet up into the chair, and Amelia sat down next to her.

Amelia's eyebrows rose. "This is a good view."

Both women laughed.

Ella folded her hands in her lap. The laughter faded. "Dearest Jesus," she prayed.

The emotions were catching up with Adam. But maybe it was just the intensity of the game he was playing with Caleb. He darted around Caleb and put up the layup. He missed. He almost never missed that shot. He leaned over with his hands on his knees, and Caleb retrieved the ball.

"You okay, man?"

Adam took in a few shaky breaths. "I don't know." He let another breath out through his mouth.

"What's going on?"

He opened his mouth to talk, but nothing came out. He scrunched his face and tried to find the words that he was looking for. "I can't do it anymore, Caleb?"

"What basketball?"

He looked up at his normally astute friend to find a teasing smile. Adam shook his head. He straightened back up and took the ball Caleb tossed back to him. "No, I can't do any of this on my own. The pastor's sermon this morning really hit home. God's grace, for the first time in my life, actually makes sense. It's a gift, freely given, even though we don't deserve it. I never understood that before."

"Pretty powerful, isn't it?"

"Yeah, seems too good to be true." Adam spun the basketball between his hands. "Would God really give His grace to me? This poor excuse for a man. A man that betrayed his closest friend and threw her to the lions. A man who walked away from God because he was afraid of being labeled a hypocrite. One who's killed? Someone who's slept with… too many women… who's run to a bottle of liquor instead of Him? One who's fearful of tomorrow? Would God really give His grace to me?"

"Absolutely. If God can give his grace to me, Adam, he can give it to you. I've told you my story before. I've lied. I've cheated. Heck, I've murdered. There is no limit to God's grace. It's free to anyone who will humble themselves before Him and accept it."

Adam set the basketball on the grass, and moisture filled his eyes. "But how? How do I go from that man that I was to who He wants me to be?"

"Just call out to Him, Adam. Just say His name. Talk to Him. Remember that verse we talked about a few weeks ago. 'He gives grace to the humble'?"

Adam nodded, and the tears escaped the captivity of his eyes.

"Just humble yourself before Him, Adam."

He swallowed past the lump forming in his throat. His body felt like it was collapsing beneath him. *Humble yourself.* He fell to his knees. "Jesus..." his voice shook as he uttered the name of the only One who could save him from himself, from his life of self-destruction. The only One who could save him from his sins. The only One who could give him peace. "Jesus, here I am."

Adam felt Caleb kneel down beside him and place his hand on Adam's shoulder. Adam prayed for Christ to come in and take control of his life. He prayed for forgiveness of his sins and for wholeness.

An old hymn that Adam had learned as a boy came to his mind,

What can wash away my sin, nothin' but the blood of Jesus

What can make me whole again, nothin' but the blood of Jesus

Oh, precious is the flow, that makes me white as snow

No other fount I know, nothin' but the blood of Jesus, nothin' but the blood of Jesus.

The Voice, the Presence that Adam had been avoiding and ignoring for almost twenty years embraced him. The God of the universe filled him with His Spirit. The peace that Adam had been searching for in women and liquor finally filled his being in a way that he never expected. Jesus was the answer. The only answer.

CHAPTER 21

Ella opened her eyes and looked at the guys outside. Her heart stopped. She reached over and grabbed Amelia's arm. The words Amelia had been praying came to an abrupt halt. Adam and Caleb were both on their knees, and even from where she sat, Ella could see that Adam was crying. Tears rushed to Ella's eyes at the sight.

"Oh, sweet Jesus, thank you!" Amelia said.

Ella couldn't speak. The boy she had been praying for since the day she accepted Jesus as her Savior at the age of seven had finally embrace his Redeemer. Her jaw trembled, and tears tumbled out of her eyes and down her cheeks. She looked at Amelia whose eyes also glistened with tears. The women embraced.

Ella pulled back, sure she had a stupid grin on her face. "Amelia! I can't believe it! Do you really think... is he really...?"

"I think so. I could scream!"

"Me too!" They laughed. "It's all I can do to hold myself here."

"I know, but we need to wait until they come in."

"I know... but Ah!"

"Let's keep praying."

"Definitely." Ella tried to settle herself, and Amelia prayed.

"Thank you, Jesus, for what you're doing in Adam's heart. We ask that you keep moving in him, drawing him closer and closer to your heart."

They kept praying until they heard the side door by the kitchen open.

Ella jumped out of her seat but held herself back until she saw Adam's face. She took a few steps toward him, and he approached her.

"So, guess what?" Adam said. "I did it. I accepted Christ!"

Hearing him say it made her heart explode with joy. She ran the rest of the way to him and threw her arms around his neck. "Oh, Adam, that's awesome!" she whispered in his ear. His arms encompassed her, and he lifted her off the ground. He set her down, and she pulled him out to arm's length. "I have been praying for you and this moment almost daily for the past twenty-five years."

His eyes widened. "Really?"

"Oh, yeah." She nodded and hugged him again.

"Hey, my turn." Amelia tapped Ella on the shoulder.

They laughed. Ella reluctantly pulled herself away from Adam and let Amelia hug him, too.

"Time to celebrate." Amelia pulled away from the hug. "Adam, you pick what we have for dinner. We need to celebrate!"

"Celebrate?"

"Yes!" Amelia said. "When the prodigal came home there was a party."

"Well, how 'bout pizza?"

"Good choice."

Ella said, "You should call Becca."

Amelia agreed. "Yes, you should. And tell them to join us for dinner."

"All right." Adam went over to where he had left his phone on the kitchen counter and dialed Becca's phone number. He put the phone on speaker and tucked his arm back around Ella.

Becca answered on the third ring. "Hey," her voice sounded concerned, "What's going on?"

"Can you guys come over to Caleb and Amelia's?"

"Sure, is everything okay?"

Ella held in a giggle at how Adam tried to suppress his smile. "Just come over for dinner, okay?"

"Okay. We'll be there shortly. Dani's still napping, but we'll be there as soon as she wakes up. Is that okay?"

"Of course. See you soon."

They hung up, and Ella couldn't contain her giggles any longer. "You couldn't tell her on the phone?"

"No, what fun would that be? I want to see her face. I know she's been praying for me for a long time too."

Ella hugged Adam close again. She couldn't believe that he had finally turned to Jesus. It was the happiest moment of her life.

———••———

Ella was stirring the brownie mix when Adam came up behind her and reached for the batter. "Hey!" She swatted his hand, but he managed to get a finger covered in the chocolaty goodness.

He stuck his finger in his mouth and winked at her.

She shook her head and leaned towards him. He wrapped his arm around her waist.

"Becca, Jared, and the girls still aren't here?" she asked.

"Not yet. Are those brownies for me?"

"Mostly, but you have to share with everyone else."

"I guess I could do that."

"Can you grab me that pan?" She nodded her head towards the pan that sat on top of the stove.

"Sure." He slid his hand across her waist as he walked to the other end of the kitchen. He set it beside the mixing bowl and stuck another finger in the batter.

"Adam!"

"What?" He gave her a toothy grin.

He stayed very close while she poured the batter in the pan. After sticking the brownies in the oven, she turned around and nearly collided with Adam. She didn't hesitate to wrap her arms around him. It had become second nature.

He pulled her away slightly, so she could see his face. "You are really okay with all this physical contact? No flashbacks looming nearby?"

She smiled. "None! I can't believe it. But I'm finally able to associate touch with something else. And I have you to thank for that."

He smiled. "You are most welcome." He winked at her again sending her heart fluttering away. "And

Ella," his voice became more serious, "thank you for always praying for me."

"You're welcome. I am so thankful that God heard them, and that you responded to Him."

Becca's voice broke the silence that had fallen. "Oops, we're interrupting a moment."

They laughed and turned towards her and Jared.

"Who's going to tell me what's going on? Adam, it sounded serious on the phone." She walked the rest of the way into the kitchen holding Dani in her arms.

"Let me take Dani." Ella raised her hands to take the toddler.

"Sure." The worry lines on Becca's face deepened.

Jared came up behind his wife; his forehead was also deeply furrowed.

"Well," Adam said solemnly, "I have some news... I decided it was time to admit that I can't do this whole life thing on my own." He turned on his thick, southern 'preacher' voice that Ella hadn't heard him use since they were kids. "I decided it was high time to turn from my worldly indulgences, as my momma would say. And I decided to accept God's free gift of salvation." His voice returned to normal. "But seriously, I did, I gave my life over to Christ today."

Becca's eyes widened. The news soaked in. "Really!?"

Adam nodded.

"Oh, my word! That's like totally awesome! Adam!" She flew towards him and embraced him.

Jared was right behind her. "Adam, that's fantastic! I'm so excited for you. But man, you had us worried."

Adam flashed a sheepish look. "Sorry about that. But I had to tell you in person."

Becca eventually let Adam go, and Jared hugged him.

"All right, enough hugging, everyone." Amelia climbed onto one of the bar stools at the breakfast bar. "What's everyone want on their pizza?"

"Ah, the pregnant woman wants food again," Adam teased. "Big surprise there."

Everyone chuckled. Ella slipped her hand in Adam's, and Amelia took pizza orders. They all chatted while they waited for the pizza, the mood light and celebratory over Adam's decision. But the mood changed after dinner and the kids had run off to play.

"Ella"—Becca leaned forward on the dining room table—"Jared and I would like to invite you to come stay with us for a while. I know you're well settled here, but I'm worried that it may have gotten out where you are staying. Or simply that he's had enough time to find you."

Ella leaned back in her chair. She didn't want to think about it, even though she knew Becca was right.

"I think it's a good idea." Adam put his hand on her arm.

She nodded but stared off. Adam squeezed her arm. She looked up and met his eyes. His eyes relaxed when he saw that she hadn't gone down the tunnel that stress often brought on. She gave him a smile to set him further at ease.

"When?" she asked.

"Tomorrow?" Becca suggested.

"That would be good."

The conversation lightened a little bit again, but Ella was restless about the idea of being displaced again. She knew it was the safest thing to do, but part of her hated to put another family with little kids at risk. She was just ready for this to all be over. She wanted her own space again, but where would home be? She could never live in her apartment again, not after knowing someone bent on killing her had gotten in there. She'd given so little thought to it in the last few weeks, but she couldn't think about it, not until this was all over.

Becca, Jared, and the girls left after everyone had some brownies. Amelia and Caleb took the kids up to bed, so Adam and Ella settled on the couch for a few minutes.

"What's up with you and Becca?" Adam took her hand in his.

She scrunched her eyebrows, confused by his question. "What do you mean?"

"You seem really closed off to her."

"I don't mean to be."

"I didn't figure, but give her a chance."

"I don't?" She turned her body to face him.

"I don't know, but she's like family to me, so I want you two to get along."

"Well, looks like I'm going to have a chance to get to know her a lot better." She gave him a smile.

"Definitely."

"I've always been intimidated by her. She's so sophisticated and put together. And I'm such a hot mess all the time."

Adam chuckled. "I think she'll surprise you."

"Maybe."

"No, definitely. I know her better than you do. You will for sure be surprised if you think she always has everything together."

"She doesn't?"

"You'll find out."

"Okay." She snuggled close to him and enjoyed a few moments rest.

"I'll pick you up from school tomorrow and take you to Becca's to get settled," he said a few moments later.

"I'd appreciate that."

Adam let out a big yawn.

"You're tired." She rubbed the back of his hand with her thumb.

"Yeah, I guess. Are you?"

"I suppose. Probably should go to bed soon."

Amelia came around the corner. "Yes, you should."

Whining, Adam said, "But Mom..."

"Don't 'but mom' me, young man!"

All three of them burst into laughter, and Adam stood to his feet pulling Ella with him. They continued to laugh, and Adam and Ella walked to the front door hand in hand.

"I'm already looking forward to seeing you tomorrow." Adam brushed a strand of hair out of Ella's face.

"Likewise." Without thinking, she reached up and stroked the two-day old stubble on his cheek. Her entire body flooded with heat. She pulled her hand back and looked at the floor. It was too soon.

He pulled her into a hug saving her from the desires she wasn't yet ready to face. "Good night, Ella."

"Good night, Adam."

He kissed the top of her head before pulling away and disappearing out the front door. She closed it behind him and leaned against it. She tried to catch her breath. She couldn't believe the intensity of the emotion she was feeling.

"You know he wants to kiss you, right?"

Ella jumped at Amelia's voice. She looked up and saw her friend standing at the bottom of the stairs in front of her. "Yes, but I'm not ready for that."

"Didn't figure you were. Just making sure you knew."

"Oh, I do! I've seen that look on his face plenty of times in the past." She smiled and walked across the foyer to Amelia.

"Can I just say how happy I am for you two? You're just too cute together."

Ella's cheeks warmed. "Yeah? It's all so unreal. We haven't really talked about it yet."

"That comes in time. I think your actions are speaking louder than words."

"I suppose." Ella shuffled her foot and looked at her friend. "Amelia, I can't thank you enough for opening your home to me."

"You don't need to. I'm going to miss having you around. It's been a joy having you here."

Ella reached out and hugged Amelia. Hugging a friend was not something Ella was used to, but she was so grateful that it was something she could do again.

Adam moaned and rolled over in bed. *Ruff!* "Oh, shut up, Rusty!" The dog stuck his nose into his face. Adam pushed him away, "Let me sleep, Boy!" The shrill of his cell phone pulled Adam's attention from the dog. That's why Rusty was barking. He glanced at the clock. The bright red numbers read "3:26." Adam's blood pressure shot through the roof as his heart pounded. Who was calling at three in the morning? Was Ella okay?

He scrambled to untangle himself from the sheet. *Maybe we should have moved her to Becca's tonight!* He tried to catch his breath and grabbed the phone off the bedside table. The sight of Amelia's phone number on the display double the speed of his pulse. He bolted upright and jabbed at the green answer button, but it didn't cooperate. "Arg!" He jabbed it again. It answered, and he jerked the phone to his ear. "What's wrong!?"

"Ella's fine. My maternal instincts made me check on her as soon as I got the call."

"What call?"

"We've got a homicide out at the old Nelson farm."

"Why are they calling us in on it?"

"Becca called. It's Hillary."

"No." Adam's stomach sank. "Want me to pick you up?"

"If you would."

"Of course. See you in ten to fifteen minutes."

They hung up, and Adam swung his legs off the side of the bed. He leaned his elbows on his knees and rubbed his face. Hillary was dead. That made four victims. The killer's goal was five. And that left Ella as his final target. Adam had to keep her safe. God had to keep her safe. *Oh Jesus, please, I beg you. Protect my girl.*

His legs shook, but he stood and walked across the room and retrieved the jeans he had left draped across the chair he kept in his bedroom. They got stuck on the exposed screw on the back of the chair. "Oh, for the love!" He freed them and hoped there wasn't a hole.

The dog barked as he slid his legs into his pants. "Hold on, Rusty. I'll let you out before I go. Don't worry." He had a doggy door on the back door that was in the utility room, but he kept that room closed at night, so the dog wouldn't set off the alarm going in and out at night.

He let the dog out and finished getting ready to walk out the door. He went to the back porch when he was ready to go. The motion activated light by the back door had gone out, so Adam stuck his hand out of the door and waved his arm and called the dog. "Rusty! Come on boy, time to come in."

The light came on. Adam jumped as the light illuminated the porch. Nothing was there. He was just being hyper-aware. *Of nothing!*

"Rusty! Let's go!" The dog wasn't coming. What was going on? "RUSTY!" His heart raced again.

He was about to turn inside to get a flashlight when the dog came bounding up the steps onto the porch. "There you are; you, old lug. You had me worried. Now get inside I have to go."

Adam left his house without incident, coffee in hand, and found himself praying as he drove to Amelia's house. Once he picked her up, they drove out to the edge of town to a little old farmhouse that hadn't been occupied for several years since the last of the local Nelson's had passed away. The children of Farmer Nelson had debated what to do with the property for years.

Adam pulled up behind Jared's truck. They climbed out of the car and entered the little old farmhouse. Adam caught a glimpse of the body that was tied to a bed in the back room and stopped Amelia. "You're not going to want to go in there."

She nodded and turned to look around the rest of the house. Adam steeled himself against what he knew he would see in the room ahead of him. He had to remove his own personal emotion from this. He couldn't think about the fact that this vile man wanted to do the same thing to the woman he was growing to love more every day.

He closed his eyes and swallowed. He entered the room. No matter how strong the wall he put up to protect his heart was, nothing could stop the anger that welled up in him. His blood boiled at the sight of the brutally beaten and murdered woman that lay on the bed, hands duct taped above her head. Just like the others. Her throat was slit as well.

Adam could feel the tips of his ears and his forehead grow red with anger. He clenched his hands. He had to keep this from happening to Ella.

"Hey." Jared's hand came to rest on Adam's shoulder.

Adam looked at his friend and superior and let out a shaky breath. "Hey. Didn't expect to see you here too. Figured you'd be home with the girls."

"Amy came over. Becca's a mess, blaming herself."

"But from what she told me, Hillary wasn't the most cooperative when it came to staying hidden and safe."

"No. But you know Becca."

He nodded.

———••———

Adam twirled his pen as he sat at the conference room table with Amelia, Gavin, and Becca.

Gavin tried to comfort his partner. "Palmer, we did all we could!"

Emotions were running high for all of them. They had stayed at the crime scene until dawn, at which point, they had come back to the station to piece together what happened. They now, at eleven o'clock, had a pretty good idea of the timeline of events.

The Captain and Sergeant came in the room. Jared leaned up against the door and the Captain leaned on the table and said, "Run me through what happened. I want to know where we went wrong. Tell me everything." He pulled out a chair, sat down, and crossed his arms.

Adam leaned forward in his chair. "The last time Hillary was seen was Friday evening. Riley picked her up from work, per the usual, and took her to where she was staying with a friend on the west side of town."

"Yep," Gavin said. "Dropped her off. Her friend was home, and nothing seemed out of place, so I left. Just like we've done for three weeks. But on Saturday afternoon the friend said she had to run an errand and Hillary insisted that she would be fine at the house by herself. When the friend got back, Hillary was gone."

"But why didn't the friend call?" Captain Baker asked. "We could have been out looking for her."

"Because Hillary left a note. Said she was going to stay with her mom for the weekend up in Greensboro."

"But she didn't," Becca said. "Her mom said that she hadn't even called on Saturday."

"Where did the note come from?" The Captain asked.

Amelia answered, "Best we can figure is that the unsub forced her to write it."

Adam tapped his pen on the table. "Also, from what Henry said, Hillary's beating began on Saturday afternoon."

"What was the time of death?" asked the Captain.

"Around eleven last night." Gavin looked as if he might be sick.

The Captain rubbed his chin. "He kept her for over twenty-four hours? That's a huge escalation." They all nodded. "Any viable suspects?"

Adam set his pen on the table. "We combed through our entire list last week and came up blank. No one stood out. We went back to the video tapes of who could have dropped the flowers on my desk and came up with nothin' as to whom the last mystery person was."

"So that's most likely our guy?"

"Yep, but we can't figure out who it is. He definitely knew where the cameras were and how to avoid being seen on them. We went back through that entire day. And nothing helped us figure out who he was. We talked to everyone who was around, and no one could identify who it was."

"How does someone walk into a police station set flowers on a detective's desk and no one notices anything?"

"We can only assume he belonged. No red flags were set off, so no one noticed."

"So, make note of every person that works in this building and have their whereabouts for the entire weekend accounted for, even if they were on duty, I want to know exactly where they were. Figure out who it was!" Captain Baker lifted himself to his feet and walked out the door.

Adam leaned forward and dropped his head onto his arm on the table.

"What does he think we've been trying to do!?" Becca sounded like she was about to start crying. Adam couldn't blame her.

Maybe it was just his exhaustion, but he was barely holding it together. He wouldn't be okay until Ella was safe in his arms. He lifted his head and looked around at his friends. He knew each one was a believer and now he was too. "So, this is the point in the case where you guys normally pray in your mind constantly, isn't it?"

Becca's eyes met his and her grief gave way to compassion. "Oh, Adam, that started the second I heard that Ella was a target."

Tears rushed into his eyes. He pressed the heels of his hands into his eye sockets. He wiped his eyes. "Guys, we have to get his scumbag."

Jared spoke from where he leaned against the wall. "I'm beginning to think we need to double our efforts to keep Ella safe. Any routine you guys have fallen into needs to change."

"I think the change we're making in where she's staying is timely," Amelia said.

Jared nodded. "Definitely. I'd send a couple of uniforms to the school, but I seriously don't even know who to send."

"Well," Gavin said, "let's try to make that list."

Adam dropped his hands on the table in frustration. "Lists haven't been working for us this case. Who are we missing? Is everyone that is in the building regularly even in the system? There has to be someone that has fallen beneath the radar."

"Wait"—Jared pushed off the wall and looked at Adam—"who was it that you said Ella was talking to the other night when God told you to protect her?"

"Scott Rebus."

"He wasn't on our list before?" Gavin asked.

Adam shook his head.

"Why not?" He pressed.

Everyone stared blankly at one another. Adam grabbed his laptop and flipped it open. "Is his file not in the system yet? He's only been working back here for what three weeks?"

Becca twirled her hair. "That timing is awfully suspicious."

"But what about the tapes?" Jared asked. "Could he be our mystery man?"

"Probably not," Amelia said. "He was on the tape, and we talked to him."

Adam's computer finally brought up the personnel files. "Well, he wasn't on the list because his file isn't in the system yet."

Amelia said, "But he's a dead end anyway. If he was clearly on the tape, why would he come back in disguise?"

Adam ran his hands through his hair, "Cuz that would take our suspicion off of him."

"Yeah, but that would take some serious forethought," Amelia said.

"Well," Adam turned to face Amelia more, "forethought is what put Patrick on that tape; remember that mysterious note Patrick claimed sent him upstairs. If he hadn't been on footage, we might not have spent so much time thinking he could be our perp."

Amelia tilted her head to the side. "Valid point, but I just don't see it being Scott. I know you don't like him, but he's a nice guy. Been nothing but helpful around here."

"Of course you'd say that, he dotes on you all the time, but maybe that's just because he's trying to find out about Ella."

"You're just being paranoid, Adam. Maybe he's just being a gentleman and helping a pregnant lady out."

Becca stood. "Enough you two. I think Scott was around the station this weekend. Let's check into that. Whoever killed Hillary probably didn't leave her out at the farm. She was in really bad shape, like she was tortured the entire time she was gone. If Scott was here for any length of time, he's not our guy."

"That's awfully simplistic, Palmer." Adam stood, too. "If he wanted to establish an alibi that would be the perfect way to do it. He couldn't have been here the entire time. That would give him opportunity."

"One step at a time." Jared lifted his hands. "Let's talk to Scott. But let's do it in a non-interrogating way. Let's ask him about who was around when he was here. Then we can ask them about him and such. Riley and Johnson why don't you two focus on that. Palmer and Jamison, get duty rosters and see what people who weren't here at the station were doing. But, Jamison, I want you at that school before the bell rings. We're not going to let anything happen to my daughter's favorite teacher."

Adam nodded.

Amelia shoved the squad room door open. This was a waste of time. Scott was a great guy; she didn't get any weird feeling around him or sense that he was trouble. Wouldn't she have some sort of intuition telling her if he was the least bit menacing?

"Johnson."

She turned and found Gavin had followed her out of the squad room.

He fell into step beside her. "Ready to find Scott?"

"After I grab a snack."

A smirk grew on Gavin's face. "You're going to have a gigantic baby if you keep eating like this."

She looked up at Gavin. "You mean I'm going to be gigantic?"

"Never. At 5'2" I'm pretty sure gigantic could never describe you." A spark of life briefly masked the sorrow that normally plagued the detective's blue eyes.

She squeezed his arm and entered the breakroom. She walked across the empty room and pulled a protein bar from the cabinet. "I wish we had a better candidate." She ripped the packaging open and took a bite.

Gavin shook his head. "He's the perfect candidate."

"You really think he could have done any of it?"

"How could you not?" Gavin shuffled his feet.

Amelia leaned back against the counter. But before she could go into her defense of Scott, he walked in. Good, he could come to his own defense. "Just the man we wanted to talk to."

Scott face beamed. "Why, color me honored, what could the beautiful Amelia Johnson want to talk to me about?"

She shook her head. She hated the flattery, but that just seemed to be Scott's way. "We're trying to get tabs on everyone who works here, specifically whoever was around this weekend."

"I was here. What can I help with?"

She wanted to point that out to Gavin. *See he was here! He couldn't have killed Hillary.* "I'd love to get a list of people you saw. And approximate times you saw them."

"Anything I can do to help."

She pushed off the counter and pulled her notepad out of her back pocket along with her pen.

Gavin puffed up his chest and took a step closer to Scott. "Were you here the whole weekend, Scott?"

Scott turned and met Gavin's stance. Both men tried to stand a little taller as they stared at the other. "A man has to sleep."

"Put the rulers away, boys. Scott, mind giving me a list?"

"Sure." Scott turned back to her and sat with her at a little table. He gave her a list of over a dozen names and various times he remembered seeing the people. The list included Saturday and Sunday, morning and afternoon.

Once he finished giving her all he could remember Scott left her and Gavin alone in the breakroom. "See!" She looked up at Gavin who had remained standing with his arms crossed the whole time.

"I don't see anything but a clever man who knows how to make an alibi. I still think he's a viable possibility."

She stood so fast her chair flew backwards.

Gavin caught it before it crashed to the floor.

"You're being a fool Gavin. It couldn't be him. He just alibied himself out. If even half of these people say they saw him too, he's clear. Why are you so insistent that he's guilty?"

"Why are you being so pigheaded?"

She grunted and pushed him out of her way. She stormed out of the breakroom. How did Becca work with Gavin?

CHAPTER 22

Ella laughed. Aidan shared his favorite moment of the day as the students sat on their desks with their backpacks on waiting for the bell to ring. This was their ritual every day. Once the students were ready to go home, they would come back and sit on their desks, the only time they were allowed to, and take turns telling about how their day had gone. Aidan's story today about laughing so hard at lunch that milk came out of his nose made everyone laugh.

The bell rang, and the kids jumped down from their desks. Half of them came to hug her before running out the door, a few yelled, "Bye, Miss Perkins!" and a few other simply vanished. She giggled with a few of the girls before they left and started cleaning the board as a few last students exited her classroom.

Movement by the door caught her eye. "Adam!" She dropped the eraser on the tray and walked to him with a spring in her step.

"Ella!" He rushed at her and drew her into his arms with a fierceness that nearly knocked the breath out of her. His arms wrapped tightly around her. He stroked her hair and kissed her head.

"Adam, what's wrong?" Her insides became a jumbled mess. She could sense his fear. When he didn't answer she pushed him back enough to see his face. "Tell me."

"It's Hillary. The other survivor from seventeen years ago..."

"No..." Ella felt her knees turn to pudding, collapsing beneath her. Adam's arms kept her from falling to the ground. "He killed her?"

Adam nodded and pulled her back into his arms. Her head fell against his chest. She clenched her arms around his waist and held him tight. Her heart thundered. That could be her. Knowing Hillary had been murdered changed everything. The whole situation came back to the front of her mind. Her developing relationship with Adam had distracted her from the real threat out there. Her body shook.

Adam's hands ran up and down her back. "Shh... we're going to keep you safe."

"You say that with such confidence... but why are you so scared. Adam, you're shaking as badly as I am." She didn't want to, but she pulled back again to see his face. She reached up and held the sides of his face.

Tears filled Adam's eyes. "I can't lose you."

"I know. I really don't think you will."

"You can't know that."

"You're right I can't. And as scared as I am, I have a peace in my soul that God's got this. Just like He always does. We have to trust Him."

Adam nodded, and Ella wrapped her arms around his neck. They held one another, and Ella pleaded with the Lord in her heart. Words couldn't form in her prayer: it was a prayer of emotion rather than words. She knew the Lord could protect her; she trusted that he would.

Her legs grew tired from being on her toes to hug Adam's neck, so she pulled away. "Give me a minute to gather my things and we can get out of here."

"That would be good." He stuffed his hands in his pockets, and she turned towards her desk.

Adam inserted the key Becca had given him into the door and unlocked it. He turned the knob and swung the door open. "Welcome to your new home."

"Thanks, Adam."

He followed her through the door into Becca and Jared's house and punched in the code in the alarm. "Becca said to make yourself at home. She and Jared will be home for dinner."

"Are you going to stick around once they get back?" The tightness of her voice gave away the unease that she was trying to hide.

"Of course. I pretty much told Becca I'd be staying before she even asked." He winked at her. Her shoulders dropped, and a bit of her tension faded. "Let's take your stuff upstairs. Becca said you can sleep in Dani's room. There's a daybed in there and Dani hardly ever sleeps in there anyway. Apparently, she's been giving Becca a run for her money in the sleep department."

"Yet, Becca still looks so put together."

"Pretty sure you can credit coffee and makeup for that." They walked up the stairs, and Adam said, "Becca's taking Hillary's murder personally."

"She is?"

"She was lead on keeping her safe."

"That would be hard."

Adam pointed to Dani's room. "Definitely. I think it will make her even more determined to keep you safe."

They walked into the nursery painted in lavender and adorned with owls. He set Ella's bag down and waited for her to put her pillow and other things down. Desire was growing inside him, leaving him feeling lightheaded. Once she released her things and turned towards him, he reached out and pulled her to his chest. His heart fluttered. She looked up at him, her beautiful brown eyes so warm and inviting. He stroked the hair away from her face. Her lips parted slightly. He smiled; his heart sped up. He slowly lowered his face closer to hers.

She looked down.

His eyes slammed shut.

"Not yet, Adam."

"I'm sorry." He opened his eyes.

She looked back at him. "No, don't apologize. I'm... just scared." She let out a shaky breath.

"Scared?"

"I know; it sounds stupid."

"It's not stupid. Been a while since you kissed anyone?"

"You could say that!" She pulled away and picked her school bag back up. "Let's go find a snack. Think Becca has anything good?"

Just like that the conversation was done, but his body was still reeling. He wanted to kiss her so badly. Really, he wanted more than that, but he knew Ella. That would wait until she was his wife. Was he really thinking about matrimony? He laughed at himself and followed Ella out the door and down the stairs. She chatted away about her day, and they searched Becca's cabinets and settled on some popcorn.

They laughed as it took a bit to figure out how to use Becca's popcorn popper. Ella chuckled. "Seriously, didn't think it would take a PhD to make popcorn! This is why I buy microwave popcorn."

"Yeah, but Becca's popcorn is never burnt. Can you say the same for yours?"

She scrunched her nose at him. "Not if I'm using *my* microwave."

He laughed. He reached over and pulled her close and kissed the top of her head. She looked up with him with rosy cheeks.

They settled on the couch, and Ella started grading papers and such. Being up for over twelve hours was starting to catch up with Adam. He had consumed ungodly amounts of caffeine, but it had all worn off.

"Adam, just lay down and go to sleep." She scooted away from him and towards the edge of the couch. She laid a pillow next to her legs and patted it.

"If you insist." He was grateful she didn't leave and encouraged him to stay next to her because that was right where he wanted to be. He laid his head on the pillow and let his legs hang of the end of the couch. He slid his hand under the pillow, but it ran into Ella's leg. He rubbed her leg and left his hand in contact. He closed his eyes, and she stroked his hair. The evil he had seen that morning faded into oblivion, and he drifted off to sleep.

Hushed voices brought him back to consciousness, but he refused to open his eyes. Sleep was too sweet, and Ella's voice sweeter. She was talking to someone, probably Becca. Yep, definitely Becca. He shifted slightly but realized a hand was resting on his chest. His lips turned upward. It had to be Ella's. He brought his hand up to meet it.

"Looks like Sleeping Beauty over here is finally going to join us in the land of the living." Ella's voice was light and relaxed.

Without opening his eyes, he said, "Eh. If I have to."

"Dinner is nearly ready, so yeah, you have to."

He opened his eyes. "Dinner? How long did I sleep?" He looked up at Ella who was still sitting where she had been when he fell asleep.

"Almost two hours."

"You let me sleep that long?"

She shrugged. "It helped me catch up on my work. I got all my grading done."

"Well, that's good." He let go of her hand and forced himself to sit up.

"Ada-Ada!" He smiled at Dani as she toddled over to him.

"Hey, little one! Come to Uncle Adam."

The toddler threw herself into Adam's arms. He picked her up and tickled her. She snuggled herself against his chest. How he loved this little girl!

He looked over at Ella. She was smiling at him. "She really likes you, huh?"

"Yeah, we're pretty tight; right, Munchkin? Fist bump?" Dani gave him the cutest little fist bump. "I taught her that!"

Ella laughed. "That's so cute!"

Dani wiggled down from his arms, and he and Ella stood and joined Becca in the kitchen. They helped Becca finish getting dinner ready, and they all sat down and had a nice dinner. Adam and Ella cleaned up dinner, and Jared and Becca spent a few minutes with the girls before bedtime. Adam didn't want the day to end. He didn't want to leave Ella. He wanted to sleep with her in his arms. He wanted to be sure she was safe. But he knew that wasn't possible. He had to trust God with her safety.

"Adam, you still look exhausted," Ella said.

He wandered over from the kitchen to where she sat on the couch. Jared and Becca had taken the girls up for bed, and they were alone for a few moments. "Here's your water." Adam handed her the glass.

"Thanks. You can go home. I'll be okay."

"I know. I just..." He sat down next to her and slid his arm across the back of the couch.

She turned towards him and smiled. Her hand traced his jaw-line. He hadn't shaved since Friday and hadn't showered since yesterday. He knew he needed to go home, but it felt as if his heart would rip out of his chest and stay behind if he left. She wrapped her arms around his neck and buried her head in his shoulder. His arms went around her and pulled her as close as he could. His heart pounded, and his breaths were shaky. She had no idea what she was doing to him.

"I'll be fine." She pulled back and looked him in the eye. "Go home and get some rest. I'll see you tomorrow."

"Ella's right." Jared's voice boomed behind him. "I could pull rank on you, but I'll stick to the friend side of it. Go home and go to bed."

He turned to see Jared. "Fine, but can I ask what progress y'all made after I left this afternoon."

"Well, Becca took a nap on the Captain's couch, but Amelia and Gavin talked to our potential suspect and most of the people he remembered seeing. Really doesn't seem that it could be him, despite your suspicions."

"Really?" His hope deflated. Part of him had hoped that it was Scott, but that was likely just because he didn't like the man.

"Yeah. He was around quite a bit. Amelia had talked about putting together a timeline of when he was sighted at the station, but I'm not sure how far she got on that before we decided we needed to look elsewhere before we spent too much time on him. We did have at least ten eyewitnesses."

"Any other possibilities?"

"Nothing promising."

Ella leaned further into him, and he tightened his arm around her. Maybe they shouldn't talk about it in front of her, but if they didn't, she'd ask him anyway.

"You guys will get him," she said with confidence.

"I hope so." He kissed her forehead.

Shortly after Adam left, Ella came out of the bathroom and put her things back in her temporary room. She was so grateful for the place to stay with friends that were trained to keep her safe, but she missed having a little autonomy. She was an independent woman, more because that's what life had dealt her than anything. She had adored being part of Amelia's family, but they still weren't *her* family. Maybe one day she would have a family. It wasn't something she ever really considered a possibility since she was a kid, but maybe she could imagine it with Adam. She fanned her warm cheeks with her hand.

She picked up her Bible and went back out of the bedroom and down the stairs. She was ready for bed, but not ready to sleep. Maybe if Becca was up she would see if she had any of her infamous tea. She rounded the corner at the bottom of the steps and headed towards the kitchen. She stopped in her tracks when she saw Becca in the kitchen. Becca slammed the tea kettle she had been filling on the stove and slammed a cabinet when she pulled out a mug.

Ella didn't know what to do. She didn't want to invade Becca's privacy, but would she be able to sneak back up the stairs? Becca turned and leaned against the counter. Ella then noticed the tears streaming down Becca's face. Becca looked up, saw Ella, and wiped her face. "Come in, Ella. Don't mind me."

"Are you sure? I'm sorry."

"Don't be. I'm just a hot mess today."

"Adam said it was a rough one." Ella walked the rest of the way into the kitchen.

"Yeah, it was. This case is just hitting too close. I have a hard time not letting cases get to me, especially when people we love are in harm's way. I would never forgive myself if something happened to you."

Ella's face warmed.

"We can't let anything happened to the woman that managed to tame Adam's wild side."

"I can't take credit for that. God gets all that."

"Indeed, He does, but I think He's used you."

She shrugged. "I guess."

"Don't be so modest. I've been praying for Adam and talking to him about God for a long time, but nothing broke through until you came into his life."

"Again, all God. His timing in everything is perfect. God used everything that's happened in Adam's life lately to draw him to Himself."

"So true. I'm still so grateful you are in his life. He's like a kid brother to me, and I've hated to see his life spiral out of control. But watching God work in it is amazing. And seeing how much he loves you…" Becca smiled wider. "It's just wonderful."

"Loves me?"

"Oh, yes, honey. That man loves you without a doubt."

"I still can't get over that he would want to be with me. I'm nothing like the girls he's dated over the years, am I?"

"No, I suppose not. But he was never really interested in any of those women. I honestly think he went out with them to maintain the persona he had built up."

"I don't get it."

"Me neither, but I don't think he's ever been in a relationship for longer than a few months. None of the girls he dated were more than a physical relationship. I've never seen him look at a woman like he looks at you. And when he put his hat on your head when you guys left the pub that night, I knew he loved you."

"Really?"

"Oh yeah, he never lets anyone even touch that hat. Plus, you're wearing his favorite sweatshirt."

Ella fanned her face again.

The tea kettle whistled, and Becca pulled it off the burner. "Would you like some too?"

"Yes, please."

Becca pulled out another mug and plopped a tea bag in each one. She filled the mugs with water. "Shall we sit on the couch?"

"Sounds like a plan."

The ladies went and sat and continued to chat. The wall Ella had felt when it came to getting to know Becca dissolved into nothing, and Ella found herself with a new friend.

After nearly an hour of talking, Ella said, "I'm sorry, Becca."

Becca tilted her head and scrunched her eyes. "For what?"

"I totally misjudged you. I never thought we could connect. You always seem so put together and sophisticated, and I'm, well, I'm the opposite."

Becca laughed. "Oh, Ella. But now you've seen the real me: a hot mess, crying and slamming cabinet doors."

Ella laughed, too. "And a good friend."

Ella climbed up on the step stool outside her classroom to hang some new artwork on the bulletin board Tuesday after school. She was surprised Adam wasn't there yet. The kids had only left a few minutes ago, but yesterday he had been there right away. A piece of her stomach felt uneasy, but he would probably be there soon. She'd give him five minutes, just long enough to hang the kids' pictures, then she'd allow herself to worry enough to call him.

"Hey, Ella."

She looked down and saw Lesley Peters one of the school's fourth grade teachers. "Hi, Lesley, how'd your day go?" She and Lesley weren't really friends, just acquaintances. They didn't really have much in common other than school.

"Not too bad. Kids were a bit squirrelly, but that's not unusual. How 'bout yours?"

"It was good." *Why is this so awkward?*

"So, I saw you've been hanging out with Adam Jamison. What's going on there? Because that surprises me. No offense, but you don't really seem like his type?"

Ella's throat constricted. "Um... well, we were friends as kids and have been reconnecting."

"Oh yeah? I didn't suspect he would be the type of guy you would hang out with either."

"What do you mean?" She knew what it meant but was curious to hear what Lesley would come up with.

"Well, just you're so uptight and he's so... such a player. I mean he's good, so I can't blame ya, but I thought you were a bit of a prude, so I didn't think you'd be getting it on."

Ella stared at Lesley. "Wait, what?"

Lesley's eyes grew wide. "Oh, you're not sleeping with him? I just assumed, seeing the way you two act and knowing the way Adam is."

"The way Adam is?"

"Yeah, don't you know? Adam is quite the ladies' man. He's gotten around." Lesley smiled.

"You?"

"Yeah, we had a little thing for a while. He's a great guy, but don't expect commitment, that's not his thing."

This conversation was getting to be too much for Ella. She stapled the final picture to the bulletin board. She needed an out but didn't want to be rude. She stepped off the ladder and looked down the hall. Adam was here. She closed her eyes briefly and swallowed the lump in her throat.

His smile did little to settle her queasiness. He had been intimate with this other teacher. How many other women would she run into in her hometown that had slept with her Adam? Why had he been so flippant with something so sacred?

"Hey, Ella!" His upbeat tone gave evidence that he had gotten a good night sleep last night and had a smooth day at work. "Hi, Lesley."

"Hi, Adam." Lesley smiled at him. "You're looking well."

"I am. You?"

"No complaints. Good to see you. I've got papers to grade. You two kids have a good night."

"Thanks." Adam looked at Ella.

She couldn't do or say anything. She was frozen, afraid she would say something she would regret. The heat grew in her face, part embarrassment, part anger. She didn't have a right to be angry, but she was. She hadn't been mad when she heard about his one-night stand, but something was really happening between them now.

She kept her mouth shut and simply walked past Adam and into her classroom. She busied herself with papers on her desk. Adam came in the room and shut the door. He didn't typically do that, but he had probably figured something was bothering her. He was a detective after all.

"Ella?"

She pursed her lips. What was she going to say?

His hand on her back made her jump, but he didn't remove it. "What's going on? Talk to me."

She was trying to bite her tongue, but she was going to have to say something. He was going to keep pressing her. "Nothing. I'm fine. How was your day?" The flatness of her voice surprised her.

"Oh, no you don't." He took her shoulders and spun her to face him. "Don't shut me out."

She sighed, but the anger didn't dissipate. "Have you seriously slept with every woman in this town?" She wished she could suck the words back in. The harshness of her words pushed him back.

His hands dropped from her, and he stepped away. His smile was gone. His eyes dropped to the floor. "Lesley." It was a statement not a question.

"Yeah. Made a point to say that you've gotten around."

His eyes closed.

"She also assumed that if you were hanging out with me that we must be sleeping together."

"I'm sorry."

Her voice softened. "You don't have to apologize."

"But I do." He looked back up at her and reached for her hands. "I know we haven't talked about what's going on here between us. We've talked about everything but that. But I hope something will come of it, and so I do need to apologize to you. I never in a million years expected to have you in my life again, but if I had known I would never... never have been with so many women."

"So many? How many, Adam?"

"Do you really want to know the answer to that question?"

"You know the answer?"

"I could figure it out."

She let go of his hands. "Figure it out?! You have to calculate? Holy cow, Adam!"

His shoulders dropped further. "I'm sorry."

She pinched the bridge of her nose. She didn't know what to do with this information.

"Have you never had sex, Ella?"

She looked up at him with a furrowed brow. "Well, obviously I have. How else would I have a case file at the police station?"

"That's not sex. What that guy *did* to you is not sex!"

"What do you call it then?"

"Rape. A crime. A sick perversion of something good."

She turned back to her desk and tossed a few things in her bag. He let her quietly gather her things. She just wanted to get out of the classroom. They walked out to his car in quietness. He opened the car door for her like he always did. He was a gentleman. How many times had that helped him get a woman in bed? She needed to stop. Why was this bothering her so much?

"I'm sorry, Adam."

He slid into the seat next to her. "Don't be. I'm the one that should have kept my pants on."

"I guess we're both damaged goods coming into... whatever this is we have going on."

He let go of the key that he had put in the ignition without starting the car and turned towards her. "Damaged goods? Me? Yes, but not you."

"Uh, yeah, I'm not a virgin, Adam. That was taken from me."

"That doesn't make you damaged goods. You survived a horrible attack. You are NOT damaged goods, and for all intents and purposes you are a virgin. Who made you think you weren't?"

She looked out of the car and off into the distance. She took in a deep long breath and let it out slowly before answering. "I dated, well, we didn't call it dating, we courted, this one guy, Miles, when I was in college. We were getting pretty serious, talking about marriage and all, so he started trying to be more affectionate, holding my hand and such. But I, as you can imagine, struggled with any physical affection—"

"Wait, you were talking marriage but hadn't been holding hands? Kissing?"

"Oh, no, he wanted to wait until the altar before kissing, and you were only supposed to hold hands if you were really serious. But anyway, one day he put his arm around me, and I had a flashback. Not a bad one, but still... he asked me about it and confronted me about being cold towards him. So, I thought it was time to tell him what happened, we were thinking we would get married after all. Well, I told him, and he freaked. Broke off our relationship. Said he wouldn't marry someone who wasn't a virgin."

"What a jack—"

"Adam!"

"Sorry, but it's true. What kind of low life breaks up with a girl because she was raped? That... that's just not right!" He slammed his fist against the steering wheel.

Her lips curled up.

He scooted across the bench seat of the old Chevy. One arm behind her across the seat and the other tucked her hair behind her ear and cupped the side of her face. "Ella, you are precious. In my sight and I know in God's. There is nothing damaged about you. What happened *to* you was awful, but it doesn't define who you are sexually, or any way. And if God wills it, I'll help you one day see that God has other ideas about sex. I've got a road to face figuring that out myself, but I know that God made it to be good. I realize that I've abused what He designed, and I confess that to you and Him. Please forgive me."

"I do, Adam." Tears welled up in her eyes. She fanned her face. "You wanna have sex with me?"

"Uh, yeah. But I realize that will only happen if we get married."

"You think you'd wanna marry me?"

"Since I was seven years old. That never changed, and the more I get to know who you are now, the more I know it's still as true today."

She smiled and leaned her face into his hand.

"Ella?"

She opened her eyes and met his deep gray eyes that reached into her being and comforted her heart. "Yeah?"

"I love you."

Her eyes filled with tears. "I know."

He pulled her into his arms, and she wrapped her arms around him and buried her face in his neck. He stroked her back and her hair.

"Wait a minute." He pulled her back to arm length.

Her heart stopped. Did he feel gypped that she didn't say I love you back. She just wasn't sure she was ready and didn't want to just say it as a response.

"If you didn't kiss that one guy, did you kiss anyone else? Any other boyfriends?"

Her heart thumped again. "He was the only one other than you that I ever dated."

"So, am I the only one you've ever kissed?"

Her cheeks turned to fire. "Yep."

He leaned up against the kitchen counter and steepled his fingers in front of his mouth. This was perfect. He would finally have Ella Perkins. Earlier today he had heard Adam tell the Sergeant that he would take Ella home after picking her up this afternoon. And since he finally knew where she was staying, he would get her tonight.

No one was home and the lock and alarm had been easy to bypass, so he had slipped into the house without being noticed. The stint he did with a security firm installing that exact model of alarms had made that task simple. Now he would wait in a quiet corner, and they wouldn't see him coming. She would not get the upper hand again. And he didn't care who got in the way. If he had to put a bullet in Adam's chest, so be it. He never liked that punk anyway. In fact, he anticipated having to kill him. He never left Ella's side. He would grab Ella, shoot Adam, and take Ella somewhere they could be alone since he would have to get Ella out of the cop's house.

He had watched Adam and Ella get in Adam's car at the school and left before they did. It was just a matter of minutes before they arrived. He could taste the victory before him.

Ella would be his final kill in Hazel Hill. Then he could move on to the next place he had lived. It was time to finish what he started with the five women that lived in that New Mexico town.

He pushed off the counter and made his way up the stairs to scope out the best place to wait for Ella. Maybe the closet would work. If she didn't come up right away, he could wait until she went to bed. He didn't like having to play it by ear so much. He'd rather have a plan in place. He had; she was supposed to be his third in this spree, but they had foiled it. That wouldn't happen this time. He was ready to play the deck, regardless of how it was dealt. He would have Ella. He checked in the first bedroom. Yes, this had to be the one she was staying in. He pulled open the bi-fold doors and slipped inside. He could wait.

CHAPTER 23

Adam held his hand out for Ella as she walked around the front of the car. He had actually told her he loved her. She slipped her hand into his and his heart soared. He loved her so much. They walked to the door, hand in hand.

"I'm looking forward to a nice, relaxing evening. I just wish I didn't have any papers to grade."

"I wish you didn't either." He winked at her. Her cheeks turned a couple shades pinker.

She pulled her hand away and dug out the keys. She unlocked and opened the door. They entered the quiet house, and Adam punched in the alarm code. He kicked the door closed and pulled Ella into his arms. She squeezed him tight. She smiled up at him, and he kissed her forehead.

"I'm going to run up and change into something more comfortable. I don't know why I wore these pants today; I really don't like them."

He smiled at her. "Okay. They look good on you though."

She blushed again. "I get the impression that you would think I look good in a brown paper bag."

"Yeah, you could pull it off." He raised his eyebrows at her.

She shook her head and turned and ran up the stairs. He stood there appreciating the view as she went up. *Thank you, God, for bringing Ella and me together. Help me to do right by her.*

"A-a-dam?" Ella's voice shook as she called from upstairs.

He took the stairs two at a time and found her in the hallway with her yoga pants in her shaking hand. "What's wrong?" He pulled her into his arms.

"I don't know," she whispered. "I just got a really uneasy feeling. I thought the closet door was closed all the way when I left this morning."

He kept his left arm tightly around Ella and pulled his pistol off his hip with his right. "Okay. Let's make sure it's nothing." He removed his arm from her. "Stay behind me but close."

She nodded and followed him into the room. The closet was on the right along the same wall as the door. The closest of the pair of bi-fold doors was slightly ajar. He squared himself with the closet and pointed his gun at the door. He took three deep breaths and motioned for Ella to open the door.

She nodded and moved next to the closet. Staying to the side she clutched the knob and pulled the door open and jumped to the side.

There was nothing.

He released the air trapped in his lungs. He stepped forward and opened the other side. The shelves on that side made it impossible for anyone larger than Callie to fit in there.

"Oh, I feel so silly." Ella ran her hand down her face.

Adam holstered his gun and reached for her. "Don't. Better safe than sorry, right?"

She nodded and fell into his arms.

"Let's check the rest of the house, just to be sure."

"I won't argue with that."

"How 'bout you lock this door and change while I give the whole house a once over?"

She nodded.

He checked under the bed before closing the door and waited until Ella locked it before making his way through the rest of Jared and Becca's house. He checked all the closets, under the beds, showers, the garage, laundry room, and every other corner of the inside of the house, being sure all the doors and windows were locked as he made his way through. When he made it back upstairs he knocked on the door. "All clear."

The door opened. "Okay, good. Thanks."

"Anytime." He gave her another hug and kissed her head before they went downstairs.

"Kinda wish we had gone back to my place today," he said as they settled on the couch for Ella to get her grading done.

"Sorry. You're probably bored. Why don't you watch something?" She handed him the TV remote from the end table.

He took the remote. "That won't be too distracting?"

"Nah. I'll be fine. And thanks for coming back here today. I know Becca appreciates it since she won't have to make dinner."

"That's the least we can do for her." He flipped the TV on and changed the channel to ESPN. He slouched into the couch and leaned his head back. He kicked off his shoes and put his feet up on the coffee table.

He opened his eyes and stretched. He must have fallen asleep; apparently, he still needed to catch up. Ella was no longer next to him. He looked around the room and found her in the kitchen. He looked at his watch. How on earth was it already 5:45!

He stood and ambled to the kitchen. "Sorry I fell asleep." He came up behind Ella and slid his arms around her waist and leaned his head against hers.

She hugged his arms. "Don't worry about it. Apparently, you were tired. But you're up now. Time to help with dinner." She stepped away and smiled at him.

A knock on the front door startled them both. "Stay here. I'll go see who it is."

Instinctively he reached for his gun as he peered through the peep hole. His hand left his side and opened the door. "Amelia? What are you doing here?"

"Nice to see you, too. Can we come in?"

"Of course." He stepped aside, and Molly and Carter came in followed by Amelia. He closed the door and relocked it once Amelia was inside. "Still, why are you here? Not that I mind, just curious."

"Well, we turned onto our street, and Caleb called and said not to go home."

"Why?"

"He wouldn't say. Is Ella safe?"

"I'm right here." Ella joined them in the foyer.

"Good; that's why we came here." Amelia and Ella exchanged smiles.

He wanted more answers though. "Where was Caleb? Was he at the house?"

"I doubt it. Should be getting off work in about half an hour."

"Hmmm…"

Ella came over and took his hand. "You think he had one of his little premonitions?"

The sound of the garage opening distracted from Ella's question.

He said, "Sounds like Becca's home."

The three moved towards the kitchen while they waited for Becca to come into the house. A moment later Becca and the girls came inside. "Hey, guys. Good, you're here," she said when she looked at Amelia. The girls went into the family room where Molly and Carter were.

"What's up?" Amelia said.

Becca set her briefcase on the counter. "Jared just called me and said that Caleb called. They're headed to your house to check on an uneasy feeling Caleb had."

Ella's hand tightened around Adam's.

"Caleb's leaving work early? That's not a good sign." The creases in Amelia's forehead deepened.

Becca said, "Why don't you and the kids plan on staying for dinner? Caleb can join us too."

"I'd like that. Do you have enough?"

"We can throw some chicken nuggets in for the kids; they'll probably like that better anyway."

Ella and Becca moved into the kitchen to finish fixing dinner. Adam took a hold of Amelia's shoulder and directed her away from ear shot of anyone else. "What do you think is going on?"

She looked back and forth, checking to be sure no one was listening. "I'm not sure, but I left my phone sitting on my desk earlier today..."

"And..."

"Well, there was a text in there yesterday to my mom about Ella... and Carter's room..."

"Are you saying someone looked at your phone?"

"I don't know! I didn't mean to leave my phone on my desk, but I had to run to the bathroom... I'm used to you being there... and not having to be so cautious. It was stupid."

"Wait, did it say that she was staying here now?"

"No. It said, 'Since Carter has been sleeping with Molly with Ella there he hasn't come in our room.'"

"Amelia! Your mom knew Ella was staying there?"

"Not until yesterday. I mean she knew a friend was staying with us because the kids have stayed over there a lot more recently. But I *never* told her it was Ella, honestly. And she doesn't know where Ella is now, don't worry. I haven't told anyone she's here."

"Okay. But based on that text it's possible he might think she was still there."

Amelia nodded.

"Did you tell Becca your phone could have been seen? Did she by chance see who picked up your phone?"

"She was in the bathroom too."

He sank backwards.

"Adam, he could be in my house, and my husband is about to go in there." Her lip began to quiver.

He pulled her into a hug. "He'll be okay."

She squeezed him but pulled back. "I know, but still...".

"I know. So, we pray."

"Oh, it does a heart good to hear you say that." Her shoulders relaxed.

He squeezed her shoulder.

"Everything okay?" Ella came around the kitchen island.

"Yeah," Amelia answered. "Just worried about Caleb."

"No doubt," Ella said.

Adam's phone rang. He pulled it off his belt. It was Jared. "Jamison."

"Hey, we're at Caleb's. I want you to join us. And tell Becca to sweep the house and turn on the alarm after you leave, including the outside sensors. Are Amelia and the kids there too?"

"Yep. They're here. I swept the inside of the house thoroughly a couple hours ago. But I'll run the perimeter before I leave."

"Okay. Good. See you in a few."

Jared hung up without giving him any other indication of what was going on. He turned back towards the three ladies, worry etched into each of their faces.

"What is going on?" Ella was shaking.

"I don't know. Jared just wants me to join them. I'm going to walk the perimeter and make sure all is safe here, and Becca, Jared wants you to turn on the alarm to def-con five."

"You're the only one that calls it that," Becca said; one side of her lips curled up.

"Yeah, but I wish you had had that system three years ago."

"You and me both."

Adam looked back at Ella. Her eyes were glazing over. "Ella?" She didn't respond. He closed the gap between them and put his arms around her. "Elly, you're safe." He ushered her out of the kitchen toward the foyer. "Babe," she was shaking, the flashback was in full swing. "You're safe. Do you smell the chicken cooking? You're here with me at Becca's house." He sang the first hymn that came to his mind, and she buried her face in his chest. *Be Thou my vision, O Lord of my heart, naught be all else to me save that Thou art. Thou my best dah, dah dah, dah dah dah dah-ah, Thou in me dwelling, and I with thee one.* He couldn't remember any more of the words.

He felt her relax in his arms, and her trembling subsided. "You okay?"

She kept her head buried in his chest and shrugged.

He stroked her hair and back. "It'll be okay."

"That's what you keep saying... Adam," she looked up at him, "I don't want you to leave."

"I know, but I have to. You're safe with Becca and Amelia. Trust me I wouldn't leave you with them if I didn't trust them implicitly."

"I know. I'm not worried about me. I'm worried about you."

He cupped the sides of her face in his hands. He tilted her head forward and kissed her forehead. "I'll be careful. I love you."

She smiled and nodded. He was grateful that she believed him.

"I'll be back as fast as I can."

She threw her arms around his neck pulling him down to herself. He wrapped his arms around her waist and pulled her up until her toes barely touched the ground. "Please."

Adam pulled up in front of Amelia and Caleb's house behind a squad car. He jumped out, walked up the path, and went through the open front door. Jared and Caleb stood there talking to Gavin.

"Hey, y'all."

"What took you so long?" Gavin teased.

Caleb's lips turned up. "He had to say good-bye to Ella. That takes him forever."

"Everything okay there?" Jared's tone much more serious than the other guys.

"Yeah. Stress like this is a trigger for Ella."

Gavin said, "Oh. I didn't realize."

"It's okay." Adam looked back at Jared. "What's going on?"

"Let me show you."

Adam followed Jared up the stairs to Carter's room. The closet door was ajar. A shudder coursed through Adam's body. What if this had been the room Ella had walked in earlier.

Several crime scene techs, including Jocelyn were in the room. The open window caught his eye. "Bet they didn't leave that open this morning before they left."

"Probably not," Jared said. "Not to mention when we walked around the house when we first got here the window was closed."

"What?! So, you just missed him?"

"Looks like it." Jared turned and looked out the window.

Adam crossed his arms. "So, he did read Amelia's phone."

Jared's head jerked back around. "What?"

Adam explained about Amelia's phone.

"He must have been real smooth. I was at my desk most of the day today."

"Who was there?"

"Same people who are always there."

"He may have walked by and swiped it and then slipped it back. It wouldn't be unexpected for someone to walk past her desk."

Jared nodded.

Adam walked over and looked out the window. It was a full two story drop with no bushes or anything to soften the fall. "That couldn't have felt good to drop from."

"No," Caleb's voice came from the doorway, "but totally doable; I've done similar."

"So how did you miss him?"

Jared answered, "Well, like I said when we got here, we walked the perimeter first. We then entered the house. We're guessing he heard us enter, but since we didn't talk, he probably realized it wasn't you and Ella and decided to make an escape. Would have had him if he hadn't jumped. I was in Molly's room when I heard the thump of him hitting the ground, but I didn't see anything and couldn't get outside fast enough."

Caleb said, "Glad we decided to move her."

Adam swallowed. "Me too."

Adam walked out of the sandwich shop with a bag full of subs for the team. He had volunteered to get their late lunch since he was too antsy to focus on the leads, or lack thereof . He was still on edge after yesterday and was counting the minutes until it was time to go pick up Ella. She had an early release today, so it was t-minus 42 minutes. Deliver lunch, eat, and pick her up.

The more he thought about the fact that someone had been inside Carter's closet, the angrier he became. And to top it off, Ella had just been sleeping in that room two nights earlier... it was too close. The night the creep had tried to get her off the street had been bad enough, but that had been his fault. This was different. Personal space had been violated. The kids he cared about, in addition to the woman he loved, being put in danger was more than he knew what to do with.

He walked across the parking lot towards his car that was parked next to the curb under a tree that created a little shade from the midday sun. A pair of coated-metal picnic tables sat under the tree and were empty even though they were often a popular spot for patrons of the sandwich shop to sit, especially on such a beautiful day.

God, I'm new to this whole 'relying on You' thing. I know we haven't talked much yet, but I just don't know what to do at this point. Give me wisdom in how to protect those I love, and some divine intervention to show us who the killer is would be great.

Adam opened the passenger's side door and set the bag on the seat. Footsteps sounded on the concrete behind him.

"Hey, Jamison. How *is* your sister?" Scott's voice was like fingernails on a chalkboard.

Adam took in a sharp breath and slammed the car door before turning around and facing the man that made his skin crawl. "Scott. My sister is none of your business."

"Oh, come on Adam, your sister and I were close. I'm just checking in on an old friend."

Adam stepped on the curb with Scott to make himself taller. "She's made it very clear that she never wanted to have anything to do with you ever again, so I think that includes telling you anything about her today."

"You're a spoil sport. Where's she living these days? She find herself another man? Although, I'm not sure how she could have found anyone as good as me."

"Would you give it a rest already? I'm not talking to you about her."

"What are you getting so riled up about? I'm just asking some friendly questions. No need to get your panties all in a twist."

Adam's blood boiled. He'd like nothing better than to clock the man, but he took a calming breath and kept his cool. His hands were starting to shake, so he shoved his keys back in his pocket and stepped towards the back of the car, careful not to put his back towards Scott.

"I haven't seen her around town. She live in these parts? If she is still in the area, I'd love to hook up with her. Remind her of what it's like to be with a real man."

Adam clenched his fists as his heart pounded in his ears. He could feel his arms tremble. *God, help me not beat this man senseless.*

Scott took another step closer to Adam, putting himself with in Adam's reach. "Did I ever tell you how great your sister was in bed? She was a wild woman. Amazing really for how young she was."

Adam glanced around the parking lot. It was almost two and the lunch rush had died. There were only a dozen cars in the strip-mall's lot. He really needed an out. He needed someone to walk out and give him an excuse to get away from Scott, but Scott just stepped closer.

"So, Adam, tell me, how's Ella in bed? I almost envy the man who got to take a stab at her seventeen years ago."

Adam couldn't contain himself any longer. Adrenaline coursed through his blood. He pulled his hand up and without a thought, pulled his arm back before sending it forward. His fist collided with skin, and then the bone of Scott's jaw met the bones in Adam's hand. Scott's head wrenched at the contact, and he sidestepped in attempt to stay on his feet.

Scott's fist came flying at Adam's face and collided with Adam's cheekbone. He stumbled to the right. He regained his footing and lunged at Scott. Adam shoved Scott, but Scott grabbed his shirt and pulled Adam with him. Adam's knuckles collided with the edge of the table, but he caught his balance and pushed himself back upright. Scott punched Adam in the side. His ribs compressed sending the air from his lungs. Adam sent another punch at Scott's head ignoring the pain in his hand.

"ADAM JAMISON!" a familiar female voice called from beyond his car, but he wasn't sure who it was.

Adam managed to block a punch coming his way. Two sets of footsteps came up beside them.

"Break it up!" A man's voice boomed, and he grabbed Adam's shoulder and sent him stumbling backwards off the curb and against his car. "Knock it off!" It was Tyrone Washington, a firefighter from Caleb's station. Ty stepped between them blocking Scott from lunging at Adam again.

Adam smacked the side of his car and stormed around the back. AJ Jackson was the other firefighter with Ty. "What on earth, Adam?" She grabbed his arm.

He jerked his arm away and winced at the pain that surged in his cheek, side and hand. His entire body shook. Why had he let Scott get to him?

He looked back past Ty, but Scott was gone. "Where'd he go?"

Ty turned towards Adam. "He just took off. You want me to go after him so you can arrest him?"

"No."

AJ grabbed his hand. "Let me look at your hand."

He let her raise his arm. He clenched his fists again. His knuckles ached. AJ examined his hand. It was bloody. He should never have hit Scott, and he knew it. But he had just kept pushing. It was almost as if he wanted Adam to punch him.

Adam walked into the squad room with the sandwiches and resisted rubbing his cheek again. Ty and AJ had checked him over and insisted he press charges, but he knew he couldn't. As it was, he could be in so much trouble. He had thrown the first punch.

None of the team was in the squad room, so Adam went to the conference room. He found them there.

"It's about time!" Gavin declared.

Amelia stood and walked towards him. "What on earth happened to you?"

Becca looked up and jumped out of her seat. She came over and grabbed his chin and moved his head back and forth.

"Just had a little altercation, but I'm fine."

"With whom?" Jared crossed his arms and leaned back in his chair.

"Doesn't matter."

The door closed behind him. "I'd beg to differ." The Captain's voice was serious.

Adam turned. "Sir, I promise, it doesn't matter."

"But it does. Scott Rebus is in my office claiming you assaulted him in a parking lot."

The bag of sandwiches dropped from his hand.

CHAPTER 24

Ella looked up from hugging her students goodbye and saw Gavin Riley walk into her classroom. Her insides froze. What was he doing here? Where was Adam?

Gavin waved at her and smiled.

She could trust him, right? Adam wouldn't have let him come get her if he didn't trust him, right? *Come on, Ella, you go to church with Gavin. God, I can trust him, right?*

The kids ran out the door and Gavin walked over. "Hey, Ella."

"Gavin. What's going on? Where's Adam?"

"He's fine. Didn't Becca text you?"

"I haven't looked." Ella walked over to her desk and picked up her phone. Sure enough, a new message from Becca was there stating that Gavin was on his way and that Adam was fine. "Would you like to explain why you both insist that Adam is fine?"

Gavin pressed his fist into his palm and smiled. "Because he's... fine."

"Now I don't believe you."

Gavin's face turned serious. "He'll have to explain. I'll take you to the station when you're ready."

She packed up quickly, and they headed out the door.

Ella walked through the door of the police station that Gavin held open for her. They walked across the lobby towards the detectives' squad room. Her chest was tight. She wanted, no needed, to see Adam. She walked past the Captain's office; inside Jared was talking to Scott Rebus. She looked back at them when Scott said, "I'm pressing charges. He needs to be on desk duty. He shouldn't be carrying a gun if he can't keep his anger in check." He pulled an ice pack away from his left cheek revealing a developing shiner.

"What happened to him?" Ella whispered to Gavin.

"I'll let Adam explain."

She raised her eyebrows at him.

They approached Becca who was standing by their desks. Gavin asked, "Where'd they put Adam?"

"He's still in the conference room."

Ella turned and headed straight there.

"Ella, wait," Becca called after her.

Ella pivoted to look at her friend.

"Ah, never mind, just go see him."

She furrowed her brow but didn't wait for anyone to say anything else. In a few more steps she was at the conference room door. She turned the door handle and swung the door open with such fury that it slammed into the wall behind it. "Adam!"

He looked up at her from where he sat with his feet up on the table. He also had an ice pack to his face, and his knuckles looked worse for the wear. She walked to him, and he dropped his feet from the table.

She pulled out a chair next to him and pulled the ice pack away from his eye to see the damage. "What happened?"

"Scott."

"Good gracious, Adam."

"You should see the other guy." His voice was thin rather than light. His attempt at humor unsuccessful.

"I did. And I think you need to work on your right hook."

A slight smile flashed through his eyes, but his jaw was rigid and his shoulders tight. He was still agitated.

Jared came in the door in a huff. "Your turn, Jamison?"

Adam sat up straight and leaned forward defensively. "Look, he started it."

"The Captain isn't impressed."

Adam tossed the ice pack on the table. "Of course not, Scott's his little pet. You saw the Captain's response to our looking at Scott as a suspect."

Captain Baker came in. "I want to hear your side now."

"Doesn't anyone want to listen to my side first?"

The Captain crossed his arms. "No. We're more inclined to believe you, Jamison."

Adam relaxed an iota.

Ella had never seen him so angry. She didn't know what to do other than sit back and listen. She wanted to step in and say something, but she had nothing to contribute.

"Were you the one to throw the first punch?" Captain Baker asked.

"Physical or verbal?"

"Physical."

"Yes."

Ella's heart sank. Adam could be in a lot of trouble. What if his gun *was* taken away? She shuttered at the thought. Adam's gun brought a sense of safety, a line of defense.

"But he started it." Adam practically spit the words out.

"Now you sound like one of my third graders," she muttered.

Adam heard it and scowled at her. Her heart shrank back.

The Captain continued, "He wants to press charges, Adam. I'm working my best to keep that from happening, but I'm not sure how much I can do. I will have to take some disciplinary action."

"You going to take my gun? I have to protect Ella."

"I know. That's why I refuse to do that. Instead I'm going to give you a few days paid leave, so that it looks like I did something. You're a great detective, but I don't want to be visible in my playing of favorites."

"You're favoring me over Scott?"

"Yes, unless you tell me you punched him for no reason."

"No, sir. He…" Adam swallowed. "He was trashing my sister and Ella."

"I figured it would be something related to Heather or Ella. And I believe you; you've never given me a reason not to. And during your time off you have an under the table assignment. Twenty-four-hour protection duty. You keep Ella safe; do you understand?"

"Yes, sir."

"Guys"—the Captain looked at Jared and back at Adam before looking at Ella—"I don't think Ella should spend more than a night or two, at the most, in the same location. Mix it up. Don't give him any reason to know where she is. He got too close last night, again."

Jared crossed his arms. "What if we drop a rumor about where she might be and set up a trap to catch him?"

"Might be worth pursuing. Ella, I'm not sure school is the best choice either at this point."

"Actually, sir, we have a long weekend starting tomorrow. They are scheduled teacher workdays, but I think Mr. Withers will understand. We don't have school again until Monday."

"Perfect. Looks like you and Adam can have some quality time. You keep him out of trouble; he keeps you safe."

She smiled at the Captain, and he winked at her.

"We'll get him, Miss Perkins. Sergeant Johnson, tell your detectives they have until Monday to get this guy."

"Yes, sir."

The Captain left, and Jared looked at them. "Our house is safe, Ella. Do one more night there, and we'll find another place for you for tomorrow."

"Okay." Jared left, and she turned to face Adam again. His face was still taut. She reached out to him, but he stood instead of taking her hand. What was wrong? Was he still agitated about his altercation with Scott?

He moved towards the door.

"Adam?"

He dropped his shoulders and turned around.

"Are you mad at me?" Her stomach came up to her chest.

His eyes softened. "I didn't appreciate you throwing me under the bus in front of my boss. I get it. 'He started it' sounds immature, but I... I don't know what else to say."

She felt like she'd been punched in the gut. "I'm sorry, Adam. I had at least three kids say that to me today, but I should never have said that, especially in front of the Captain." She looked down at the floor and fiddled with her hands in her lap. "I'm sorry."

Adam came back towards her, knelt on the floor in front of her, and took her hands. "I know. Let's get out of here."

She met his eyes. Letting go of one hand she reached up and traced around the wound on his face. "Okay, and maybe we should work on your defenses. He shouldn't have been able to get a punch in."

He smiled at her. "You're going to show *me* how deflect a punch?"

"Yep, and work on that right hook. You could have done more damage."

He laughed. "So, should we spend tomorrow at the gym and you can show me all the things you learned in kickboxing that they didn't teach me at the academy?"

"Yep, that sounds like a plan."

Ella took the board book Dani offered her and pulled the toddler onto her lap. She read the book to her while Adam and Callie cleaned up after dinner. Becca had run out to the store once they had finished eating, and since Jared still hadn't been able to come home Ella and Adam had offered to watch the girls. Ella's heart floated. It was fun to watch Adam interact with the girls and hear them call him uncle.

Dani wriggled down again and waddled over to the basket of books and retrieved another. As Ella waited for the little one to come back to the couch, her eyes fell on Adam's overnight bag. After leaving the station they had gone to Adam's for a while and played with Rusty. Adam had packed a bag for the night. He was taking the Captain's orders seriously. He wasn't going to leave her side; twenty-four-hour protection. Her heart fluttered.

"Ook, ook," Dani said, pulling Ella's attention back.

She read the next book, and Callie came over and hovered around them. Adam followed Callie into the family room and winked at Ella before looking at Callie and asking, "Did mean Miss Perkins give you homework?"

Callie giggled. "Yes."

Ella shook her head at the glint in Adam's eye.

"Why don't we get it done now so you have the next four days free?"

The eight-year-old groaned.

"He's got a point, Callie. It won't take you long; just get it out of the way."

Adam said, "I'll help you. It's that or wait for your mom. Who would you rather do it with?"

"You." She scurried across the room and got her backpack. The two sat at the table working on Callie's homework while Ella read yet another story to a sleepy Dani.

When Ella finished *Good Night, Moon* Dani tapped the tips of her fingers together. "More? You want me to read that one again."

She nodded.

"Okay." But before she could finish reading it again the little girl had fallen asleep in her arms. "Oh, sweetie, you were tired." She shifted the little girl against her chest and settled deeper into the couch. She soaked in the sleeping baby's warmth, but the weight of Dani's body was nothing compared to the heaviness in her heart. She had held babies from time to time over the last sixteen and a half years, but holding someone else's baby wasn't the same as holding the child that you carried inside your body for nine months. Would she ever be called Mommy? After her breakup with Miles she just assumed it would never happen. She had let go of the dream and embraced spinsterhood. No one would ever want her to mother their children. She looked over to the kitchen table where Adam sat next to Callie helping her process her math problems. Tears welled up in her eyes. All her hopes and dreams that had been murdered years ago had been resurrected.

Jesus, is it possible? Could motherhood really be part of my future? What plans do you have for Adam and me? Could we really have something permanent? But will we survive? Or will the monster hunting me ruin it all? Oh, Jesus, please keep us safe.

She tried to blink back the tears, but they were coming on too strong. They silently rolled down her cheeks in steady streams.

"Thanks, Uncle Adam."

"Anytime, Callie. Why don't you go put your pj's on before you play?"

"Okay."

Ella listened to Callie run up the stairs, but she kept her head down, unsure how she would explain the tears. But Adam came over anyway.

He sat down next to her and put his arm across her shoulders. "You okay?"

She nodded. She kissed the toddler's head before looking back up at Adam.

"You want this"—he motioned to Dani and the hallway were Callie had just disappeared—"one day?"

She nodded again.

Adam wiped the tears from her cheeks and pulled her closer. "Me too." He kissed her head.

"You do?"

"With you and only you."

Adam unzipped the side pocket of his bag and pulled out an old, leather-bound Bible. Ella had gone upstairs to get ready for bed but promised to come back down in a little bit. While she was gone, he would take a minute to look at his Bible again. When he opened it for the first time in twenty years on Sunday, the whole gamut of emotions had washed through him. His dad had given him this book when he was just learning to read. Told him that this book had all the answers he would ever need. He just needed to read it and take it to heart. Too bad his dad hadn't taken his own advice. He barely spoke to the man anymore. Just a call on Adam's birthday and one on Christmas. Heather insisted that Adam give their dad another chance, but he just didn't know what to say. But something was stirring in Adam's heart, it was probably the Holy Spirit tugging him towards reconciliation. But the Holy Spirit would need to do a little more work before Adam could bring himself to pick up the phone and call his dad. But maybe they could talk beyond pleasantries and trivial chit-chat when his dad called in a couple of weeks on Adam's birthday.

He stood and walked over to the couch where he would be sleeping. Jared and Becca hadn't put up a fight at all about him staying here. They understood.

"Adam, here's some blankets and such." Becca walked into the room.

He set his Bible on the coffee table and took the stack of blankets from Becca.

"Wasn't sure what you'd want…"

"Thanks."

"You're welcome. I can only imagine how you're feeling every night when you have to leave her somewhere. I know you trust that we'll keep her safe, but it's not the same, is it?"

"No, it's not."

Becca wandered towards the kitchen. "You really love her, don't you?"

Adam smiled as his cheeks filled with heat. He followed her and leaned on the breakfast bar, and Becca filled the kettle with water. "Yes, yes, I do."

"I'm so happy for you, Adam. I can't wait until this is all over and we can all go out for karaoke again. I want to hear the two of you sing again."

His heart did somersaults. "Sounds like fun."

"Have you figured out another place for Ella to stay tomorrow?"

"I have."

"And...?"

"I'm not telling. Not going to tell anyone. I just can't risk talking about it at all."

"Fair enough."

Plus, you wouldn't approve. He knew Ella would baulk at his idea as well, but he didn't care at this point. Staying alive was more important at this point than propriety.

He looked toward the stairs to see Ella rounding the corner at the bottom. His heart flipped again. She was beautiful. How was it possible that a woman could make pajama pants, a ponytail, and his baggy sweatshirt look so amazing?

"Oh, you've got it bad." Becca's voice was just loud enough for him to hear.

He shot her a scowl that he couldn't keep as a smile took over his face. "You could say that."

"Hey, Ella. Would you like a cup of tea, too?" Becca asked.

"That'd be great, thanks." Ella walked over to him and put her hand on his back.

"Oh, can't bother to ask me, though could you?" Adam teased Becca.

"Where are my manners?" Sarcasm seeping from her voice. "Would you like some, Mr. Jamison?"

"Nah, I'm good."

"That's what I thought." Becca turned and pulled two mugs out of the cabinet.

Ella laughed. The sweet sound toyed with his heart.

He put his arm around her as they waited for Becca to pour water over the tea bags.

"Here you go." Becca slid Ella's tea across the breakfast bar. "Good night, you two. I'm headed to bed. Don't stay up too late. Oh wait, neither of you have to work tomorrow, but still, what kind of mother would I be if I didn't say it." She gave them a toothy grin.

Ella laughed.

"Sure thing, Mom. Good night."

Becca left, and Adam looked down at Ella who had wrapped her hand around her mug. "Shall we snuggle on the couch?"

"Yes, please." She moved away from the counter. "I seriously can't believe I'm okay with that."

"Me neither, but I'm glad you are."

They went to the couch and settled in close to one another.

"Is that your Bible, Adam? The one you had as a kid?"

"It is." He leaned forward and picked it up. "I've been trying to read it some over the last few days."

"Awesome."

He flipped it open to Psalm 146. "Read this while I ate breakfast this morning. 'Do not put your trust in princes, in mortal men, who cannot save... Blessed is he whose help is the God of Jacob, whose hope is in the LORD his God, the Maker of heaven and earth, the sea and everything in them— the LORD, who remains faithful forever.'"

Ella had leaned close and looked at the words with him. "Adam, what a perfect reminder right now. Thank you for sharing."

Her face was so close to his, but she looked down. When she looked back up her brow was furrowed, and she was biting her lower lip.

"What's wrong?" he asked.

Her eyebrows relaxed. "Nothing. I'm just trying to figure out how to say something."

He tilted his head. Her eyes sparkled, confusing him further. "You can tell me anything."

"I know. I just want to say it right... I can't believe how close we've gotten again." Her eyes held his steady, but her hands were fidgeting. "I'm so happy. But more than that..." She took in a deep breath and let it out slowly between her lips. "I love you, Adam."

His heart swelled. She loved him! "I love you too."

"I know." Her cheeks were as red as a firetruck.

He pulled her close. He never wanted to let go.

CHAPTER 25

Adam bent over and rested his gloved hands on his knees as he tried to catch his breath. He looked up at Ella who had her boxing gloves back up ready to dish out a few more punches. Sparring had been a great idea, but she was giving him a run for his money in the ring. He would never have guessed how skilled she had become in boxing.

"I thought you said you took kickboxing, as in martial arts, not boxing!" he said.

"I have a well-rounded education in all methods of self-defense."

"I'd call those last few punches more offense than defense."

She laughed. "A good defense is a good offense, right? Now come on, you aren't tired yet, are you?" Her smile was going to undo him. She was beautiful with her hair in a sloppy bun, no makeup, and her forehead glistening with sweat. Her snug t-shirt revealed her curves. He longed to draw her in and give her a kiss, a deep, intense kiss that would express the love that overwhelmed his heart.

He let a long breath out through his mouth and righted himself again putting his mouth guard back in place. He pulled his hands up to a defensive position in front of his face and waited for Ella to take another shot. She bounced toward him, light on her feet. She made a quick jab to his left and hooked a punch at his right. He blocked both, he threw back two quick jabs with his right hand, but she responded by coming close and throwing her leg behind his. Before he knew what happened, he fell backwards and landed flat on his back. Ella knelt on one knee next to him and put a gloved hand on his chest, but he wasn't giving up so easily. He grabbed her and pulled her down and rolled her to his other side and pinned her to the mat.

They were both laughing. But the overwhelming urge to kiss her despite their mouth guards sucked the air out of his lungs. He patted the side of her helmet and pulled himself away. He stood and offered her a hand up.

Once she was on her feet, she gave him a playful shove and strode away. "Oh, no you don't." He grabbed her hips and spun her back around and into his arms. She laughed so hard her mouth guard fell out. He pulled his out, keeping her as close as possible. Maybe he could finally kiss her. Desire showed in her eyes. They sparkled, and her lips parted, but he waited. He didn't want to kiss her before she was ready. He was beyond ready, but he wanted to honor her in every possible way. He lifted his head and pulled her closer instead. She leaned her head against his chest and hugged his waist.

"I love you, Ella."

"I love you, too."

Was this really happening? Was he really holding Ella in his arms? Hearing her say that she loved him back? It almost seemed too good to be true. But he needed to focus on something else or he was going to kiss her. "I talked to Heather this morning."

"When did you do that?"

"While you were upstairs getting ready."

"Did you tell her about your decision to follow Christ?"

"I did that on Sunday. I called her so late that I woke her up."

"No wonder you were so tired on Monday."

He nodded. "Today, after I told her about what happened with Scott, we talked about you."

"Oh yeah?"

"Yeah. She's really happy to hear that we're... whatever we are."

"And what are we, Mr. Jamison?"

He shrugged. "I don't know, what do the kids call it these days?"

"Hooking up?"

"Oh, no, babe, that is not what that means!"

"Oh!" Her eyes were as big as saucers.

"Well, what did we call it when we were kids, going out?"

"So, I'm your girlfriend?"

"Absolutely!"

Her eyes disappeared with the breadth of her smile. Her cheeks had already been flushed from boxing, but they took an even deeper shade of red. His heart soared. Ella Perkins was once again his girlfriend. Life was perfect.

Ella pulled her things out of the bed of the truck Adam was borrowing. She couldn't believe she had agreed to this. Staying at his house had to be one of the most foolish things. Not that she thought they would do something they shouldn't, but it just wasn't wise. It wouldn't look good. But then again, who knew? Adam had told her explicitly that while he did tell Caleb, he hadn't told anyone else. Not even Amelia or Becca. And a rumor had gone out that she was staying at a safehouse. Maybe the team that was going to set up there would catch the guy.

She adjusted the bag on her shoulder as they walked to the front door together.

Adam inserted the key into the door and was about to turn it when Ella's heart stopped. She grabbed Adam's hand and stopped him from unlocking the door.

"What is it?"

"Rusty. Why isn't Rusty barking? He always barks when you unlock the door if not before!"

"It's okay. Mrs. Williams, my neighbor who helps out with him, took him to the groomers today. She'll let him in the yard when she brings him back in a few hours."

She released the tension in her body with a large sigh. "Oh, okay. That scared me, especially after what that monster did to the cat."

"No doubt. Sorry I didn't tell you. I just didn't even think about it."

"That's okay."

Adam opened the door, and once they were inside, they set her things down. She stood and waited for Adam to punch in the code on his alarm.

She had wanted to kiss him at multiple points while they had been sparring, but she was still scared. She didn't know what she was doing. Thirty-three years old and she hadn't kissed anyone in almost twenty years! Would it be like riding a bike? But Adam had kissed plenty, what if he didn't like the way she kissed?

He turned back towards her and smiled and raised his eyebrows suggestively. Her heart flipped. She jabbed at him playfully in attempt to relieve the tension she felt. But it didn't help, this tension was different than any she was familiar with. "I had fun today."

He grabbed her and pulled her close. "So, did I." There was that look in his eyes again. He wanted to kiss her. "Ella, you're driving me mad."

She tilted her head to the side and tried to give him a confused look.

He chuckled. "Can I kiss you yet?" He stroked her face.

All air vanished from her lungs. "You sure you want to kiss me? I really don't know much..."

"Oh, yes, I do. If my memory serves me correctly you weren't too bad."

"That's because you had no idea what you were doing back then either."

"True enough, but I'm sure you'll remember what you're doing." His face inched closer to hers. "Just follow my lead."

Her heart pounded as her mouth watered. She swallowed. She rested her hands on his chest. They were both still sweaty and stinky from sparring, but that didn't matter. Adam's fingers traced her face;

her skin tingled at his touch. She reached her hand up and traced his hairline. Her eyes fell upon his shiner from yesterday's scuffle with Scott. She loved his passion, even if it got him in trouble. He had stood up for his sister. Her fingers traced along his strong jaw, and his hand slid into her hair and gently rested on the nape of her neck. She let her hand slide back to his chest. His face came closer to hers. His other hand on her waist drew her even closer raising her to her toes; their bodies touched. She looked at Adam's lips. When they were too close to see, she closed her eyes. His lips touched hers. All sounds of the world vanished as all she could hear was blood surging in her ears. His lips were gentle and moved slowly. She responded mirroring his actions. The salty taste of his lips... her heart floating... the stirrings in her soul... all things she was unacquainted with but wanted to know better. His lips pulled back slightly, but she took the lead and kissed him again. She felt his lips curl upward under hers as he kissed her back. This time she pulled back. She opened her eyes and looked deep into his gray eyes, the color of the North Carolina sky right before a storm. She couldn't move. She didn't want to. The silly grin on his face made her heart flutter a little more. She bit her lower lip for a moment before Adam came in for another kiss. She giggled and returned his kiss.

He pulled her back to arm's length. "Ok..." He let out a heavy breath. "That's enough for now."

She giggled again. She felt like she could cry out of sheer bliss.

"I love you."

"Not as much as I love you." She grabbed the front of his t-shirt and pulled him down for another little kiss. She walked over to her things. She pulled out her water bottle and took a long swig before turning around again.

Adam stood there smiling at her. "You should go take that shower you were wanting. When you're done, I'll take a quick one, and we can start dinner."

"Sounds like a plan. What shall we do after dinner?"

"Movie marathon?"

"Perfect, unless of course Amelia calls and says they caught the monster, then we can go out and sing a little karaoke!"

"Even better."

She smiled at him. Oh, how she hoped this would all be over soon, and they could start exploring what their future could hold without the constant threat looming over their heads. She grabbed the bag she would need and kissed Adam one more time before disappearing into the bathroom.

Adam could barely keep his feet on the ground after kissing his sweetheart. He floated down the hallway on cloud nine. Ella's sweet voice floated out of the bathroom as he turned into the utility room.

A mighty fortress is our God, A bulwark never failing;

One of his favorite hymns, even though as a kid he had not fully appreciated the meaning behind the words. He grabbed the laundry basket full of clean clothes from off the floor in front of the dryer. He peeked in the washer to make sure it was empty. Ella's voice came strong through the walls.

Our helper He, amid the flood of mortal ills prevailing:

He turned out of the laundry room and walked into his bedroom. The hairs on the back of his neck stood up.

For still our ancient foe Doth seek to work us woe;

The cold steel of the barrel of a gun pressed into the back of his head. The laundry basket dropped to the floor.

His craft and pow'r are great, and armed with cruel hate, on earth is not his equal.

"On your knees, Jamison," like fingernails on a chalkboard, an all too familiar voice commanded. He had no choice but to obey as the gun pressed into his head forced him forward.

Ella's voice still rang down the hall.

Did we in our own strength confide, Our striving would be losing;

They wouldn't survive this without God on their side. *God help us!*

"In the chair now. And don't you make a sound, or I'll cut out your—no, Ella's tongue."

Were not the right Man on our side, The Man of God's own choosing:

Dost ask who that may be? Christ Jesus, it is he,

Adam sat in the chair and his captor duct taped his hands together behind the chair and taped his legs to the chair. The man kept himself to the side making it impossible for Adam to fight.

Lord Sabbaoth, his name, From age to age the same, And he must win the battle.

"I thought you preferred knives not guns."

The man sneered. "I do what I must. Now shut up while I go get the little tramp. And remember what I said about Ella's tongue."

Oh God! Adam's insides ignited into raging lava. He was staring death in the face. How were they going to survive? *Jesus, we need your divine intervention. Give us a way out!*

The wood of the bathroom door cracked and slammed open. It had been kicked in. Ella screamed.

CHAPTER 26

Amelia tapped her pen on her desk. She was so sick of not knowing who was trustworthy around the station. Knowing that a killer walked in their midst was driving her crazy. She reached into her desk and pour herself a couple of antacids. The heartburn was worse today than it had ever been. The anxiety of the case wasn't helping.

"Riley," she called over to Gavin who had just put his feet up on his desk. "Do you have any other ideas?"

"Would I have put my feet up if I did?"

She pressed her lips together.

"We'll get him."

"I hope so."

Her cell phone rang Caleb's unique ringtone. She pulled it out of her blazer pocket, never again would she leave it on her desk. "Hey, Babe."

"Hi, is everything going all right today?"

"Yeah..." She didn't like it when he randomly asked questions like that. "All's been quiet here."

"Okay. Are Adam and Ella still there?"

"No, they said goodbye when they left the gym maybe an hour ago."

"Hmm... okay. Maybe I'll shoot Adam a line."

"What's wrong, Caleb?"

"I don't know; that's why I called."

Ella shook. The monster dragged her down the hallway and into Adam's room. Her heart and mind swirling like a tornado. *Jesus, please let Adam be okay.*

He had turned the lights off as soon as he burst into the bathroom. And the hall was so dark that she couldn't see the face of the man whose hand grasped her arm so tightly it would leave a bruise tomorrow, if she survived the night by some miracle. He threw her onto the floor once they were in the room.

"Ella!"

She looked up and could barely see Adam restrained to a chair.

The familiar voice of her attacker said, "You know the drill, Ella. On your knees. And put your hands out in front of you."

She complied. He had the upper hand; she couldn't take him out. Her mind refused to play out an option to defend against him this time. He wrapped duct tape around her wrists so tightly it hurt. He grabbed her and threw her on the bed and taped her hands to the headboard. She tried to kick him, but he was ready for that and was able to avoid her kicks.

"Oh, Ella. So spirited. Well, your fate is sealed."

She wasn't going to let him win. He may kill her body, but God had her soul. She picked up where she left off singing "A Mighty Fortress."

And tho this world, with devils filled, Should threaten to undo us,

We will not fear, for God hath willed His truth to triumph thro' us:

The Prince of Darkness grim, We tremble not for him;

His rage we can endure, for, lo, his doom is sure, One little word shall fell him.

Their captor laughed. The laugh was haughty and sounded like pure evil. "Sing all you want. It changes nothing. Your God cannot save you now." He flipped on the light that was on Adam's bedside table.

"You."

He smiled but said nothing.

God, help us. There was one more verse she hadn't sung yet. A reminder of that God is God over all earthly woes. So, she sang it, even while the monster that now had a face cut her shirt and her pants off her body. Leaving her exposed.

That word above all earthly pow'rs, No thanks to them, abideth;

The Spirit and the gifts are ours Thro' him who with us sideth:

Let goods and kindred go, this mortal life also;

He ran the tip of his knife down the length of her nearly naked body. Her whole body shuddered. This really was happening. It would all end here for her and Adam.

The body they may kill: God's truth abideth still, His kingdom is forever.

———•———

As if pregnancy didn't increase her anxiety everyday anyway, now Caleb was feeling unsettled again. Some days it was such a blessing to have a husband who had such a keen sense of the spiritual realm, but today it just increased her heartburn.

"What's up, Johnson?" Gavin asked, his feet still propped up on the corner of his desk.

"Caleb's just being Caleb again. He's going to call and check on Adam."

"They're fine."

"I hope so."

Captain Baker walked up behind Gavin, and as soon as he noticed his boss, Gavin dropped his feet to the floor, and he sat up straight. Amelia chuckled.

"So, what's up guys? Working hard or hardly working?"

"Taking a break for a minute. Feeling stuck though. I just don't know where else to look. Oh, and since you know my husband, you should know that he's feeling uneasy."

"Oh, that's not good. Does he have a lead for us? Maybe he should have become a cop. Apparently, we could use a little more intuition around here."

Before she could answer one of the front desk people came in escorting a young man. They walked straight to Amelia.

"Detective Amelia Johnson?"

"Yes, that's me." She stood.

"May I see some identification? I'm under strict orders to only give this to Amelia Johnson or Adam Jamison."

She glanced down at the badge he was wearing. The laboratory they had left Kyle's DNA sample with.

"Absolutely! That was so fast!" She pulled out her ID and showed him.

"We make a special point of speeding along law enforcement requests." He had her sign a paper.

She took the package and inhaled deeply. This was it. Inside was hopefully the identification of their killer.

"What is it, Johnson?" Gavin stood and came over.

"Is that what I think it is?" The Captain pointed at the package.

She nodded.

"Let's go to my office. Riley, you can come too. Where are Becca and Jared?"

"Went to get coffee."

"Here we are."

The Captain clasped his hands together. "Good. Everyone in my office. Hopefully this is the break we need." The five went to the Captain's office and closed the door and blinds. "All right, open it, Amelia."

She took a deep breath and opened the well secured envelope. She slid the piece of paper out and set the envelope down on the Captain's desk.

Jared asked, "You guys going to fill us in to what this is?"

The Captain answered, "Not unless it's helpful. Well?" he asked Amelia.

She read the document. *We were able to compare the DNA you provided us with all North Carolina police records, employees of the departments along with criminals. The results are attached.* She flipped the paper and scanned the lab report until she found the only piece of information she cared about. She found it. "99% paternal match." Her hands shook and the documents dropped to the Captain's desk.

"What is it, Amelia?" Becca came close and put her hand on Amelia's shoulder.

Amelia looked up at the Captain. "It's Scott Rebus."

Captain Baker took a step back as if blown away by the information. "I trusted him. I was a fool."

"He fooled us all, Captain." Amelia couldn't believe she had thought he was innocent.

"Now, I think it's time to fill us in," Jared said.

The Captain explained the source of the DNA sample, about the child, and the trip to Charlotte.

"Is he here today? Let's go arrest him," Gavin said.

"I haven't seen him at all today," Jared said.

Fear washed over Amelia. "I have to call Adam!" She pulled out her cell and dialed Adam's as fast as she could. It went straight to voicemail. She tried again. Same.

"Try Ella." Becca said, the worry lines digging deeper into her forehead, much as Amelia imagined hers had.

She dialed Ella's. Straight to voicemail. Her heart raced. This wasn't good.

"Where are they staying?" Gavin asked.

"I don't know. He wouldn't tell anyone."

"Surely he told someone."

Jared walked closer. "Maybe he told Caleb."

"Good thought." Amelia dialed her husband's phone. He answered on the second ring. "Did Adam tell you where he's taking Ella tonight?"

"He did, but I'm not supposed to tell you."

"Caleb, I appreciate your loyalty, but we know who the killer is. And I can't reach Adam or Ella!" The fear started catching up with her. "Oh, Caleb, he could have already killed them. He could be killing them right now, it's been over an hour since they left."

"Calm down, Hun. I'm coming to the station."

"But you're working."

"Yep, I'm bringing my crew. We'll stay with you all and be on hand when we get to where they are... just in case."

"Ok, but we need to know where we're going? Warrant and all."

"You won't need one. I'll be there in less than five. I love you."

"I love you too. Hurry."

Adam swallowed the bile that rose into his mouth at the sight of Scott touching Ella. He had to get out of this duct tape, but his arms shook with anger. *Think, Adam. No. Pray.* He closed his eyes briefly. *Hey God, really could use some help here! How do I get out of this tape? He didn't wind it around too much. You think I could pull out of it? God, I have to do something. I can't sit here and watch him hurt Ella. The screw!* Adam shifted his hands to where the exposed screw stuck out of the back of the chair.

"This is new for me, Jamison, having someone watch. I have to say I like it." He moved away from Ella and came close to Adam. "It's a whole new rush to have someone who loves the girl watch me decimate her." He spun the knife in his hand. "And who better than Heather's bratty little brother. I've been thinking about how I want this to go. Initially, I had thought I'd make it simple and just put a bullet in your head. But where's the fun in that? I saw how close you were getting to Ella and that's when I realized that maybe I could expand my business."

Adam wiggled his hands. He had to get out.

"Oh really, you're going to fight it. It's time to give up."

He jabbed the tape against the screw; he almost had his hands out, but he stopped.

"Let's be clear about how this is going to go down. I'm going to take my sweet time with the lady over there. And you're going to watch." He pointed the knife at Adam's face. "And if you don't watch I'll make her suffer even more. Her pain is my favorite part, so I'll start by cutting off one finger at a time. So, pay attention. After that we'll play it by ear. But you annoyed me too much when we were younger and that whole fist fight yesterday, yeah, I'm going to kill her first. Then, I'll kill you."

Adam's jaw was locked in place. Ella was sniffling; her sobs caused her to hiccup.

Scott stepped back toward her and backhanded her across her face.

Adam lunged forward, but the duct tape kept him secured to the chair. "Keep your hands off of her, Scott!"

Tsk, tsk, tsk. "You're much too feisty, Jamison. That's just not going to work. I don't want you actually getting free. Hmmm... let's start the dying process with you." Scott stood over Adam and leaned one hand on the arm of the wooden chair and with the other hand pointed the knife at Adam. "Now, if I stab you here"—he poked the knife at Adam's chest—"I'd have to contend with bone, not to mention you'd die quite quickly. And I don't want that."

Adam's pulse raced, and his stomach churned at the smell of the man's foul breath.

"Now, your abdomen is a good place to stab you, but again, I don't want to hit that major artery running down the center so, let's see, off center, right about here should suffice."

Adam was so close to having the duct tape off his hands, but it wasn't quite off. He needed more time. But he didn't have it. He looked over to Ella. Their eyes met. The longing in her eyes matched his heart. She lipped the words "I love you."

With the best Han Solo expression he could muster considering the circumstances, he lipped, "I know." He needed to hold her again, they had to survive this.

Scott pulled his hand back.

"Scott don't!" Ella shouted her voice cracking under the weight of her emotions.

Scott snorted and plunged the knife into Adam's abdomen.

Ella screamed. "NO!"

When Scott pulled the knife out the intensity of the pain registered. He groaned. His body collapsed forward, the stinging and burning sensation overtook his whole torso. The world went fuzzy for a moment. *Oh Jesus, send in the cavalry! But they don't know where we are or that we need them. Send your angels. Give Caleb one of those feelings he gets. He credits them to you. Now would be good.* He tried praying to keep his mind off the pain. He needed to apply pressure, but he couldn't do anything.

Scott's voice cut into his thoughts. "Now, that's good."

Adam opened his eyes. The look of satisfaction on Scott's face was downright terrifying. This man really got pleasure from causing pain. Adrenaline surged through Adam's body. He wasn't going to let this end here. He wasn't going to let Scott win. He worked again at the duct tape on his wrists.

CHAPTER 27

Gavin eased the chain link gate open as quietly as possible. They still weren't a hundred percent sure what the situation was, but they were taking positions around Adam's house. Gavin's truck, the one he had loaned Adam so that Adam's Chevy didn't act as a neon sign to where they were, was parked in the driveway, pointing to them being here, but that didn't mean they were still. Gavin made his way closer to the house. He was trying to get a clue as to whether or not they were here.

Amelia's voice crackled in his earpiece, "Anything, Riley?"

"Nothing. The windows are all covered," he whispered. "Can't tell if there is a light on, let alone if anyone is inside."

He crept further along the house. As he approached one of Adam's bedroom windows, he stopped and tried to see in. This window was also completely covered, so he listened. Nothing. He moved on to the next window along the back of the house, also part of the back bedroom in the little bungalow. Same deal. But an unseen force urged him to wait before he moved on.

Muffled by drywall, insulation, and siding, he heard the unmistakable sound of Ella scream!

"They're in there!" Gavin fought to keep his voice low. "Did anyone else hear that scream?"

"Scream?" Amelia asked.

"Yes, and it sounded like Ella. Can we go in?" Gavin moved back towards the back door on the porch.

"Not yet. We need eyes!"

Ella screamed again as Scott came close to her with the knife dripping with blood. Adam's blood.

"Now you," Scott came onto the bed next to her. "It's time to have a little fun. Does this bother you?" He held the knife close to her face. "Your love's blood dripping all over you?"

She tried to turn her face away, but he touched the knife to her jaw and forced her to look at his by pressing the side of the wet knife against her skin.

A drip of blood fell on her chest. Adam was dying in the chair across the room, and she was helpless to do anything to save him. She had to get free. She pulled at the duct tape that bound her hands to the headboard. But he had used a majority of the role to tape her hands.

"That's it. Struggle." He snorted a sinister laugh.

He liked that she was fighting the restraints, but what was she to do. She couldn't give up. Their lives depended on it.

"How did you find us?" Adam coughed out. Ella's heart broke at the sight of the strain in his face because of the pain.

"As soon as I heard that stupid rumor, I knew she wasn't going to be there. You've been entirely too careful so far. I didn't think you'd actually be stupid enough to bring her here, but I had hoped. And if you had shown up without her, I had a plan."

Adam leaned his head back. The tight muscles in his face and neck proved that he was in so much pain. "Oh, my gosh. The front door."

Scott looked towards the door. "What about it?"

"Ella, did you lock the front door?"

Ella shook her head. Why would Adam be worried about the door right now?

"Mrs. Williams. What if she comes in? I think I forgot to lock the door."

Scott tossed the bloody knife on the foot of the bed. "For crying out loud. You really are the worst security guard. You'd think, with a killer after you, you'd lock the door." Scott turned on his heals and left the room.

"Adam!" She pulled at the tape and tried to twist her hands.

"We'll be okay." He struggled back and forth. "I almost... There!" Adam's arms snapped out of the duct tape. The blood was soaking his shirt, but he moved as if he wasn't hurt. He reached down and pulled the tape off his feet. He gripped his stomach as he stood and stumbled towards the bed. "Now..." he moaned. "Let's get you out."

He grabbed the knife Scott had left on the bed and crawled towards her. Blood seemed to pour out of his wound. He reached up and cut her hands out of the duct tape. He was losing too much blood. Her hands fell free, and Adam dropped to the bed next to her; he was struggling to stay conscious. "Get... my gun!"

She rolled over to the bedside table. Her wrists hurt from struggling against Scott and the tape. Would she be able to grasp the gun tightly enough to shoot the man who was trying to kill them? And could she really shoot someone, possibly taking their life? Adam had taught her to shoot to kill. And their lives now depended on her. She pulled open the drawer. She glanced back over at Adam, he was unconscious, he needed to get to the hospital immediately. Her fingers met the cold steel of Adam's pistol. Her wrist ached, but she tightened her grasp on the heavy weapon.

"What do you think you are doing?" Scott sneered.

Her eyes shot up and met his. He pulled his side arm. She pulled the gun from the drawer.

CHAPTER 28

Amelia couldn't stand the waiting. She was running point from the van like Jared had ordered. The SWAT unit along with the detectives were positioned and ready to breech on her command, but she couldn't risk that he had a knife to Ella or Adam's neck. They needed eyes on the situation. Were they even still alive?

Pkew Pkew Pkew Pkew Pkew Pkew! The unmistakable sound of gun fire resonated through the silence surrounding Adam's house. Amelia jerked the radio mic to her mouth and yelled, "NOW! Breech! Go, go, go!"

She jumped out of the van and ran to the house faster than she knew her swollen legs would take her. The SWAT were in the door first followed by Jared and Becca. If she hadn't been so pregnant, she would have pushed past them. Her partner was in this house somewhere possibly dead.

"Clear."

"Clear," various voices called from throughout the house.

"Back here!" Gavin shouted from the back of the house near where he had gone in through the back door.

Amelia pushed Jared out of the way and ran to the bedroom. She stepped over Scott who was bleeding and struggling for breath on the floor with multiple gunshot wounds in his chest. Her eyes went to the bed. Ella sat on the bed, barely dressed, cradling Adam and pressing a bloody blanket to Adam's abdomen. She rushed to Ella's side. Someone called for the EMTs.

A gun sat on the bed next to Ella. Had Ella shot Scott?

"Sergeant!" She looked at Jared and pointed to the gun. He nodded and went over and collected it.

Ella was shaking. Amelia wished she still had her blazer for Ella's shoulder's. Her friend was staring at Adam. "Ella?"

"Where's Caleb?" Ella's voice was loud.

"I'm here."

Amelia looked up to see her husband stepping over Scott. He tossed her the blanket in his hands as he went around to the other side of the bed. She draped the blanket over Ella's shoulders.

Caleb asked, "Can you tell me what happened, Ella?"

———•———

Ella's ears rang from the gun shots making it nearly impossible to hear Caleb. She could see that he was speaking to her. "Huh?" Her brain was also foggy. The adrenaline from the whole situation made it hard to process the sounds she could hear. She opened her mouth and tried to pop her ears that helped a little.

"Ella, can you tell me what happened? Was Adam shot or stabbed?

"Stabbed."

"Okay. You can move your hands now."

She looked down and saw Caleb's hands on hers. She pulled her hands back and looked at them. They were covered in Adam's blood. Her whole body shook. Amelia wiped Ella's hands with a towel and tried to direct her away from Adam, but she couldn't. She ran her hands through his hair.

"Ella, let Caleb help him."

"Ok." She leaned down and kissed Adam's warm lips.

"Let's go over here, Ella." Amelia pulled her away by the shoulders, but she kept her hand on Adam as long as possible. "Let me look at you." Ella willingly turned as Amelia directed her to sit on the side of the bed turned away from where Caleb and his partner worked on Adam. "Are you hurt? Is any of this blood yours?"

She stared at Amelia. As hard as it was with the ringing, she understood what Amelia asked, but she didn't know the answer. Had she been shot? Had Scott gotten a round off before she put him down? She didn't know. "I... I don't know."

"Okay, that makes sense. Let me look you over to be sure."

She nodded. It was like she wasn't even in her body. The shock was overwhelming. She needed Adam, but Adam was dying on the other side of the bed. Amelia lifted the blanket to check her body but kept her body hidden from those around them.

"Looks like you're okay, Ella. Let's get you cleaned up and dressed."

Ella couldn't move.

Amelia leaned over until her face was even with Ella's and reached up and wiped the tears from her face. "He's in the best hands. They're going to get him to the hospital, and Adam is going to make it through this. You hear me?"

She nodded. She looked back at Adam. They were loading him onto a backboard, so they could move him to the stretcher that had somehow come into the room. She couldn't look to where Scott had fallen. She didn't want to know if he was alive or dead. Had she killed him? They started rolling Adam out of the room. She jumped to her feet. "Wait, I have to stay with him."

Amelia's hand grasped her arm. "No, hun. They have to get him to the hospital ASAP. Let's get you cleaned up and dressed, and I'll take you there myself, all right?"

She turned to her friend. The flood gates opened. Amelia pulled her into her arms and let her cry on her shoulder. As the sobs subsided, she raised her head and looked at Amelia. Her friend had been crying too. They smiled weakly at one another.

"Clothes?"

"Bathroom."

She stood and let Amelia guide her out of the bedroom. Scott was no longer there. Amelia led her to the bathroom, but as she turned into the room the memory of Scott busting down the door came rushing back. She froze, and the tunnel drew her in.

"Ella, you're safe. You're right here with me, Amelia. We have to get your clothes so you can go to the hospital to be there for Adam."

She was able to pull herself out of it long enough to get her clothes out of her bag and grab Adam's sweatshirt she had kept since last week. But she couldn't change in there. She went into Adam's spare room that held his workout equipment and pulled on her jeans and t-shirt as fast as she could. She had to get to the hospital. She needed to see Adam.

Jocelyn took a deep breath before going into her cousin's house that was currently a crime scene. She had seen Ella before Amelia took her to the hospital to check on Adam. Ella had pulled her into a hug unlike anything she had ever expected from Ella. They had been friends since they were kids, never very close, but friends none the less. And Adam. Her cousin was in the hospital with a stab wound. How was she supposed to go in and take crime scene photographs of his house? These things weren't supposed to happen to family. She prayed as she stepped over the threshold, but her words felt empty.

Her heart quickened slightly when her eyes fell on Gavin Riley. She moved toward the hallway.

"Hey," he said to her.

"Hi, how bad is it?"

His head wavered side to side. "Not too bad, just don't think about where you are, and you'll be fine." His hand came to rest on her shoulder.

"Easier said than done, Gavin."

"I know." He squeezed her shoulder.

"Where's the bulk of the evidence? I'll start there."

"The bedroom."

"Okay." She patted Gavin's side and moved back to the living room. She set her bag down. The other techs were pulling out their equipment to start taking samples, she followed suit and pulled out her camera. She attached her flash, checked her settings, and put an empty memory card in. She went down the hall towards Adam's bedroom, but glanced into the utility room where Gavin was with Becca.

"You think that's how he made it in?" Becca asked.

Jocelyn stopped and turned into the little room.

"Anything picture worthy in here?" she asked before Gavin could answer Becca.

"Maybe." Gavin looked at her. "I think he came in through the back door. But there isn't any sign of forced entry."

"Did he find Adam's spare key?"

"Maybe, you know where he keeps it?"

"I do. But it's not easy to find. But how would he have gotten through the alarm? Shouldn't the alarm agency have been notified of an unauthorized entrance?"

"That's the part I figured out. I've been churning around in my mind how he got into Amelia's house, so when I saw that Adam has the same system, I checked it. Probably could take pics of this." He motioned to the keypad by the back door and slid on a rubber glove.

Jocelyn took pictures of each screen he showed her and Becca.

"Looks like he knew how to circumvent the alarm code, like he knew the system inside and out. Here's when Adam and Ella would have arrived. Adam punched in the code in the front door unit. But this time before that? I know Adam and Ella were at the gym during that time. Plus this"—he pointed to an icon on the side of the screen—"shows that it was an technician code rather than Adam's."

"Nice work, Riley," Becca said.

Jocelyn smiled at Gavin and headed towards Adam's bedroom. She stopped before entering the room and photographed the blood that was all over the doorway and floor. She was sure to get the bullet holes in the wall before the techs removed the bullets. Once she had finished those, she had to steel herself for what she would see when she entered the bedroom. But her efforts weren't enough. Her stomach churned at the sight of the blood covering Adam's bed.

A hand rested on her back, and Jocelyn jumped. She turned to see Gavin.

"You okay?"

"Not really, but I just have to do my job. I've seen worse, but…"

"This is different."

She nodded.

"We'll go to the hospital as soon as you're done, all right?"

"That would be good." She turned back towards the scene and swallowed the lump in her throat and got her job done.

Ella pushed her way through the automatic doors of the hospital emergency room and ran to the desk. "Where is he? Adam Jamison. They just brought him in an ambulance."

Amelia came up beside Ella. The young woman behind the counter said, "I'm sorry. Are you family?"

Amelia held up her badge. "I'm Detective Johnson. He's a cop and my partner. She's with me and is also his girlfriend. Can you please find out how he is?"

"Detective Johnson? Related to Caleb Johnson?"

"Yes! That's my husband; he brought Adam in."

"Okay, give me a moment, and I'll go see what I can find out. You can go in the waiting room over yonder." The woman motioned around a corner and stood. She disappeared through the double doors that said, "Emergency Treatment Area."

Ella knew she should go to the waiting area, but her body wasn't responding to that knowledge.

Amelia took her elbow and without a word guided her towards the waiting area. Once in the room full of chairs decorated in brown and beige tones, Amelia spoke. Ella could hear the strain in her voice even though she masked it behind soft words. "Ella, why don't we sit?"

"I can't. I have to see Adam."

"I get it, but they aren't going to let us see him until they've finished patching him up."

Ella's lungs deflated, and she looked up at her friend. Amelia was struggling with this too. *Adam is her partner!* She needed to not forget that she wasn't the only one who loved Adam.

The double doors to the ER opened and Caleb came through. Ella's chest tightened.

"Hey." He came to where they stood and took his wife into his arms.

"How is he?" Ella asked.

"He's doing... ok. They will be taking him to surgery soon. The knife didn't hit anything too vital, but they need to repair the damage and close off any bleeders."

Ella took a deep breath and let it out slowly, but her anxiety didn't ease up.

Caleb put his hand on her shoulder. "He's going to make it."

She looked in his eyes and nodded. She looked down at her hands that she was wringing. Despite having washed them at the house, Adam's blood was still dried under and around her fingernails. Her hands started to shake again.

"He's going to be okay," Amelia reiterated Caleb's promise.

Movement at the entrance caught her eye as she looked back up at Amelia. It was Jared and Adam's mom.

"Ella." Adam's mom came up to her.

"Mrs. Jamison." They both hesitated; they hadn't interacted in years. Mrs. Jamison still lived in the large white house three doors down from her mom, but the mothers' friendship had never been very deep, and Ella's mom had always judged Adam's mom more harshly than she intended. So, after the kids drifted, their moms naturally did as well.

"I'm so sorry, Ella." Mrs. Jamison pulled her into a hug. "Adam's told me how close y'all have been getting."

Ella released the tall, older woman. "They say he's going to be okay."

Tears slipped out of Mrs. Jamison's eyes. "Because of you. Sergeant Johnson said you saved his life."

Ella shrugged.

After wiping a tear off her own cheek, Mrs. Jamison reached toward Ella and in a dear, motherly fashion brushed the strains of Ella's hair that had found their way out of her ponytail again out of her face, just as she had when Ella was a little girl running around playing with her son. Ella smiled. But Mrs. Jamison's hand froze beside Ella's head. Her eyes grew wide and her pupils dilated. "Is... is that Adam's blood?"

Ella's hand darted up to her hairline. She must have at one point pushed her hair out of her face while her hands were still wet with the blood of the man she loved. "I'm sorry; I tried to clean it up."

Mrs. Jamison's body wavered.

Caleb said, "Mrs. Jamison, why don't you sit?"

Jared stepped in behind her and led her to a chair. "Take a few deep breaths, Mrs. Jamison."

Ella sat but stood again, unsure of what to do.

Amelia asked Caleb, "Should we move to the surgical waiting room?"

He said, "I'll go check again if they've moved him to surgery yet." Caleb turned and left.

Amelia turned to Ella. "Let's go see if the reception desk can hook us up with a washcloth and towel, and maybe we can get you cleaned up a bit better."

"Probably a good idea."

———•———

Ella paced the surgical waiting room. The room was filled with loved ones, yet Ella felt alone. Adam had become such a rock in her life in the last few weeks that she wasn't sure what to do without him by her side. *Oh Jesus, I know you're here with me now, but I want Adam here too. But he's still in surgery. It's been,* she looked at the clock, *almost two hours already. Why hasn't the doctor come in yet and said he's fine? I don't think I can take much more of this waiting.*

She continued pacing and looked around at the people who had gathered. Adam's mom was there, and Amelia, Caleb, and Jared were all present. Jocelyn, Gavin, and Captain Baker had come with Becca about twenty minutes ago, although Becca was not in the room now. But the biggest surprise to her were her parents. They sat on the opposite side of the room from Mrs. Jamison. Her mom was warming up to the idea that Adam and Ella were moving forward in their relationship, but she and Ella's father were still very skeptical. They hadn't even been open to having dinner with Adam yet. But they were here, and Ella appreciated it even if they still had no idea how to comfort their only daughter.

Becca walked through the door and came straight to Ella and handed her a Styrofoam cup full of brown liquid. "Coffee? I think I remembered how you like it."

"Thank you." Ella smiled and took the coffee.

Becca gently grasped Ella's upper arm. "How are you holding up?"

She shrugged and shook her head. "I don't know. I just want Adam." Her hands started to shake.

Becca took the cup back and set it down on a table. "Come here." She opened her arms and pulled Ella into a hug. Ella melted into her new friend's arms, and the tears started flowing again.

She ran out of tears and pulled back from Becca's shoulder. "I'm sorry; your shoulder is all wet."

"Do you really think I care about that right now?" Ella smiled.

"Let's sit."

Ella sat in the chair next to the table that held her coffee. She picked it up and took a sip. She grimaced.

"Not enough sugar?"

"I don't think it would matter."

"Got to love hospital coffee."

Ella chucked lightly at Becca's comment. But the light faded, and her mind started to play back why they were here. And it was coming like a flashback. That stupid tunnel was closing in, and she could see Scott's face, the mean, sinister look he had as he reached for the gun on his hip. She hadn't had a choice, had she?

"Ella..." Becca touched Ella's arm.

Ella jerked out of the flashback and spilled her coffee on her knee.

"Oh, no. I'm so sorry," Becca said.

"Don't worry about it." Someone handed her a few napkins, and she dabbed at the mess.

"You were having a flashback?"

"Yeah... I never heard what happened to Scott. I don't know if he made it."

"I didn't either. Do you want to know?"

"I guess; I'll have to know eventually."

"Jared," Becca called across the room to where Jared sat next to Ella's dad.

"Excuse me, sir." Jared got up and walked over to them. He squatted in front of them and cocked his head to the side ready to listen to his wife.

In hushed tones, Becca asked, "Did you hear if Scott made it or not?"

"I know he was still alive when they arrived at the hospital, but I don't know past that. I can go find out."

Ella didn't want to know, but she needed to. "Would you?"

"I will. I'll be back in a few. But, Ella, regardless of whether he makes it or not, you did the right thing. I wasn't joking when I told Mrs. Jamison that you saved Adam's life." Jared squeezed her shoulder and stood. She smiled at him as best she could with the weight of life and death hanging on her shoulders.

Jared nearly ran over someone when he walked out of the door. She couldn't see who it was until they came fully into the room. "Heather!" Ella stood and moved toward Adam's big sister.

Two young boys burst past Heather. "Grandma!" They shouted in unison and ran to Mrs. Jamison.

Ella looked back at Heather who opened her arms to her. "Oh, Ella. Look at you. You've turned into a gorgeous woman."

She embraced the woman who looked so much the same as she had twenty years ago, just an older version that sported crow's feet and gray hair mixed in to her long, curly dark hair. "You look amazing too. And your boys. What handsome young men! But how on earth are you here already? I thought you lived in DC."

"I do. I left as soon as I could after I got off the phone with Adam this morning, what I need to tell him can't be said over the phone. So, I was only a couple hours out when Mom called me to say that Adam was in the hospital. Is he okay? What happened?"

"We... we were attacked. Adam was stabbed and is in surgery right now."

"Oh, my word." Her hands flew to her mouth. "Are you okay?" She reached out to Ella.

"Eh." She shrugged. "I'll be better when I know Adam is okay."

Heather nodded. "Let's sit and catch up. I can't think about Adam without losing it, so let's talk about something else."

"I could use that."

"Adam said you're a teacher?"

They sat and talked about anything and everything except Adam. Thirty minutes passed before anyone else came in or out of the door. But Ella's chest tightened when Jared and a doctor came into the room talking to one another. Jared's long frown caused her pulse to quicken. Bad news. But who? Ella jumped to her feet.

A smile came onto the older, black doctor's face as he spoke to the room, "Adam is out of surgery and in recovery. We were able to stitch him up without any complications."

A collective sigh washed through the room. Adam's mom stood and approached the doctor, but before Ella was able to listen in and join the conversation, Amelia came up to her. "Do you want to go home and take a shower and get some sleep? I'm sure it will be hours before he's awake."

"I want to see him first. Maybe a shower, but if they'll let me, I'd rather camp out in his room. I want to be there when he wakes up."

"That makes sense to me."

"Plus, Amelia, I don't know where home is right now."

"My house is always open to you, but I think your parents could offer you some space too."

"That's true."

Jared came over to them. "Hey, Ella?"

She looked into Jared's somber eyes. "He didn't make it, did he?"

Jared pressed his lips together and shook his head.

All the air escaped Ella's lungs. She had killed a man.

Heather turned towards them. "Who didn't make it?"

Ella tried to answer but speech was impossible without air in her lungs. But she made eye contact with Heather. She had killed Heather's ex-boyfriend.

Amelia's voice cut into her shock. "Ella, breathe. It's okay. You did what you had to."

Ella took in a slow breath, and Jared said, "You saved Adam's life by shooting Scott. The doctor said Adam wouldn't have made it if he had arrived thirty minutes later."

"Scott? Scott Rebus?" Heather's voice was flat.

Ella's eyes locked with Heather's. Ella nodded.

Heather dropped her shoulders as if a giant weight had been lifted off her shoulders.

"You aren't surprised?"

"I wish I was. I'm so sorry, Ella!"

"Sorry for what?"

"Not now. I'll tell you when Adam is up to hearing too."

"Okay."

"Let's just go see him."

Ella nodded.

CHAPTER 29

Where was he? What had happened? Adam tried to open his eyes, but his brain was so foggy that he couldn't remember anything. Scott. He had stabbed Adam, but why didn't he feel the pain he had? Ella. She had grabbed his gun before he passed out. He vaguely remembered gun shots. What happened to her? Was she okay?

"Ella!" He finally opened his eyes and shouted her name.

"Hey! I'm right here." The sound of an angel filled his ears. Maybe he was dead. He turned towards the sound and his eyes fell upon God's most beautiful creation.

"Are you okay?"

"I'm fine." Her warm fingers slid around his hand.

Adam looked around; he was in a small hospital room. He tried to sit up but couldn't. *There's the pain.*

"Don't try to move." She placed the hand not holding his on his chest to keep him lying in the hospital bed. "You had to have surgery to close up the wound and have been out longer than they expected." She reached up to his head and ran her fingers through his hair. His heart fluttered.

Deep in her eyes there was a shadow of sorrow. "Are you sure you're okay? You weren't hurt? What happened after I cut you free?"

Her eyes dropped to where their hands gripped one another. "I killed him. I didn't want to kill him, but I had to stop him."

He tightened his grip on her hand and pulled on her hand until she looked back up at him. "You did good."

"I guess. But what matters is you are going to be just fine, and now I'm safe."

"Exactly."

"Oh, I was supposed to call the nurse when you woke up." She reached across him to get the call button.

His heart raced at her closeness. He just wanted to pull her into his arms, but he was becoming more aware of the pain in his abdomen. Instead, he put his hand gently on her back keeping her close after she pushed the button and talked to the nurse.

Ella's hair was in the same messy bun it had been all day, and it looked like she still hadn't gotten a shower. "You haven't left the hospital yet, have you?"

"I couldn't. Amelia encouraged me to, but I just couldn't leave you."

He looked up at the clock it was after eleven. The last five hours were not part of his memory at all. But the bags under Ella's eyes and the creases in her forehead told him that they had been excruciatingly long for her. "You should get some sleep. You can go; not that I want you to, but I'll be okay."

"I'm not going anywhere. The nurse brought me a pillow and some blankets. I'm sleeping on the couch... that is if I can sleep." Fear flashed through her eyes. "Adam, I don't want to close my eyes."
Of course. "Stay close. I'll be here for you."
Her lips curled up into a tired smile.
The nurse came into the room and checked on him. Ella stepped back but stayed close enough to keep her hand in his. Once the nurse finished her check and her instructions for him regarding his IV pain meds, the round older woman looked at Ella. "And how are you doing?"
"I'm okay."
"Hun, I don't believe you. But in any case, both of you need to get some sleep. Technically, he's my patient, but let me know if you need anything either, okay?"
Ella nodded. "Will do. Thank you."
Adam kept his eyes on Ella, and the nurse left. Ella turned her face back towards him and blushed when she caught him staring. "Come closer."
She leaned in towards him. He stroked her hair out of her face. He wanted to say so much but was unsure what to say at the same time. "I love you."
"I know. I love you too." She came closer and closer, until their lips met. The kiss could only graze the surface of the passion he felt for her. And he could sense the same passion in the way she kissed him. She pulled back and smiled.
"That should help you sleep," he said.
She giggled. "I'm not sure about that. But maybe."

Adam clenched his teeth and tried to shift in the hospital bed. Ella stirred next to him, and he tightened his arm around her. It had been a long night for both of them. The pain had woken him on several occasions. He had tried too hard to be a tough guy and limit the pain meds, but Ella had caught on and pushed the morphine drip for him. She had woken up to several nightmares. He wished he hadn't been stuck in the bed unable to move. But at one point he woke up to her with her head on the side of the bed, and he had insisted she crawl in next to him. She had argued, afraid she would hurt him, but they had both slept better in each other's arms.

He looked up at the large clock on the wall. It was already after ten. *Guess Ella isn't going to get any breakfast from the cafeteria.* Maybe one of their friends could bring her something once she woke up.

He stroked her hair away from her face and took in the beauty of the woman whose head lay on his shoulder. *Thank you, Jesus, for hearing my prayers and saving our lives.*

The door opened revealing a different nurse from the night before. The tall, dark woman in scrubs greeted him with a smile. "Good morning. I'm Keisha, and I'm your nurse today." She padded quietly across the room and kept her voice low. "How are you feeling this morning?"

"Eh. Okay, all things considered."

Ella stirred beside him. She smiled and opened her eyes.

"Sorry, Hun, didn't mean to wake ya," Keisha said.

"No worries." Ella smiled at him and kissed his cheek before easing herself up and out of the bed.

He didn't want her to leave his side, and the cold spot left where her warm body had just been increased his longing for her closeness. But Keisha's voice brought his focus away from Ella. "Hun, I'm sorry, I can't recall your name."

"Ella."

"That's right, Ella, will you be the one helping Adam change his dressings? Because I'd like to start teaching ya, so y'all feel real comfortable with it before he's discharged."

"Umm..." Ella looked like a deer in headlights.

Adam chuckled and answered for her. "I'll probably change them myself mostly, but it wouldn't hurt for her to know how. That is if you can handle it, Ella."

"I guess..." Her eyes narrowed, and she frowned.

He tried not to laugh at her disgust. "Really don't like the medical stuff, huh?"

"I'm not sure."

"You'll be fine. You were always good at helping patch me up when we were kids."

"That was different. I didn't have PTSD."

"Touché."

Her disgust gave way to a smile, and she winked at him. She stepped closer to the bed and took his hand. "All right, just show me."

Adam looked over at Keisha who was trying to suppress a giggle. "You two are adorable. I'm impressed with your good natures considering the circumstances. So, here's what you do." Keisha showed them how to care for his wound, and Ella handled it beautifully. Once that was done, Keisha helped him raise the bed, so he was in more of a sitting position, and she finished checking Adam's vitals and made sure they didn't need anything else. "All right, just ring if y'all need anything at all. And when you're ready there are several people waiting outside to come in and see you. I'm supposed to limit visitors to three at a time, but I know you cops don't like that rule, so my only stipulation is that you tell everyone to leave if you get tired. And Ella, if you see him getting weary, you kick 'em out. Y'all hear me?"

"Yes, ma'am," Adam said.

Ella nodded. "Will do."

"You can send them in." Adam wanted to be alone with Ella, but he knew that his friends and family would want to see him too.

As soon as Keisha was out of the room Ella surprised Adam by leaning close and kissing him. Heat rose in his cheeks. She winked at him again; his heart danced.

The door to his room swung open, and his sister appeared.

"Heather!" He wanted to jump out of bed and hug her, but he had to wait until she came to him.

"Adam!" They embraced. She pulled away and slapped him on the arm. "What were you thinking? Getting stabbed and all?"

"Right, did that on purpose!" They both laughed. "When did you get here?"

"Ella didn't tell you?"

He shook his head.

"It slipped my mind," Ella said from where she still stood next to his bed.

"I got here while you were in surgery last night."

"How is that possible?"

Heather's face turned down. "Because after we got off the phone yesterday, I knew I had to tell you the truth about Scott, but I wanted to tell you in person. I should have told you, or someone, years ago." Heather turned and pulled a chair up next to the bed and sat.

Ella sat on the edge of the bed. Adam put his hand on her thigh, and she took it in her hand. With his other hand he reached out for his sister's. She took it into both of her hands and leaned forward placing her forehead on their hands. "Oh, Adam, this is all my fault." She looked up at him with tearful eyes.

"How is anything about this your fault?"

"If I had recognized the truth back in high school. If I had come forward, he wouldn't have been able to hurt you, either of you."

"What are you talking about, Heather?"

Heather bit the side of her lip and rubbed the back of her neck. "When Scott and I were dating twenty-five years ago, he... he pushed me to do more than I wanted to."

Adam's insides lurched. "He raped you?"

Heather's eyes dropped back to her hands that held Adam's. "I didn't recognize it as that then. I thought because he was my boyfriend that somehow, it was my fault."

"Absolutely not."

Her eyes softened into a slight smile. "I know that now. It took a long time and a lot of work, but I see what he did was wrong. But what is my fault is that I didn't come forward. I didn't tell you right away when you told me Scott was back in town. But Ella, if I had said something back then, maybe... maybe I could have spared you so much hurt."

Ella reached across Adam and took Heather's hand. "No, you can't think that way, Heather. What happened is done and over. There's no use dwelling on the what ifs because they aren't. We are all here, alive, and safe. That's what matters." Tears formed in Ella's eyes. "I'm so sorry you went through that, Heather."

"Same, Ella."

Adam shifted. He groaned and grabbed his wound. "I just wish we had figured out it was him before last night."

"You're telling me!" Ella's eyes grew wide.

He laughed which just made his abdomen hurt more.

"Sorry." Ella must have noticed the grimace he tried to hide.

After a moment of quiet passed Heather said, "Mom is with the boys at home and will come by later. She understood that I wanted to talk to you. Also, there are some others waiting in the hallway to see you. Should I let them in now?"

"Sure."

Heather disappeared. A moment later, Amelia and Becca came rushing into the room followed by Caleb, Jared, and Heather. Becca came over to him and patted his head.

"That was too close, Mister."

"Tell me about it. You're not the one lying in a hospital bed."

"I'm glad you're okay." Becca squeezed his shoulder.

"Me too." Amelia said coming around next to Ella. She handed Ella a bag. "A few things I thought you'd like to have since I can't convince you to leave."

"Thanks." Ella hugged her. "I'll leave for a bit at some point."

"Sure, you will," Amelia teased.

"If I have any say"—Adam raised his pointer finger—"I'm fine with her staying here as much as she wants."

"We all know you think that." Jared laughed.

Adam's eyes met Ella's. Her cheeks turned pink as she smiled at him.

He winked at her.

Ella pulled the car into the parking spot and turned to Adam. "Are you sure you're up to this tonight? I'm sure everyone will understand if we change plans and do something more low-key."

"Thanks, babe, but I'm fine, really."

It had only been a week since Adam had been released from the hospital, but it was his birthday, and he insisted that they celebrate with karaoke. She had secretly learned a song for them to sing tonight, and she couldn't wait to surprise him, but she also didn't want him to push himself too hard. "If you say so. But we're leaving if I notice you're getting too tired."

"I love having you take care of me." He reached across the car and pulled her close and planted a kiss on her lips. "Even if you can be a bit overbearing. As if living with my mom wasn't bad enough."

The twinkle in his eye made her laugh. "You know I can't help myself. I just love you too much."

"I love you too."

They got out of the car and slowly walked hand in hand to the restaurant. Inside they were greeted by all their friends. Ginger hugs were given to Adam as happy birthday wishes were shared. Ella sat in a chair between Adam and Jocelyn.

"How's he doing, for real?" Jocelyn leaned close to Ella.

"He's doing all right. Keeps trying to push himself to do more than he should, but I made sure he took a nap after I got home from school this afternoon."

"Good."

"Where's Patrick? He still have hard feelings with everyone for suspecting him of being the attacker?"

"Uh, I... I guess."

Gavin pulled out the chair on the other side of Jocelyn and sat. "He's on duty tonight anyway."

Adam slid his arm across the back of her chair pulling her attention away from Jocelyn and Gavin. She leaned into him, and the waitress took everyone's drink orders. Once everyone had ordered, Ella sat up straight and turned towards Adam. "Time to sing."

"Really?"

"Yep." She stood. "Will you sing with me?"

"Of course." He took her hand, and everyone cheered them on as they made their way to the stage. The MC handed them the mics, and Adam sat on a stool. The music began.

"You know this one, right?" she asked him during the intro.

"I do. Do you?"

"I do."

They sang the popular love duet together, and Ella's heart soared. She loved Adam more than she thought possible. They sang the last few notes, and Adam pulled her close and wrapped his arm around her waist. When the music faded, she turned and kissed him without any regard to the eyes of everyone in the restaurant being glued to them. Ella pulled away from the kiss. Everyone was giving them a standing ovation. But she knew it was for Adam more than her. A police officer wounded in the line of duty.

"They're clapping for you, ya know." Adam stood and put his arm around her shoulders and leaned a little heavier on her than normal.

She put her arm tightly around his waist and supported his weight, and they walked back to the table. "Not hardly, love."

They sat and after everyone congratulated. Amelia clanged her knife against her glass. "Well, I have an announcement. Since my partner is on desk duty for the foreseeable future, I decided, well, I was also ordered by my superiors, to officially go on desk duty myself since I have"—she rubbed her tummy—"a little boy to think of."

"A boy!?" Ella exclaimed. "I thought you guys weren't going to find out?"

"We weren't, but let's just say he wasn't shy during my ultrasound this afternoon."

Everyone laughed.

Adam leaned in close to her ear. "Do you want to find out when we have a baby?"

She froze for a second before turning to him. "Getting a little ahead of yourself there, aren't you, Adam?"

He shrugged his shoulders while sporting a goofy grin. "Eh. Just preparing for the inevitable future."

"Oh, so if you can see the future, why don't you go ahead and tell me if we'll have a boy or girl, because I want to know as soon as possible."

"My foresight isn't that good. But you know what I do see?"

"What?"

"Me kissing you."

"That's no surprise."

"True." He leaned in and kissed her sweetly on the lips.

EPILOGUE

Four Months Later

Ella slipped her hand in Adam's as they walked down the path towards the lake. It was an unseasonably warm February evening. The last four months had been the happiest in her life. Every day wasn't roses, but nearly. Adam's stab wound had healed well without any complication. Her parents had come around and learned to love Adam again and now fully supported their growing relationship.

Adam had lived with his mom for a month after the attack but had moved back to their little dream house. Ella still had a difficult time going inside. The place they had dreamed of as kids had been stained with the blood of a man who had tried to kill them. The memories of pulling the trigger still haunted her every time she walked to the end of that hallway, but she was making progress with the new counselor she was seeing. And God was healing her.

Adam's voice cut into her thoughts as they walked along the path. "The contractor came over today."

"Oh yeah?" While the memories couldn't be changed, the house could be.

"Yep, he thinks our ideas for renovating the house are totally feasible."

Her heart bounced. Was this really happening? He was talking to someone about adding on to the house. "So, second story isn't out of the question?"

"Nope. The foundation is in perfect shape for it. Two more bedrooms and a bathroom. Plenty of room for babies."

"Slow down, Mister. You have to marry me before we can talk babies."

His gentle chuckle drew her eyes to his face. "I know." He pulled her hand and took her down by the water.

There on the sand was a blanket laid out with a basket. Adam's guitar rested up against the basket.

"Wha..."

"Let's sit."

"Okay. I thought we were celebrating Valentine's Day tomorrow?"

He sat on the blanket and picked up his guitar. "We are. But this is something different."

Ella lowered herself onto the blanket next to Adam.

He started strumming. "Ella"—he plucked the strings of the guitar—"I wrote a little song for you when we were younger, but I never got to sing it to you. Mostly because I was too embarrassed, but... well, we drifted, and I pushed you away. I found the piece of paper I wrote it on stuffed in my Bible and have been working on making it something worthy of you, and I think it's ready to share with you now."

Tears welled up in Ella's eyes. A song for her? She pressed her lips together and just waited. Adam's rich baritone filled the quiet of dusk.

Down by the lake, we swam and played,
Down by the lake, we fell in love,
We were only children, but that didn't matter
Down by the lake
Years have gone by, and I thought I lost you
Years have gone by, but God found me
Things change but they stayed the same
Years have gone by
I love you, I always loved you
I love you, more than I knew
God brought us back to have and to hold
I love you
Please marry me, be mine forever
Please marry me, I'll be yours too
Won't you say yes, would you please say yes.
Please marry me.

He put down his guitar and shifted until he was kneeling on one knee. He reached into the basket and pulled out a little jewelry box.

Ella's hands covered her mouth and tears streamed out of her eyes.

"Well, Eleanor Grace Perkins. You are the most beautiful woman I have ever known, inside and out. You bring out the best in me. You've taught me how to love and shown me who God is. You are the most forgiving and kind human being. I cannot fathom life without you. I don't want to. I would be honored if you would be my wife. I promise to take care of you and love you all the days of my life. Will you marry me?"

She lifted herself to her knees and threw her arms around his neck. "Yes!"

His arms encompassed her and held her tight. "I love you."

"I love you."

He pulled back enough to kiss her. He lifted the ring out of the box and slipped it onto her finger.

She returned to his arms, and they sat there and dreamed of the future for a while until Adam's phone beeped.

"What's up?" she asked.

He looked at his phone and laughed. "That dear partner of mine is apparently getting impatient."

He turned the phone and showed her the text from Amelia. *"Well, you guys coming or not? I highly doubt she said no, so, where are you? Baby wants to eat."*

Ella laughed. "Where're we going?"

"My mom's."

"Amelia's at your mom's?"

"Yep, her and all of our friends."

"You really were banking on me saying yes?"

"It's not like we hadn't talked about it. So yeah, I was quite confident."

They stood and gathered their things and walked back up the path. Adam's car was waiting for them. "That was not there when we came."

Adam just smiled.

Less than five minutes later they were walking up the steps to his mom's house. Inside all their friends and family were waiting to celebrate. Ella welcomed the hugs and congratulations from everyone.

Everyone ate pizza and mingled but Ella couldn't help but notice Jocelyn standing in the corner of the kitchen barely picking at her pizza. Ever since they were kids Jocelyn had been the life of a party, talking to anyone and everyone. Something wasn't right. Ella pulled Adam down, kissed his cheek, and whispered, "I'll be back."

"Okay." He kissed her forehead before she turned towards Jocelyn.

"Hey, Jocelyn. How are you doing?"

"Hey, Ella. Congrats. I'm so happy for you and Adam."

"Thanks. You all right?"

"Eh. I haven't been feeling that great."

"Yeah?" Ella tucked her hair behind her ear.

Jocelyn shifted to her other foot. "Yeah, not sure why. I'm headed to the doctor on Tuesday. I'm sure it's nothing. Just a little heartburn. My mom has always had bad reflux. I'm sure that's all it is. Makes eating pizza less than appetizing."

"I'm sure. Don't worry about feeling like you have to eat that. Come join us."

"I guess."

Ella took Jocelyn's hand and pulled her over to join the group of detectives. Amelia handed Adam little baby Jonathan, and Ella's heart did a little flip. Adam cradled the one month old in his arms. Ella put her arm around Adam and cooed at the baby.

"Oh, Adam," she whispered, "you're going to make a great daddy one day."

He smiled at her. "I hope so." Jonathan started fussing so Adam bounced the baby, but he didn't calm down.

"I'll take him. He probably wants to eat again." Amelia took the baby.

Once Adam's arms were free again, he turned to Ella. "Can I steal you away for a moment?"

"Of course."

He winked at her, and they slipped out the door into the backyard. "I just needed to do this."

Before she could ask what Adam pulled her close and pressed his lips against hers. Her heart took flight, and she kissed him back. Once their lips parted, she wrapped her arms around his neck.

"I love you, Ella," he said softly in her ear.

"I love you, Adam."

Also By Liz Bradford

A Shot at Redemption - Book Four - The Detectives of Hazel Hill- Coming 2020!

Gavin Riley has been a detective with the Hazel Hill PD for two years, and while he and his partner, Becca Palmer, have by no means closed every case, too many unsolved cases in a row has left Gavin doubting his ability to do his job. Are his personal mistakes distracting him from doing his job well? He can't let them, especially when a sniper decides to terrorize the city of Hazel Hill. Gavin must tap into his training as a former Army sniper to help find the killer before he finds his way into the sniper's cross hairs.

Forensic photographer, Jocelyn North, knew she shouldn't have gotten as close to Gavin as she did, but he had always been such a good friend to her so it was too late by the time she realized it had gone too far. Now she was pregnant with his baby. She needs to tell him, but she also needs to tell Patrick, her husband. How will either of them react? Will God punish her and Gavin for their mistakes or do they have a shot at redemption?

A Shot at Redemption is a unique romance that shows how we must face the consequences of our sin and how God can redeem even our most foolish mistakes.

Book Five (title to be determined) - Coming late 2020!

A FRIGHTFUL NOEL - Prequel Christmas Novella

If you haven't read it yet, be sure to grab Liz's prequel to The Detectives of Hazel Hill series.

Can a gang execution, a pregnant witness, and a mountain-brewed snowstorm be the perfect recipe for a Christmas miracle?

Doug Ramirez, a detective for the Hazel Hill Police Department, and his wife, Paige, an EMT for the HHFD, thought they'd be dancing the night away even when the rest of North Carolina was hunkering down for a massive snow storm, but when Doug is called out to investigate a body in gang ridden area of the city, the dancing will have to wait. Doug and his partner, Rebecca Palmer, arrive on the scene of a gang execution and find a scared and pregnant witness to the murder. Their focus changes from hunting a murder to protecting this young girl from the killers. The snowstorm swirling overhead only increases the risk on everyone's lives. Will they all make it through the night alive?

Follow Liz on Facebook or subscribe to receive her newsletter via email to be among the first to get updates regarding upcoming releases.

Stay Connected

Thanks for reading ON YOUR KNEES!

Let's connect. Sign up for my mailing list and get a free short story about Rebecca Palmer:

To get the story go to

http://eepurl.com/dGuIjr

Like and Follow me on Facebook:
www.facebook.com/lizbradfordwrites

Follow me on Amazon (and don't forget to leave a review of ON YOUR KNEES):
www.amazon.com/author/lizbradford

Follow me on BookBub:
www.bookbub.com/profile/liz-bradford

Author's Note

Thank you for reading ON YOUR KNEES. I hope you have enjoyed reading this story as much as I loved writing it. I've tried to figure out why I love it so much, but I think it's the characters. Something about Adam and Ella. Maybe it's just because they developed in my head for a long time before I was finally able to sit down and write their story.

People are always asking writers, "Where do you get your ideas?" I was just asked this very question by one of my sweet younger cousins at a family reunion. And honestly, I have no idea where the ideas for Adam and Ella's story stemmed from. Although, I do remember, during one of my early drafts of NOT ALONE, I was struck by Adam's unexpected response that the killer was delivering his own sense of Biblical punishment. I had to think, where did that unexpected response come from? I knew there had to be a backstory to that. And can I say, I was honestly surprised when I discovered his dad's past. (Be sure to pick up book four when it comes along to discover more about Adam's dad's redemption story.)

My husband thinks I'm a little crazy when I say that I didn't see part of a character's story coming, but as much as I create the characters in my head, it truly feels like they are independent of my mind. However, I do believe that God has given me the stories I write. I pray when I write, especially when I reach a difficult part or I'm stuck. I pray that God will guide my words and that He would use the words I write to touch someone's heart. I pray that if there is any part of Adam and Ella's story that strikes a chord in your heart that you would seek God in that area. Reach out to a pastor or another believer so they can pray with you and for you. And I'd love to hear from you too. Dear Reader, you are always in my prayers!

James 4:6-8

And he gives grace generously. As the Scriptures say,

"God opposes the proud but gives grace to the humble.

So humble yourselves before God. Resist the devil, and he will flee from you.

Come close to God, and God will come close to you..."

Acknowledgements

First and foremost, Thank you, Jesus, for Your grace and mercy and for giving me the opportunity to write these stories. I pray that they honor You, Lord.

Thank you to my family, Ken, Mom, Dad, my girls. Thank you for your support and encouragement.

Thank you to my dear friend, Becky Shaulis. Thank you for your friendship. Thank you for your professional input and analysis of the Ella's PTSD and Adam's drinking problem.

Thank you to my editor, Teresa. Thanks for teaching me so much. It is so much fun working with you.

Thank you to my cover designer, Alyssa. Thank you so much for blowing my mind with yet another beautiful cover design.

Thank you to my formatter, Kari. Thanks for making my book beautiful and easy to read.

Thank you to my readers. I pray this story encourages to fall to your knees at Jesus' feet and trust Him with your life.

Made in the USA
Columbia, SC
07 May 2020